W9-BVV-316

RANDOM
HOUSE

LARGE
PRINT

SAVING FAITH

David Baldacci

RANDOM HOUSE
LARGE PRINT

A Division of Random House, Inc.
Published in Association with Warner Books, Inc.
New York 2000

This book is a work of fiction. All characters, incidents, and dialogue, except for incidental references to public figures, products, or services, are imaginary and are not intended to refer to any living persons or disparage any company's products or services.

First Large Print Paperback edition September 2000
Copyright © 1999 by Columbus Rose, Ltd.

All rights reserved under International and Pan-American Copyright Conventions. Published in the United States of America by Random House Large Print and simultaneously in Canada by Random House of Canada Limited, Toronto. Distributed by Random House, Inc. New York. This edition published in association with Warner Books, Inc.

Library of Congress Cataloging-in-Publication Data

Baldacci, David
Saving Faith: a novel / David Baldacci.
    p.   cm.
    ISBN 0-375-72798-1
    1. Large type books. I. Title.
    [PS3552.A446S28   1999]
    813'.54—dc21   99-36764
    CIP

Random House Web Address:
www.randomlargeprint.com

Printed in the United States of America

1 3 5 7 9 8 6 4 2

This Large Print Edition published in accord with the standards of N.A.V.H.

To Aaron Priest,
my friend

ACKNOWLEDGMENTS

To my dear friend Jennifer Steinberg, for tracking down so much information for me. You'd make a great PI!

To my wife, Michelle, for always telling me the truth about the books.

To Neal Schiff at the FBI for his continued help and cooperation with my novels.

A very special thanks to FBI Special Agent Shawn Henry, who was very generous with his time, expertise, and enthusiasm, and who helped me avoid some serious gaffes in the story. Shawn, your comments made the book much better.

To Martha Pope for her valuable, insightful knowledge on Capitol Hill matters, and her patience with a political neophyte. Martha, you'd make a great teacher!

To Bobby Rosen, Diane Dewhirst, and Marty Paone for sharing their experiences and institutional memories with me.

To Tom DePont, Dale Barto, and Charles Nelson of NationsBank for assistance on financial and tax matters.

To Joe Duffy for enlightening me on foreign aid policy and procedures. And to his wife, Anne Wexler, for sharing her valuable time and insight with me.

A very, very special thanks to my friend Bob Schule for going above and beyond the call of duty in helping me on this book, for not only providing fascinating details about his long and distinguished career in Washington, but also for casting a wide net among his friends and colleagues in order to help me better understand politics, lobbying, and how Washington really works. Bob, you're a wonderful friend and a true professional.

To Congressman Rod Blagojevich (D. Ill) for allowing me a glimpse into the life of a member of Congress.

To Congressman Tony Hall (D. Ohio) for helping me better understand the plight of the world's poor, and how that issue plays out (or doesn't) in Washington.

To my good friend and family member Congressman John Baldacci (D. Maine) for his support and assistance with this project. If everyone in Washington were like John, the plot of this book would seem totally implausible.

To Larry Benoit and Bob Beene for their help on everything from lobbying to the nuts and bolts of governing, to all the little nooks and crannies in the U.S. Capitol building. To them I owe one of my favorite scenes in the book.

To Mark Jordan of Baldino's Lock and Key for educating me on the ways of security and phone systems and how to crack them. Mark, you're the best.

To Steve Jennings for reading every word as usual and helping to make them better.

To my dear friends David and Catherine Broome for exposing me to the North Carolina settings and for their continued encouragement and support.

To all those other people who contributed to this novel but for various reasons wish to remain anonymous. I couldn't have done it without all of you.

To my editor and my friend Frances Jalet-Miller. Her skill, encouragement, and gentle persuasion are all that any writer could ever want in an editor. To many more books together, Francie.

Last, but absolutely not least, to Larry, Maureen, Jamie, Tina, Emi, Jonathan, Karen Torres, Martha Otis, Jackie Joiner, and Jackie Meyer, Bruce Paonessa and Peter Mauceri, and all the rest of the Warner Books family. It takes *all* of us to make this happen.

All the people listed above gave me the knowledge

and help I needed to write this novel. How I used that assistance to conjure up all sorts of shenanigans, misdeeds, outright crimes, and depictions of felonious and conspiratorial souls in *Saving Faith*, however, is my responsibility alone.

SAVING FAITH

CHAPTER 1

The somber group of men sat in a large room that rested far belowground, accessed by only a single, high-speed elevator. The chamber had been secretly built during the early 1960s under the guise of renovating the private building that squatted over it. The original plan, of course, was to use this "super-bunker" as a refuge during a nuclear attack. This facility was not for the top leaders of American government; it was for those whose level of relative "unimportance" dictated that they probably wouldn't be able to get out in time but who still rated protection afforded no ordinary citizen. Politically, even in the context of total destruction, there must be order.

The bunker was built at a time when people believed it possible to survive a direct nuclear hit by burrowing into the earth inside a steel cocoon. After the holocaust that would annihilate the rest of the country, leaders would emerge from the rubble with absolutely nothing left to lead, unless you counted vapor.

The original, aboveground building had been leveled long ago, but the subterranean room remained under what was now a small strip mall that had been vacant for years. Forgotten by virtually all, the chamber was now used as a meeting place for certain people in the country's primary intelligence-gathering agency. There was some risk involved, since the meetings were not related to the men's official duties. The matters discussed at these gatherings were illegal, and tonight even murderous. Thus additional precautions had been necessary.

The super-thick steel walls had been supplemented by a copper coating. That measure, along with tons of dirt overhead, protected against prying electronic ears lurking in space and elsewhere. These men didn't particularly like coming to this underground room. It was inconvenient, and ironically, it seemed far too James Bondish even for their admittedly cloak-and-dagger tastes. However, the truth was the earth was now encircled with so much advanced surveillance technology that virtually no conversation taking place on its surface was safe from interception. One had to dig into the dirt to escape his enemies. And if there was a place where people could meet with reasonable confidence that their conversations would not be overheard even in their world of ultra-sophisticated peekaboo, this was it.

The gray-headed people present at the meeting were all white males, and most were nearing their agency's mandatory retirement age of sixty. Dressed quietly and professionally, they could have been doctors, lawyers or investment bankers. One would probably not remember any of the group a day after seeing them. This anonymity was their stock-in-trade. These sorts of people lived and died, sometimes violently, over such details.

Collectively, this cabal possessed thousands of secrets that could never be known by the general public because the public would certainly condemn the actions giving rise to these secrets. However, America often demanded results—economic, political, social and otherwise—that could be obtained only by smashing certain parts of the world to a bloody pulp. It was the job of these men to figure out how to do so in a clandestine manner that would not reflect poorly on the United States, yet would still keep the country safe from the pesky international terrorists and other foreigners unhappy with the stretch of America's muscle.

The purpose of tonight's gathering was to plot the killing of Faith Lockhart. Technically, the CIA was prohibited by presidential executive order from engaging in assassination. However, these men, though employed by the Agency, were not representing the CIA tonight. This was their private agenda, and there was little disagreement that the woman had to die, and soon; it was critical for the well-being of the country. These men knew this, even if American presidents did not. However, because of another life that was involved, the meeting had become acrimonious, the group resembling a cadre of posturing members fighting on Capitol Hill over billion-dollar slices of pork.

"What you're saying, then," one of the white-haired men said as he poked the smoke-filled air with a slender finger, "is that along with Lockhart we have to kill a federal agent." The man shook his head incredulously. "Why kill one of our own? It can only lead to disaster."

The gentleman at the head of the table nodded thoughtfully. Robert Thornhill was the CIA's most distinguished Cold War soldier, a man whose status at the Agency was unique. His reputation was unassailable, his compilation of professional victories unmatched. As associate deputy director of Operations, he was the Agency's ultimate free safety. The DDO, or deputy director of operations, was responsible for running the field operations that undertook the secret collection of foreign intelligence. The operations directorate of the CIA was also unofficially known as the "spy shop," and the deputy director was still not even publicly identified. It was the perfect place to get meaningful work done.

Thornhill had organized this select group, who were as upset as he about the state of affairs at the CIA. It was he who had remembered that this bloated underground time capsule existed. And it was Thornhill who had found the money to secretly bring the chamber back to working condition and upgrade its facilities. There were thousands of little taxpayer-funded toys like that sprinkled around the country, many of them gone to complete waste. Thornhill suppressed a smile. *Well, if governments didn't waste their citizens' hard-earned money, then what would be left for governments to do?*

Even now, as he ran his hand over the stainless steel console with its quaint built-in ashtrays, sniffed the filtered air and felt the protective coolness of the earth all around, Thornhill's mind wandered back for a moment to the Cold War period. At least there was a measure of certainty with the hammer and sickle. In truth, Thornhill would take the lumbering Russian bull over the agile sand snake that you never knew was out there until it flung its venom into you. There were many who wanted nothing more in life than to topple the United States. It was his job to ensure that never happened.

Gazing around the table, Thornhill gauged each man's devotion to his country and was satisfied it matched his own. He had wanted to serve America for as long as he could remember. His father had been with the OSS, the World War II–era predecessor to the CIA. He had known little of what his father did at the time, but the man had instilled in his son the philosophy that there was no greater thing to do with one's life than to serve one's country. Thornhill had joined the Agency right out of Yale. Right up until the day he died, his father had been proud of his son. But no prouder than the son had been of the old man.

Thornhill's hair was a shining silver, which lent him a distinguished air. His eyes were gray and active, the angle of his chin blunt. His voice was deep, cultured; technical jargon and the poetry of Longfellow flowed from his mouth with equal ease. The man still wore three-piece suits and favored pipe smoking over cigarettes. The fifty-eight-year-old Thornhill could have quietly finished out his time at the CIA and led the pleasant life of a former public servant, well traveled, erudite. He had no thought of going out quietly, and the reason was very clear.

For the last ten years, the CIA's responsibilities and budgets had been decimated. It was a disastrous development, for the firestorms that were popping up across the world now often involved fanatical minds accountable to no political body and possessing the capability to obtain weapons of mass destruction. And while just about everyone thought high-tech was the answer for all the ills of the world, the best satellites in the world couldn't stroll down alleys in Baghdad, Seoul or Belgrade and take the emotional temperature of the people there. Computers in space could never capture what people were thinking, what devilish urges were lurking in their hearts. Thornhill would always choose a smart field operative willing to risk his or her life over the best hardware money could buy.

Thornhill had just such a small group of skilled operatives within the CIA, completely loyal to him and his private agenda. They had all worked hard to regain for the Agency its former prominence. Now Thornhill finally had the vehicle to do that. He would very soon have under his thumb powerful congressmen, senators, even the vice president himself, and enough high-ranking bureaucrats to choke an independent counsel. Thornhill would see his budgets revive, his manpower skyrocket, his agency's scope of responsibility in the world return to its rightful place.

The strategy had worked for J. Edgar Hoover and the FBI. It was no coincidence, Thornhill believed, that the Bureau's budget and influence had flourished under the late director and his allegedly "secret" files on powerful politicians. If there was one organization in the world that Robert Thornhill hated with all his soul, it was the FBI. But he would use whatever tactics he could to bring his agency back to the forefront, even if it meant stealing a page from his most bitter foe. *Well, watch me do you one better, Ed.*

Thornhill focused again on the men clustered around him. "Not having to kill one of our own would, of course, be ideal," he said. "However, the fact is, the FBI have her under 'round-the-clock stealth security. The only time she's truly vulnerable is when she goes to the cottage. They may place her in Witness Protection without warning, so we have to hit them at the cottage."

Another man spoke up. "Okay, we kill Lockhart, but let the FBI agent live, for God's sake, Bob."

Thornhill shook his head. "The risk is too great. I know that killing a fellow agent is deplorable. But to shirk our duty now would be a catastrophic mistake. You know what we've invested in this operation. We cannot fail."

"Dammit, Bob," the first man to protest said, "do you know what will happen if the FBI learns we took out one of their people?"

"If we can't keep a secret like that, we have no business doing what we do," Thornhill snapped. "This is not the first time lives have been sacrificed."

Another member of the group leaned forward in his chair. He was the youngest of them. He had, however, earned the respect of the group with his intelligence and his ability to exercise extreme, focused ruthlessness.

"We've only really looked at the scenario of killing Lockhart to forestall the FBI's investigation into Buchanan. Why not appeal to the FBI director and have him order his team to give up the investigation? Then no one has to die."

Thornhill gave his younger colleague a disappointed look. "And how would you propose going about explaining to the FBI director why we wish him to do so?"

"How about some semblance of the truth?" the younger man said. "Even in the intelligence business there's sometimes room for that, isn't there?"

Thornhill smiled warmly. "So I should say to the FBI director—who, by the way, would love to see us all permanently interred in a museum—that we wish him to call off his potentially blockbuster investigation so that the CIA can use illegal means to trump his agency. Brilliant. Why didn't I think of that? And where would you like to serve *your* prison term?"

"For chrissakes, Bob, we *work* with the FBI now. This isn't 1960 anymore. Don't forget about CTC."

CTC stood for the Counter Terrorism Center, a cooperative effort between the CIA and the FBI to fight terrorism by sharing intelligence and resources. It had been generally deemed a success by those involved. To Thornhill, it was simply another way for the FBI to stick its greedy fingers into his business.

"I happen to be involved in CTC in a modest way," Thornhill said. "I find it an ideal perch on which to keep tabs on the Bureau and what they're up to, which is usually no good, as far as we're concerned."

"Come on, we're all on the same team, Bob."

Thornhill's eyes focused on the younger man in such a way that everyone in the room froze. "I request that you never say those words in my presence again," Thornhill said.

The man paled and sat back in his chair.

Thornhill clenched his pipe between his teeth. "Would you like me to give you concrete examples of the FBI taking the credit, the glory for work done by our agency? For the blood spilled by our field agents? For the countless times we've saved the world from annihilation? How they manipulate investigations in order to crush everyone else, to beef up their already bloated budget? Would you like me to give you instances in my thirty-six-year career where the FBI did all it could to discredit our mission, our people? Would you?" The man slowly shook his head as Thornhill's gaze bored into him. "I don't give a damn if the FBI director himself came down here and kissed my shoes and swore his undying allegiance to me—I will not be swayed. Ever! Have I made my position clear?"

"I understand." As he said this, the younger man managed not to shake his head in bewilderment. Everyone in this room other than Robert Thornhill knew that the FBI and CIA actually got along well. Though they could be ham-handed at times in joint investigations because they had more resources than anyone else, the FBI was not on a witch hunt to bring down the Agency. But the men in this room also understood quite clearly that Robert Thornhill believed the FBI was their worst enemy. And they also knew that Thornhill had, decades ago, orchestrated a number of Agency-authorized assassinations with cunning and zeal. Why cross such a man?

Another colleague said, "But if we kill the agent, don't you think the FBI will go on a crusade to find out the truth? They have the resources to scorch the earth. No matter how good we are, we can't match their strength. Then where are we?"

Some grumbling rose from the others. Thornhill looked around warily. The collection of men here represented an uneasy alliance. They were paranoid, inscrutable fellows long used to keeping their own counsel. It had truly been a miracle to forge them together in the first place.

"The FBI *will* do everything they can to solve the murder of one of their agents and the chief witness to one of their most ambitious investigations ever. So what I would propose doing is to give them the solution we desire them to have." They looked curiously at him. Thornhill sipped water from his glass and then took a minute to prime his pipe.

"After years of helping Buchanan run his operation, Faith Lockhart's conscience or good sense or paranoia got the better of her. She went to the FBI and has now begun telling them everything she knows. Through a little foresight on my part, we were able to discover this development. Buchanan, however, is completely unaware that his partner has turned against him. He also doesn't know that we intend to kill her. Only we know." Thornhill inwardly congratulated himself for this last remark. It felt good, omniscience; it was the business he was in, after all.

"The FBI, however, may suspect that he does know about her betrayal or may find out at some point. Thus, to the outside observer, no one in the world has greater motivation to kill Faith Lockhart than Danny Buchanan."

"And your point?" the questioner persisted.

"My point," said Thornhill tersely, "is quite simple. Instead of allowing Buchanan to disappear, we tip off the FBI that he and his clients discovered Lockhart's duplicity and had her and the agent murdered."

"But once they get hold of Buchanan, he'll tell them everything," the man quickly responded.

Thornhill looked at him as a disappointed teacher to pupil. Over the last year, Buchanan had given them everything they needed; he was now officially expendable.

The truth slowly dawned on the group. "So we tip the FBI about Buchanan *posthumously*. Three deaths. Correction, three murders," another man said.

Thornhill looked around the room, silently gauging the reaction of the others to this exchange, to his plan. Despite their protestations about killing an FBI agent, he knew that three deaths meant nothing to these men. They were from the old school, which quite clearly understood that sacrifices of that nature were sometimes necessary. Certainly what they did for a living sometimes cost people their lives; however, their operations had also avoided open war. Kill three to save three million, who could possibly argue with that? Even if the victims were relatively innocent. Every soldier who ever died in battle was innocent too. Covert action, quaintly referred to as the "third option" in intelligence circles, the one between diplomacy and open war, was where the CIA could really prove its worth, Thornhill believed. Although it was also at the heart of some of the Agency's worst disasters. Well, without risk there was never the possibility for glory. That epitaph could be put on his tombstone.

No formal vote was taken by Thornhill; none was needed.

"Thank you, gentlemen," Thornhill said. "I'll take care of everything." He adjourned the meeting.

CHAPTER 2

THE SMALL, WOOD-SHINGLED COTTAGE STOOD
alone at the end of a short, hard-packed gravel road,
its dirt shoulders laced with the tangled sprawl of
dandelion, curly dock and chickweed. The ram-
shackle structure rested on an acre of cleared flat
land, but was surrounded on three sides by woods
where each tree struggled to find sunlight at the expense of its neighbor. Because of wetlands and other
development problems, the eighty-year-old home
had never had any neighbors. The nearest community was about three miles away by car, but less than
half that distance if one had the backbone to challenge the dense woods.

For much of the last twenty years the rustic cottage
had been used for impromptu teen parties, and on occasion by the wandering homeless looking for the

comfort and relative safety of four walls and a roof, however porous. The cottage's discouraged current owner, who had recently inherited the beast, had finally opted to rent it out. He had found a willing tenant who had paid the full year's rent in advance, in cash.

Tonight the calf-high grass in the front yard was pushed low and then straightened in the face of a strengthening wind. Behind the house a line of thick oaks seemed to mimic the movements of the grass as they swayed back and forth. It hardly seemed possible, yet except for the wind, there were no other sounds.

Save one.

In the woods, several hundred yards directly behind the house, a pair of feet splashed through a shallow creek bed. The man's dirty trousers and soaked boots attested to the difficulty with which he had navigated the congested terrain in the dark, even with the aid of a three-quarters-full moon. He paused to scrape his muddy boots against the trunk of a fallen tree.

Lee Adams was both sweaty and chilled after the punishing trek. At forty-one years of age, his six-foot-two body was exceptionally strong. He worked out regularly, and his biceps and delts showed it. Keeping in reasonably good shape was a necessity in his line of work. While he was often required to sit in a car for days on end, or in a library or courthouse reviewing microfiche records, he also, on occasion, had to climb trees, subdue men even larger than he was or, like now, slog through gully-filled woods in the dead of night. A little extra muscle never hurt. However, he wasn't twenty anymore either, and his body was letting him know it.

Lee had thick, wavy brown hair that seemed perpetually in his face, a quick, infectious smile, pronounced cheekbones and an engaging set of blue eyes that had caused female hearts spontaneously to flutter from fifth grade onward. He had suffered enough broken bones during his career, though, and other assorted injuries, that his body felt far older than it looked. And that's what hit him every morning when he rose. The creaks, the little pains. Cancerous tumor or merely arthritis? he sometimes wondered. What the hell did it really matter? When God punched your ticket, He did so with authority. A good diet and messing around with weights or pitter-pattering on the treadmill wasn't going to change the Man's decision to pull your string.

Lee looked up ahead. He couldn't see the cottage just yet; the forest clutter was too thick. He fussed with the controls of the camera he had pulled from his knapsack while he took a series of replenishing breaths. Lee had made this same trek several times before but had never gone inside the cottage. He had seen things, though—peculiar things. That's why he was back. It was time to learn the secret of this place.

His wind having returned, Lee trudged on, his only

companions the scurrying wildlife. Deer, rabbit, squirrel and even beaver were plentiful in this still-rural part of northern Virginia. As he walked along, Lee listened to the flit of flying creatures. All he could envision were rabid, foaming bats blindly cleaving the air around his head. And it seemed that every few steps he would run straight into a twister of mosquitoes. Though he had been paid a large amount of cash up front, he was seriously considering increasing his daily fee on this one.

When he approached the edge of the woods, Lee stopped. He had a great deal of experience spying on the haunts of people and their activities. Slow and methodical was the best way, like a pilot's checklist. You just had to hope nothing happened to make you improvise.

Lee's bent nose was a permanent badge of honor from his time as an amateur boxer in the Navy, where he had taken out his youthful aggression in a square of roped canvas against an opponent of like weight and ability. A pair of stout gloves, quick hands and nimble feet, a cagey mind and a strong heart had constituted his arsenal of weapons. The majority of the time, they had been enough for victory.

After his military stint, things had worked out mostly okay for him. Never rich, never actually poor despite being mostly self-employed over the years; never quite alone, though he had been divorced for almost fifteen years. The only good thing from that marriage had just turned twenty. His daughter was tall, blond and brainy, as well as the proud bearer of a full academic scholarship to the University of Virginia and a star on the women's lacrosse team. And for the last ten years, Renee Adams had had no interest whatsoever in having anything to do with her old man. A decision that had her mother's full blessing, if not her insistence, Lee well knew. And his ex had seemed so kind on those first few dates, so infatuated with his Navy uniform, so enthusiastic in tearing up his bed.

His ex-wife, a former stripper named Trish Bardoe, had married on the rebound a fellow by the name of Eddie Stipowicz, an unemployed engineer with a drinking problem. Lee thought she was heading for disaster and had tried to get custody of Renee on the grounds that her mom and stepfather could not provide for her. Well, about that time, Eddie, a sneaky runt Lee despised, invented, mostly by accident, some microchip piece of crap that had made him a gazillionaire. Lee's custody battle had lost its juice after that. To add insult to injury, there had been stories on Eddie in the *Wall Street Journal, Time, Newsweek* and a number of other publications. He was famous. Their house had even been featured in *Architectural Digest*.

Lee had gotten that issue of the *Digest*. Trish's new home was grossly huge, mostly crimson red or eggplant so dark it made Lee think of the inside of a coffin. The windows were cathedral-size, the furniture large enough to become lost in and there were enough wood moldings, paneling and staircases to heat a typical midwestern town for an entire year. There were also stone fountains sculpted with naked people. What a kicker! A photo of the happy couple was included in the spread. In Lee's opinion they might as well have captioned it "The Nerd and the Bombshell strike it rich in poor taste."

One photo had captured Lee's complete attention, however. Renee had been poised on the most magnificent stallion Lee had ever seen, on a field of grass that was so green and perfectly trimmed that it looked like a pond of sea glass. Lee had carefully cut that photo out and put it away in a safe spot—his family album of sorts. The article, of course, made no mention of him; no reason that it should. The one thing that had ticked him off, though, was the reference to Renee as Ed's daughter.

"Stepdaughter," Lee had said out loud when he read that line. "Stepdaughter. That one you can't take away, Trish." Most of the time he felt no envy for the wealth his ex-wife now had, for it meant that his daughter would never want. But sometimes it still hurt.

When you had something for all those years, something you had made with a part of yourself, and loved more than it was probably good to love anything, and then lost it—well, Lee tried never to dwell for long on that loss. Big tough guy that he was, when he did let himself think about the massive hole dead center in his chest, he ended up blubbering like a baby.

Life was so funny sometimes. Funny like when you get a clean bill of health one day and drop dead the next.

Lee looked down at his muddy pants and worked a painful cramp out of his weary leg at the same time he swatted a mosquito out of his eye. Hotel-size house. Servants. Fountains. Big horses. Sleek private jet. . . . Probably all a real pain in the ass.

Lee hugged the camera to his chest. It was loaded with 400-speed film that Lee was "turbocharging" by setting the camera's ISO speed to 1600. Fast film required less light, and with the shutter opening for shorter periods of time, there was far less likelihood that camera wobble or vibration would distort any photos. He slipped on a 600mm telephoto lens and flipped down the lens' attached tripod.

Peering between the branches of a wild dogwood, Lee focused on the rear of the cottage. Scattered clouds drifted past the moon and deepened the darkness around him. He took a series of shots and then put the camera away.

As he stared at the house, the problem was he couldn't tell from here if the place was occupied or not. It was true he couldn't see a light on, but the place might have an interior room not visible from here. Added to that, he couldn't see the front of the house, and there might be a car parked there, for all he knew. He had observed the traffic and foot patterns on his other trips here. There hadn't been much to see. Few cars came down this road, and no walkers or joggers did. All the cars he had seen had turned around, obviously having made a wrong turn. All, that is, except one.

He glanced up at the sky. The wind had died down. Lee roughly calculated that the clouds would obscure the moonlight for a few minutes more. He slung the pack across his back, tensed for a moment, as though marshaling all of his energy, and then slid out of the woods.

Lee glided noiselessly until he reached a spot where he could squat behind a copse of overgrown bushes and still observe the front and back of the house. While he watched the house, the shades of darkness grew lighter as the moon reappeared. It seemed to be lazily watching him, curious as to what he was doing here.

Though isolated, the cottage was only a forty-minute drive from downtown D.C. That made it very convenient for any number of things. Lee had made inquiries about the owner and found him to be legitimate. The renter, however, had been a little tougher to pin down.

Lee pulled out a device that looked like a cassette recorder but was actually a battery-powered lock-pick gun, along with a zippered case, which he opened. He felt the different lock picks inside, then selected the one he wanted. Using an Allen wrench, he secured the pick into the machine. Lee's fingers moved quickly, confidently, even as another bank of clouds passed over, deepening the darkness once more. Lee had done this so many times that he could have closed his eyes and his fingers would carry on, manipulating his tools of felony with enviable precision.

Lee had already checked out the locks on the cottage with his spotting scope during daylight. That had also disturbed him. Deadbolt locks on all the exterior doors. Sash locks on both the first- *and* second-story windows. All the hardware looked new too. On a falling-down rental in the middle of nowhere.

Despite the cool weather, a bead of nervous sweat surfaced on Lee's forehead as he thought about this. He touched the 9mm in his belt clip holster; the metal was comforting. He took a moment to put the single-action pistol in a cocked-and-locked position—a round in the firing chamber, the hammer cocked and the safety set.

The cottage also had a security system. That had been a real stunner. If he was smart, Lee would pack his tools of criminality and go home, reporting failure to his employer. However, he took pride in his work. He would see it through at least until something happened to make him change his mind. And Lee could run very fast when he needed to.

Getting into the house wouldn't be all that difficult, particularly since Lee had the pass-code. He'd managed to get it the third time he'd been here, when the two people had come to the cottage. He had already confirmed the place was wired, so he had come prepared. He had beat the couple here and waited while they did whatever they were doing inside. When they had come out, the woman had entered the pass-code to arm the system. Lee, hiding in the same copse he was in now, just happened to have a bit of electronic wizardry that snatched that code right out of the air like a fly ball neatly falling into a glove. All electrical current produces a magnetic field, like a little transmitter. When the tall woman had punched in the numbers, the security system had thrown off a discrete signal for each digit, right into Lee's electronic mitt.

Lee checked the cloud cover once more, slapped on a pair of latex gloves with reinforced fingertip and palm pads, readied his flashlight and took another deep breath. A minute later he moved out from the cover of the bushes and made it quietly to the back door. He slipped off his muddy boots and set them next to the door. He didn't want to leave traces of his visit. Good private investigators were invisible. Lee held the light under his arm while he inserted the pick in the door lock and activated the device.

He used the pick gun partly for speed and partly because he didn't crack enough locks to be that proficient at it. A pick and tension tool required constant use to allow the fingers the level of sensitivity required to detect the proximity of the shear line, the subtle descent of the tension tool as the lock's tumblers began to do their little jig. Using a pick and tension tool, an experienced locksmith could pick the lock faster than Lee could with his pick gun. It was a true art and Lee knew his limitations. Soon, he felt the dead bolt sliding back.

When he eased open the door, the silence was broken by the low beeping sound of the security system. He quickly found the control pad, punched in six numbers and the beeping sound immediately stopped. As Lee closed the door softly behind him, he knew he was now a felon.

The man lowered his rifle and the red dot emanating from the weapon's laser scope disappeared from the wide back of an unsuspecting Lee Adams. The man holding the rifle was Leonid Serov, a former KGB officer specializing in assassination. Serov had found himself without gainful employment after the breakup of the Soviet Union. However, his ability to efficiently kill human beings was much in demand in the "civilized" world. Fairly well pampered as a communist for many years, with his own apartment and car, Serov had grown wealthy literally overnight as a capitalist. If he had only known.

Serov didn't know Lee Adams and had no idea why he was here. He had not noticed him until Lee had made his break for the bushes near the house, because

Lee had come through the woods on the side farthest from the Russian. The sounds of his presence, Serov correctly surmised, had been covered by the wind.

Serov checked his watch. They would be coming soon. He inspected the elongated suppressor attached to the rifle and then rubbed its long snout gently, like a favorite pet, as though bestowing the notion of infallibility onto the polished metal. The rifle's stock was a special composite of Kevlar, fiberglass and graphite that provided remarkable stability. And the weapon's bore was not rifled in the conventional way. Instead it had a rounded rectangular profile, known as polygonal boring, with a right-hand twist. This type of rifling was supposed to increase muzzle velocity by upward of eight percent, and, more important, a ballistics match on a bullet fired from this gun was virtually impossible because there were no lands or grooves in the barrel that would make distinctive markings on the bullet as it exploded from the weapon. Success really was all in the details. Serov had built his entire career on that one philosophy.

The place was so isolated that Serov had mulled over perhaps removing the suppressor and relying on his skill as a marksman, his high-tech scope and his well-conceived exit plan. His confidence was justified, he believed. Just like the tree falling, when you kill someone in the middle of nowhere, who can hear him die? And he had known some suppressors to greatly distort the flight path of a bullet, with the unacceptable result that no one had died, except for the would-be assassin once his client had learned of the failure. Still, Serov had personally supervised this device's construction and was confident it would perform as designed.

The Russian shifted quietly, working out a cramp in his shoulder. He had been here since nightfall but was used to lengthy vigils. He never tired during these assignments. He took life seriously enough that preparing to extinguish another's kept his adrenaline high. With risk always came invigoration, it seemed. Whether you were mountain climbing or contemplating murder, it ironically made you feel more alive to have the possibility of death so close.

His escape route through the woods would take him to a quiet road where a car would be waiting to whisk him to nearby Dulles Airport. He would go on to other assignments, other places probably far more exotic than this. However, for his particular purpose, this setting had its virtues.

Killing someone in the city was the most difficult. Setting up where you would shoot, pulling the trigger and then escaping, all were vastly complicated by the fact that witnesses and the police were only a few anxious steps away in any direction. Give him the country, the isolation of the rural life, the cover of trees, the separation of homes, and like a tiger in a cattle pen he would kill with numbing efficiency every day of the week.

Serov sat on a stump a few feet from the tree line and only about thirty yards from the house. Despite the thickness of the woods, this spot allowed a clear field of fire: A bullet only needed an inch or so of free space. The man and woman, he had been told, would enter the house from the rear door. Only they would never make it that far. Whatever the laser touched, the bullet would destroy. He was confident he could hit a lightning bug from twice the distance he was confronted with here.

Things were set up so perfectly that Serov's instincts told him to be on high alert. Now he had an excellent reason not to fall into that trap: the man in the house. He was not the police. Law enforcement types didn't slink through the bushes and break into people's homes. Since he had not been made aware beforehand of the man's presence tonight, he concluded that the man was not on his side. However, Serov did not like to deviate from an established plan. He decided that if the man remained in the house after the bodies fell, he would follow through on his original plan and escape through the woods. If the man interfered in any way or came outside after the shots were fired—well, Serov had plenty of ammo, and the result would be three bodies instead of two.

C H A P T E R 3

Daniel Buchanan sat in his darkened office
and sipped black coffee of such strength that he could
almost feel his pulse rise with each swallow. He ran
a hand through hair that was still thick and curly but
had gone from blond to white after thirty years toil-
ing in Washington. After another long day of trying
to convince legislators that his causes were worthy of
their attention, the level of exhaustion was intense,
and enormous amounts of caffeine were increasingly
becoming the only remedy. A full night of sleep was
not typically an option. A catnap here or there, closing his eyes while being driven around to the next
meeting, the next flight, occasionally blanking out
during an interminably long congressional hearing,
even an hour or two in his bed at home—that was his

official rest. Otherwise, he was working the Hill in all its near-mystical facets.

Buchanan had grown into a six-footer with wide shoulders and sparkling eyes, and possessing an enormous appetite for achievement. A boyhood friend had entered politics. While Buchanan had no interest in holding office, his lively wit and natural powers of persuasion had made him a perfect lobbyist. He had been an instant success. His career had been his only obsession. When he was not pushing the legislative process Buchanan was not a comfortable man.

Sitting in the chambers of various congressmen, Buchanan would hear the voting buzzer go off and watch the TV every member had in his or her office. The monitor gave them the current bill up for vote, the tally for and against and the time they had left to scurry like ants to the floor and cast their ballot. With about five minutes remaining on a vote, Buchanan would conclude his meeting and hurry down the corridors looking for other members he needed to talk to, the Whip Wind-up Report clutched in his hand. It gave the daily voting schedules, which helped Buchanan determine where certain members might be—critical information when you were tracking dozens of moving targets who probably didn't want to talk to you.

Today Buchanan had managed to grab the ear of an important senator by riding the private underground

subway to the Capitol for a floor vote. Buchanan left
the man feeling fairly confident of help. He wasn't
one of Buchanan's "special" people, but Buchanan
was aware that you never knew where help could
come from. He didn't care that his clients weren't
popular or that they lacked a constituency that
would hook a member's attention. He would just
keep hammering away. The cause was a virtuous one;
the means were therefore susceptible to a lower standard of conduct.

Buchanan's office was sparsely furnished and lacked
many of the normal accoutrements of a busy lobbyist.
Danny, as he liked to be called, kept no computer, no
diskettes, no files, no records of anything of importance here. Paper files could be stolen, computers
could be hacked into. Telephone conversations were
bugged all the time. Spies were listening with everything from drinking glasses pressed to walls, to the
latest gadgets that a year before hadn't even been invented but that could suck up streams of valuable information right out of the air. A typical organization
bled confidential information the way a torpedoed
ship shed its sailors. And Buchanan had a lot to hide.

For over two decades Buchanan had been the top influence peddler of them all. In some important ways
he had laid the groundwork for lobbying in Washington. It had evolved from highly paid lawyers dozing at congressional hearings to a world of numbing
complexity where the stakes couldn't possibly be

higher. As a Capitol Hill hired gun, he had successfully represented environmental polluters in battles
with the EPA, allowing them to spread death to an
unsuspecting public; he had been the lead political
strategist for pharmaceutical giants who had killed
moms and their kids; next a passionate advocate for
gun makers who didn't care if their weapons were
safe; then a behind-the-scenes player for automobile
manufacturers who would rather fight than admit
they were wrong on safety issues; and finally, in the
mother of all cash cows, he had spearheaded the efforts of tobacco companies in bloody wars with everyone. Back then Washington could not afford to ignore
him or his clients. And Buchanan had earned an enormous fortune.

Many of the strategies he had concocted during
that time had become staples of current legislative
manipulation. Years ago he had had congressmen
float bills on the House floor he knew would be de-
feated, in order to rip away platforms for change
later. Now that tactic was routinely employed in
Congress. Buchanan's clients hated change. He had
constantly fought rearguard actions as those who
wanted what his clients had nipped at his heels. How
many times had he avoided outright political disaster by flooding members' offices with letters, propaganda, thinly veiled threats to drop financial
support. "My client will support you for reelection,
Senator, because we know you'll do right by us. And,

by the way, the contribution check is already in your campaign account." How many times had he said those words.

Ironically, it was the spoils of lobbying for the powerful that had led to a dramatic change in Buchanan's life over ten years ago. His original plan had been to build his career first and then settle down with a wife and raise a family. Deciding to see the world before he took on these responsibilities, Buchanan had driven through western Africa in a sixty-thousand-dollar Range Rover on a photography safari. In addition to the beautiful animals, he had seen squalor and human suffering of unmatched depth. On another trip, to a remote region of the Sudan, he had witnessed a mass burial of children. An epidemic had swept the village earlier, he was told. It was one of the devastating diseases that routinely afflicted the area, killing off the young and elderly. What was the disease? Buchanan had asked. Something like measles, he was told.

Another trip he had watched as billions of American-produced cigarettes were unloaded on Chinese docks, to be consumed by people who already spent their lives wearing masks because of abysmal air pollution. He was witness to birth-control devices that had been banned in the United States being dumped by the hundreds of thousands in South America with one set of instructions written only in English. He had viewed shacks next to skyscrapers in Mexico

City, starvation next to crooked capitalists in Russia. Though he had never been able to go there, North Korea, he knew, was a certified gangster state where it was believed that ten percent of the population had starved to death in the last five years. Every country had its schizophrenic story to tell.

After two years of this "pilgrimage," Buchanan's passion for marriage, having a family of his own, had evaporated. All the dying children he had seen became his children, his family. Fresh graves would still come by the millions for the young, the old, the starving of the world, but not without a fight that had become his. And he brought to it all that he had, more than he had ever given to the tobacco, chemical and gun behemoths. To this day he recalled in precise detail how this revelation of sorts had come: returning from a trip to South America, an airplane lavatory, him on his knees, his stomach sickened. It was as though he had personally murdered every dying child he had seen on that continent.

With eyes freshly opened, Buchanan started marching to these places to see precisely how he could help. He had personally brought a shipment of food and medicine to one country, only to discover there was no way to transport it to the interior regions. He had watched, helpless, as looters stripped his "care" package clean. Then he started working as an unpaid fundraiser for humanitarian organizations ranging from CARE to Catholic Relief Services. He had done well, but the dollars amounted to a drip into a bottomless bucket. The numbers were not in their favor; the problem was only getting worse.

That's when Buchanan turned to his mastery of Washington. He had left the firm he had founded, taking only one person with him: Faith Lockhart. For the last decade his clients, his wards, were the most impoverished countries in the world. In truth, it was difficult for Buchanan to regard them as geopolitical units; he saw them as fragile clusters of devastated people under various flags who had no voice. He had dedicated the remainder of his life to solving the unsolvable problem of the global have-nots.

He had used all of his immense lobbying skills and contacts in Washington, only to find that these new causes paled in popularity to those he had represented before. When he had gone to Capitol Hill as an advocate of the powerful, the politicians had greeted him with smiles, no doubt with visions of campaign contributions and PAC dollars dancing in their heads. Now they gave him nothing. Some members of Congress bragged that they didn't even have passports, that the United States already spent far too much on foreign aid. Charity starts at home, they had said, and let's damn well keep it there.

But by far the most common retort was, "Where's the constituency, Danny? How does feeding the Ethiopians get me reelected in Illinois?" As he was quickly ushered from office after office, he sensed that they all looked at him with pity: Danny Buchanan, perhaps the greatest lobbyist ever, was now muddled, senile. It was so sad. Sure, it was a good cause and all, who can doubt that, but get real. Africa? Starving babies in Latin America? I've got my own problems right here.

"Look, if it ain't trade, troops or oil, Danny, why the hell are you here wasting my time?" one highly regarded senator had told him. That could be the quintessential statement on American foreign policy.

Could they be that blind? Buchanan had asked himself over and over. Or was he the utter fool?

Finally, Buchanan decided he had only one option. It was completely illegal, but a man pushed to the precipice could not afford allegiance to pristine ethics. Using the fortune he had amassed over the years, he had taken to bribing, in very special ways, certain key politicians for their assistance. It had worked wonderfully. The aid to his clients had grown, in so many different ways. Even as his own wealth was dissipated, things were looking up, Buchanan believed. Or at least things were not getting worse; he would count the holding of precious, hard-won ground as a success. It had all worked well, until about a year ago.

As if on cue, the knock on his office door startled him from his reverie. The building was closed, supposedly secure, the cleaning crews long since departed. He didn't get up from his desk. He simply watched as the door swung inward, the silhouette of a tall man framed against the opening. The man's hand reached out and flicked on the light.

Buchanan squinted as the glare of the overheads hit him. When his eyes adjusted to the brightness, he watched as Robert Thornhill took off his trench coat, smoothed down his jacket and shirt and sat down across from him. The man's movements were graceful, unhurried, as though he had plopped down for a leisurely drink at his country club.

"How did you get in here?" Buchanan asked sharply. "The building is supposed to be secure." For some reason Buchanan could sense that others lurked right outside the door.

"And it is, Danny. It is. For *most* people."

"I don't like you coming here, Thornhill."

"I'm courteous enough to use your given name. I'd appreciate reciprocity on that point. A small thing, to be sure, but at least I'm not demanding that you address me as *Mister* Thornhill. That's the norm between master and servant, isn't it, Danny? You see, I'm not so bad to work for."

The man's smug look was designed, Buchanan knew, to drive him to such distraction that he couldn't think clearly. Instead he leaned back in his chair and settled his hands across his middle.

"To what do I owe the pleasure of your visit, *Bob?*"

"Your meeting with Senator Milstead."

"I could easily have met him in town. I'm not sure why you insisted that I go to Pennsylvania."

"But this way you get one more opportunity to make your pitch for all those starving masses. You see, I do have a heart."

"Does it even make a dent in whatever you call a conscience that you're using the plight of millions of men, women and children who consider it a miracle to see the sun rise, to further your own selfish agenda?"

"I'm not paid to have a conscience. I'm paid to protect the interests of this country. *Your* interests. Besides, if having a conscience were the criteria, there would be no one left in this town. In fact, I applaud your efforts. I have nothing against the poor and helpless. Good for you, Danny!"

"Sorry if I don't buy that."

Thornhill smiled. "Every country in the world has people like me. That is, they do if they're smart. We get the results everybody wants, because most 'everybody' lacks the courage to do it himself."

"So you play God? Interesting line of work."

"God is conceptual. I deal in facts. Speaking of which, you powered your agenda by illegal means; who are you to deny me the same right?"

In truth, Buchanan had no response to this statement. And Thornhill's intractably calm demeanor only reinforced the helplessness he felt.

"Any questions about the meeting with Milstead?" Thornhill asked.

"You have enough on Harvey Milstead to put him away for three lives. What are you really after?"

Thornhill chuckled. "I hope you're not accusing me of having a hidden agenda."

"You can tell me, Bob, we're partners."

"Maybe it's as simple as wanting you to jump when I snap my fingers."

"Fine, but a year from now, if you pop up like this, you may not leave under your own power."

"Threats from a solitary lobbyist to *me*." Thornhill sighed. "But not so solitary. You have an army of one. How is Faith? Doing well?"

"Faith is not a part of this. Faith will never be a part of this."

Thornhill nodded. "You're the only one in the crosshairs. You and your fine group of felonious politicians. America's best and brightest."

Buchanan stared coldly at his antagonist and said nothing.

"Things are coming to a head, Danny. The show will be coming to a close soon. I hope you're ready to exit cleanly."

"When I leave, my trail will be so clean, not even your spy satellites will be able to pick it up."

"Confidence is inspiring. Yet so often misplaced."

"Is that all you wanted to tell me? Be prepared to escape? I've been ready to do that since the first minute I met you."

Thornhill stood. "You focus on Senator Milstead. Get us some good, juicy stuff. Get him to talk about the income he'll have when he retires, the nominal tasks he'll have to perform as window dressing. The more specific, the better."

"It heartens me to see you enjoying this so much. Probably a lot more fun than the Bay of Pigs."

"Before my time."

"Well, I'm sure you've made your mark in other ways."

Thornhill bristled for a moment and then his calm returned. "You'd make a fine poker player, Danny. But try to remember that a bluff when one is holding nothing of value is still a bluff." Thornhill put on his trench coat. "Don't trouble yourself, I can find my way out."

In the next instant Thornhill was gone. The man appeared and disappeared at will, it seemed. Buchanan leaned back in his chair and let out a quick breath. His hands were trembling and he pressed them hard against the desk until the quivering stopped.

Thornhill had thundered into his life like an exploding torpedo. Buchanan had become, essentially, a lackey, now spying on those he had been bribing for years with his own money, now collecting a wealth of material for this ogre to use as blackmail. And Buchanan was powerless to stop the man.

Ironically, this decline in his material assets and now his work in the service of another had brought Buchanan directly back from whence he had come. He had grown up on the illustrious Philadelphia Main Line. He had lived on one of the most magnificent estates in that area. Stacked fieldstone walls—like thick gray brushstrokes of paint—outlined the grass perimeters of the vast, perfect lawns, on which was situated a sprawling twelve-thousand-square-foot house with broad, covered porches, and a detached quadruple-car garage with an apartment overhead. The house had more bedrooms than a dormitory, and lavish baths with costly tile and the luster of gold on something as commonplace as a faucet.

It was the world of the American blue bloods, where pampered lifestyles and crushing expectations existed side by side. Buchanan had observed this complex universe from an intimate perspective, yet he was not one of its privileged inhabitants. Buchanan's family had been the chauffeurs and maids and gardeners, the handymen, nannies and cooks to these blue bloods. Having survived the Canadian border winters, the Buchanans had migrated south, en masse, to a gentler climate, to less demanding work than that required by ax and spade, boat and hook. Up there they had hunted for food and cut wood for warmth, only to watch helplessly as nature mercilessly culled their ranks, a process that had made the survivors stronger, their descendants stronger still. And Danny Buchanan was perhaps the strongest of them all.

Young Danny Buchanan had watered the lawn and cleaned the pool, swept and repainted the tennis court, picked the flowers and vegetables and played, in a properly respectful manner, with the children. As he had gotten older, Buchanan had huddled with the younger generation of the spoiled rich, deep in the privacy of the complex flower gardens, smoking, drinking and exploring each other sexually. Buchanan had even acted as pallbearer, weeping sincerely as he bore two of the young and the rich who had wasted their privileged lives, mixing too much whiskey with a racing sports car, driving too fast for impaired motor skills. When you lived life that fast, often you died fast as well. Right now Buchanan could see his own end rushing headlong at him.

Buchanan had never felt comfortable in either group—the rich or the poor—since then. The rich he would never be a part of, no matter how much his bank account swelled. He had played with the wealthy heirs, but when mealtime came, they went to the formal dining room while he trudged to the kitchen to break his bread with the other servants. The baby blues had attended Harvard, Yale and Princeton; he had worked his way through night school at an institution his betters would openly mock.

Buchanan's own family was now equally foreign to him. He sent his relatives money. They sent it back. When he went to visit, he had found they had nothing to talk about. They neither understood nor cared about what he did. However, they made him feel that there was nothing honest about his life's occupation; he could see that in their tightly drawn faces, their mumbled words. Washington was as foreign as hell itself to all that they believed in. He lied for money, large sums of it. Better he had followed in their tread: honest if simple work. By rising above them, he had fallen far below what they represented: fairness, integrity, character.

The path he had chosen during the last ten years had only deepened this solitary confinement. He had few friends. Nevertheless, he did have millions of strangers across the world who deeply depended on him for something as basic as survival. Even Buchanan had to admit, it was a bizarre existence.

And now, with the coming of Thornhill, Buchanan's foothold had dropped another rung on the ladder leading to the abyss. Now he could no longer even confide in his one indisputable soul mate, Faith Lockhart. She knew nothing about Thornhill, and she never would know of the man from the CIA; this was all that was keeping her safe. It had cost him his last thread of real human contact.

Danny Buchanan was now truly alone.

He stepped to the window of his office and looked out at majestic monuments known around the world. Some might argue that their beautiful facades were just that: Like the magician's hand, they were designed to guide the eyes away from the truly important business of this city, transacted usually for the benefit of a select few.

Buchanan had learned that effective, long-term power came essentially from the gentle force of rule of the few over the many, for most people were not political beasts. A delicate balance was called for, the few over the many, *gently*, civilly; and Buchanan knew that the most perfect example of it in the history of the world existed right here.

Closing his eyes, he let the darkness envelop him, let new energy spill into his body for the fight tomorrow. It promised to be a very long night, however, for in truth, his life had now become one long tunnel to nowhere. If he could only ensure Thornhill's destruction as well, it would all be worth it. One small crack in the darkness, that would be all Buchanan needed. If only it could be so.

CHAPTER 4

THE CAR MOVED DOWN THE HIGHWAY AT
precisely the speed limit. The man was driving, the
woman next to him. Both sat rigidly, as though one
feared a sudden attack from the other.

As a jet, landing gear down, roared over them like
a swooping hawk on its way in to Dulles Airport,
Faith Lockhart closed her eyes and pretended for a
moment that she was on that plane, and instead of
landing, it was beginning some far-flung journey. As
she slowly opened her eyes, the car took an exit off the
highway and they left the unsettling glare of sodium
lights behind. They were soon sailing past jagged
rows of trees on both sides of the road, the wide,
grassy ditches deep and soggy; the dull pulse of flat-
looking stars was now their only source of light other
than the car's twin beams stabbing the darkness.

"I don't understand why Agent Reynolds couldn't come tonight," she said.

"The simple answer is, you're not the only investigation she has going, Faith," Special Agent Ken Newman replied. "But I'm not exactly a stranger, am I? We're just going to talk, like the other times. Pretend I'm Brooke Reynolds. We're all on the same team."

The car turned onto another, even more isolated road. On this stretch the trees were replaced by denuded fields awaiting the final scrape of the bulldozers. In a year's time there would be almost as many homes here as there had been trees before, as suburban sprawl continued its push. Now the land simply looked ravaged, naked. And bleak, perhaps because of what was to come. In that regard, the land and Faith Lockhart were as one.

Newman glanced over at her. Although he didn't like to admit it, he felt uneasy around Faith Lockhart, as though he were seated next to a ball of wired C-4 with no idea when it might explode. He shifted in his seat. His skin was a little raw where the leather of his shoulder holster usually rubbed against his skin. Most people developed a callus at that spot, but his skin just kept blistering and then peeling off. Ironically, he felt that the twinge of pain gave him an edge because he never relaxed; it was a clear warning that if he let down his guard, that small discomfort could become a fatal one. Tonight, however, because he was wearing body armor, the holster wasn't scrap-

ing his skin; the pain and heightened sense of aware-
ness were not nearly as strong.

Faith could feel the blood rush through her ears, all
senses elevated, the way they were when you were
lying in bed late at night and hearing a strange, troubling sound. When you were a child and that happened, you raced to your parents' bed and climbed in,
to be wrapped up, consoled by loving, understanding
arms. Her parents were dead and she was now thirty-
six years old. Who was out there for Faith Lockhart?

"And after tonight, it'll be Agent Reynolds instead
of me," Newman said. "You're comfortable with her,
aren't you?"

"I'm not sure 'comfort' applies to situations like
this."

"Sure it does. It's very important, in fact. Reynolds
is a straight shooter. Believe me, if it weren't for her,
this thing would be going nowhere. You haven't exactly given us much to go on. But she believes in you.
So long as you don't do anything to destroy that confidence, you have a powerful ally in Brooke Reynolds.
She cares about you."

Faith crossed her legs and folded her arms across
her chest. She was about five-five, and her torso was
short. Her bosom was flatter than she would have
liked, but her legs were long and well shaped. If
nothing else, she could always count on her legs to
get attention. The defined muscles in her calves and
thighs, visible through her sheer stockings, were

enough to cause Newman's gaze to flicker over them several times with what appeared to be mild interest, she noted.

Faith swatted her long auburn hair out of her face and rested her hand on the bridge of her nose. A few white strands of hair floated among the darker. They were not yet noticeable, but that would change with time. In fact, the pressure she was under would un-doubtedly accelerate the aging process. Besides hard work, agile wits and poise, Faith's good looks, she knew, had helped her career. It was shallow to believe that one's features made a difference. Yet the truth was they did, particularly when one dealt with an overwhelmingly male audience, as she had for her en-tire career.

The broad smiles she received when entering a sen-ator's office were not so much due to her gray mat-ter, she knew, as to the above-the-knee skirts she favored. Sometimes it was as simple as dangling a shoe. She was talking about children dying, families living in sewers in far-off lands, and these men were fixated on toe cleavage. God, testosterone was a man's greatest weakness and a woman's most power-ful advantage. At least it helped to level a playing field that had always been tilted in favor of the males.

"It's nice to be so well loved," said Faith. "But picking me up in an alley. Coming out here in the middle of nowhere in the dead of night. That's a lit-tle much, don't you think?"

"Your walking into the Washington Field Office just wasn't an option. You're the star witness in what could be a very important investigation. This place is safe."

"You mean it's perfect for an ambush. How do you know we haven't been followed?"

"We've been followed, all right. By our people. If anyone else had been around, believe me, our people would've noticed it before sending us on. We had a tail car until we turned off the highway. There's nobody back there."

"So your people are infallible. I wish I had that kind of people working for me. Where do you find them?"

"Look, we know what we're doing, okay? Relax." Even as he said this, though, he checked the mirror again.

He glanced at the cell phone lying on the front seat, and Faith could easily read his thoughts. "Suddenly wanting backup?" Newman glanced sharply at her but said nothing. "Okay, so let's get to the principal terms," she said. "What do I really get out of all this? We've never quite nailed it down." When Newman still didn't respond, she studied his profile for a minute, sizing up his nerve. She reached over and touched his arm.

"I took a lot of risk to do what I'm doing," she said. She felt him tense through his suit jacket where her fingers rested. She kept her fingers there, applied slightly more pressure. Her fingertips could now distinguish the material of his jacket from that of his shirt. As he turned slightly toward her, Faith was able to see the bulletproof vest he was wearing. The saliva in her mouth suddenly evaporated, along with her composure.

Newman glanced at her. "I'll give it to you straight. What exactly your deal will be, that's not up to me. So far, you haven't really given us anything. But play by the rules and everything will be okay. You'll cut your deal, you'll give us what we need and pretty soon you'll have a new identity selling seashells on Fiji, while your partner and his playmates become long-term guests of the government. Don't revel in it, don't think too much about it, just try to survive it. Remember, we're on your side here. We're the only friends you have."

Faith sat back, finally drawing her gaze from the body armor. She decided it was time to drop her bombshell. She may as well try it out on Newman instead of Reynolds. In some ways, Reynolds and she had hit it off. Two women in a sea of men. In many subtle ways, the female agent had understood things a man never would have. In other ways, however, they had been like two alley cats circling around fish bones.

"I want to bring in Buchanan. I know I can get him to do it. If we work together, your case will be much stronger." She said all of this quickly, vastly relieved to have it finally out.

Newman's face betrayed his astonishment. "Faith, we're pretty flexible, but we're not cutting a deal with the guy who, according to you, masterminded this whole thing."

"You don't understand all the facts. Why he did it. He's not the bad person in all this. He's a good guy."

"He broke the law. According to you, he corrupted government officials. That's enough for me."

"When you understand why he did it, you won't think that way."

"Don't pin your hopes on that strategy, Faith. Don't do that to yourself."

"What if I say it's both or none?"

"Then you're making the biggest mistake of your life."

"So it's either me or him?"

"And it shouldn't be that tough a choice."

"I'll just have to talk to Reynolds, then."

"She'll tell you the same thing I just did."

"Don't be so sure. I can be pretty persuasive. And I also happen to be right."

"Faith, you have no idea what's involved here. FBI agents don't decide who to prosecute. The U.S. Attorney's Office does. Even if Reynolds sided with you, and I doubt she will, I can tell you there's no way in hell the lawyers will go along. If they try to take down all these powerful politicos and cut a sweetheart deal with the guy who got them into it in the first place, they're gonna lose their asses, and then

their jobs. This is Washington, these are eight-hundred-pound gorillas we're dealing with here. There'll
be phones ringing off the hook, a media frenzy, behind-the-scenes deals going a mile a minute, and at
the end of the day, we'll all be toast. Trust me, I've
been doing this for over twenty years. It's Buchanan
or nothing."

Faith sat back and stared at the sky. For a moment,
amid the clouds, she envisioned Danny Buchanan
slumped over in a dark, hopeless prison cell. She
could never let it come to that. She would have to
talk to Reynolds and the attorneys, make them see
that Buchanan had to be given immunity too. That
was the only way it could work. But Newman
sounded so sure of himself. What he had just said
made perfect sense. This was Washington. As suddenly as the strike of a match, her confidence completely deserted her. Had she, the consummate
lobbyist, who had been tallying political scorecards
for God knew how long, failed to account for the political situation here?

"I need a bathroom," Faith said.

"We'll be at the cottage in about fifteen minutes."

"Actually, if you take the next left, there's a
twenty-four-hour gas station about a mile down the
road."

He looked at her in surprise. "How do you know
that?"

She stared back with a look of confidence that

masked a rising panic. "I like to know what I'm getting into. That includes the people and the geography."

He didn't answer, but hung the left, and they were soon at the well-lit Exxon, which had a convenience store component. The highway had to be nearby, despite the isolation of the surroundings, because semis were parked up and down the lot. The Exxon obviously catered to open-road truckers. Men in boots and cowboy hats, Wrangler jeans and windbreakers, with trucking- and automotive-parts' logos stenciled across them, strode across the lot. Some patiently filled their rigs with fuel; others sipped hot coffee, tiny wisps of steam heat rising past tired, leathery faces. No one paid attention to the sedan as it pulled up next to the rest room located on the far side of the building.

Faith locked the bathroom door behind her, put the toilet lid down and sat on it. She didn't need to use the facilities; she needed time to think, to control the panic hitting her from all sides. She looked around, her eyes absently taking in the handwritten scribbles on the chipping yellow paint covering the block walls. Some of the obscene language almost made her blush. Some of the writings were witty— belly-rocking funny, even—in their crudeness. They probably surpassed anything the men had composed to decorate their rest room next door, although most males would never concede this possibility. Men were always underestimating women.

She stood, splashed cold tap water on her face and dried it with a paper towel. About that time her knees decided to give, and she locked them, her fingers curling tightly around the stained porcelain of the sink. She had had nightmares about doing that at her wedding: locking her knees and then passing out because of it. Well, one less thing to worry about now. She'd never had a lasting relationship in her life, unless one counted a certain young man in fifth grade whose name she couldn't remember but whose sky-blue eyes she would never forget.

Danny Buchanan had given her lasting friendship. He'd been her mentor and substitute father for the last fifteen years. He had seen potential in her where no one else had. He had given her a chance when she so desperately needed one. She had come to Washington with boundless ambition and enthusiasm and absolutely no focus. Lobbying? She knew nothing about it, but it sounded exciting. And lucrative. Her father had been a good-natured if aimless wanderer, dragging his wife and daughter from one get-rich scheme to the next. He was one of nature's cruelest concoctions: a visionary lacking the skills to implement that vision. He measured gainful employment in days instead of years. They all lived one nervous week to the next. When his plans went awry and he was losing other people's money, he would pack up Faith and her mother and flee. They'd been homeless on occasion, hungry more often than not; still, her father had always gotten back on his feet, however totteringly. Until the day he died. Poverty was a lasting, powerful memory for her.

Faith wanted a good, stable life, and she wanted to be dependent on no one for it. Buchanan had given her the opportunity, the skills to accomplish her dream, and much more than that. He had not only vision, but also the tools to execute his sweeping ideas. She could never betray him. She was in breathless awe of what he had done and was still trying so hard to do. He was the rock she had needed at that stage of her life. However, in the last year their relationship had changed. Ever more reclusive, he had stopped talking to her. Danny was irritable, snapping for little reason. When she pressed him to tell her what was troubling him, he withdrew even more. Their relationship had been so close that the change had been even harder for her to accept. He became stealthy, stopped inviting her to travel with him; they no longer even engaged in their lengthy strategy sessions.

And then he had done something entirely original and personally devastating: He had lied to her. The matter had been purely trivial, but the implications were serious. If he spun lies in small areas, what was he holding from her of importance? They had one final confrontation and Buchanan had told her that no possible good could come from his sharing what troubled him. And then he dropped the real stunner.

If she wanted to leave his employ, she was free to do so, and maybe it was time she did, he had strongly intimated. His employ! The father telling his precocious daughter to get the hell out of the house was more the effect upon her.

Why did he want her to go away? And then it finally dawned on her. How could she have been so blind? They were on to Danny. Somebody was on to him, and he didn't want her to share his fate. She had point-blank confronted him on that issue. And he had point-blank denied it. And then insisted that she leave. Noble to the end.

And yet if he wouldn't confide in her, she would map a separate course for them. After much deliberation she had gone to the FBI. She knew there was a chance it was the FBI that had somehow discovered Danny's secret, but this might make it easier, Faith had thought. Now a thousand doubts assailed her for the decision to approach the Bureau. Did she really believe the Bureau would just fall all over themselves inviting Buchanan into the prosecution's fold? She cursed herself for giving them Danny's name, although he was very famous in a town of famous people; the FBI would not have failed to make the connection. They wanted Danny to go to prison. Her for Danny. That was supposed to be her choice? She had never felt more alone.

She looked at herself in the bathroom's cracked mirror. The bones of her face seemed to be pushing through her skin, her eye sockets hollowing right in front of her. A centimeter of skin between her and nothing. Her grand vision, the way out for them both, had suddenly become a free fall of insane, dizzying proportion. Her wayward father would have just packed up and fled into the night. What was his daughter supposed to do?

Lee PULLED OUT HIS PISTOL AND POINTED IT ahead of him as he moved through the hallway. With his other hand he swung the flashlight in slow, steady arcs.

The first room he peered into was the kitchen, containing a small 1950s-era refrigerator, GE electric range and tattered black-and-yellow-checked linoleum flooring. The walls were discolored in places by water damage. The ceiling was unfinished, the joists and the subfloor above clearly visible. Lee gazed at the old copper pipes and the newer grafts of PVC as they made a series of right angles through the exposed, darkened wall studs.

There was no aroma of food here, only a smell of grease, presumably hardened in the stove-top burners and in the bowels of the vent, along with probably a few trillion bacteria. A chipped Formica table and four bent-metal, vinyl-backed chairs stood in the center of the kitchen. The counters were barren, no dishes visible. There were also no towels, coffeemaker or condiment canisters, nor any other item or personal touch that might have suggested the kitchen had been used in the last decade or so. It was as though he had stepped back in time, or happened upon a bomb shelter put into service during the hysteria of the fifties.

The small dining room was across the hallway from the kitchen. Lee looked at the waist-high wood paneling, darkened and cracked over the years. He had a sudden chill, though the air was stale and oppressive inside. The house apparently had no central heating, nor had Lee seen any wall-mounted air conditioners. There had been no heating oil tank outside either, at least aboveground. Lee eyed the chill-chasers bolted along the bottom of the walls, their power cords plugged into electrical outlets. As in the kitchen, the ceiling here was unfinished. The electrical line to the dust-ridden chandelier ran through holes bored in the exposed joists. Electricity, Lee deduced, must have come to the home after it was first built.

As he moved down the hallway toward the front of the house, Lee was unable to see the invisible trip beam, positioned at knee height, that stretched across the hall. He pierced this security perimeter, and from somewhere in the house a barely audible click was heard. Lee jerked for a moment, pointing his gun in wide circles, and then relaxed. It was an old house, and old houses made lots of noises. He was just being jumpy, yet he had a right to be. The cottage and its location were right the hell out of a *Friday the 13th* movie.

Lee entered one of the front rooms. There, under the sweep of his flashlight, he saw that the furniture had been moved up against the walls, and there were footprints and drag patterns in the layers of dust on the floor. In the center of the room were a number of folding chairs and a rectangular-shaped table. A stack of Styrofoam coffee cups rested at one end of the table next to a coffeemaker. Packets of coffee, creamer and sugar lay next to the coffeemaker.

Lee took all this in and jerked when he saw the windows. Not only were the heavy drapes drawn tight, but also the windows had been boarded over with big sheets of plywood, the drapes dangling from underneath the wood.

"Shit," Lee muttered. He quickly discovered that the small square windows set in the front door had been covered over with cardboard. He pulled out his camera and snapped some shots of all these puzzling items.

Wanting to complete his search as soon as possible, Lee hurried up the stairs to the second floor. He cautiously opened the door to the first bedroom and peered in. The bed was small and made, and its smell of mildew hit him immediately. The walls here were unfinished as well. Lee put his hand against the exposed wall and immediately felt air from the outside coming through the cracks. He was startled for a moment when he saw a slender line of light coming from the top of the wall. Then he realized it was the moonlight coming through a gap where wall was supposed to meet roof.

Lee carefully nudged open the closet door. It still let out a prolonged squeak that made him catch a breath. No clothes, not even a single hanger. He shook his head and went into the small connecting bathroom. Here, there was a more modern, drop-down ceiling, linoleum floor with a pebble design and plasterboard walls covered with peeling flower-patterned wallpaper. The shower was a one-piece fiberglass unit. However, there were no towels, toilet paper or soap. No way to shower or even freshen up.

He went through into the other, adjoining bedroom. Here, the smell of mildew on the bedcovers was so strong he almost had to hold his nose. The closet here was empty as well.

None of this was making sense. He stood in the pool of moonlight coming through the window, felt his neck tickled by the drafts of air pushing through the cracks in the walls and shook his head. What was Faith Lockhart doing here if not using it as some kind of love nest? That was what his initial conclusion had been, even though he had only seen her with the tall woman. People swung lots of ways. But not even with cement up their noses could they have been having sex on these sheets.

Returning downstairs, he went across the hallway

and into the other front space, which Lee assumed was the living room. The windows here had been boarded over as well. There was a bookshelf notched into one of the walls, although no books were on it. As in the kitchen, the ceiling was unfinished. As Lee swung his light upward, he spied the short pieces of wood tacked between the joists at forty-five-degree angles, forming a line of X's across the ceiling. The wood was clearly different from that used for the original construction; it was lighter and of a different grain. Additional support? Why had that been necessary?

He shook his head in the manner of a man resigned to his fate. Now added to Lee's list of worries was the possibility that the damn second floor would collapse at any minute on his head. He envisioned his obit headlined something like: LUCKLESS PI FELLED BY BATHTUB/SHOWER COMBO; WEALTHY EX-WIFE REFUSES COMMENT.

As Lee shone his light around, he froze. Set into one wall was a door. A closet, most likely. Nothing unusual about that, except that this door was secured by a deadbolt. He went over and examined the lock more closely, glancing at the small pile of wood dust on the floor directly under the lock. Lee knew it had been left over when the person installing the lock had drilled the hole through the wooden door. Exterior deadbolts. A security system. A deadbolt recently installed on an *interior* closet door in a crappy rental in the boonies. What could be so valuable here to go to all this trouble?

"Shit," Lee said again. He wanted to leave this place, but he could not take his eyes off the lock. If Lee Adams had one fault—and it could hardly be considered a fault for someone in his line of work—it was that he was a very curious man. Secrets plagued him. People attempting to hide things came close to infuriating him. As a "lunch pail" kind of guy utterly convinced that great monied forces stalked the earth creating all kinds of havoc for ordinary folk like him, Lee believed in the principle of full and fair disclosure with all his substantial heart. Putting action to that belief, he wedged the flashlight under his armpit, holstered his gun and pulled out his lock-pick kit. His fingers worked nimbly as he slipped a fresh pick into the lock-pick gun. He took a deep breath, inserted the pick in the lock and turned on the machine.

When the deadbolt slid back, Lee took another deep breath, pulled his pistol and pointed it at the door as he turned the knob. He didn't really believe that anyone had locked himself in a closet and was about to jump him, but then again, he had seen stranger things happen. Someone might be on the other side of this door.

When he saw what was in the closet, a part of him wished the problem were as simple as someone preparing to ambush him. He swore under his breath, holstered his pistol and ran.

In the closet the blink of red lights from the stacks of electronic equipment shone forth now in the open doorway.

Lee raced into the other front room and shone his light around the walls in even patterns, moving higher and higher. Then he saw it. There was a camera lens in the wall next to the molding. Probably a pinhole lens, designed specifically for covert surveillance. It was impossible to see in the poor lighting, but the beam from the flashlight was reflecting off it. As he moved the beam around, he hit a total of four camera lenses.

Holy shit. The sound he had heard earlier. He must have tripped some device that had triggered the cameras. He raced back to the living room closet, flashed his light on the front of the video machine.

Eject! Where the hell was eject? He found the button, hit it and nothing happened. He punched it again and again. He hit the other buttons. Nothing. Then Lee's gaze closed on the *second* small infrared portal in the front of the machine, and the answer hit him. The machine was controlled by a special remote, its function buttons overridden. His blood ran cold with the possibilities this sort of arrangement suggested. He thought about putting a bullet into the thing, to make it cough up the precious tape. But for all he knew, the damn thing was armored and he'd end up eating his own slug off the ricochet. And what if it had a real-time satellite link and the tape was only a backup? Was there a camera in here? People could be looking at him right now. For one ridiculous second, he thought about giving them the finger.

Lee was about to run again but then had a sudden

inspiration. He fumbled in his knapsack, his usually steady fingers now not quite so dexterous. His hands closed around the small case. He whipped it out, fought with the lid for an instant and then managed to pull out the small but powerful magnet.

Magnets were a popular burglary tool because they were ideal for locating and popping window pins once you had cut through the glass. Otherwise, the pins would defeat the most accomplished burglar. Now the magnet would play the reverse role: not helping him break in, but rather assisting him in making what he hoped would be an invisible exit.

He palmed the magnet and then ran it in front of the video machine and then over the top. He did it as many times as he could in the one minute he had allowed himself before fleeing for his life. He prayed that the magnetic field would obliterate the images on the tape. *His* images.

He threw the magnet back in his bag, turned and ran for the door. God only knew who might be on their way here. Lee suddenly stopped. Should he go back to the closet, rip the VCR out and take it with him? The next sound Lee heard drove all thoughts of the VCR from his mind.

A car was coming.

"Sonofabitch!" hissed Lee. Was it Lockhart and her escort? They had come here every *other* evening. So much for a pattern. He raced back down the hall, threw open the back door, burst through and hurdled the concrete stoop. He landed heavily in the slick grass, his shoeless feet slipped and he fell hard. The impact knocked the breath out of him and he felt a sharp pain where his elbow had struck at an odd angle. But fear was a great painkiller. Within a few seconds he was up and chugging for the tree line.

He was halfway to the woods when the car pulled into the driveway, its light beams bouncing a little as the car moved from flat road to uneven ground. Lee took another few strides, hit the tree line and dove under cover.

The red dot had lingered for a few moments on Lee's chest. Serov could have taken the man so easily. But that would warn the people in the car. The former KGB man aimed the rifle at the driver's-side door. He hoped the man who had now made it to the woods would not be stupid enough to try anything. He had been very lucky up until now. He had escaped death not once, but twice. One should not waste that much luck. It would be in such poor taste, Serov thought as he once more sighted through the laser scope.

Lee should have kept running, but he stopped, his chest heaving, and crept back to the tree line. His curiosity had always been his strongest trait, sometimes too strong. Besides, the people behind all the electronic equipment probably had already identified him. Hell, they probably knew the dentist he used and his preference for Coke over Pepsi, so he might as well stick around and see what was coming next. If the people in the car started for the woods, he would do his best impersonation of an Olympic marathoner, shoeless feet and all, and dare anyone to catch him.

He crouched down and took out his night-vision monocular. It utilized forward-looking infrared, or FLIR, technology, which was a vast improvement over the ambient light intensifier, or I-squareds, Lee had used in the past. FLIR worked by detecting, in essence, heat. It needed no light to operate, and unlike the I-squareds, it could distinguish dark images against dark backgrounds, with the heat transferred into crystal-clear video images.

As Lee focused the contraption, his field of vision was now a green screen with red images. The car appeared so close that Lee had the sense that he could reach out and touch it. The engine area glowed particularly brightly, since it was still very hot. He watched the man as he climbed out of the driver's side. Lee didn't recognize him, but the private investigator tensed as he watched Faith Lockhart climb out of the car and join the man. They were side by side at this point. The man hesitated as though he had forgotten something.

"Damn," Lee hissed between clenched teeth. "The door." Lee focused for a moment on the back door to the cottage. It was standing wide open.

The man had obviously seen this. He turned, facing the woman, and reached inside his coat.

*   *   *

In the woods, Serov fixed his laser point on the base of the man's neck. He smiled contentedly. The man and woman were lined up nicely. The ammo the Russian was chambering was highly customized, military-style ordnance with full metal jackets. Serov was a careful student of both weapons and the wounds they caused. With its high velocity, the bullet would have minimal projectile deformity as it passed through its target. However, it would still cause devastating injury when the kinetic energy the bullet carried was released and then rapidly lost in the body. The initial wound track and cavity would be many times larger than the size of the bullet before it partially closed. And the destruction to tissue and bone would occur radially, akin to the epicenter of an earthquake, with terrible damage resulting a great distance away. It was quite beautiful, in its own way, Serov felt.

Velocity was the key to kinetic energy levels—the Russian was well aware—which, in turn, determined damage force on the target. Double the weight of a bullet and it doubled the kinetic energy. However, Serov had long ago learned that when you doubled the velocity at which the bullet was fired, the kinetic energy was *quadrupled*. And Serov's weapon and ammo were at the top end of the scale on velocity. Yes, beautiful indeed.

However, because of its full metal jacket, the bullet could also easily pass through one person and then strike and kill another. This was not an unpopular result for soldiers who were going at it in combat. And for hired killers with two targets. However, if another bullet was required to kill the woman, so be it. Ammo was relatively cheap. Consequently, so were humans.

Serov took a slight breath, became absolutely still and lightly squeezed the trigger.

"Oh my God!" Lee shouted as he watched the man's body twist and then pitch violently against the woman. They both dropped to the ground as though sewn together.

Lee instinctively started to race out of the woods to help. A shot hit the tree right next to his head. Lee instantly dropped to the ground and sought cover as another shot hit near him. Lying on his back, his body shaking so hard he could barely focus the damn monocular, Lee scanned the area where he thought the shots had come from.

Another shot hit close to him, kicking up wet dirt in his face, stinging his eyes. Whoever was out there knew what he was doing and was loaded for dinosaur. Lee could sense the shooter methodically closing in on him grid by grid.

Lee could tell that the shooter was using a suppressor, because each shot sounded like someone slapping a wall hard with the palm of his hand. *Splat. Splat. Splat.* They could have been balloons exploding at a child's party, not cone-shaped pieces of metal flying at a million Mach seeking to wipe out a certain PI.

Other than the hand holding his monocular, Lee tried not to move, tried not to breathe. For one terrifying instant he saw the red line of the laser dart near his leg like a curious snake, and then it was gone. He didn't have much time. If he just stayed here, he was a dead man.

Laying his gun on his chest, Lee stretched his fingers out and carefully groped for a moment in the dirt until his hand closed around a stone. Using just the flick of his wrist, he tossed the stone about five feet away, waited; and when it hit a tree, a bullet struck the same spot a few seconds later.

With his infrared eye, Lee instantly zeroed in on the heat of this last muzzle flash, as oxygen-deprived, super-hot gas escaping from the rifle barrel collided with the outside air. This simple reaction of physical elements had cost many a soldier his life as it revealed his position. Lee could only hope for the same result now.

Lee used the muzzle flash to fix on the man's thermal image amid the cover of trees. The shooter wasn't that far away, well within range of Lee's SIG. Realizing he would probably get only one attempt, Lee slowly gripped his gun and raised his arm, trying to locate a clear line of fire. Keeping his gaze on his target through the monocular, Lee clicked off the safety, said a silent prayer and fired eight shots from his fifteen-round mag. They were all aimed fairly close together, increasing his chances of a hit. His pistol shots were much louder than the rifle's suppressed ones. On all sides of him wildlife fled the human conflict.

One of Lee's shots miraculously found its mark, mainly because Serov had moved right into the path of the shot as he was attempting to shift to a closer position. The Russian grunted in pain as the bullet entered his left forearm. For a split second it stung, then the dull throbbing came as the bullet ripped through soft tissue and veins, shattered his humerus and finally came to rest in his clavicle. His left arm immediately became heavy and useless. After killing a dozen people in his career, always with a gun, Leonid Serov finally knew what it felt like to be shot. Clutching the rifle in his good hand, the ex-KGB agent took the professional way out. He turned and ran, blood splattering on the ground with each step.

Through the FLIR, Lee watched him run for a few moments. From the way the man was retreating, Lee was pretty certain that at least one of his shots had scored a hit. He decided it would be both stupid and unnecessary to chase an armed and wounded man. Besides, he had something else to do. He grabbed his bag and ran toward the cottage.

WHILE LEE AND SEROV WERE EXCHANGING FIRE, Faith struggled to get her breath back. The collision with Newman had taken most of her wind and left a throbbing pain in her shoulder. With convulsive strength she was able to roll him off. She felt a warm and sticky substance on her dress. For a terrifying moment she thought she had been shot. Faith couldn't have known it, but the agent's Glock pistol had acted as a mini-shield, deflecting the bullet as it left his body. It was the only reason she was still alive. For a moment she stared at what was left of Newman's face and felt herself growing sick.

Pulling her gaze away, Faith managed to squat low in the driveway and slid her hand into Newman's pocket, then pulled out his car keys. Faith's heart was pumping so frantically that it was difficult for her mind to focus. She could barely hold the damn car keys. Still crouching, she eased open the driver's-side door.

Her body was shaking so hard she didn't even know if she could drive the car once she got in it. Then she was inside, slammed the door shut and locked it. When the engine caught, she put the car in gear, hit the gas and the engine flooded and died on her. Swearing loudly, she turned the key again; the engine caught. She made a more cautious movement on the gas pedal and the engine remained purring.

She was about to hit the gas when her breath caught in her throat. A man stood at the driver's-side window. He was breathing heavily and looked as scared as she felt. What really held her attention, though, was the gun pointed directly at her. He motioned for her to roll the window down. She contemplated hitting the gas.

"Don't try it," he said, seemingly reading her thoughts. "I'm not the one who shot at you," he said through the glass. He added, "If I were, you'd already be dead."

Finally Faith edged down the window.

"Unlock the door," he said, "and move over."

"Who are you?"

"Let's go, lady. I don't know about you, but I don't want to be here when someone else shows up. They might be a better shot."

Faith unlocked the door and slid over. Lee holstered his gun, threw his bag in the back, got in, slammed the door shut and backed out. Right at that instant the cell phone on the front seat rang, causing them to both jump. He stopped the car and they looked down at the phone and then at each other.

"It's not my phone," he said.

"It's not mine either," replied Faith.

When the ringing stopped, he asked, "Who's the dead guy?"

"I'm not telling you anything."

The car hit the road and he shifted to drive and punched the gas. "You might regret that decision."

"I don't think so."

He appeared confused by her confident tone.

She slipped her seat belt on as he took a curve a little fast. "If you shot that man back there, then you'll shoot me regardless of what I tell you or not. If you're telling the truth and you didn't shoot him, then I don't think you'll kill me simply because I won't talk."

"You have a very naive perspective of good and bad. Even good guys have to kill on occasion," he said.

"Are you speaking from experience?" Faith edged closer against the door.

He hit the auto door lock. "Now, don't go and throw yourself out the car. I just want to know what's going on. Starting with who's the dead guy."

Faith stared at him, her nerves completely shattered. When she finally spoke, her voice was very weak. "Do you mind if we just go somewhere, anywhere, so I can just sit and think for a bit?" She curled her fingers and added hoarsely, "I've never seen anyone killed before. I've never almost been . . ." Her voice rose as she said this last part and she started to tremble. "Please pull over. For God's sake, pull over! I'm going to be sick."

He skidded the car to a stop on the shoulder and hit the auto unlock button. Faith threw open the door, leaned out and vomited.

He reached across and put his hand on her shoulder, squeezing tightly until she stopped shaking. He spoke in a slow, steady tone. "You're gonna be okay." He paused and waited until she was able to sit back up and close the door before continuing. "First we need to ditch this car. Mine's on the other side of the woods. It'll only take a few minutes to get there. Then I know a place where you can be safe. Okay?"

"Okay," Faith managed to say.

Barely twenty minutes later, a sedan pulled into the cottage's driveway and a man and woman got out. The metal of their weapons reflected off the light thrown from the car's headlights. Approaching the dead man, the woman knelt down and looked at the body. If she hadn't known Ken Newman very well, she might not have recognized him. She had seen human death before, yet she still felt something rising from her stomach to her throat. She quickly stood and turned away. The pair searched the cottage thoroughly and then did a quick sweep of the tree line before coming back to the body.

The large, barrel-chested fellow looked down at Ken Newman's body and uttered a curse. Howard Constantinople was "Connie" to all who knew him. A veteran FBI agent, he had seen just about everything in his career. However, tonight was new territory even for him. Ken Newman was a good friend of his. Connie looked as though he might burst into sobs.

The woman stood next to him. At six feet one, she matched Connie's height. Her brunette hair was cut very short, curving over her ears. Her face was long, narrow and intelligent, and she was dressed in a stylishly fitting pantsuit. Both the years and the stress of her occupation had hammered fine lines around her mouth and around her dark, sad eyes. Her gaze swept the surrounding area with the ease of someone accustomed not only to observing but also to making accurate deductions from what she observed. There was an edge to her features that clearly demonstrated a powerful internal anger.

At age thirty-nine, Brooke Reynolds had attractive features and a tall, lean physique that would make her appealing to men for as long as she desired the attention. However, immersed as she was in the middle of a bitter divorce that had wreaked havoc on her two young children, she questioned whether she would ever again want the companionship of a man.

Reynolds had been christened, over the objections of her mother, Brooklyn Dodgers Reynolds by her overzealous baseball-fan father. Her old man had never been the same when his beloved ball club went to California. Almost from day one, her mother had insisted she be called Brooke.

"My God," Reynolds finally said, her gaze fixed on her dead colleague.

Connie looked over at her. "So what do we do now?"

She shook off the net of despair that had settled over her. Action was called for, swift but methodical. "We have a crime scene, Connie. We don't have much choice."

"Locals?"

"This is an AFO," she said, referring to an assault on a federal officer, "so the Bureau will be in the lead." She found she couldn't take her gaze from the body. "But we'll still have to work with the county and state people. I have contacts with them, so I'm reasonably sure we can control the information flow."

"With an AFO we have the Bureau's Violent Crime Unit. That breaks our Chinese wall."

Reynolds took a deep breath to quell the tears she felt rising to her eyes. "We'll do the best we can. The first thing we have to do is secure the crime scene, not that it's going to be too difficult out here. I'll call Paul Fisher at HQ and fill him in." Reynolds mentally went up her chain of command at the Bureau's Washington Field Office, or WFO. The ASAC, SAC and ADIC would have to be notified; the ADIC, or assistant director in charge, was the head of the WFO, really only a notch below the director of the FBI himself. Soon, she thought, there would be enough abbreviations here to sink a battleship.

"Dollars to donuts the director himself will be out here too," Connie added.

The walls of Reynolds's stomach started to burn. An agent being killed was a shock. An agent losing his life on her watch was a nightmare she would never wake up from.

An hour later, forces had converged on the scene, fortunately without any media. The state medical examiner verified what everyone who had even remotely seen the devastating wound already knew: namely, that Special Agent Kenneth Newman had died from a distant gunshot entry wound to the upper neck, exiting from his face. While the local police stood guard, the VCU, or Violent Crime Unit, agents methodically collected evidence.

Reynolds, Connie and their superiors gathered around her car. The ADIC was Fred Massey, the ranking agent at the scene. He was a small, humorless man who kept shaking his head in exaggerated motions. His white shirt collar was loose around a skinny neck, his bald head seeming to glow under the moonlight.

A VCU agent appeared with a videotape from the cottage and a pair of muddy boots. Reynolds and Connie had noted the boots when they had searched the cottage, but had wisely opted against disturbing any evidence.

"Someone was in the house," he reported. "These boots were on the back stoop. No forced entry. The alarm was deactivated and the equipment closet was open. Looks like we maybe got the person on tape. They tripped the laser."

He handed the tape to Massey, who promptly handed it over to Reynolds. The act was far from subtle. All this was her responsibility. She would either get the credit or take the fall. The VCU agent put the boots in an evidence bag and went back into the house to continue searching.

Massey said, "Give me your observations, Agent Reynolds." His tone was curt, and everyone understood why.

Some of the other agents had openly shed tears and cursed loudly when they saw their colleague's body. As the only woman here, and Newman's squad supervisor to boot, Reynolds didn't feel she had the luxury of dissolving into tears in front of them. The vast majority of FBI agents went through their entire careers without ever even drawing their sidearms except for weapons recertification. Reynolds had sometimes wondered how she would react if such a catastrophe ever hit home. Now she knew: Not very well.

This was probably the most important case Reynolds would ever handle. A while back, she had been assigned to the Bureau's Public Corruption Unit, a component of the illustrious Criminal Investigation Division. After receiving a phone call from Faith Lockhart one night and secretly meeting the woman on several occasions, Reynolds had been named the squad supervisor of a unit detailed to a special. That "special" had the opportunity, if Lock-hart was telling the truth, to topple some of the biggest names in the United States government. Most agents would die for such a case during their careers. Well, one had tonight.

Reynolds held up the tape. "I'm hoping this tape will tell us something of what happened here. And what happened to Faith Lockhart."

"You think it's likely she shot Ken? If so, a nation-wide APB goes out in about two seconds," Massey said.

Reynolds shook her head. "My gut tells me she had nothing to do with it. But the fact is we don't know enough. We'll check the blood type and other residue. If it only matches Ken's, then we know she wasn't hit as well. We know Ken hadn't fired his gun. And he had on his vest. Something took a chunk out of his Glock, though."

Connie nodded. "The bullet that killed him. Through the back of the neck and out the front. He had his weapon out, probably eye-height, the slug hit and deflected off it." Connie swallowed with difficulty. "The residue on Ken's pistol supports that conclusion."

Reynolds stared sadly at the man and continued the analysis. "So Ken might have been between Lock-hart and the shooter?"

Connie slowly shook his head. "Human shield. I thought only the Secret Service did that crap."

Reynolds said, "I spoke with the ME. We won't know anything until the post and we can see the wound track, but I think it was most likely a rifle shot. Not the sort of weapon a woman ordinarily carries in her purse."

"So another person waiting for them?" Massey ventured.

"And why would that person kill and then go inside the house?" Connie asked.

"Maybe it was Newman and Lockhart who went in the house," Massey surmised.

Reynolds knew it had been years since Massey had worked a field investigation, but he was still her ADIC and she couldn't very well ignore him. She didn't have to agree with him, though.

Reynolds shook her head decisively. "If they had gone in the house, Ken wouldn't have been killed in the driveway. They'd still be in the house. We interview Lockhart for at least two hours each time. We got here a half hour after they would have, tops. And those weren't Ken's boots. But they are men's boots, about a size twelve. Odds are a big guy."

"If Newman and Lockhart didn't go in the house, and there are no signs of forced entry, then this third party had the pass-code to the alarm." Massey's tone was clearly accusatory.

Reynolds looked miserable, but she had to keep going. "From where Ken fell, it looked like he had just gotten out of the car. Then something must have spooked Ken. He pulls his Glock and then takes the round."

Reynolds led them over to the driveway. "Look at the rut marks here. The ground around here is reasonably dry, but the tires really gouged the dirt. I think somebody was getting out of here in a hurry. Hell, fast enough that he ran out of his boots."

"And Lockhart?"

"Maybe the shooter took her with him," Connie said.

Reynolds thought about this. "It's possible, but I don't see why. They'd want her dead too."

"In the first place, how would a shooter know to come here?" Massey asked, and then answered his own question. "A leak?"

Reynolds had been considering this possibility from the moment she had seen Newman's body. "With all due respect, sir, I don't see how that could be the case."

Massey coldly ticked off the points on his fingers. "We've got one dead man, a missing woman and a pair of boots. Put it all together and I'm looking at a third party being involved. Tell me how that third party got here without inside information."

Reynolds spoke in a very low tone. "It could be a random thing. Lonely place, possible armed robbery. It happens." She took a quick breath. "But if you're right and there is a leak, it's not complete." They all looked at her curiously. "The shooter obviously didn't know about our last-second change of plan.

That Connie and I would be here tonight," Reynolds explained. "Ordinarily, I would've been with Faith, but I was working another case. It didn't pan out and I decided at the last minute to hook up with Connie and come out here."

Connie glanced over at the van. "You're right, no one could have known about that. Ken didn't even know."

"I *tried* to call Ken about twenty minutes before we got here. I didn't want to just suddenly appear. If he heard a car pull up to the safe house without prior warning, he might have gotten spooked, shot first and asked questions later. He must have already been dead when I tried to reach him."

Massey stepped toward her. "Agent Reynolds, I know you've been handling this investigation from the beginning. I know that your use of this safe house and the closed-circuit TV surveillance of Ms. Lockhart were all approved by the appropriate parties. I understand your difficulties in pursuing this case and gaining this witness's trust." Massey paused for a moment, seeming to select his words with great care. Newman's death had stunned them all, although agents were often in harm's way. Still, there would be definite blame assessed in this case, and everyone knew it.

Massey continued, "However, your approach was hardly textbook. And the fact is, an agent is dead."

Reynolds plunged right in. "We had to do this very quietly. We couldn't exactly have surrounded Lockhart with agents. Buchanan would've been gone before we had enough evidence for prosecution." She took a long breath. "Sir, you asked for my observations. Here they are. I don't think Lockhart killed Ken. I think Buchanan is behind it. We have to find her. But we have to do it quietly. If we put out an APB, then Ken Newman has probably died in vain. And if Lockhart is alive, she won't be for long if we go public."

Reynolds looked over at the van just as its doors closed on Newman's body. If she had been escorting Faith Lockhart instead of Ken, the odds were that she would have lost her life tonight. For any FBI agent, death was always a possibility, however remote. If she were killed, would Brooklyn Dodgers Reynolds fade in her children's memory? She was certain her six-year-old daughter would always remember "Mommy." She had doubts about three-year-old David, though. If she were killed, would David, years from now, only refer to Reynolds as his "birth" mother? The thought itself was nearly paralyzing.

One day she had actually taken the ridiculous step of having her palm read. The palm reader had warmly welcomed Reynolds, given her a cup of herbal tea and chatted with her, asking her questions that tried to sound casual. These queries, Reynolds knew, were designed to gather background information to which the woman could add appropriate mumbo-jumbo as she "saw" into Reynolds's past, as well as her future.

After examining Reynolds's hand, the palm reader

had told her that her life line was short. Significantly so, in fact. The worst she'd ever seen. The woman said this as she stared at a scar on Reynolds's palm. Reynolds knew it was the result of falling on a broken Coke bottle in her backyard when she was eight.

The reader had picked up her cup of tea, apparently waiting for Reynolds to plead for more information, presumably at an appropriate premium over the initial fee. Reynolds had informed her that she was strong as a horse with years in between even a simple bout of flu.

Death needn't be by natural causes, the palm reader had replied, her painted eyebrows rising to emphasize the obvious point.

On that, Reynolds had paid her five dollars and walked out the door.

Now she wondered.

Connie scuffed the dirt with his toe. "If Buchanan is behind this, he's probably long gone by now anyway."

"I don't think so," Reynolds replied. "If he runs right after this, then he's as good as admitting guilt. No, he'll play it cool."

"I don't like this," Massey said. "I say we APB Lockhart and bring her in, assuming she's still living."

"Sir," Reynolds said, her voice tight, edgy, "we can't name her as a subject in a homicide when we have reason to believe she wasn't involved in the murder, but may well be a victim herself. That opens the Bureau to a whole civil-action can of worms if she does turn up. You know that."

"Material witness, then. She damn well qualifies for that," said Massey.

Reynolds looked directly at him. "An APB is not the answer. It's going to do more harm than good. For everybody involved."

"Buchanan has no reason to keep her alive."

"Lockhart is a smart woman," Reynolds said. "I spent time with her, got to know her. She's a survivor. If she can hang on for a few days, we have a shot. Buchanan can't possibly know what she's been telling us. But we do an APB naming her as a material witness, we just sign her death notice."

They were all silent for a bit. "All right, I see your point," Massey finally said. "You really think you can find her on the Q.T.?"

"Yes." What else could she say?

"Is that your gut talking, or your brain?"

"Both."

Massey studied her for a long moment. "For now, Agent Reynolds, you focus on finding Lockhart. The VCU people will investigate Newman's murder."

"I'd have them lockstep the yard looking for the slug that killed Ken. Then I'd search the woods," Reynolds said.

"Why the woods? The boots were on the stoop."

She glanced over at the tree line. "If I were here to ambush someone, that"—she pointed toward the woods—"would be my first tactical choice. Good cover, excellent line of fire and a hidden escape route. Car waiting, gun disposed of, a quick trip to Dulles Airport. In an hour the shooter's in another time zone. The shot that killed Ken entered the back of his neck. He's facing away from the woods. Ken must not have seen his attacker, or else he wouldn't have turned his back." She eyed the thick woods. "It all points there."

Another car pulled up and the director of the FBI himself climbed out. Massey and his aides hurried over, leaving Connie and Reynolds alone.

"So what's our plan of action?" Connie asked.

"Maybe I'll try to match those boots to my Cinderella," Reynolds said as she watched Massey talking to the director. The director was a former field agent who, Reynolds knew, would take this catastrophe extremely personally. Everybody and everything associated with it would be subject to intense scrutiny.

"We'll cover all the usual bases." She tapped her finger against the tape. "But this is really all we have. Whoever's on this tape we hit hard, like there's no tomorrow."

"Depending on how this turns out, we might not have many tomorrows left, Brooke," said Connie.

CHAPTER 8

LEE GRIPPED THE STEERING WHEEL SO HARD HIS fingers were turning white. As the police car, lights blazing, raced past him going in the opposite direction, he let out an enormous breath and then pushed hard on the accelerator. They were in Lee's car after having ditched the other. He had scrubbed down the inside of the dead man's car, but he could have easily missed something. And nowadays equipment existed that could find things completely invisible to the naked eye. Not good.

As Faith watched the swirling lights disappear into the darkness, she wondered if the police were heading to the cottage. Did Ken Newman have a wife and kids? she wondered. There had been no wedding band on his finger. Like many women, Faith had the habit of making that quick observation. Yet he'd seemed like the fatherly type.

As Lee maneuvered the car through the back roads, Faith's hand moved up, down and then drew a vertical line across her chest as she finished crossing herself. The near-automatic movement conveyed a subtle sense of surprise to her. She added a silent prayer for the dead man. She whispered another prayer for any family he might have. "I'm so sorry you're dead," she said out loud, to help assuage her mounting feelings of guilt for simply having survived.

Lee looked over at her. "Friend of yours?"

She shook her head. "He was killed because of me. Isn't that enough?"

Faith was surprised at how easily the words of prayer and remorse had come back to her. Because of her nomadic father, her attendance at mass over the years had been sporadic. But her mother had insisted on Catholic schools wherever the family happened to venture, and her father had followed this rule after his wife had died. Catholic school must have ingrained something in her other than the constant bite of the ruler on her knuckles from Sister Something-or-other. The summer before her senior year, she had become an orphan, her travels with her father abruptly cut short by a heart attack. She was sent to live with a relative who did not want her and who took pains to show no attention to her. Faith had rebelled however she could. She smoked, she drank, she ceased to be virgin Faith long before it was fashionable to do so. At school the daily tugging down of her skirt to below her knees by the nuns only made her want to pull the damn thing up to her crotch. All in all, it was a truly forgettable year in her life, followed by several more as she struggled through college, tried to gain some direction in her life. Then for the past fifteen years she had thought her rudder was flawless, the grand movements of her life fluid. Now she was floundering, speeding toward the rocks.

Faith looked at Lee. "We need to call the police, tell somebody that he's back there."

Lee shook his head. "That opens a whole other can of worms. That is definitely not a good idea."

"We can't just leave him back there. It's not right."

"Do you suggest we go to the local precinct and try to explain this thing? They'll put us in straitjackets."

"Dammit! If you won't do it, I will. I am *not* leaving him back there for the squirrels."

"All right, all right. Calm down." He sighed. "I guess we could place an anonymous call in a little while, get the cops to check it out."

"Fine," said Faith.

A few minutes later, Lee noticed that Faith was fidgeting.

"I have another request," she said.

The woman's demanding style was really starting to annoy him. Lee tried not to think about the hurt in his elbow, the irritating specks of cold dirt in his eyes, the unknown dangers that lay ahead.

"Like what?" he said wearily.

"There's a gas station near here. I'd like to wash up." She added quietly, "If that's okay."

Lee looked down at the stains on her clothes and his expression softened. "No problem," he said.

"It's down this road—"

"I know where it is," Lee said. "I like to get the lay of the land where I'm working."

Faith simply stared at him.

In the bathroom Faith tried not to focus on what she was doing as she painstakingly cleaned the blood off her clothing. Still, every couple of minutes she felt like ripping off all her clothes and scrubbing herself down using the soap from the dispenser and the stack of paper towels on the dirty sink.

When she climbed back in the car, her companion's look said what his mouth didn't.

"I'll make it, for now," she said.

"By the way, my name's Lee. Lee Adams."

Faith said nothing. He started the car and they left the gas station.

"You don't have to tell me your name," he said. "I was hired to follow you, Ms. Lockhart."

She eyed him suspiciously. "Who hired you to do that?"

"Don't know."

"How could you possibly not know who hired you?"

"I admit it's a little unusual, but it happens, on occasion. Some people are embarrassed about hiring a private detective."

"So that's what you are, a private eye?" Her tone was one of contempt.

"It can be a very legit way of earning a buck. And I'm as legit as they come."

"And how did this person come to hire you?"

"Other than the fact that I've got a killer Yellow Pages ad, I don't have a clue."

"Do you have any idea what you're mixed up in, Mr. Adams?"

"Let's just say I have a better idea now than I did a little bit ago. Getting shot at is the one thing that has always captured my undivided attention."

"And who shot at you?"

"The same guy who nailed your friend. I think I winged him, but he got away."

Faith rubbed her temples and looked out into the darkness. His next words startled her.

"What are you, Witness Protection?" Lee waited. When she didn't answer, he continued. "I did a ten-second down-and-dirty on your friend while you were busy choking out the car. He had a Glock nine-millimeter and a Kevlar vest, for all the good it did him. The shield on his belt said FBI. I didn't have time to check for ID. So what was his name?"

"Does it matter?"

"It might."

"Why Witness Protection?" she asked.

"The cottage. Special locks, security system. It's a safe house, of sorts. Nobody's living there, that's for sure."

"So you've been inside."

He nodded. "At first I thought you were having an affair. A couple minutes inside told me it wasn't a love nest. Strange house, though. Hidden cameras, tape-recording system. Did you know you were on stage, by the way?"

The astonished look on her face answered his question.

"If you didn't know who hired you, how were you engaged to follow me?"

"Easy enough. Phone message said a packet of information on you and an advance on my fee would be delivered to my office. They were. A file on you, and a big chunk of cash. It said to follow your movements, and I did."

"I was told I wasn't being followed."

"I've gotten pretty good at it."

"Apparently."

"Once I knew where you were going, I just got here ahead of you. Pretty simple."

"Was the voice a man's or woman's?"

"Couldn't tell; it was scrambled."

"Didn't that make you suspicious?"

"Everything makes me suspicious. One thing's for sure, whoever's after you, they ain't playing around.

The ammo the guy was using back there could have wasted an elephant. I got to see it up close and personal."

He fell silent, and Faith could not bring herself to say anything else. She had several credit cards in her purse, all with virtually limitless spending power. And they were all useless to her, because as soon as one went through the swipe machine, they would know where she was. She put her hand in her purse and touched the Tiffany pewter ring holding the keys to her beautiful home and her luxury car. Useless as well. In her wallet was the grand sum of fifty-five dollars and a few pennies. She had been stripped bare except for this cash and the clothes on her back. Her impoverished childhood had come roaring back in all its tarnished, hopeless memory.

She did have a large sum of cash, but it was in a safe-deposit box at her bank in D.C. The bank would not be open until tomorrow morning. And there were two other items she kept in that box that were even more critical to her: a driver's license and another credit card. They were both under a fake name. They had been relatively easy to set up, but she had hoped she would never have to use them. So much so that she had kept them in her bank instead of a more accessible place. Now she shook her head at such stupidity.

With those two cards she could go just about anywhere. If everything collapsed on top of her, she had often reminded herself, this would be her way out.

Well, she thought now, *the roof's gone, the walls are creaking, the killer tornado's at the window and the fat lady is in the limo on the way back to the hotel. It's time to pull the tent and call it a life.*

She looked at Lee. What would she do with him? Faith knew that her most pressing challenge was surviving the rest of the night. Maybe he could help her do that. He seemed to know what he was doing, and he had a gun. If she could just get in and out of her bank without too much trouble, she would be okay. There were about seven hours between now and the bank's opening. They might as well have been seven years.

CHAPTER 9

THORNHILL SAT IN THE SMALL STUDY OF HIS
lovely ivy-draped old home in a much-sought-after
neighborhood in McLean, Virginia. His wife's family
had money, and he enjoyed the luxuries that money
could buy, as well as the freedom it gave him to be a
public servant his entire career. Right now, though,
he was not feeling much comfort.

The message he had just received was unbelievable to
him, and yet all plans had the potential for failure. He
looked at the man sitting across from him. This person
was also a veteran at the Agency, and a member of
Thornhill's secret group. Philip Winslow shared
Thornhill's ideals and concerns. They had spent many
a night in Thornhill's study, both reminiscing about
past glories and devising plans that would ensure there
would be many future triumphs as well. They were
both Yale graduates, two of the best and brightest.

They had come along at a time when it was considered honorable to serve one's country. And the CIA had gotten its share of the Ivy League's best back then. They had also come from a generation in which a man did whatever it took to protect his country's interests. A man with vision, Thornhill believed with all his heart, had to be willing to take risks to achieve that vision.

"The FBI agent was killed," Thornhill said to his friend and colleague.

"And Lockhart?" Winslow asked.

Thornhill gave one brief shake of his head. "She's disappeared."

Winslow summed it up. "So we take out one of the Bureau's finest and let the real target get away." He clinked the ice in his drink. "Not good, Bob. The others won't be happy to hear that."

"Just to get all the good news out, our man was also shot in the process."

"By the agent?"

Thornhill shook his head. "No. There was someone else there tonight. Unknown as yet. Serov has been debriefed. He gave a description of the man who was at the cottage. We're doing computer generations of him right now. We should know his identity shortly."

"Could he tell us anything else?"

"Not at present. Mr. Serov is being detained, for now, in safe quarters."

"You know the Bureau will go after this tooth and nail, Bob."

"More precisely," Thornhill said, "they will do everything in their power to find Faith Lockhart."

"Who do they suspect?"

"Buchanan, of course. It's logical," Thornhill replied.

"So what do we do with Buchanan?"

"For now, nothing. We'll keep him informed. Of at least our version of the truth, that is. We'll keep him busy at the same time we keep close tabs on the FBI. He has a trip out of town this morning, so we're covered there. However, if the FBI's investigation gets too close to Buchanan, we'll provide him with an early death and provide our professional brethren with all the sordid facts of how Buchanan tried to have Lockhart murdered."

"And Lockhart?" Winslow asked.

"Oh, the FBI will find her. They're quite good at that sort of thing, in their limited way."

"I don't see how that helps us. She talks, and Buchanan goes down and takes us with him."

"I hardly think that," Thornhill said. "When the FBI finds her, we will be there as well, if we don't find her first. And this time we won't miss. With Lockhart gone, Buchanan will soon follow. Then we can move forward with our original plan."

"God, if it could only work."

"Oh, it will work," said Thornhill with his usual optimism. To last as long as he had in this business, one had to have a positive attitude.

CHAPTER 10

LEE PULLED THE CAR INTO THE ALLEYWAY AND
stopped. His gaze swept over the darkened landscape. They had driven around for over two hours
until he felt reasonably sure they had not been followed, and then he had made the phone call to the
police from a pay phone. Although they seemed relatively safe now, Lee still kept one hand resting on
the grip of his pistol, ready to pull it in an instant,
to terminate their enemies with the salvos from his
deadly SIG. That was a joke.

These days you could kill from a sky away, with a
bomb smarter than a man, taking the most important
thing a human being had without so much as a
"Hello, you're dead." Lee wondered if, during the
millisecond it took to cremate the poor bastards, the
brain moved fast enough to spark the thought that

the Hand of God had struck them down instead of something manufactured by man, the idiot. For a crazy moment, Lee scanned the sky looking for a guided missile. And depending on who was involved in all this, maybe it wasn't so crazy after all.

"What did you tell the police?" Faith asked.

"Short and sweet. The location of the place and what happened."

"And?"

"And the dispatcher was skeptical but did his best to keep me on the line."

Faith looked around the alley. "Is *this* the safe place you mentioned?" She took in the darkness, the hidden crevices, the garbage can and the distant tap of footsteps on pavement.

"No, we leave the car here and walk to the safe place. Which, by the way, is my apartment."

"Where are we?"

"North Arlington. It's being yuppified, but it can still be dangerous, especially this time of night."

She stayed right next to him as they made their way down the alley and out onto the next street, which was an avenue of old but nicely kept-up attached rowhouses.

"Which one's yours?"

"The big one at the end there. Owner's retired, lives in Florida. He's got a couple of other properties. I troubleshoot for him, and he gives me a break on the rent."

Faith started to walk out of the alley, but Lee stopped her. "Give me a sec, I want to check things first."

She clutched his jacket. "You are not leaving me here alone."

"I'm just making sure there's nobody there waiting to throw us a surprise party. Anything looks weird, give a shout and I'm back in two shakes."

He disappeared and Faith edged into the crevice of the alley. Her heart was beating so loud, she half expected a window to open and a shoe to come sailing out at her. When she thought she could not take being alone anymore, Lee reappeared.

"Okay, it looks good. Let's go."

The outer door to the building was locked, but Lee opened it with his key. Faith noted the video camera bolted to the wall above her head.

Lee looked at her. "My idea. I like to know who's coming to see me."

They went up four flights of stairs to the top floor and down the hallway to the last door on the right. Faith eyed the three locks on the door. Lee opened each of them with another key.

When the door opened, she heard a beeping sound. They went inside the apartment. On the wall was an alarm panel. Screwed into the wall above it was a piece of shiny copper on a hinge. Lee flipped the copper shield down so that it covered the alarm panel. He reached his hand underneath the copper plate and hit some buttons on the panel and the beeping sound stopped.

He looked over at Faith, who was watching him closely.

"Van Eck radiation. You probably wouldn't understand."

She hiked her eyebrows. "You're probably right."

Next to the alarm panel was a small video screen built into the wall. On the screen Faith could see the front stoop of the building. It was obviously the video link to the surveillance camera outside.

Lee locked the front door and then put his hand on it. "It's steel, set in a special metal frame I built myself. It doesn't matter how strong the lock is. What usually gives is the frame. A lousy two-by-four if you're lucky. A crook's Christmas present handed out by the building industry. I've also got pick-proof window locks, outside motion detectors, piggyback cellular on the alarm system's phone link. We'll be okay."

"I take it you're somewhat security-minded?" she said.

"No, I'm paranoid."

Faith heard something approaching from down the hall. She flinched, but relaxed when she saw Lee smile and move toward the sound. A second later an old German shepherd wandered around the corner. Lee squatted and played with the big dog, who rolled over on his back. Lee accommodated the animal with a belly rub.

"Hey, Max, how you doing, boy?" Lee patted Max's head and the dog affectionately licked his owner's hand.

"Now, this thing is the best security device ever invented. Don't have to worry about electrical outages, batteries going dead or somebody turning his loyalties."

"So your plan is that we stay here?"

Lee looked up at her. "You want something to eat or drink? We might as well work on this over a full stomach."

"Hot tea would be nice. I couldn't really look at food right now."

A few minutes later they were sitting at the kitchen table. Faith sipped on herbal tea while Lee worked on a cup of coffee. Max dozed under the table.

"We have a problem," Lee began. "When I went in the cottage I tripped something. So I'm on the video-tape."

Faith looked stricken. "My God, they could be on their way here right now."

"Maybe that's a good thing." Lee looked at her sharply.

"And why is that?"

"I'm not into helping criminals."

"So you think I'm a criminal?"

"Are you?"

Faith fingered her teacup. "I was working with the FBI, not against them."

"Okay, what were they doing with you?"

"I can't answer that."

"Then I can't help you. Come on, I'll give you a ride to your place." Lee started to rise from his chair.

She gripped his arm. "Wait, please wait." The thought of being left alone just then was paralyzing.

He sat back down and waited expectantly.

"How much do I have to tell you before you'll help me?"

"Depends on what sort of help you want. I'm not doing anything against the law."

"I wouldn't ask you to."

"Then you've got no problem, other than somebody wanting to kill you."

Faith took a nervous sip of her tea while Lee watched her.

"If they know who you are from the video, should we be just sitting here?" she asked.

"I messed with the tape. Ran my magnet over it."

Faith looked at him, a glint of hope in her eyes. "You think you were able to erase it?"

"I can't tell for sure. I'm not an expert in that stuff."

"But at the very least it might take some time for them to reconstruct it?"

"That's what I'm hoping. But we're not exactly dealing with the Camp Fire girls here. The recording equipment also had a security system built in. Chances are if the police try to force the tape out, it might self-destruct. Personally, I'd give the forty-seven bucks I have in the bank if that did happen.

I'm a man who likes his privacy. But you still need to fill me in."

Faith didn't say anything. She just stared at him, like he had just made an unwanted pass at her.

Lee cocked his head at her. "I tell you what. I'm the detective, okay? I'll make some deductions and you tell me if I'm right or not, how's that?" When Faith still said nothing, he continued. "The cameras I saw were only in the living room. And the table, chairs, coffee and stuff were set up in the living room only. Now, I tripped the laser or whatever it was going in. That apparently set off the cameras."

"I guess that would make sense," Faith said.

"No, it doesn't. I had the access code to the alarm system," said Lee.

"So?"

"So I put in the code and disarmed the security system. So why have the trip device still operating? The way it was set up, even when the guy you were with disarmed the security system, he would still have engaged the cameras. Why would he want to record himself?"

Faith looked deeply confused. "I don't know."

"Hello, so they'd have you on film without you knowing it. Now the out-of-the-way place with the CIA-level security in place, the Feds, the cameras and taping equipment, all point to one thing." Lee paused as he thought about exactly how he was going to phrase this. "They brought you there to interrogate you. But maybe they're not sure of your level of cooperation, or they think somebody might try to pop you, so they film the interrogations just in case you turn up missing later on."

Faith looked at him with a resigned smile. "Terribly prescient of them, don't you think? The 'turning up missing' thing."

Lee stood and stared out the window as he thought things through. Something very important had just occurred to him. Something that he should have thought about a lot sooner. And even though he didn't know the woman, he was feeling kind of crappy about what he had to say. "I've got some bad news for you."

Faith looked startled. "What do you mean?"

"You're under interrogation by the FBI. Presumably you're also in their protective custody. One of their guys gets popped protecting you and I probably wounded the guy who killed him. The Feds have my face on their tape." He paused for a moment. "I've got to turn you in."

Faith jumped up. "You can't do that! You can't! You said you'd help me."

"If I don't, then I'm looking at some serious time in a place where guys get way too friendly with other guys. At the very least I lose my PI license. I'm sure if I knew you better I'd feel even worse about doing this, but at the end of the day I'm not sure even my grandma would be worth that much trouble." He slipped on his jacket. "Who's your principal handler?"

"I don't know his name," Faith said coldly.

"Do you have a phone number?"

"It wouldn't do any good. I doubt he'd be able to take the call now."

Lee eyed her dubiously. "Are you telling me the dead guy back there is your only contact?"

"That's it." Faith told this lie with a completely straight face.

"The guy was your handler and he never bothered to tell you his name? That's not exactly textbook FBI."

"Sorry, that's all I know."

"Is that right? Well, let me tell you what I know. I saw you at that cottage three other times with a woman. A tall brunette. What, did you sit around calling her Agent X?" He leaned right into her face. "Bullshit Rule Number One: Make damn sure the person you're lying to can't prove same." He hooked an arm around hers. "Let's go."

"You know, Mr. Adams, *you* have a problem you may not have thought about."

"Is that right? Care to share it?"

"What exactly are you going to tell the FBI when you bring me in?"

"I don't know, how about the truth?"

"Okay. Let's look at the truth. You were following me because someone you don't know and can't identify instructed you to. Which means we only have your word for that. You were able to follow me even though the FBI assured me no one could. You were in that house tonight. Your face is on the tape. An FBI agent is dead. You fired your gun. You say you shot the other man, but you have no way to prove another man was even there. So the proven facts are we have you at the house and me at the house. You fired your gun and an FBI agent is dead."

"The ammo that killed that guy is not something my pistol happens to chamber," he said angrily, releasing her arm.

"So you threw the other gun away."

"Why would I snatch you from the place, then? If I was the shooter, why wouldn't I have killed you back there?"

"I'm not saying what *I* think, Mr. Adams. I'm just suggesting to you that the FBI might suspect you. I suppose if there's nothing in your past to make them suspicious, the FBI might believe you." She added offhandedly, "They'll probably just investigate you for a year and then drop it if nothing turns up."

Lee scowled at her. His recent past was squeaky clean. Going back a little further, the waters got a little murkier. When he was first starting out as a PI, he had done some things he would never even consider doing now. Not illegal, but still hard to explain to straightlaced federal agents.

And then there was the restraining order his ex had gotten right before Lucky Eddie had struck patent gold. Claimed Lee was stalking her, was perhaps violent. Lee would have become violent if he had gotten hold of the little shit. Every time Lee thought about the bruises on his daughter's arms and cheek when he had made an unexpected visit to their rat-trap apartment he almost had a stroke. Trish claimed Renee had fallen down the stairs. Stood there and lied to his face, when Lee could see the imprint of what he knew was a knuckle against his daughter's soft skin. He had taken a crowbar to Eddie's car and would've taken one to Eddie if the guy hadn't locked himself in the bathroom and called the cops.

So did he really want the FBI snooping around his life for the next twelve months? On the other hand, if he let the woman walk away and the Feds tracked him down, then where would he be? Everywhere he turned, he ran into a nest of snakes.

Faith spoke in a pleasant tone. "Do you want to drop me at the Washington Field Office? They're at Fourth and F Streets."

"Okay, okay, you've made your point," Lee said hotly. "But I didn't ask for this crap to be dropped in my lap."

"And I didn't ask for you to become involved in this either. But . . ."

"But what?"

"But if you weren't there tonight, I wouldn't be alive right now. I'm sorry I haven't thanked you before. I'm thanking you now."

Despite his suspicions, Lee felt his anger slowly receding. Either the woman was sincere or she was one of the slickest operators he'd come across. Or maybe it was a little slice of both. This was Washington, after all.

"Always glad to help a lady," he said dryly. "Okay, supposing I decide not to turn you in. What do you have in mind to pass the night away?"

"I need to get away from here. I need some time to think things through."

"The FBI is not going to just let you walk away. I'm assuming you've cut some sort of deal."

"Not yet. And even if I had, don't you think I have good grounds to declare them in default?"

"What about the people who tried to kill you?"

"Once I have some space, I can decide what to do. I'll probably end up just going back to the FBI. But I don't want to die. I don't want anyone else associated with me to die." She stared very deliberately at him.

"I appreciate your concern, but I can take care of myself. So where do you plan to run, and how do you plan to get there?"

Faith started to say something and then stopped. She looked down, suddenly wary.

"If you don't trust me, Faith, none of this works," Lee prodded gently. "If I let you walk, that means I'm going to bat for you big-time. But I haven't made that decision yet. A lot depends on what you're thinking. If the Feds need you to bring down some powerful people—and what I've seen so far clearly rules out this being shoplifting material—then I'm going to have to side with the Feds."

"What if I agreed to come back so long as they could give guarantees as to my safety?"

"I guess that sounds reasonable. But what guarantee is there that you'll come back at all?"

"What if you come with me?" she said quickly.

Lee stiffened so much that he accidentally kicked Max, who came out from under the table and looked at him pitifully.

Faith rushed on. "It's probably only a matter of time before they identify you on the tape. The person you shot, what if he identifies you to whoever hired him? It's obvious that you're in danger too."

"I'm not sure—"

"Lee," Faith said excitedly, "did it ever occur to you that the person who hired you to follow me had you trailed as well? You could very well have been used to set up the shooting."

"Well, if they could follow me, they could follow you," he countered.

"But what if they wanted to frame you for all this somehow?"

Lee blew the air from his cheeks as the hopelessness of his situation set in. Sonofabitch, what a night. How the hell hadn't he seen it coming? Anonymous client. Bag full of cash. Mystery target. Lonely cottage. Had he been in a frigging coma or what? "I'm listening."

"I have a safe-deposit box in a bank in D.C. In that box I have cash, and some pieces of plastic with another name on them that'll let us go about as far as we need to. The only problem is they might be watching my bank. I need your help."

"*I* can't access your safe-deposit box."

"But you can help me scope the place out, see if anyone's watching. You're obviously better at that than I am. I go in, clean out the box and get out as fast as possible while you cover me. Anything looks suspicious, we run like hell."

"It sounds like we're planning to rob the place," he said angrily.

"I swear to God all the things in that box are mine."

Lee put a hand through his hair. "Okay, maybe that works. Then what?"

"Then we head south."

"South where?"

"The Carolina shore. Outer Banks. I have a place there."

"Are you listed as the owner? They can check that."

"I bought it in the name of a corporation and signed the papers under my other name, as an officer. But what about you? You can't travel under your own name."

"Don't worry about me. I've been more people in my life than Shirley MacLaine, and I've got the papers to prove it."

"Then we're all set."

Lee looked down at Max, who had settled his big head in his lap. Lee gently stroked the dog's nose.

"How long?"

Faith shook her head. "I don't know. A week, maybe."

Lee sighed. "I guess I can have the lady downstairs take care of Max."

"Then you'll do it?"

"Just so long as you understand that while I don't mind helping somebody who needs it, I'm not playing the world's greatest sucker either."

"You don't strike me as someone who would ever play that role."

"If you really want a laugh, tell my ex-wife that."

CHAPTER 11

OLD TOWN ALEXANDRIA WAS LOCATED IN northern Virginia next to the Potomac River, about a fifteen-minute drive south of Washington, D.C. The waters were the primary reason the city had been established, and it had flourished as a seaport for a very long time. It was still an affluent and desirable place to live, although the river no longer played a prominent role in the town's economic future.

It was a setting of both old wealth and freshly monied families nestled within the graceful brick, stone and wood-frame structures of late eighteenth and early nineteenth century architecture. A few of the streets were covered in the very same rolling cobblestone that had supported the treads of Washington and Jefferson. And of the young Robert E. Lee at his two boyhood homes, which were set across from each

other on Oronoco Street, itself named after a particular brand of long-ago Virginia-grown tobacco. Many
of the town's sidewalks were brick and had buckled
up around the numerous trees that had shaded the
homes, streets and inhabitants for so long. A number
of the wrought-iron fences that encircled the court-
yards and gardens of the homes were painted the color
of gold on their European-inspired spikes and finials.

At this early hour the streets of Old Town were
quiet except for the drizzle of rain and the rush of
wind among the branches of the aged, knobby trees
whose shallow roots clutched at the hard Virginia
clay. The street names reflected the colonial origins
of the place. Driving through town, one would pass
King, Queen, Duke and Prince Streets. Off-road
parking was scarce here, so the narrow avenues were
lined with virtually every make and model of vehicle. Placed against the two-hundred-year-old homes,
the chrome, rubber and metal hulls seemed oddly out
of place, as though a time warp had whisked the automobile back to the era of horse and buggy.

The narrow four-story brick townhouse that was
wedged among a line of others along Duke Street was
by no means the grandest in the area. There was a
lone, tilting maple in the small front yard, its split
trunk covered with leafy suckers. The wrought-iron
fencing was in good but not superb condition. The
home had a garden and courtyard out back, yet the
plantings, dripping fountain and brickwork there

were unremarkable when compared with others located but a few steps away.

Inside the home, the furnishings were far more elegant than the outside of the place would have led the observer to expect. There was a simple reason for this: The outside of the home was something Danny Buchanan could not hide from curious eyes.

The first traces of the pink dawn were just starting to nudge at the edges of the horizon as Buchanan sat, fully dressed, in the small oval-shaped library off the dining room. A car was waiting to take him to Reagan National Airport.

The senator he was meeting with was on the Appropriations Committee, arguably the Senate's most important committee, since it (and its subcommittees) controlled the government's purse strings. More importantly for Buchanan's purposes, the man also chaired the Subcommittee on Foreign Operations, which determined where most foreign aid dollars went. The tall, distinguished senator with the smooth manners and confident tones was a longtime associate of Buchanan's. The man had always enjoyed the power that came with his position and he had consistently lived beyond his means. The retirement package he had waiting from Buchanan would be almost impossible for a human being to exhaust.

Buchanan's bribery scheme had started out cautiously at first. He had analyzed all the players in Washington who even remotely might further his goals, and whether they could be bribed. Many members of Congress were wealthy, but many others were not. It was often both a financial and familial nightmare for people to serve in Congress. Members had to maintain two residences, and the Washington metro area was not cheap. And their family often did not come with them. Buchanan approached the ones he figured he could corrupt and began a long process of feeling them out on possible involvement. The carrots he dangled were small at first but quickly grew in size if the targets showed any enthusiasm. Buchanan had selected well, because he had never had a target not agree to exchange votes and influence for rewards down the road. Perhaps they felt that the difference between what he proposed and what occurred in Washington every day was marginal at best. He didn't know if they cared that the goal was a worthy one. However, they hadn't gone out of their way to increase foreign aid to any of Buchanan's clients on their own.

And they had all seen colleagues leave office and grab the gold of lobbydom. But who wanted to work that hard then? Buchanan's experience was that ex-members made terrible lobbyists anyway. Going back hat in hand to lobby former colleagues over whom you no longer had any leverage was not appealing to these overly proud folk. Much smarter to use them when they were the most powerful they would ever be. Work them hard first. And then pay them grandly later. What could be better?

Buchanan wondered if he could really hold it together during the meeting with a man he had already betrayed. But then, betrayal was doled out in large doses in this town. Everyone was constantly scrambling for a chair before the music stopped. The senator would be understandably upset. Well, he would have to stand in line with the rest.

Buchanan suddenly felt tired. He didn't want to get in the car or climb on another plane, but he had no say in the matter. *Still a member of the Philadelphia servant class?*

The lobbyist focused his attention on the man who was standing before him.

"He sends his compliments," the burly man said. To the outside world he was Buchanan's driver. In reality he was one of Thornhill's men keeping close tabs on their most important charge.

"And please send Mr. Thornhill my sincerest wishes that God should decree he not grow one day older," said Buchanan.

"There have been important developments of which he would like you to be aware," the man said impassively.

"Such as?"

"Lockhart is working with the FBI to bring you down."

For a brief, dizzying moment Buchanan thought he would vomit all over himself. "What in the hell are you talking about?"

"This information was just discovered by our operative inside the Bureau."

"You mean they entrapped her? Made her work for them?" *Just like you did to me.*

"She voluntarily went to them."

Buchanan slowly regained his composure. "Tell me everything," he said.

The man responded with a series of truths, half-truths and outright lies. He told them all with equal, practiced sincerity.

"Where is Faith now?"

"She's gone underground. The FBI is looking for her."

"How much has she told them? Should I be making plans to leave the country?"

"No. It's very early in the game. What she's told them thus far would not warrant prosecution of any kind. She's told them more of the process of how it was done, but not who was involved. However, that's not to say they can't follow up what she's told them. But they have to be careful. The targets aren't exactly flipping burgers at McDonald's."

"And the vaunted Mr. Thornhill doesn't know where Faith is? I hope his omniscience isn't failing him now."

"I have no information about that," said the man.

"A poor state of affairs for an intelligence-gathering agency," Buchanan said, even managing a smile. A log in the fireplace let out a loud pop, and a fat wad of sap shot out and hit the screen. Buchanan watched it dripping down the mesh face, its escape halted, its existence over. Why did he suddenly feel the remainder of his life had just been symbolically played out?

"Perhaps I should try to find her."

"It's really not your concern."

Buchanan stared at him. Had the idiot really said that? "*You* won't be the one going to prison."

"It'll work out. You just continue right on."

"I want to be kept informed. Clear?" Buchanan turned to the window. In its reflection he studied the man's reaction to his sharply spoken words. But what were they really worth? Buchanan had clearly lost this round; he had no way of winning it, actually.

The street was dark, no visible movement, just the familiar sounds of squirrels corkscrewing up the trees and then leaping from branch to branch in their never-ending game of survival. Buchanan was engaged in a similar contest, but even more dangerous than hopping across the slippery bark of thirty-foot-tall trees. The wind had picked up some; the beginnings of a low howling sound could be heard in the chimney. A bit of smoke from the fire drifted into the room with the backdraft of air.

The man looked at his watch. "We need to leave in fifteen minutes to make your flight." He picked up Buchanan's briefcase, turned and left.

Robert Thornhill had always been careful in how he contacted Buchanan. No phone calls to the house or office. Face-to-face meetings only under conditions such as these where it would not raise suspicions, where surveillance by others could not be maintained. The first meeting between the two had been one of the few times in Buchanan's life that he had felt inadequate in the face of an opponent. Thornhill had calmly presented stark evidence of Buchanan's illegal dealings with members of Congress, high-ranking bureaucrats, even reaching inside the White House. Tapes of them going over voting schemes, strategies to defeat legislation, frank discussions of what their fake duties would be once they left office, how the payoffs would occur. The CIA man had uncovered Buchanan's web of slush funds and corporations designed to funnel money to his public officials.

"You now work for me," Thornhill had said bluntly. "And you will go right on doing what you are doing until my net is as strong as steel. And then you will stand clear, and I will take over."

Buchanan had refused. "I'll go to prison," he had said. "I'll take that over indentured servitude."

Thornhill, Buchanan recalled, had looked slightly impatient. "I'm sorry if I wasn't clear. Prison isn't an option. You either work for me or you cease to live."

Buchanan had paled in the face of this threat, but still held firm. "A public servant embroiled in murder?"

"I'm a special type of public servant. I work in extremes. It tends to justify what I do."

"My answer's the same."

"Do you also speak for Faith Lockhart? Or should I consult her personally on the matter?"

That remark had struck Buchanan like a bullet to the brain. It was quite clear to Buchanan that Robert Thornhill was no bully. There was not a hint of bluster in the man. If he said something as innocuous as, "I'm sorry it's come to this," you would probably be dead the next day. Thornhill was a careful, deliberate, focused person, Buchanan had thought at the time. Not unlike himself. Buchanan had gone along. To save Faith.

Now Buchanan understood the relevance of Thornhill's safeguards. The FBI was watching him. Well, they had their work cut out for them, for Buchanan doubted they were in Thornhill's league when it came to clandestine operations. But everyone had an Achilles' heel. Thornhill had easily found his in Faith Lockhart. Buchanan had long wondered what Thornhill's weakness was.

Buchanan slumped in a chair and studied the painting hanging on the library wall. It was a portrait of a mother and child. It had hung in a private museum for almost eighty years. It was by one of the acknowledged—but lesser known—masters of the Renaissance period. The mother was clearly the protector, the infant boy unable to defend himself. The wondrous colors, the exquisitely painted profiles, the subtle brilliance of the hand that had invented this image so clearly evident in every brushstroke, never failed to enrapture anyone who saw it. The gentle curl of finger, the luminosity of the eyes, each detail still so vibrant almost four hundred years after the paint had hardened.

It was perfect love on both sides, uncomplicated by silent, corrosive agendas. At one level it was the simple thread of biological function. At another it was a phenomenon enhanced by the touch of God. This painting was his most prized possession. Unfortunately, it would soon have to be sold, and perhaps his home as well. He was running out of money to fund the "retirements" of his people. Indeed, he felt guilty for still owning the painting. The funds it could generate, the help it could bring to so many. And yet just to sit and gaze at it was so soothing, so uplifting. It was the height of selfishness, and brought him more pleasure than just about anything else.

But maybe it was all moot at this point. The end was coming for Buchanan. He knew that Thornhill would never let him walk away from all of this. And he had no illusions that he would let Buchanan's people enjoy any retirement whatsoever. They were his slaves-in-waiting. The CIA man, despite his refinement and pedigree, was a spy. What were spies but living lies? However, Buchanan would honor his agreement with his politicians. What he had promised them in return for helping him would be there, whether they would be able to enjoy it or not.

As the light of the fire played over the painting,

the woman's face, it seemed to Buchanan, took on the characteristics of Faith Lockhart—not the first time he had observed this. His gaze traced the set of full lips that could turn petulant or sensual without warning. As his eye ran down the long, gracefully formed face, the hair golden, not auburn, in just the right splash of angled light, he always thought of Faith. She had a pair of eyes that held you; the left pupil slightly off center added depth to make Faith's countenance truly remarkable. And it was as though this flaw of nature had empowered her to see right through anyone.

He remembered every detail of their very first meeting. Fresh out of college, she had bounded into his life with the enthusiasm of a newly minted missionary, ready to take on the world. She was raw, immature at certain levels, largely ignorant of the ways of Washington, astonishingly naive in various respects. And yet she could also command a room like a movie star. She could be funny and then turn serious on a dime. She could stroke egos with the best of them and still get her message across, without overtly pushing the issue. After five minutes talking to her, Buchanan knew she had what it took to flourish in his world. After her first month on the job, his intuition proved correct. She did her homework, worked tirelessly, learned the issues, dissected the players down to the level needed to do the job and then went deeper. She understood what everyone needed in order to walk away a winner. Burning bridges in this town meant you didn't survive. Sooner or later, you needed help from everyone, and memories were exceptionally long in the capital city. As tenacious as a wolverine, she had endured defeat after defeat on a number of fronts, but continued to pound away until she was victorious. He had never met anyone like her before or since. They had been through more together in fifteen years than couples married a lifetime. She was really all the family he had. The precocious daughter he was destined never to have. And now? How did he protect his little girl?

As the rain drifted across the roof and the wind strummed its peculiar sounds down the aged fire-brick of his Old Town chimney, Buchanan forgot about his car and his flight and the dilemmas confronting him. The man continued to stare at the painting in the soft glow of the quietly crackling fire. And it was clearly not the work of the grand master that fascinated him so.

Faith had not betrayed him. Nothing Thornhill could ever tell him would change that belief. But now she was in Thornhill's way, which meant she was in mortal danger. He stared at the painting. "Run, Faith, run just as fast as you can," he said under his breath, with all the anguish of a desperate father seeing violent death racing after his child. In the face of the protector mother in the painting, Buchanan felt even more powerless.

CHAPTER 1 2

BROOKE REYNOLDS SAT IN RENTED OFFICE
space about ten blocks from the Washington Field
Office. The Bureau sometimes took off-site space for
agents engaged in sensitive investigations, where
something overheard even in the cafeteria or hallway
could have disastrous effects. Virtually everything
the Public Corruption Unit did was of a sensitive nature. The usual targets of the unit's investigation
were not bank robbers wearing masks and waving
guns. They were often people one read about on the
front pages of the newspapers or saw being inter-
viewed on the TV news.

Reynolds leaned forward and slipped out of her
flats, rubbing her aching feet against the legs of her
chair. Everything about her was tight, raw and hurting: Her sinuses were almost completely closed, her

skin feverish, her throat scratchy. But at least she was alive. Unlike Ken Newman. She had driven straight to his home after first calling ahead to let his wife know she had to see her. Reynolds hadn't said why, but Anne Newman had known that her husband was dead. Reynolds had heard it in the tone of the few words the woman had managed to speak.

Normally, a person of a higher level than Reynolds would accompany her to the home of a bereaved spouse, to show that the Bureau did care, from top to bottom, when it lost one of its own. However, Reynolds had not waited for anyone else to volunteer to come with her. Ken was her responsibility, including telling his family that he was dead.

When she had arrived at the house, Reynolds had gotten right down to it, figuring a drawn-out monologue would only prolong the woman's obvious agony. Reynolds's compassion and empathy for the bereaved woman had been unhurried, however, and sincere. She had held Anne, consoled her as best she could, broken down in tears with her. Anne had taken the absence of information well, Reynolds had thought, far better than she probably would were the roles reversed.

Anne would be allowed to see her husband's body. Then it would be autopsied by the state's chief medical examiner. Connie and Reynolds would attend the post along with representatives from the Virginia State Police and the commonwealth's attorney office, all of whom were under strict confidentiality orders.

They would also have to count on Anne Newman to help keep angry and confused family members under control. It was a potentially weak link in the chain, expecting a woman in personal agony to help a government agency that couldn't even tell her all the circumstances of her husband's death. But it was all they had.

As she had left the stricken woman's home—the kids had been away with friends—Reynolds had the distinct feeling that Anne blamed her for Ken's death. And as Reynolds had walked back to her car she couldn't really disagree with that. The guilt Reynolds was feeling right now was like a crusty barnacle sunk into her skin, a free radical roaming inside her body, seeking a place to nest, grow and eventually kill her.

Outside the Newmans' home she had run into the director of the FBI as he had come to offer his own condolences. He conveyed heartfelt sympathy to Reynolds for the loss of one of her men. He told her that he had been briefed on her conversation with Massey and that he concurred in her judgment. However, he made it clear that results had better be both quick and substantial.

As Reynolds now eyed the considerable clutter of her office, it occurred to her that the mess well symbolized the disorganization, some would say dysfunction, of her personal life. Matters of importance from many open cases lay across her desk and small conference table. They were wedged onto her shelves, had mutated into piles on her floor and even found their way onto the couch where she often slept, far away from her children.

But for her live-in nanny and the nanny's teenage daughter, Reynolds didn't know how she could possibly keep a halfway normal life for her kids. Rosemary, a wonderful woman from Central America who loved the children nearly as much as Reynolds did and was fanatical about keeping the house clean, the meals cooked and the clothes laundered, was costing Reynolds over a quarter of her entire salary and was more than worth every penny. But after the divorce was final it would be very tight. And Reynolds's ex would not be paying any alimony. His work as a fashion photographer, though lucrative, came in quick bursts followed by long periods of deliberate inactivity. Reynolds would be lucky if she didn't end up paying *him* alimony. And child support from him, while she would seek it, would be a joke. The man may as well have had "deadbeat dad" engraved on his forehead.

She looked at her watch. The FBI lab was working on the videotape right now. Because the existence of her "special" was unknown within the FBI except for very select personnel, any lab work that was required was supposed to be sent over under a dummy case name and file number. It would be nice to have separate laboratory facilities and personnel, but that

would entail enormous expense that just didn't figure in the Bureau's budget. Even elite crime fighters
had to live within the allowance Uncle Sam gave
them. Normally a liaison agent at the main agency
would work with Reynolds's team to coordinate any
lab submissions and findings with Reynolds. However, Reynolds didn't have time for normal channels.
She had personally delivered the tape to the lab and
with her superior's blessing it had received a very
high priority.

After meeting with Anne Newman she had gone
home, cuddled for as long as she could with her
sleeping kids, showered, changed and driven right
back to work. All the time she had been thinking of
that damn tape. As if in response to her thoughts, the
phone rang.

"Yes?"

"You better come over," said the man. "And just so
you know, it's not good news."

CHAPTER 13

Faith awoke with a start. She looked at her watch. It was nearly seven. Lee had insisted that she get some rest, but she hadn't expected to be out so long. She sat up, feeling thickheaded. Her body was aching and when she swung her legs over the side of the bed, she felt a little sick to her stomach. She still had her suit on, but she had slipped off her shoes and pantyhose before lying down.

She got off the bed, padded into the adjoining bathroom and looked at herself in the mirror. "God," was all she could manage to say. Her hair was matted flat, her face a mess, her clothes filthy and her brain felt like cement. Such a pleasant way to begin the day.

She turned on the shower and stepped back into the bedroom to undress. She had taken off her clothes

and was standing naked in the middle of the bedroom when Lee knocked on the door.

"Yes?" she said anxiously.

"Before you get in the shower, we need to do something," Lee said through the door.

"Is that right?" The odd tone of his words sent a
chill up her spine. She quickly put her clothes back
on and stood rigidly in the middle of the room.

"Can I come in?" He sounded impatient.

She went over and edged open the door. "What
is—" Faith almost screamed when she saw him.

The man looking at her was not Lee Adams. This
man had a buzz cut, the hair dyed blond and damp,
a matching short beard and mustache, and he wore
glasses. And instead of dazzling blue, his eyes were
brown.

The man smiled as he watched her reaction. "Good,
it passed the test."

"Lee?"

"We can't quite walk past the FBI as ourselves."

Lee held out his hands. Faith saw the scissors and a
box of hair coloring.

"Short hair is easier to take care of, and personally
I think it's a myth that blondes have more fun."

She looked at him dully. "You want me to cut my
hair? And then color it?"

"No, I'll cut it. And if you want, I can color it for
you too."

"I can't do that."

"You have to do that."

"I know it seems silly under the circumstances—"

"You're right, it does seem silly under the circumstances. Hair grows back, but once you're dead, you're dead," he said bluntly.

She started to protest but then realized he was right.

"How short?"

He cocked his head, examining her hair from different angles. "How about a short, Joan of Arc do? Boyish, but cute."

Faith just stared at him. "Wonderful. Boyish, but cute—my lifetime ambitions realized with a few snips and a bottle of hair color."

They went into the bathroom. Lee sat her down on the toilet and began to cut while Faith kept her eyes tightly shut.

"Want me to do the color too?" Lee asked when he was done.

"Please. I'm not sure I can look at it right now."

It took some time under the sink, and the smell of chemicals contained in the coloring mix was tough to take on an empty stomach, but when Faith finally managed to look in the mirror she was pleasantly surprised. It didn't look as bad as she would have thought. The outline of her head, now more fully revealed, was actually a nice shape. And the dark color went well with her skin tones.

"Now grab a shower," Lee said. "The color won't

rinse out. Blow dryer's under the sink. There'll be some clean clothes on the bed."

She eyed his big frame. "I'm not your size."

"Not to worry. I run a full-service resort."

Thirty minutes later, Faith emerged from the bedroom in jeans and a flannel shirt, jacket and low-heeled boots that Lee had left for her. From power suit to college student. She felt years younger. The short black hair encircled her face, which she left au naturel. Fresh start all around.

Lee sat at the kitchen table. He studied her new appearance. "Looks good," he said approvingly.

"You did it." She looked at his wet hair and a thought struck her. "Do you have a second bathroom?"

"Nope, just the one. I showered while you were sleeping. I didn't use the hair dryer because I was afraid it would wake you. You'll find I'm a very considerate soul."

She recoiled slightly. It was a creepy revelation, that he had been lurking around while she was asleep in his bed. She got this sudden image of a maniacal, scissors-toting Lee Adams leering while she lay there tied to the bed, naked and helpless.

"God, I must have really been out," she said as casually as she could.

"You were. I actually grabbed some shut-eye too." He continued to study her appearance. "You know, you look better without makeup."

Faith smiled. "Your lies are very much appreciated."

She smoothed down her shirt. "By the way, do you always keep women's clothes around your apartment?"

Lee pulled on a pair of socks and then some tennis shoes. He wore jeans and a white T-shirt that was spread taut across his chest. The veins in his biceps and smooth forearms rippled, and Faith hadn't really noticed before how thick his neck was. His torso narrowed dramatically at his waist, the pants slightly loose there, giving him a hard V-shape. His thighs looked ready to burst through the denim. He caught her staring and Faith quickly looked away.

"My niece Rachel," he said. "She goes to law school at Michigan. She clerked at a law firm here last year and stayed with me, rent-free. Only she earned more money in one summer than I do in about a year. She left some of her stuff. Lucky you're about the same size. She'll probably be back next summer."

"Tell her to be careful. This town has a way of destroying people."

"I don't think she'll have your problems. She wants to be a judge one day. No felons need apply."

Faith's face flushed. She took a mug from the sink rack and poured a cup of coffee.

Lee stood. "Look, that was out of line. I'm sorry."

"I deserve a lot worse than that, actually."

"Fine, I'll let other people do the honors."

Faith poured a cup of coffee for him and sat down at the table. Max came into the kitchen and nudged her hand. She smiled and petted the dog's broad head.

"Max taken care of?"

"All set." He checked his watch. "The bank opens shortly. We'll have just enough time to pack. We'll get your stuff, head to the airport, get our tickets and fly, fly away."

"I can call down and arrange for the house from the airport. Or should I try from here?"

"No. Phone logs can be checked."

"I didn't think of that."

"You're going to have to start to." He took a sip of coffee. "Hope the place is available."

"It will be. I happen to own it. Or at least my other identity does."

"Small place?"

"Depends on what you call small. I think you'll be comfortable."

"I'm easy." He carried his coffee into the bedroom and came out a few minutes later wearing a navy blue sweater over his T-shirt. His mustache and beard were gone and he had a baseball cap on. He was carrying a small plastic bag.

"The evidence of our makeovers," he explained.

"And no disguise?"

"Mrs. Carter's used to me keeping odd hours, but if I barge in looking like somebody else, it'll be a little much for her this early in the morning. And I don't want her being able to give anyone a description later on."

"You are good at this," said Faith. "That's reassuring."

He called Max. The big dog obediently padded from the small living room into the kitchen, stretched his body and then sat next to Lee. "If the phone rings, don't answer it. And stay away from the windows."

Faith nodded and then he and Max were gone. She took her coffee and walked around the small apartment. It was a curious cross between a messy college dorm and a more mature person's home. In what should have been the dining room, Faith found a home gym. Nothing fancy, no high-dollar, high-tech machines, just barbells, a weight bench and squat rack that were set up throughout the space. In one corner was a heavy punching bag and next to it a speed bag. Boxing and weight gloves, hand wraps and towels were neatly arranged on a small wooden table next to a box of white powder. A medicine ball sat in another corner.

On the walls were some photos of men in Navy whites. Faith picked out Lee quite easily. He looked pretty much the same at eighteen as he did now. However, the years had weathered his face, cut in lines and angles that made him even more attractive, even more seductive. Why was aging so damn tilted in favor of men? There were black and white photos of Lee in the boxing ring, and one of him with his hand raised in victory, a medal resting against his wide chest. His expression was calm, as though he had expected to win; in fact, as though he would not accept losing.

Faith gave the heavy bag a small punch with a

loosely made fist, and her hand and wrist instantly throbbed. In that moment she recalled how big and thick Lee's hands were, the knuckles resembling a miniature mountain range. A very strong, resourceful, tough man. A man who could take punishment. She just hoped he would remain on her side.

She went into the bedroom. On the nightstand next to his bed was a cell phone and next to that a portable panic-button device. Faith had been too exhausted to notice them last night. She wondered if he slept with his pistol under his pillow. Was he really just paranoid or did he know something the rest of the world didn't?

It suddenly occurred to her: Wasn't he afraid she might make a run for it? She went back into the hallway. The front was covered; he would see her leave that way. But there was a back door off the kitchen that went down a fire escape. She went over to the door and tried to open it. It was locked. Deadbolted. The kind you could only open with a key even from inside. The windows also had key locks. It angered Faith, being trapped like this, but the truth was she had been trapped long before Lee Adams popped up in her life.

She continued looking through the apartment. Faith smiled at the collection of record albums housed in their original covers, and a framed poster from the movie *The Sting*. She doubted if the man had a CD player or even cable TV. She opened another door and went into the room. She started to turn on the light and then paused as a sound caught her attention. She stepped to the window, inched back the blinds and looked out. It was fully light outside now, although the sky was still gray and gloomy. She didn't see anyone, but that meant nothing. She could be encircled by an army and she'd never know it.

She turned the light on and looked around, surprised. A desk, file cabinets, a sophisticated phone system and shelves filled with manuals surrounded her. There were large pegboards on the wall with memo cards tacked to them. On the desk were neatly arranged files, a calendar and the usual desktop accessories. Apparently, Lee's home also served as his place of business.

If this was his office, maybe the file on her was here. Lee would probably be gone for a few more minutes. She started to sift carefully through the papers on his desk. Then she went through the desk drawers and then moved on to the file cabinets. Lee was very organized and he had a lot of clients—mostly businesses and law firms, from the file labels she was seeing. Defense lawyers, she assumed, since prosecutors had their own detective force.

The ringing phone made her almost leap out of her shoes. Trembling, she went over to it. The base unit had an LCD readout. Lee obviously had caller ID, because the number of the person calling him was displayed on the readout. It was long distance, with a

215 area code. Philadelphia, she recalled. Lee's voice came on and told the caller to leave a message after the beep. When that person started talking, Faith froze.

"Where is Faith Lockhart?" asked the voice of Danny Buchanan. Danny sounded very distressed as he fired more questions: What had Lee found out? He wanted answers and he wanted them immediately. Buchanan left a phone number, then hung up. Faith felt herself backing away from the phone. She stopped and stood still, transfixed by what she had just heard. A full minute passed as numbing thoughts of betrayal swirled through her mind like confetti in a parade. Then she heard a sound behind her and whirled around. Her scream was short, sharp, leaving her momentarily breathless. Lee was staring at her.

Buchanan looked around the crowded airport. He had taken a risk in calling Lee Adams directly, but his options now were few. As his eyes roamed the area, he wondered which of the people it was. The old lady in the corner with her big purse and hair in a bun? She had been on Buchanan's flight. A tall, middle-aged man had been pacing the aisle while Buchanan had been on the phone. He too had been on the flight from National.

The truth was Thornhill's people could be anywhere, anyone. It was like being attacked by nerve gas. You never saw the enemy. A sense of profound hopelessness gripped Buchanan.

Buchanan's greatest fear had been that Thornhill would either try to get Faith involved in his scheme, or suddenly find her a liability. He might have pushed

Faith away, but would never abandon her. This was why he had hired Adams to follow her. As the end drew near, he had to make sure she remained safe.

Buchanan had looked in the phone book, of all places, and used the simplest logic he could think of. Lee Adams had been the first person listed under private investigators. Buchanan almost laughed out loud now at what he had done. But unlike Thornhill, he didn't have an army at his beck and call. For all he knew, Adams hadn't reported in because he was dead.

He paused for a moment. Should he just flee to the ticket counter, book the first flight available to anywhere remote and then lose himself? Easy to fantasize about, quite another thing to implement. He envisioned trying to escape: Thornhill's heretofore invisible army would suddenly materialize and descend upon him from the shadows, displaying official-looking badges to anyone bold enough to intervene. Then Buchanan would be taken to a quiet room in the bowels of the Philadelphia airport. There Robert Thornhill would be calmly waiting with his pipe and his three-piece suit and his casual arrogance. He would calmly ask Buchanan, did he want to die right this very minute? Because Thornhill would certainly accommodate him if he did. And Buchanan would have absolutely no response.

Finally Danny Buchanan did the only thing he could do. He left the airport, climbed in his waiting car and drove to see his friend the senator, to put another nail in the man's coffin with his smiling, disarming manner and the listening device he was wearing, which looked exactly like skin and hair follicles and was so advanced that it wouldn't set off the most sophisticated of metal detectors. A surveillance van would follow him to his destination and record every word said by Buchanan and the senator.

As a backup, in case the transmission from his listening device was somehow interfered with, Buchanan's briefcase had a tape recorder built into its frame. A slight twist on the briefcase handle activated the recorder. It too was undetectable by even the most sophisticated airport security. Thornhill really had thought of everything. *Damn the man.*

On the drive over, Buchanan comforted himself with a deliriously inspiring fantasy involving a pleading, broken Thornhill, an assortment of poisonous snakes, boiling oil and a rusted machete.

If only dreams could come true.

The person sitting in the airport was clean-cut, mid-thirties, dressed in a dark, conservatively cut suit and working on a laptop computer—meaning he mirrored about a thousand other business travelers all around him. He seemed busy and focused, even talking to himself at times. He gave the appearance, to the casual passersby, of a man preparing for a sales pitch or compiling a marketing report. He was actually quietly talking into the tiny microphone embedded in his necktie. What looked like infrared data ports on the backside of his computer were really sensors. One was designed to capture electronic signals. The other was a sound wand that collected words and posted them onto the screen. The first sensor quite easily snagged the phone number Buchanan had just called and automatically transmitted it to the screen. The voice sensor had been a little garbled, what with so many conversations going on at the airport; but enough had come through to make the man excited. The words "Where is Faith Lockhart?" stared back at him from the screen.

The man conveyed the telephone number and other information to his colleagues back in Washington. Within seconds a computer at Langley had produced the account holder of the phone and the address to which the phone number was registered. Within minutes a very experienced team of professionals completely in allegiance to Robert Thornhill—who had been waiting for just such a mission—was dispatched to Lee Adams's apartment.

Thornhill's instructions were simple. If Faith Lockhart was there, they were to "terminate" her, as it was so benignly termed in official espionage parlance, as though she would simply be fired and asked to collect her personal belongings and leave the building, instead of having a bullet fired into her head. Anyone with her would suffer the same fate. For the good of the country.

CHAPTER 15

YOU SCARED THE HELL OUT OF ME." FAITH couldn't stop trembling.

Lee moved into the room and looked around. "What are you doing in my office?"

"Nothing! I was just wandering. I didn't even know you had your office here."

"That's because you didn't need to know that."

"I thought I heard a sound outside the window when I came in here."

"You did hear a sound, but it didn't come from the window." He pointed to the doorjamb.

Faith noted the rectangular piece of white plastic attached to the wood there.

"It's a sensor. Anybody opens the door to my office, it trips the sensor and triggers my beeper." He took the device out of his pocket. "If I hadn't had Max to calm down at Mrs. Carter's, I would've been up here a lot sooner." He scowled at her. "I don't appreciate this, Faith."

"Hey, I was just looking around, killing time."

"Interesting choice of words: 'killing.'"

"Lee, I'm not plotting against you. I swear it."

"Let's finish packing. Don't want to keep your bankers waiting."

Faith avoided looking at the phone again. Lee must not have heard the message. He had been hired by Buchanan to follow her. Had he killed the agent last night? When they got on the plane, would he some-how manage to push her out at thirty thousand feet and laugh riotously while she plummeted screaming through the clouds?

But he could have killed her at any point from last night to now. Leaving her dead at the cottage would have been the easiest move. That's when it hit her: It would have been the easiest move unless Danny wanted to know how much she had told the FBI. That would explain why she was still alive. And also why Lee was so eager to get her to talk. Once she did, then he would kill her. And here they were flying off together to a North Carolina beach community that would be largely deserted this time of year. She slowly walked out of the room, a condemned woman on the way to her execution.

Twenty minutes later, Faith closed the small travel bag and slid her purse strap over her head and onto her shoulder. Lee came into the bedroom. He had put back on the mustache and beard, and the baseball cap was gone. In his right hand were his pistol, two boxes of ammo and his belt holster.

Faith watched as he loaded the items into a special hard-sided container. "You can't take a gun on a plane," she said.

"You're kidding, really? When did they start that shit?" He closed the container and locked it, pocketing the keys before looking at her. "You *can* take a gun on a plane if you disclose the weapon when you check in and fill out a declaration form. They ensure that the weapon is unloaded and in an approved case." He rapped his knuckles against the hard-sided aluminum case. "Which it is. They check that the ammo is a hundred rounds or fewer and is in the manufacturer's original or otherwise FAA-approved packaging. Again, I'm cool. Then they mark the bag with a special tag and it goes to the cargo bay, where it would be real hard for me to get to if I was thinking about skyjacking the plane, wouldn't you agree?"

"Thanks for the explanation," Faith said curtly.

"I'm not a damn amateur," he said hotly.

"I never said you were."

"Right."

"Okay, I'm sorry." She hesitated, intensely desiring to establish some sort of truce, for a number of reasons, her survival being chief among them. "Would you do me a favor?"

He looked at her suspiciously.

"Call me Faith."

The door buzzer startled them both.

Lee checked his watch. "Little early for visitors."

Faith watched in amazement as his hands moved like a machine. Within twenty seconds the pistol was out of the container and fully loaded. He put the container and the ammo boxes in his small travel bag and hoisted it over his shoulder. "Get your bag."

"Who do you think it is?" Faith felt her pulse throbbing in her ears.

"Let's go find out."

They stepped quietly into the hallway and Faith followed Lee to the front door.

He checked the TV screen. They both saw the man standing there on the front stoop of the building, a couple of packages in his arms. The familiar brown uniform was clearly visible. As they watched, he hit the buzzer once more.

"It's just the UPS man," Faith said, letting out a relieved breath.

Lee didn't take his eyes off the screen. "Is that right?" He hit a button on the screen that obviously moved the camera, as Faith found herself now staring at the street in front of the building. Something that should have been there wasn't.

"Where's his truck?" she said, her fear abruptly returning.

"Excellent question. And the fact is I know the UPS guy on this route real well, and that's not him."

"Maybe he's on vacation."

"Actually, he just got back from a week in the islands with his new bride. And he never comes at this time of the morning. Which means we've got a big problem."

"Maybe we can get out through the back."

"Yeah, I'm sure they forgot to cover the rear."

"There's only the one man."

"No, he's the only one we can see. He's got the front. They probably want to flush us out the back right into their arms."

"So we're trapped," she managed to whisper.

The buzzer rang again and Lee reached out his finger to hit the intercom button.

Faith grabbed his hand. "What the hell are you doing?"

"I'm going to see what he wants. He'll say UPS and I'm going to let him in."

"You're going to let him in," Faith repeated dully. She glanced at his pistol. "What, and have a shootout in your apartment building?"

Lee's face hardened. "When I tell you to move, you move your ass like a T-Rex is breathing down your neck."

"Move? Move where?"

"Just follow me. And no more questions."

Lee hit the intercom button, the man identified himself and Lee touched the door release. As soon as he did, he activated the apartment's alarm system, whipped open the front door, grabbed Faith by the arm and pulled her out into the hallway. There was a door across from Lee's apartment. It had no apartment number on it. As Faith listened to the UPS man's footsteps echoing in the building down below, Lee already had unlocked the door. They were through it in an instant and he quietly closed and locked the door behind them. The place was very dark, but Lee obviously knew his way around here. He led her to the back, through another door that opened up into what looked like a back bedroom, from the little Faith could see.

Lee opened another door in the room and motioned Faith in. She stepped through and almost immediately felt a wall against her. When Lee joined her, it was a very tight fit, like a telephone booth. He closed the door and the darkness became blacker than anything Faith had ever experienced before.

He startled her when he spoke, his breath tickling her ear. "Right in front of you there's a ladder. Here are the rungs." He gripped her hand and guided it until her fingers touched the rungs. Lee continued whispering. "Give me your bag and start climbing. Take it slow. I'll sacrifice speed for silence right now. I'll be right behind you. When you get to the top, just stop. I'll take it from there."

As she began to climb, Faith started feeling severely claustrophobic. And, because she had lost her bearings, she was becoming queasy. Now would be such a perfect time to lose the contents of her stomach, little though it was.

She moved her hands and feet slowly as she went up. Then, gaining confidence, she started to pick up her pace. That was a mistake because her foot missed a rung, she slipped and her chin painfully clipped one of the rungs. But then Lee's strong arm was round her in an instant, holding her up. She took a moment to steady herself, tried to ignore the pain in her chin and kept climbing until she felt the ceiling above her head and then stopped.

Lee was still on the rung right below her. Then he suddenly moved up on the same rung she was on, his legs on either side of hers so that her legs were pinched between his. He leaned against her with increasing force, and she wasn't sure what he was trying to do. It was becoming painful to breathe with her chest pushed up hard against the ladder rungs. For one terrifying moment she thought he had lured her in here to rape her. Suddenly a blast of light hit her from above and he moved away from her. She looked up, blinking rapidly. The view of the blue sky was so wonderful after the terror of the darkness that she felt like screaming in relief.

"Go up and onto the roof, but keep low. As low as you can," Lee whispered urgently into her ear.

She went up and through, dropping to her belly and looking around. The roof of the old building was flat, with a gravel and tar base. Bulky old heating units and newer air-conditioning machinery dotted the roof in various places. They made for good hiding places, and Faith slid over and squatted next to the nearest one.

Lee was still on the ladder. He listened intently and then checked his watch. The guy would be at his door right about now. He would buzz, wait for Lee to answer. They had thirty seconds at most before the guy realized no one was coming to the door. It would be nice to have a little more time than that, and also a way to draw in the other forces Lee knew were out there. He pulled his cell phone from his pocket and hit a speed-dial number.

When the person answered, he said, "Mrs. Carter, it's Lee Adams. Listen to me, I want you to let Max out in the hallway. Right, I know I just dropped him off. I know he'll head up to my apartment. That's what I want. I, uh, I forgot to give him a shot he needs. Please hurry, I really need to get out of here."

He pocketed the phone and pushed the bags up and out, then he hoisted himself through the opening and closed the hatch behind him. He scanned the roof and spotted Faith. Grabbing the bags, he slid over to her.

"Okay, we got a little time."

Down below they heard a dog start to bark loudly

and Lee smiled. "Follow me." Squatting low, they made their way to the edge of the roof. The building attached to Lee's was a little shorter so that the roof was about five feet lower. Lee motioned for Faith to take his hands. She did so and he lowered her over the edge, holding tightly until her feet touched the roof. As soon as Lee joined her, they both heard shouts coming from Lee's building.

"Okay, they've made their all-out assault. They'll go through the door and that'll trip the alarm. I don't have a call-back option with the alarm company, so there's no delay in sending the cops. A few minutes and it'll be a big mess."

"What do we do in the meantime?" Faith asked.

"Three more buildings and then down the fire escape. Move!"

Five minutes later they were running through a back alley and then out onto another quiet suburban street flanked by a number of low-rise apartment buildings. The street was lined on both sides with parked cars. In the background Faith could hear the thump of a tennis ball being hit. She could make out a tennis court surrounded by several tall pine trees in a small park across from the apartment buildings.

She watched as Lee eyed a line of cars parked at the curb. Then he jogged across to the park area and bent down. When he straightened up, he was holding a tennis ball—one of many that had landed there from years of errant shots on the court. He walked back over to Faith. She could see that he was working a hole in the tennis ball with his pocketknife.

"What are you doing?" she asked.

"Go up on the sidewalk and walk as calmly as you can. And keep your eyes open."

"Lee—"

"Just do it, Faith!"

She spun around and went up on the sidewalk, paralleling his movements as he walked on the other side of the parked cars, his eyes scanning each of the vehicles. He finally stopped at a new-looking luxury model.

"See anybody watching us?" Lee asked.

Faith shook her head.

He walked over to the car and held the tennis ball against the key lock, the hole in the ball facing the lock's opening.

Faith looked at him as if he were insane. "What are you doing?"

In response, he slammed his fist against the tennis ball, driving all the air out of the ball and into the key lock. Faith watched in amazement as all four door locks popped open.

"How did you do that?"

"Get in."

Lee slid into the car, and Faith did the same.

He poked his head under the steering column and found the wires he needed.

"You can't hot-wire these new cars. The technology—" Faith stopped talking when the car started.

Lee sat up, put the car in gear and pulled away from the curb. He looked at Faith. "What?"

"All right, so how did the tennis ball unlock the car?"

"I've got my professional secrets."

While Lee waited in the car with his eyes sharply on the lookout, Faith entered her bank, explained what she wanted to the assistant manager and managed to sign her name, all without falling over in a dead faint. *Steady, girl, one step at a time.* Fortunately, she knew the man.

The assistant manager looked curiously at her new appearance.

"Midlife crisis," she said, responding to his stare. "Decided to go for the youthful, streamlined look."

"It's very becoming, Ms. Lockhart," he said gallantly.

She closely watched him as he took her key, inserted it and the bank's duplicate key into the lock and pulled out her box. They left the vault and he set the box inside the private booth across from the vault reserved for safe-deposit box tenants. As he walked away, Faith continued to watch him.

Was he one of them? Was he going to slip away and call the police or the FBI or whoever was running around killing people? Instead he sat down at his desk, opened a white bag, extracted a glazed donut and proceeded to devour it.

Satisfied for the moment, Faith closed and locked

the door. She opened the box and stared at the contents for a moment. Then she swept it all into her bag and closed the box. The young man put the safe-deposit box back in the vault and Faith walked out as calmly as she could.

Back in the car, Faith and Lee headed down Interstate 395, where they exited on to the GW Parkway and headed south to Reagan National Airport. Going against the morning rush hour, they made good time.

Faith looked over at Lee, who stared straight ahead, lost in thought.

"You did really well back there," she said.

"Actually, we cut it closer than I would have liked." He paused and shook his head. "I'm really worried about Max, as stupid as that sounds under the circumstances."

"It doesn't sound stupid."

"Max and I have been together a long time. For years it's been only me and that old dog."

"I doubt they would have done anything to him with all those people around."

"Yeah, you'd like to think so, wouldn't you? But the fact is if they'll kill a man, a dog doesn't have a chance."

"I'm sorry you had to do that for me."

He sat up straight. "Well, a dog is still a dog, Faith. And we've got other things to worry about, don't we?"

Faith found herself nodding. "Yes."

"I guess my magnet trick didn't work so well. They must have identified me through the video. Still, that was awfully fast." He shook his head, his expression a mix of admiration and fear. "Like scary fast."

Faith felt her spirits sink. If Lee was scared, at what level of sheer terror should she be operating? "Not very encouraging, is it?" she said.

"I might be a little better prepared if you tell me what's going on."

After the man's heroics, Faith found herself wanting to confide in him. But then the phone call from Buchanan came flashing back, ringing in her ears, like the shots last night.

"When we get to North Carolina, we'll have it all out. *Both* sides," Faith said.

CHAPTER 16

THORNHILL REPLACED THE PHONE RECEIVER
and looked around his office, a disturbed expression
on his face. His men had found the nest empty, and
one of them had even been bitten by a dog. There had
been reports of a man and woman running down the
street. This was all just a little too much. Thornhill
was a patient man, used to working on projects for
many years, but still, there were limits to what he
could tolerate. His men had listened to the message
Buchanan had left on Lee's answering machine. They
had taken the tape and played it back for Thornhill
over his secure phone line.

"So you've hired a private investigator, Danny,"
Thornhill muttered to himself. "You'll pay for that
one." He nodded thoughtfully. "I'll make you pay."

The police had responded to the burglar alarm, but

when Thornhill's men had flashed official-looking IDs they had quickly backed off. Legally, the CIA had no authority to operate within the United States. Thus, Thornhill's team routinely carried several types of identification and would select one depending on who confronted them.

The patrolmen had been sent off with instructions to bury deeply all that they had seen. Still, Thornhill didn't like it. It was all too close to the edge. There were holes there, ways for people to gain an advantage over him.

He went to the window and looked outside. It was a beautiful fall day, the colors starting to turn. As he studied the pleasing foliage, he primed his pipe, but unfortunately that was all he could do. CIA headquarters was a nonsmoking building. The deputy director had a balcony outside his office where Thornhill could sit and smoke, but it was not the same. During the Cold War, the CIA offices had been as foggy as steam baths. Tobacco helped one think, Thornhill believed. It was a minor thing, yet it symbolized all that had gone wrong with the place.

In Thornhill's opinion, the CIA's downfall had accelerated in 1994 with the Aldrich Ames debacle. Thornhill still winced every time he thought of the former CIA counterintelligence officer being arrested for spying for the Soviets and later the Russians. And of course, as fate would have it, the FBI had broken the case. After that, the president had issued a directive ordering an FBI agent to be made a permanent employee of the CIA. From then on, this FBI agent oversaw the agency's counterespionage efforts and had access to all CIA files. An FBI agent on the premises! His nose in all their secrets! Not to be out-done by the executive branch, the idiotic Congress had followed with a law requiring all government agencies, including the CIA, to notify the FBI when-ever there was evidence that classified information might have been improperly disclosed to foreign powers. The result: The CIA took all the risk and gave the prize to the FBI. Thornhill seethed. It was a direct usurpation of the CIA's mission.

Thornhill's rage was building. The CIA could no longer even put people under surveillance or wiretap. If it had suspicions of someone, it had to go to the FBI and request surveillance, electronic or otherwise. If electronic surveillance was desired, then the FBI had to go to FISC, the Foreign Intelligence Surveil-lance Court, and obtain authorization. The CIA couldn't even approach FISC on its own. It had to have its hand held by Big Brother. Everything was stacked in the FBI's favor.

Thornhill's thoughts went into a tailspin as he re-minded himself that the shackles on the CIA weren't just domestic; the Agency had to get authorization from the president before commencing any covert operations overseas. The congressional oversight committees had to be told of any such operations in a timely fashion. And with the world of espionage becoming more and more complicated, the CIA and FBI found themselves continually running into each other over jurisdictional squabbles, use of witnesses and informants and the like. Though it was supposed to be a domestic agency only, the FBI, in reality, did considerable work abroad, where it focused on antiterrorism and anti-drug operations, including the collection and analysis of information. Again, that hit right at the CIA's home turf.

Was it any wonder Thornhill hated his federal counterparts? Like a cancer, the bastards were everywhere. And to drive the nail a little farther into the CIA's coffin, a former FBI agent now headed up the Center for CIA Security, which conducted internal background checks on all current and prospective personnel. And all CIA employees had to file annual financial disclosure forms that were damn well exhaustive in their content requirements.

Before he suffered a stroke thinking any more on this sore subject, Thornhill forced himself to turn his attention to other matters. If Buchanan had hired this PI person to follow Lockhart, then he very well could have been the man at the cottage last night and the person who had shot Serov. There had been permanent nerve damage to the man's arm from the gunshot wound, and Thornhill had ordered the Russian to be finished off. A hired killer who could no longer hold a weapon steady enough to kill would look for other ways to make money and could pose a small threat. It was Serov's own fault, and if there was one thing Thornhill demanded from his people, it was accountability.

So this Lee Adams was now in the mix of things, he mused. Thornhill had already ordered a complete background search on the man. In these days of computerized files, he would have a full dossier in half an hour, if not sooner. Thornhill did have Adams's file on Faith Lockhart; his men had taken that from the apartment. The notes showed that the man was thorough, logical in his approach to investigation. That was both good and bad for Thornhill's purposes. Adams had also given Thornhill's men the slip. That was not an easy thing to do. On the good side, if Adams was logical, he should be amenable to a reasonable offer, meaning one that would allow him to live.

Presumably Adams had also escaped from the cottage with Faith Lockhart. He had not reported in to Buchanan about this, which was why Buchanan had left that phone message. Buchanan was obviously unaware of what had happened last night. Thornhill would do all he could to make sure this state of affairs continued.

How would they run? A train? Thornhill doubted it. Trains were slow. And you couldn't take a train overseas. Now, a train to an airport was a more intriguing possibility. Or a cab. That seemed certainly more likely.

Thornhill eased back into his chair as an assistant entered with some files he had requested. While everything at the CIA was computerized these days, Thornhill still liked the feel of paper in his hand. He could think much more clearly with paper than when he was simply staring at the pixeled screen.

So all the usual bases were covered. What about the unusual? With the added element of a professional investigator, Adams and Lockhart might be fleeing under false identities, even disguises. He had men at all three airports and the train stations. That would only go so far. The pair could easily rent a car and drive to New York and take a plane there. Or they could go south and do the same thing. It certainly was problematic.

Thornhill hated these sorts of chases. There were too many places to cover and he had limited manpower for these "extracurricular" activities of his. At least he had the advantage of operating more or less autonomously. No one from the director of central intelligence on down really questioned him as to what he was up to. Or if they did, he was able to dance around any issue they threw at him. He got results that made them all look good, and that was his biggest weapon.

It was much better to coax the runners out, bring them to you, which was certainly possible with the right sort of bait. Thornhill just had to come up with that bait. That would take some more thinking. Lockhart had no family, no elderly parents or young children. He didn't know enough about Adams yet, but he would. If the man had just hooked up with the woman, he couldn't possibly be willing to sacrifice everything for her. Not just yet. Other things being equal, Adams was the one to focus on. And they had a communication link to him by virtue of knowing where he lived. If they needed to get a discreet message to him, they could.

Now Thornhill's thoughts turned to Buchanan. He was currently in Philadelphia meeting with a prominent senator on how best to further the agenda of one of Buchanan's clients. They had this particular fellow on enough felonious activity to make the man literally break down and plead for his miserable life. He had been a special pain in the ass to the CIA, nickle-and-diming them to death from the high perch of his Appropriations Committee seat. The payback would be so gratifying.

Thornhill envisioned walking into all these mighty politicians' offices and showing them the videos, the audiotapes, the paper trails. Of them and Buchanan plotting their little conspiracies, all the details of the future payoffs; they so eager to do Buchanan's bidding in return for all that money. How greedy they looked!

Good Senator, would you mind very much licking my boots, you whiny, squealing excuse for a human being. And then you will do exactly as I say, no more, no less, or I will crush you underfoot faster than you can say "vote for me."

Of course, Thornhill would never say that. These men demanded your respect even if they didn't deserve it. He would tell them that Danny Buchanan had disappeared and left these tapes with them. They weren't quite sure what to do with the evidence, but it appeared that the tapes should be turned over to the FBI. It seemed an awful thing to do; these fine men couldn't possibly be guilty of these sorts of things, but once the FBI started its feeding frenzy, they all knew where that would end: prison. And how could that possibly help the country? The world would laugh at us. Terrorists would be emboldened in the face of a supposedly weakened foe. And resources were so tight. Why, the CIA itself was understaffed and underfunded, its responsibility unfairly curtailed. And could you fine people perhaps do something to change that? And would you please do so at the expense of the FBI, the very bastards who would love to get their hands on these tapes so they could destroy you? Starting with getting them the hell off our backs? And we thank you very much, you fine public leaders. We knew you'd understand.

The first move in Thornhill's grand plan would be to have his new allies find a way to completely remove the FBI presence from the Agency. Next, the operations budget for the CIA would be increased by fifty percent. To start. In the next fiscal year he would get serious about the dollars. In the future, the CIA would only report to a joint intelligence committee instead of the separate House and Senate committees it was confronted with now. It was far easier to co-opt one committee. Then the hierarchy of the U.S. intelligence-gathering agencies needed to be straightened out once and for all. And the director of Central Intelligence would be at the very top of that pyramid. The FBI would be as far down the totem pole as Thornhill could bury it. And the tools of the CIA would be considerably strengthened. Domestic surveillance, the covert funding and arming of insurgency groups to overthrow enemies of the United States, even selective assassination, all would come back as weapons of choice for him and his colleagues. Right that minute Thornhill could think of five heads of state whose immediate deaths would leave the world a better, safer, more humane place. It was time to take the shackles off the best and brightest and let them do their jobs again. God, he was so close.

"Keep up the good work, Danny," Thornhill said out loud. "Pour it on until the end. That's a good man. Let them almost taste victory right before I take their lives away."

Grim-faced, he looked at his watch and rose from behind his desk. Thornhill was a man who loathed the press. He had, of course, never granted an interview in all his years at the Agency. But as senior as he was now, he occasionally had to undertake another sort of appearance, one that he equally detested. He had to testify before the House and Senate Select

Committees on Intelligence on a series of matters involving the Agency.

In these "enlightened" times, CIA personnel gave more than one thousand substantive reports to Congress in a year's time. So much for covert operations. Thornhill was able to get through these briefings only by focusing on how easily he could manipulate the idiots who were supposed to be overseeing his agency. With their smug looks, they posed to him questions formulated by their very diligent staffs, who were more knowledgeable about most intelligence matters than the elected officials they served.

At least the hearing would be in camera, no public or press allowed. To Thornhill the First Amendment's rights to an unfettered press had been the biggest mistake the Founding Fathers ever made. You had to be damn careful around the scribes; they looked for every advantage, any chance to put words in your mouth, trip you up, make the Agency look bad. It deeply hurt Thornhill that no one seemed to really trust them. Of course they lied about things; that was their job.

In Thornhill's mind the CIA was clearly the Hill's favorite whipping boy. The members loved to look tough in facing down the super-secret organization. That really played well back home: FARMER-TURNED-CONGRESSMAN STARES DOWN SPOOKS. By now Thornhill could write the headlines himself.

However, today's hearing actually promised to be

positive because the Agency had scored some serious PR points lately in the most recent Middle East peace talks. Indeed, largely through Thornhill's behind-the-scenes work, the Agency had overall fashioned a more benign, upstanding image, an image he would seek to bolster today.

Thornhill snapped his briefcase shut and put his pipe in his pocket. *Off to lie to a bunch of liars, and we both know it and we both win,* he thought. *Only in America.*

CHAPTER 17

Senator," Buchanan said, shaking hands with the tall, elegant-looking gentleman. Senator Harvey Milstead was a proven leader with high morals and strong political instincts who offered thoughtful insight on the issues. A true statesman. That was the public perception. The reality was that Milstead was a womanizer of the first order and was addicted to painkillers for a chronically bad back, medications that sometimes left him incoherent. He also had a worsening drinking problem. It was years since he had sponsored any meaningful legislation of his own, although in his prime he had helped enact laws from which every American now benefited. These days when he spoke, it was in gobbledygook that no one ever bothered to check up on because he said it with such authority. Besides, the press loved the charming guy with such genteel manners, and he held a very powerful leadership position. He also fed the media machine with a flow of appropriately timed juicy leaks, and he was quotable to a fault. They loved him, Buchanan knew. How could they not?

There were five hundred and thirty-five members of Congress—a hundred senators plus the representatives in the House. Well over three-quarters of them, Buchanan estimated perhaps a little generously, were decent, hardworking, genuinely caring men and women who believed strongly in what they were doing both in Washington and for the people. Buchanan termed them, collectively, the "Believers." Buchanan stayed away from the Believers. Touching those folk would only have earned him a quick trip to prison.

The rest of the Washington leadership were like Harvey Milstead. Most were not drunks or womanizers or shells of their former selves, but, for various reasons, they were ripe for manipulation, easy targets for the lures Buchanan was tossing overboard.

There were two such groups that Buchanan had successfully recruited over the years. Forget Republicans and Democrats. The parties Buchanan was interested in were the members of the venerable "Townies," and the group Buchanan had labeled, only somewhat tongue-in-cheek, the "Zombies."

The Townies knew the system better than anyone. They *were* the system. Washington was their town, hence the nickname. They had all been here longer than God. If you cut them, their blood would run red, white and blue, or so they liked to tell you. There was another color Buchanan had added to that mix: green.

By contrast, the Zombies had come to Congress with nary a stitch of moral fiber or whiff of a political philosophy. They had won their place of leadership with the finest campaigns that media dollars could buy. They were fabulous on sound bite TV and in the confines of tightly controlled debates. They were, at best, mediocre in intellect and ability and yet delivered the sales pitch with the verve and enthusiasm of a JFK at his oratorical best. And when they were elected, they arrived in Washington with absolutely no idea what to do. Their only goal had already been achieved: They had won their campaign.

However, despite this, the Zombies tended to stay in Congress because they loved the power and access that came with being an incumbent. And with the cost of elections going through the stratosphere, it was still possible to defeat an entrenched incumbent . . . in the same way that it was still theoretically possible to climb Mount Everest without oxygen. One only had to hold his breath for several days.

Buchanan and Milstead sat down on a comfortable leather couch in the senator's spacious office. The shelves were filled with the usual spoils of a longtime politician: plaques and medals of appreciation, silver cups, awards made of crystal, hundreds of photographs of the senator standing with people even more famous than he; in-

scribed ceremonial gavels and bronzed miniature shov-
els symbolizing political pork brought to his state. As
Buchanan looked around, it occurred to him that he had
spent his entire professional life coming to places such
as this, hat in hand, essentially begging.

It was early yet, but the man's staff was busy in the
outer suite preparing for a hectic day with Keystone
State constituents, a day laced with lunches,
speeches, appearances and pop-in-and-out dinners,
meet-and-greets, drinks and parties. The senator was
not up for reelection, but it was always nice to put on
a good show for the people back home.

"I appreciate your meeting with me on such short
notice, Harvey."

"Hard to refuse you, Danny."

"I'll get right to it. Pickens's bill is looking to
knock out my funding, along with about twenty
other aid packages. We can't let that happen. The results speak for themselves. The infant mortality rate
has been cut seventy percent. My God, the wonders
of vaccine and antibiotics. Jobs are being created, the
economy is moving from thuggery to legitimate
business. Exports are up by a third, and imports from
us are up twenty percent. So you see it's creating jobs
here too. We can't let the plug be pulled now. Not
only is it morally wrong, it's stupid from our side. If
we can get countries like this on their feet, we won't
have a trade imbalance. But you need reliable sources
of electricity first. You need an educated population."

"AID is accomplishing a lot," the senator pointed out.

Buchanan was intimately familiar with AID, or the Agency for International Development. Formerly an independent agency, it now reported to the Secretary of State, who also more or less controlled its very substantial budget. AID was the flagship of American foreign aid, with the vast majority of funds flowing through its long-standing programs. Every year it was like musical chairs to see where AID's limited budget dollars would end up. Buchanan had been caught without a seat many times, and he was so weary of it. The grant process was intensive and highly competitive, and unless you fit the template set up by AID for the programs it wanted to sponsor, you were out of luck.

"AID can't do it all. And my clients are too small a bite for IMF and the World Bank. Besides, now all I hear is 'sustainable development.' No dollars unless it goes for sustainable development. Hell, last time I looked, food and medicine were necessary for life. Doesn't that qualify?"

"You're preaching to the choir, Danny. But people count pennies around here too. The days of fat are over," Milstead said solemnly.

"My clients will take gristle. Just don't cut them off."

"Look, I just won't schedule the bill."

In the Senate, if a chairman didn't want a bill to get out of committee, he simply didn't schedule it for hearing, as Milstead was now suggesting. Buchanan had played that game many times before.

"But Pickens could end-run you on that," Buchanan said. "Word is he's dead set on getting this thing heard one way or another. And he might get a more sympathetic audience on the floor than he would in committee. Why not put a hold on the bill and run it out of session?" Buchanan suggested.

Danny Buchanan was the master at this technique. A hold was simply one senator objecting to a pending bill. The legislation would be in complete limbo until the hold was removed. Years ago, Buchanan and his allies on the Hill had used it to stunning effect in representing the most powerful special interests in the country. It took real power in Washington to make things not happen. And for Buchanan, that had always been the most fascinating aspect of the city. Why health care reform legislation or the tobacco settlement bills, propelled by intense media coverage and public clamor, simply disappeared into the yawning gulf of the Congress. And it was very often the case that special interests wanted to maintain the status quo they had worked so hard to erect. For them change was not good. Hence, a good deal of Buchanan's previous lobbying work had focused on burying any legislation that would harm his powerful clients.

The hold maneuver was also known as the "blind rolling" hold because, as in the passing of the baton on a relay team, a different senator could place a new hold when the previous one had been released, and only the leadership knew who had placed the restriction. There was a lot more to it, but at the end of the day the blind rolling hold was an enormous waste of time, and hugely effective, which explained much of politics in a nutshell, Buchanan well knew.

The senator shook his head. "I found out Pickens has holds on two of my pieces, and I'm close to cutting a deal that'll make him let go. I hit him with another hold and the sonofabitch'll clamp down on my ass like a ferret on a cobra."

Buchanan sat back and sipped his coffee as a number of potential strategies rolled through his mind. "Look, let's go back to square one. If you have the votes to knock it out, schedule it and let the committee vote on it and kill the bastard for good. Then if he takes it to the floor I can't believe he'll have the support to carry it. Shit, once it's on the floor we can hold it up forever, ask for amendments, hit it in the cloak room, cut the crap out of it pretending to want to deal for some juice on one of your bills. In fact, we're so close to the elections now we can even play the quorum call game until he yells uncle."

Milstead nodded thoughtfully. "You know Archer and Simms are giving me a little trouble."

"Harvey, you've sent enough highway construction dollars to both those bastards' states to choke every man and woman and child there. Call them on it! They don't give a damn about this bill. They probably haven't even read the staff briefing materials."

Milstead looked suddenly confident. "One way or another, we'll get it done for you. In a one-point-seven-trillion-dollar budget, it's not that big a deal."

"It is for my client. A lot of people are counting on this one, Harvey. And most of them can't even walk yet."

"I hear you."

"You should take a fact-finding trip over there. I'll go with you. It's really beautiful country, you just can't use the land for shit. God might have blessed America, but he forgot about a lot of the rest of the world. But they keep going. If you ever think you're having a bad day, it's a good memory to have."

Milstead coughed. "My schedule is really full, Danny. And you know I'm not running for reelection. Two more years and I'm out of here."

Okay, shop talk and humanitarian plea time is over, Buchanan thought. *Now let's play traitor.*

He leaned forward and casually moved his briefcase out of the way. One twist on the handle activated the recording device secreted inside. *This one's for you, Thornhill, you smug bastard.*

Buchanan cleared his throat. "Well, I guess it's never too early to talk about replacements. I need some people on Foreign Aid and Ops who'll participate in my little retirement program. I can promise them as good as I'll be paying you. They'll want for nothing. They just have to get my agenda done. I'm at the point now where I can't afford defeat on any-thing. They have to come through for me. That's the only way I can guarantee the payoff at the end. Just like you. You always come through for me, Harvey. Almost ten years and counting, and you always get it done. By hook or crook."

Milstead glanced at the door and then spoke in a very low voice, as though that made it all better. "I do have some people you might want to talk to." He looked nervous, uncomfortable. "About taking over some of my *duties*. I haven't broached the issue with them directly, of course, but I'd be surprised if they weren't amenable to some sort of arrangement."

"That's real good to hear."

"And you're right to plan ahead. The two years will go quickly."

"Christ, in two years I might not be here, Harvey."

The senator smiled warmly. "I didn't think you'd ever retire." He paused. "But I guess you have your heir apparent. How is Faith, by the way? Vivacious as ever, I'm sure."

"Faith is Faith. You know that."

"Lucky to have someone like her backing you up."

"Very lucky," Buchanan said, frowning slightly.

"Give her my best when you see her. Tell her to come up and see old Harvey. Best mind and legs in the place," he added with a wink.

To this, Buchanan said nothing.

The senator sat back against the couch. "I've been

in public service half my life. The pay is ridiculous—
chickenshit, really, for somebody of my ability and
stature. You know what I could earn on the outside.
That's the trade-off when you serve your country."

"Absolutely, Harvey. Of course it is." *The bribe
money is only your due. You earned it.*

"But I don't regret it. Any of it."

"No reason you should."

Milstead smiled wearily. "The dollars I've spent
over the years rebuilding this country, shaping it for
the future, for the next generation. And the next."

Now it was *his* money. *He* saved the country. "People never appreciate that," said Buchanan. "The
media only goes after the dirt."

"Guess I'm just making up for it in my golden
years," Milstead said, sounding a little contrite.

*After all these years a little humility, a little guilt re-
main.* "You deserve it. You served your country well.
It's all waiting for you. Just like we discussed. Better
than we discussed. You and Louise will want for nothing. You'll live like a king and queen. You did your
job, and you'll reap the rewards. The American way."

"I'm tired, Danny. Weary to the bones. Between
you and me, I'm not sure I can last two more minutes, much less two more years. This place has sucked
the life right out of me."

"You're a true statesman. A hero to us all."

Buchanan took a deep breath and wondered if
Thornhill's boys parked in the van outside were en-

joying this sappy exchange. In truth, Buchanan too was looking forward to getting out. He looked at his old friend. An expression of giddiness was on the man's features as he no doubt thought of a truly glorious retirement with his wife of thirty-five years, a woman he had cheated on many times, who had always allowed him back. And kept silent about it. The psychology of political wives would be a worthy college course, Buchanan believed.

In truth, Buchanan had a soft spot for his Townies. They actually had accomplished a lot, and in their own way were some of the most honorable people Buchanan had ever met. And yet the senator had no problem being bought.

Very soon Harvey Milstead would have a new master. The Thirteenth Amendment to the Constitution had outlawed slavery, but apparently no one had bothered telling Robert Thornhill that. He was turning his friends over to the Devil. That's what troubled Buchanan most of all. Thornhill, always Thornhill.

The men rose and Buchanan and the senator shook hands. "Thank you, Danny. Thank you for everything."

"Please, don't mention it," Buchanan said. "Please don't." He grabbed his spy briefcase and fled the room.

CHAPTER 18

D EGAUSSED?" REYNOLDS STARED AT THE TWO technicians.

"My tape has been degaussed? Will someone please explain that to me?" She had watched the video twenty times now. From every angle possible. Or rather, she had watched jagged lines and dots swarm across the screen like a World War I aerial dogfight with heavy doses of ground flack thrown in. She had been sitting here for a very long time and knew no more than when she had first walked in.

"Without getting too technical—" one of the men started to say.

"Please don't," Reynolds interjected. Her head was pounding. If the tape was useless? *Good God, it can't be.*

"'Degaussing' is the reference term used for the erasure of a magnetic medium. It's done for many reasons, some of the most common being so that the medium can be used again, or to eliminate confidential information that was recorded. A videotape is one of the many forms of magnetic media. What happened to the tape you gave us was an unwanted intrusional influence that has distorted and/or corrupted the medium, preventing its proper utilization."

Reynolds stared in wonder at the man. What the hell would his technical answer have been?

"So you're saying someone intentionally screwed with the tape?" she said.

"That's right."

"But couldn't it be a problem with the tape itself? How can you be sure someone 'intruded' upon it?"

The other technician spoke up. "The level of corruption we've seen in the images so far would preclude that conclusion. We can't be one hundred percent sure, of course, but it really does look like third party interference. From what I understand, the surveillance system used was very sophisticated. A multiplexer with three or four cameras on line, so there was no dwell time gap. How were the units activated? Motion or trip?"

"Trip."

"Motion is better. The systems these days are so sensitive they can pick up a hand reaching for something on a desk in a one-foot-square zone. Trips are obsolete."

"Thanks, I'll keep that in mind," she said dryly.

"We did a pixel zoom for detail enhancement, but still nothing. Definitely interference."

Reynolds remembered that the closet at the cottage containing the video equipment had been found open.

"Okay, how could they have done it?"

"Well, there's a wide variety of specialized equipment available."

Reynolds shook her head. "No, we're not talking a lab setting. We're looking at doing it on site, where the equipment was set up. And maybe whoever did it wouldn't have even known there was video recording equipment there. So assume that whatever they happened to have with them would have been what they used."

The techs thought for a moment. "Well," one of them said, "if the person had a powerful magnet and passed it over the recorder a number of times, that could distort the tape by rearranging the metallic particles, which would, in turn, remove the previously recorded signals."

Reynolds took a deep, troubled breath. A simple magnet could have blown away her only clue. "Is there any way to get it back, the images on the tape?"

"It's possible, but it will take some time. We can't make any guarantees until we get in there."

"Do it. But let me make this real clear." She stood, towering over the two men. "I need to be able to see what's on that tape. I need to be able to see who was in that house. You have no higher priority than that. Check with the AD if you have a conflict, but whatever it takes, twenty-four hours a day. I need it. Understood?"

The men looked at each other briefly before nodding.

When Reynolds got back to her office, a man was waiting to see her.

"Paul." She nodded at him as she sat down.

Paul Fisher rose and closed the door to Reynolds's office. He was her liaison at Headquarters. He stepped over a pile of documents as he sat back down. "You look like you're overworked, Brooke. You always look like you're overworked. I guess that's what I love about you."

He smiled and Brooke caught herself smiling back.

Fisher was one of the few people at the FBI whom Reynolds looked up to, literally, as he was easily six-foot-five. They were about the same age, although Fisher was her superior in the chain of command and had been at the Bureau two years longer. He was competent and assured. He was also handsome, having retained the tousled blond hair and trim figure of his California days at UCLA. After her marriage had started to disintegrate, Reynolds had imagined having an affair with the divorced Fisher. Even now, his unexpected visit made Reynolds feel fortunate she'd had the opportunity to go home, shower and change her clothes.

Fisher's jacket was off, his shirt draped gracefully over his long torso. He had just come on duty, she knew, although he tended to be around at all hours.

"I'm sorry about Ken," he said. "I was out of town, or I would've been there last night."

Reynolds played with a letter opener on her desk. "Not as sorry as I am. And neither of us is anywhere near where Anne Newman is on the sorry meter."

"I've talked to the SAC," Fisher said, referring to the special agent in charge, "but I want you to tell me about it."

After she told him what she knew, he rubbed his chin. "Obviously the targets know you're on to them."

"It would seem so."

"You're not that far along in the investigation, are you?"

"Nowhere near referring it to the U.S. attorney for indictment, if that's what you mean."

"So Ken's dead and your chief and only witness is MIA. Tell me about Faith Lockhart."

She glanced up sharply, being equally disturbed by his choice of words and the blunt tone he had used to say them.

He stared back at her, his hazel eyes holding a definable measure of unfriendliness, Reynolds concluded. But right now, she knew, he was not supposed to be her friend. He represented Headquarters.

"Is there something you want to tell *me,* Paul?"

"Brooke, we've always shot straight with each other." He paused and tapped his fingers against the arm of the chair as though trying to communicate with her in Morse code. "I know Massey authorized some leeway for you last night, but they're all very concerned about you. You need to know that."

"I know that in light of recent developments—"

"They were concerned *before* this. Recent developments have only heightened that level of concern."

"Do they want me to just drop it? Christ, it could implicate people who have government buildings named after them."

"It's a question of proof. Without Lockhart what do you have?"

"It's there, Paul."

"What names has she given you, other than Buchanan?"

Reynolds looked momentarily flustered. The problem was Lockhart hadn't given them any names. Yet. She had been too smart for that. She was saving that for when her deal was completed.

"Nothing specific yet. But we'll get it. Buchanan didn't do business with local school board members. And she told us some of his scheme. They work for him while in power, and when they leave office he lines up jobs for them with no real duties and megadollars in compensation and other perks. It's simple. Simply brilliant. The level of detail she's provided us could not be made up."

"I'm not disputing her credibility. But again, can you prove your case? Right now?"

"We're doing everything we can to prove it. I was going to ask her to wear a wire for us when all this happened, but you can't rush these things, you know that. If I pushed too hard, or lost her confidence, we'd end up with nothing."

"Do you want my coldly reasoned analysis?" Fisher took her silence as assent. "You've got all these name-less but very powerful people, many of whom may have things lined up in the future or currently have nice post–public service careers. What's so unusual about that? It happens all the time. They get on the phone, have lunches, whisper in ears, call in some fa-vors. That's America. So where are we?"

"This is more than that, Paul. A lot more."

"Are you saying you can trace the actual illegal ac-tivity, how the legislation was manipulated?"

"Not exactly."

"'Not exactly' is right. It's really like trying to prove a negative."

Reynolds knew he was right on that point. How did you prove someone *didn't* do something? Many of the tools Buchanan's people would have used to further his agenda were probably tools every politician used, legitimately. They were talking motivation here. *Why* somebody was doing something, not *how* they were doing it. The why was illegal, the how wasn't.

Like a basketball player not trying his best because he'd been paid off.

"Is Buchanan a director in these unknown firms where the former, unknown politicians get jobs? A stockholder? Did he put up the money? Does he have any ongoing business with any of them?"

"You sound like a defense lawyer," she said hotly.

"That's exactly my intent. Because those are the sort of questions you'll need answers for."

"We have not been able to uncover evidence directly tying Buchanan to any of it."

"Then what are you basing your conclusion on? What's your evidence that there is a connection at all?"

Reynolds started to speak and then stopped. Her face flushed and in her agitation she broke in half the pencil she was holding.

"Let me answer that for you," said Fisher. "Faith Lockhart, your missing witness."

"We'll find her, Paul. And then we're back in business."

"And if you don't find her? What then?"

"We'll find another way."

"Can you determine the identities of the bribed officials independently?"

Reynolds desperately wanted to say yes to that question, but she couldn't. Buchanan had been in Washington for decades. He'd probably had dealings with just about every politician and bureaucrat in the city. It would be impossible to narrow down the list without Lockhart.

"Anything's possible," she said gamely.

He shook his head. "Actually, it's not, Brooke."

Reynolds erupted. "Buchanan and his cronies have broken the law. Doesn't that count for anything?"

"In a court of law it counts for zero without proof," he shot back.

She slammed her fist down on the desk. "I damn well refuse to believe that. Besides, the evidence is there; we just have to keep digging."

"You see, that's the problem. It would be one thing if you could do it in complete secrecy. But an investigation of this magnitude, with the sort of important targets we're talking about, can never remain completely secret. And now we have a homicide investigation to deal with as well."

"Meaning there will be leaks," Reynolds said, wondering if Fisher suspected that those leaks might have already occurred.

"Meaning that when you go after important people, you better be damn sure of your case before any leaks do occur. You can't target people like that unless you're loaded for bear. Right now, your gun's empty and I'm not sure where you go to reload. It pretty much says in the Bureau manual, you can't hunt down public officials based on rumor and innuendo."

She looked at him coolly when he finished saying

this. "Okay, Paul, would you like to tell me exactly what it is you want me to do?"

"The Violent Crime Unit will keep you informed on its investigation. You have to find Lockhart. Since the two cases are inextricably connected, I suggest cooperation."

"I can't tell them anything about our investigation."

"I'm not asking you to. Just work with them to help clear Newman's murder. And find Lockhart."

"And beyond that? If we can't find her? What happens to my investigation?"

"I don't know, Brooke. The tea leaves are very hard to read right now."

Reynolds stood and looked out the window. Thick, dark clouds had turned day almost into night. She could see both her reflection and Fisher's in the window. He never took his eyes off her, and she doubted if he was all that interested at the moment in how her backside and long legs looked in the black knee-length skirt and matching stockings she was wearing.

As she stood there her ears picked up on a sound they usually didn't: the "white noise." At sensitive government facilities windows were potential outlets for valuable information, namely speech. To plug this leak, speakers were mounted at the windows in these facilities to filter out the sound of voices such that anyone lurking outside with the fanciest in surveillance equipment would end up with zip. The speakers accomplished this by emitting a sound akin to a small waterfall, hence the term "white noise." Reynolds, like most employees in such buildings, had tuned out the background noise; it was such a daily part of her life. Now she noticed it with stunning clarity. Was that a signal to her to notice other things as well? Things, people she saw every day and then thought no more of, accepting them for what they proclaimed to be? She turned to face Fisher.

"Thanks for the vote of confidence, Paul."

"Your career has been nothing short of spectacular. But the public sector is often like the private in one regard: It's the 'what have you done for me lately?' syndrome. I'm not going to sugarcoat this, Brooke. I've already started to hear the rumblings."

She folded her arms across her chest. "I appreciate your complete bluntness," she said coldly. "If you'll excuse me, I'll see what I can do for you lately, Agent Fisher."

As Fisher rose to leave, he moved next to her, touching her lightly on the shoulder. Reynolds recoiled slightly from this, the bite of his words still smarting.

"I've always supported you, and I will continue to support you, Brooke. Don't read this as though I'm throwing you to the wolves. I'm not. I respect the hell out of you. I just didn't want you to be blindsided on this. You don't deserve that. This messenger is friendly."

"That's good to know, Paul," she said unenthusiastically.

When he reached the door, he turned back. "We're handling the media relations from WFO. We've already had inquiries from the press. For now, an agent was killed during an undercover operation. No other details were provided, including his identity. That won't last long. And when the dam breaks, I'm not sure who can keep dry."

As soon as the door closed behind him, a cold shudder hit Reynolds. She felt as though she were being suspended over a vat of boiling something. Was it her old paranoia kicking in? Or was it simply her reasoned judgment? She kicked her shoes off and paced her office, stepping over the paper land mines as she did so. She rocked on the balls of her feet, trying to guide the massive tension she was feeling throughout her body toward the floor. It didn't come close to working.

CHAPTER 19

THE RECENTLY RENAMED RONALD REAGAN
Washington National Airport, which everyone in the
area still simply called "National," was very busy this
morning. It was loved for its convenience to the city
and its numerous daily flights, and hated for its con-
gestion, short runways and stomach-jolting tight
turns to avoid restricted airspace. However, the airport's new sparkling terminal with its row of Jeffer-
sonian-inspired domes and hulking, multitiered
parking garages with skywalks to the terminal were
very welcome to the hassled air traveler.

Lee and Faith entered the new terminal, where Lee
eyed a police officer patrolling the corridor. They had
left the car in one of the parking lots.

Faith watched the policeman's movements too. She
was wearing "eyeglasses" that Lee had given her. The

lenses were ordinary glass, but they helped to further change her look. She touched Lee's arm. "Nervous?"

"Always. It kind of gives me an edge. Makes up for a serious lack of formal schooling." He put their bags over his shoulder. "Let's grab a cup of coffee and let the line at the ticket counter die down a little, scope the place out." As they looked for a coffee shop, he asked, "Any idea of when we can get a flight out of here?"

"We fly through Norfolk and then take a commuter to Pine Island, off the Outer Banks of North Carolina. Flights to Norfolk are pretty frequent. The commuter to Pine Island you have to call ahead and schedule. Once we get the Norfolk flight scheduled, I'll call down and arrange that. They only fly during daylight."

"Why's that?"

"Because we won't be landing on a regular runway; it's more like a little road. No lights or tower or anything. Just a wind sock."

"That's comforting."

"Let me call down and check on the house."

They went over to the phone bank and Lee listened while Faith confirmed their arrival. She hung up. "All set. We can get a rental car once we get down there."

"So far, so good."

"It's a nice place to relax. You don't need to see or talk to anybody else if you don't want to."

"I don't want to," said Lee firmly.

"I'd like to ask you a question," Faith said as they walked toward a café.

"Shoot."

"How long had you been following me?"

"Six days," he promptly answered, "during which you made three trips to the cottage, including last night."

Last night, Faith thought. Was that all it had been? "And you haven't reported back to your employer yet?"

"No."

"Why not?"

"I like to do weekly reports, unless something really extraordinary happens. Believe me, if I'd had time, last night would have qualified for the mother of all reports."

"How were you to make these reports if you don't know who hired you?"

"I was given a phone number."

"And you never checked up on it?"

He looked at her with annoyance. "Nah, why should I care? Take the money and run."

She looked chastened. "I didn't mean it like that."

"Uh-huh, sure." He shifted the bags slightly and continued, "There's a special crisscross directory that'll give you the corresponding address if you have the phone number."

"And?"

"And in these days of satellite phones and nation-wide cell networks and crap like that, nothing came up. I called the number. It must have been set up just to receive calls from me, because it told Mr. Adams to leave any information on the tape. It also gave a

P.O. box in D.C. Being the ever curious type I checked that out too, but it was listed in the name of a corporation I'd never heard of, with an address that turned out to be phony. Dead end." He looked down at her. "I take my work seriously, Faith. I don't like walking into traps. Famous last words, right?"

They stopped at the small café, bought their coffee and a couple of bagels and sat down in a vacant corner of the place.

Faith took a quick breath as she sipped her coffee and nibbled on a poppyseed bagel oozing butter. Maybe he was being straight with her, but he still had a connection to Danny Buchanan. It was such a strange feeling suddenly being fearful of a man she had idolized. If things had not changed so much between them the last year, she would have been tempted to call Danny. But she was confused now, the horror of last night so crystal clear in her mind. Besides, what was she supposed to ask him: *Danny, did you try and have me killed last night? If you did, please stop, I'm working with the FBI to help you, really. And why did you hire Lee to follow me, Danny?* Yes, she had to part company with Lee, and soon.

"The report you were given, tell me what it said about me," Faith said.

"You're a lobbyist. You used to be with a big outfit, represented Fortune 500s. About ten years ago, you and a man named Daniel Buchanan started your own firm."

"Did it mention any of our current clients?"

He cocked his head. "No, is that important?"

"What do you know about Buchanan?"

"The report didn't say much about him, but I did some digging on my own, nothing you won't know. Buchanan is a legend on the Hill. Knows everybody and everybody knows him. Fought all the big battles, made a ton of money doing it. I assume you didn't do so badly yourself."

"I did well. What else?"

He stared at her strangely. "Why do you want to hear something you already know? Is Buchanan somehow mixed up in all this?"

Now it was Faith's turn to scrutinize Lee. If he was playing dumb, he was doing an exceptional job, she thought.

"Danny Buchanan is an honorable man. I owe him everything I have."

"Sounds like a good friend. But you didn't answer my question."

"People like Danny are rare. A true visionary."

"And you?"

"Me? I just help implement his vision. People like me are a dime a dozen."

"You don't strike me as so ordinary." Faith took a sip of coffee and didn't respond. "So how does one become a lobbyist?"

Faith stifled a yawn and sipped her coffee again. Her head was starting to pound. She had never needed much rest, galloping the globe, catching only plane catnaps.

But right now she felt like curling up under the table and sleeping for the next ten years. Maybe her body was reacting to the last twelve hours of horror by shutting itself down, throwing in the towel. *Please don't hurt me.*

"I could lie and say I wanted to change the world. That's what everyone says, isn't it?" She pulled a bottle of aspirin from her bag, popped two and washed them down with coffee. "Actually, I remember watching the Watergate hearings when I was a kid. All those very serious people in that room. All these middle-aged men with wide ugly ties, puffy faces, overeasy hair, talking into these clunky microphones, and all the lawyers whispering into their ears. All the media, the whole world focused right there. What the rest of the country apparently found appalling, I found extremely cool. All that power!" She smiled weakly into her coffee cup. "My demented soul. The nuns were right about me. One in particular, Sister Audrey Ann, truly believed my name was a blasphemy. 'Dear Faith,' she would say, 'live up to your Christian name, not down to your devilish urges.'"

"So you were a rabble rouser?"

"It's like if I saw a habit coming my way I just turned evil. My dad moved us around a lot, but I did well enough in school, even if I raised hell outside it. I went to a good college, ended up in Washington with all those memories of absolute power dancing in my head. I didn't have the faintest idea what to do with myself, but I knew desperately I wanted to get into the game. I did a stint on Capitol Hill for a freshman congressman and caught the eye of Danny Buchanan. He snatched me up, saw something in me, I guess. I think he liked my spirit—I was running the office with all of two months' experience behind me. The way I sort of refused to back down from anyone, even the Speaker of the House."

"I guess that is impressive for somebody right out of college."

"My philosophy was, after the nuns, politicians weren't much of a challenge."

Lee cracked a smile. "Makes me glad I went to public school." He glanced away for a second. "Don't look now, but the FBI is circling."

"What?" She whipped her head around, looking everywhere.

Lee rolled his eyes. "Oh, that was good."

"Where are they?"

He lightly smacked the tabletop. "They're nowhere. And they're everywhere. The Feds don't walk around with their badges pinned to their foreheads. You won't see them."

"So why the hell did you say they were circling?"

"It was a little test. And you failed. *I* can spot the Feds, sometimes, not always. If I ever say that to you again, I won't be kidding. They will be there. And you can't react the way you just did. Normal, slow movements. Just a pretty woman on a holiday with her boyfriend. Understand?"

"Okay, fine. But just don't pull that crap on me again. My nerves aren't well rested."

"How are you paying for the tickets?"

"How should I pay for them?"

"Your credit card. Under your other name. Don't want to flash a bunch of cash around. You buy a one-way ticket with cash leaving today, that might be a red flag for the airline. Right now, the less attention, the better. What is it, by the way? Your other name?"

"Suzanne Blake."

"Nice name."

"Suzanne was my mother's name."

"Was? Passed on?"

"Both my parents. My mother when I was eleven. My dad six years later. No brothers or sisters. I was a seventeen-year-old orphan."

"That must've been tough."

Faith didn't say anything for a long moment. Talking about her past was always hard, so she rarely did so. And she really didn't know this man. Still, there was something about Lee Adams that was comforting, solid. "I really loved my mother," she began. "She was a good woman, and long-suffering, because of my dad. He was a good person too, but one of those souls who always have an angle, a way to make a quick buck with these crazy ideas. And when his plan blew up, and it always did, we'd have to pack up and move on."

"Why was that?"

"Because other people always lost money with my

dad's grand schemes too. And they were understandably upset about it. We moved four times before my mother died. Five more times after that. We prayed for my dad every day, my mom and I. Right before she died, she told me to take care of him, and me all of eleven."

Lee shook his head. "I can't even relate to that. My parents have lived in the same house for fifty years. How did you manage to keep it together after your mother died?"

The words somehow came easier for Faith now. "It wasn't as tough as you'd think. Mom loved my dad, hated how he lived, his schemes, all the moving. But he wasn't going to change, so they weren't the happiest couple to live with. There were times I really thought she was going to kill him. When she died, it sort of became my dad and me against the world. He'd dress me up in the one nice outfit I had and show me off to all his prospective partners. I guess people would think, how can this guy be so bad, what with his little girl right there and all? When I got to be sixteen I'd even help him pitch his deals. I grew up fast. I guess that's where I got my motor mouth and my backbone. I learned to think on my feet."

"Quite an alternative education," Lee commented. "But I can see how it would serve you well as a lobbyist."

Her eyes grew moist. "On the way to every meeting, he'd say, 'This one is the one, Faith, darling. I can feel it right here,' and he'd put his hand over his heart. 'It's all for you, baby girl. Daddy loves his Faith.' And I believed him every single damn time."

"Sounds like he really ended up hurting you," Lee said quietly.

Faith shook her head stubbornly. "It wasn't like he was trying to rip people off. We're not talking Ponzi schemes or anything. He sincerely believed his ideas would work. But they never did and we'd move on. And it wasn't like we ever made any money. God, we slept in our car enough times. How many times do I remember my dad strolling into the back door of restaurants and walking out a little later with dinner he had talked them into giving him. We'd sit in the backseat and eat. He'd stare at the sky, pointing out the constellations to me. He never even finished high school, but he knew all about the stars. Said he'd been chasing enough of them his whole life. We'd just sit there far into the night, and my dad would tell me things would get better. Just down the road."

"Sounds like a man who could talk his way into anywhere. Probably would've made a good PI."

Faith smiled as she thought back. "I'd walk into a bank with him, and within five minutes he'd know everybody by name, drinking coffee, talking with the bank manager like he'd known him his whole life. And we'd walk out with a letter of recommendation and a list of local high-net-worth individuals for my dad to solicit. He just had that way about him.

Everyone liked him. Until they lost their money. And we always lost what little we had too. Dad was a stickler about that. His money went in too. He was actually very honest."

"You sound like you still miss him."

"I do," she said proudly. "He named me Faith because he said with Faith beside him, how could he ever fail?" On this Faith closed her eyes, tears trickling down her cheeks.

Lee pulled a napkin out of the holder and slipped it into her hand. She wiped her eyes.

"I'm sorry," she said. "I've never really talked about this with anyone before."

"It's okay, Faith. I'm a good listener."

"I found my dad again in Danny," she said, clearing her throat, her eyes wide. "He has the same way about him. The pluck of the Irishman. He can talk his way into seeing anybody. Knows every angle, every issue. Refuses to back down from anyone. He's taught me a lot. And not just about lobbying. About life. He didn't have it easy growing up either. We had a lot in common."

Lee smiled. "So from scams with your dad to lobbying in D.C.?"

"And some would say my job description hasn't changed." Faith smiled at her own remark.

"And some would say that the nut didn't fall far from the tree."

She bit into her bagel. "Since we're into true confessions, how about your family?"

Lee settled back. "Four of each. I'm number six."

"God! Eight kids. Your mother must be a saint."

"We gave them both enough heartache to last ten lifetimes."

"So they're both still around."

"Going strong. We're all pretty close now, although we had some rough times growing up. Good support groups when things go haywire. Help's only a phone call away. Usually, that is. Not this time, though."

"That's sounds nice. Real nice." Faith looked away.

Lee eyed her keenly, easily reading her thoughts. "Families have their problems too, Faith. Divorces, serious illnesses, depression, hard times, we've seen it all. I have to say sometimes I'd rather be an only child."

"No, you wouldn't," she said with authority. "You might think you would, but trust me, you wouldn't."

"I do."

She looked confused. "You do what?"

"Trust you."

She said slowly, "You know, for a paranoid PI, you sure make friends fast. I could be a mass murderer, for all you know."

"If you were really bad, the Feds would've had you in custody."

She put down her coffee and leaned toward him,

her expression very serious. "I appreciate the observation. But just so we're very clear on this, I've never
physically harmed even an ant in my entire life, and
I still don't consider myself a criminal, but I guess if
the FBI wanted to put me in jail, they could. Just so
we're clear," she said again. "Now, you still want to
get on that plane with me?"

"Absolutely. You've really got my curiosity up now."

She sighed and sat back, glancing down the terminal's corridor. "Don't look now, but here come a pair
who look an awful lot like the FBI."

"Seriously?"

"Unlike you, I wouldn't even attempt to joke about
something like that." She bent over and fiddled with
something in her bag. After a few anxious moments,
she sat back up as the pair passed by without looking at them.

"Lee, depending on what they've found out, they
may be looking for a man and a woman. Why don't
you stay here while I go buy the tickets? I'll meet you
at the security gate."

Lee looked uncertain. "Let me think about that."

"I thought you said you trusted me."

"I do." For a moment he envisioned Faith's dad
standing in front of him, asking for money. And damn
if Lee wasn't reaching in his pocket for his wallet.

"But even trust has its limits, right? I tell you
what, you keep the bags. I need to take my purse. If
you're really worried, you have a clear view of the se-

curity entrance from here. If I try to give you the slip, you've got me dead on. And I'm sure you can run much faster than I can." She stood. "And you know I can't call in the FBI, now, can I?"

She eyed him for a moment longer, apparently daring him to challenge her logic.

"Okay."

"What's your new name? I'll need it for your ticket."

"Charles Wright."

She winked at him. "And your friends call you Chuck?"

He gave her an uneasy smile and then Faith turned and disappeared into the crowd.

As soon as she was gone, Lee regretted his decision. Sure she had left her bag, but it only had a few clothes in it, the ones he had given her! She had her purse with her, which meant she had what she really needed: her fake ID and her money. Yes, he could see the security gate from here, but what if she just walked out the front door? What if that's what she was doing right now? Without her, he had nothing. Except some really dangerous people who now knew where he lived. People who would take great pleasure in breaking his bones one by one until he told them what he knew, which was nothing. They wouldn't be thrilled to hear that. Next stop: your standard landfill burial. That did it. Lee jumped up, grabbed the bags and headed after her.

CHAPTER 20

THERE WAS A KNOCK ON REYNOLDS'S DOOR. Connie popped his head in. Reynolds was on the phone but she waved him in.

Connie had two cups of coffee. He put one in front of Reynolds, together with two cream packets, a sugar and a swizzle stick. She thanked him with an appreciative smile. He sat down and sipped on his coffee while she finished her call.

Reynolds put down the phone and started mixing her coffee. "I would absolutely love some good news, Connie." She noted that he also had gone home, showered and changed. Rambling through the woods in the dark had probably done a real number on his suit, she assumed. His hair was still damp and the wetness made it seem more gray than usual. Reynolds kept forgetting that he was in his fifties. Connie just never seemed to change, always big, always craggy, the weatherbeaten rock upon which she clung when the riptide gripped her. As it was right now.

"Do you want lies or the truth?"

Reynolds took a sip of the coffee, sighed and leaned back in her chair. "Right now, I'm not sure."

He sat forward, perching his coffee on her desk. "I worked the scene with the VCU boys. That's where I started at the Bureau, you know. Just like old times." He put his palms flat on his knees and flexed his thick neck to work out a kink. "Damn, my back feels like Reggie White's been doing jumping jacks on it. I'm getting too old for this kind of work."

"You can't retire. I can't function without you."

Connie picked up his coffee cup. "The hell you say." It was obvious, though, that the remark had pleased him. He sat back, unbuttoned his jacket and let his belly push through. He let a minute or so pass as he presumably collected his thoughts.

Reynolds waited patiently. She knew Connie had not come down here to shoot the breeze with her. He rarely did that with anyone. Reynolds had learned that just about everything the man did had a specific purpose. Connie was a true veteran of the ways of bureaucracy and, consequently, he carried an agenda with him everywhere. While she thoroughly relied on him for his field expertise and his instincts, Reynolds never quite lost sight of the fact that she was younger, less experienced, yet was still his boss; it had to be a sore point with the man. And she was a woman, to boot, in a field that still didn't have many at her level of responsibility. She could not really blame Connie if he felt resentment toward her. And yet he had never said a negative word about her, nor had he ever dragged his feet on an assignment in order to make her look bad. On the contrary, he was methodical to a fault, and reliable as the sunrise. Still, she had to watch herself.

"I saw Anne Newman this morning. She appreciated your coming over last night. She said you were a real comfort."

This surprised Reynolds. Maybe the woman *didn't* blame her. "She took it about as well as anyone could."

"I understand the director went too. That was good of him. You know Ken and I go way back." The look on Connie's face was easily read. If the man caught up to the killer before the VCU did, there might not be any need for a trial.

"I know. I never stopped to think how hard this must be for you."

"You have enough on your mind. Besides, I'm the last person you need to worry about." Connie took a swallow of coffee. "The shooter was hit. Least it looks that way."

Reynolds immediately sat forward. "Let me have everything."

Connie momentarily smiled. "Don't want to wait

for the written report from VCU?" He crossed one thick leg over the other, hitching up his cuffed trousers as he did so. "You were right about the shooter's location. We found blood, a fair amount of it in the woods behind the house. Did a rough trajectory. The location jells with where the shot probably came from. We followed the trail as best we could, but lost it in the woods after a few hundred feet."

"Exactly how much blood? Life-threatening?"

"Hard to say. It was dark. A team's over there right now continuing the search. They're lockstepping the lawn, looking for the slug that killed Ken. They're also canvassing the neighborhood, but the place was so isolated, I'm not sure that'll pay off."

Reynolds took a deep breath. "If we find a body, that would both simplify and complicate things."

Connie nodded thoughtfully. "I see where you're going with that."

"You got a blood sample?"

"Lab's running it as we speak. Don't know what it'll be worth."

"At the very least it'll confirm whether it's human or not."

"That's true. Maybe all we'll find is a deer carcass. But I don't think so." Reynolds perked up. "Nothing concrete," he said in response to her look, "just call it my gut."

"If the guy's wounded, that should make it a little easier to track him down."

"Maybe. If he required medical attention, he wouldn't be so stupid as to go to a local emergency room. They have to report gunshot wounds. And we don't know how badly he was hurt. Might have just been a flesh wound that bled like a bitch. If so, he bandages it up, gets on a plane and poof. Gone. I mean we've got all the bases covered, but if the guy was leaving on a private plane, then we got problems. The truth is he's probably already long gone."

"Or maybe dead. Apparently he missed his primary target. Whoever hired him won't be happy about that."

"Right."

Reynolds folded her hands in front of her as she thought of the next topic she wanted to discuss. "Connie, Ken's gun was unfired."

Connie had obviously given this line of inquiry some thought because he said, "Which means, if the blood is confirmed as human, we definitely have a *fourth* person at the cottage last night. And that party shot the shooter." He shook his head wearily. "Shit, listen to us, it all sounds crazy."

"Crazy but apparently true under the facts as we know them. Think about this: Could this fourth person have killed Ken? And not the guy who was wounded?"

"Don't think so. The VCUs are looking for shell cartridges in the woods where we think the other shot came from, as confirmation. If there was a gun battle between two unknown parties, then maybe we'll find another set of ejected shells as well."

"Well, this fourth person being present may explain the door being unlocked and the cameras being tripped."

He sat up straight. "Anything on the tape yet? We had to get some faces or something."

"To put it simply, we have been degaussed."

"What?"

"Don't ask. For right now we can't count on the tape."

"Well, shit. That doesn't leave us with much."

"Specifically, it leaves us with Faith Lockhart."

"We've got all the airports, train and bus stations, rental car agencies covered. Her firm too, although I can't believe she'd go there."

"Agreed. Actually, that may be where the bullet came from," Reynolds said slowly.

"Buchanan?"

"Wish we could prove it."

"If we find Lockhart, we still may be able to. We'll have some leverage there."

"Don't count on it. Almost getting your head blown off can make you rethink loyalties," Reynolds said dryly.

"If Buchanan and his people are on to Lockhart, then they must be on to us as well."

"You said that before. A leak? From here?"

"A leak from somewhere. Here or at Lockhart's end.

Maybe she did something to make Buchanan suspicious. From all accounts, the guy's cagey as hell. He had her followed somehow. They saw her meeting with you at the house. He dug a little more, hit the truth and contracted to take her out."

"I'd like to believe *that* more than someone here selling us down the river."

"So would I. But the fact is every law enforcement agency has some bad apples."

Reynolds briefly wondered for a moment if Connie was suspicious of her. Everyone who worked at the FBI, from special agents to support staff, had top-secret security clearance. When you applied for a job at the Bureau, teams of agents would show up investigating every single piece of your past, no matter how insignificant, talking to everyone who ever knew you. Every five years a full field investigation was conducted on on-board Bureau employees. In the interim any suspicious activity involving a bureau employee or any complaints of persons asking suspicious questions of an employee were to be reported to the security officer in the employee's division. That had never happened to Reynolds, thank God. Her record was clean.

If there were suspicions of a leak or other type of security breach, it might very well be investigated by the Office of Professional Responsibility, and a polygraph exam might be ordered for the suspect employee. Other than that, the Bureau was always on the lookout for any signs that an employee was having undue personal or professional problems that might make him or her susceptible to bribes or influence by third parties.

Reynolds knew Connie was doing okay financially. His wife had died years ago from a lengthy illness that had sapped their resources, but he lived in a nice house that was worth a lot more than he had paid for it. His kids' college educations were done, and he had his pension locked in. All in all, he had a nice retirement to look forward to.

On the other hand, Reynolds knew her personal life and finances were in abysmal shape. College funds? Damn, she'd be lucky if she could continue to afford the private school tuition for first grade. And pretty soon, she wouldn't have a house to call her own. That was being sold as part of the divorce. The condo she was eyeing was about the size of the one she had rented when she had finished college. It had seemed cozy with one person. An adult and two energetic kids would quickly turn cozy into cramped. And could she afford to keep her nanny? With her hours, how could she not? She couldn't leave the kids alone at night.

In any other occupation she would probably be on the top ten soon-to-crash-and-burn list. But in the FBI, the divorce rate was such that her mess of a marriage would not create a blip on the Bureau radar. A career in the FBI was often simply not conducive to a happy personal life.

She blinked for a moment as she found Connie's gaze still upon her. Did he really suspect her of being the leak? Of causing Ken Newman to die? She knew it looked bad. On the very night when she'd had Newman substitute for her with Lockhart, he was killed. She knew Paul Fisher had been thinking that, and she was reasonably sure Connie was right now.

She composed herself and said, "There's really nothing we can do about this theory of a leak right now. Let's concentrate on what we can do."

"Fine. So what's our next move?"

"Hit all our lines of investigation as hard as we can. Find Lockhart. Let's hope she uses a credit card for plane or train tickets. If she does that, we've got her. We need to at least make an effort to find the shooter. Shadow Buchanan. Unscramble that tape and see who was in that house. I want you to act as liaison with the VCU. We have a lot of threads, if we can only grab one or two of them and hold on."

"Hey, isn't that always the case?"

"We're in a *really* tight spot here, Connie."

He nodded thoughtfully. "I heard Fisher was here. Figured he'd been by to see you."

Reynolds didn't respond to this, and Connie plunged on.

"Thirteen years ago, I was heading up a joint undercover drug operation with the DEA in Brownsville, Texas." He paused for a moment as if deciding whether to go forward or not. "Our official goal was to disrupt the flow of cocaine over the Mexican border. Our unofficial goal was to accomplish our mission without making the Mexican government look bad. For that reason, we had open lines of communication with our counterparts in Mexico City. Perhaps too open, since there was rampant corruption south of the border at all levels. But it was done that way so the Mexican authorities could share in the glory after we did all the work and scored the perps heading up the cartel. After two years of work, a huge bust was planned. But our plans got leaked and my guys walked into an ambush that left two of them dead."

"Oh my God. I heard about that case, but I didn't know you were involved in it."

"You were probably still cutting your teeth at Quantico."

Reynolds didn't know if this was a backdoor barb or not, but she chose not to respond.

"Anyway, after all that went down, I got a visit from one of the young ladder climbers at HQ who wouldn't know which end of his pistol to hold, and who politely informed me that if I didn't make things right, my ass was cooked. But there was one stipulation. If I found out our friends in Mexico sent us down the river, I couldn't use that as an excuse. International relations, I was told. I'd just have to fall on the sword for the good of the world." Connie's voice trembled a little as he said this last part.

Reynolds found she was holding her breath. It was not like Connie to talk this much. In the dictionary, the man's picture could well be found next to the word "taciturn."

He took a gulp of coffee and wiped his lips with the back of his hand. "Well, you know what? I traced the leak right to the top of the Mexican police department and I put a big X on the bastards' foreheads and walked away from it. If my superiors didn't want to do anything about it, fine. But damn if I was going to take the fall for somebody's else's shit." He eyed her steadily. "'International relations,'" he said, a bitter smile spreading across his lips as he did so. He rested his elbows on her desk.

Was this a challenge he was laying before her? Reynolds wondered. Was he expecting to leave an X on her forehead, or daring her to pin one on his?

"That's been my official motto ever since," he said.

"What's that?"

"Fuck 'international relations.'"

CHAPTER 21

Through the airport terminal drifted members of both the FBI and Central Intelligence, with the former group completely unaware of the latter's presence. Thornhill's men also had the advantage of knowing that Lee Adams was probably traveling with Faith Lockhart. The FBI agents were only looking for the woman.

Lee unknowingly passed a couple of the FBI agents dressed as businessmen with briefcases and *Wall Street Journal*s. They were equally oblivious to him. Faith had passed by the agents a moment earlier.

Lee slowed when he got near to the main ticket counter. Faith was up there speaking with a clerk. This was starting to look okay. He had a sudden feeling of guilt for not having trusted her. He edged over to a corner and waited.

At the counter, Faith displayed her new ID and purchased three tickets. Two tickets were in the name of Suzanne Blake and Charles Wright. The woman barely looked at her photo. Thank God for that, although Faith supposed people rarely looked like their ID photos anyway. The flight to Norfolk International left in about forty-five minutes. The third ticket she purchased was in the name of Faith Lockhart. It was a flight heading to San Francisco with a stopover in Chicago. It left in forty minutes. She had spotted it on the monitors. West Coast, big city. She could lose herself, drive down the coast, maybe even sneak into Mexico. She wasn't sure how she would accomplish that, but she just had to take it one step at a time.

Faith had explained that she was buying the ticket to San Francisco for her boss, who would arrive shortly.

"She'll have to hurry," the clerk said. "She still has to check in. And they're going to begin boarding in about ten minutes."

"It won't be a problem," Faith assured her. "She doesn't have any luggage, so she can check in at the gate."

The clerk handed her the ticket. Faith figured she was safe using her real name on the ticket because she paid for all of them with her Suzanne Blake credit card. And the only other ID she had to check in with was her real one. It was Faith Lockhart or nothing. Everything would be okay.

She could not have been any more wrong.

As Lee watched Faith, a thought jolted him. His gun! He had to check it before going through security or all hell would break lose. He shot across to the counter and next to a startled Faith.

He put his arm around her and gave her a quick kiss on the cheek. "Hey, babe. Sorry, the phone call took longer than I thought." He looked at the ticket agent and said casually, "I have a pistol I need to check."

The ticket agent raised her eyes slightly at this. "You're Mr. Wright?"

Lee nodded. She went about processing the necessary documents. He showed her his fake ID and she stamped his passenger ticket appropriately and entered the information in the computer. He turned over the gun and ammo, and filled out the declaration form. The agent tagged the container and they left the ticket counter.

"Sorry, I forgot about the gun." Lee looked up ahead to the security gate. "Okay, they're going to have people posted at the gate. We'll go through separately. Be cool; you don't look anything like Faith Lockhart."

Although Faith felt her heart in her throat the entire time, they went through the security gate without incident.

As they passed the flight information monitors, Lee spotted their gate. "Down this way."

Faith nodded as she noted how the gates were con-
figured here. The departure gate for the San Francisco flight was close enough to easily get to, but far
enough away from the Norfolk gate. She hid a smile.
Perfect.

As they walked along, she looked over at Lee. He
had done a lot for her. She wasn't feeling good about
what she was about to do, but had convinced herself
it was for the best. For both of them.

They reached the gate for the flight to Norfolk.
The plane would be boarding in about ten minutes,
they were told. There was a good crowd waiting.

Lee looked at her. "You better call that commuter
service for the flight to Pine Island."

Lee and Faith walked over to the phone bank and
she made that call.

"All set," Faith said. "Now we can relax."

"Right," Lee said dryly.

Faith looked around. "I need to use the rest room."

"Better hurry."

She hustled off while Lee looked after her thoughtfully.

CHAPTER 22

BINGO!" THE MAN SITTING IN FRONT OF THE computer screen said. He was in a van outside of the airport. The FBI had a designated liaison with the airlines to monitor the travel of persons the Bureau was looking for. With more than one airline sharing reservation systems and data and the advent of code-sharing, the FBI's job had been made a little easier. The Bureau had requested that the name Faith Lockhart be marked with a tag in the major airlines' reservation systems. That request had just paid an enormous dividend.

"She just made a reservation for a flight to San Francisco that leaves in about half an hour," he said into his headset microphone. "United Airlines." He passed along the flight number and gate information. "Hit it," he ordered the men inside the terminal. He picked up the phone to notify Brooke Reynolds.

Lee was leafing through a magazine someone had left on the seat next to his when two men dressed in suits flew past. A few moments later, a pair of gents in jeans and windbreakers hurried past, heading in the same direction.

Lee immediately jumped up, looked around for anyone else hustling by, saw no one moving fast and then followed after the group.

The FBI agents, followed by the men in jeans, hurried past the women's room a minute before Faith came out. The men had disappeared into the crowds by the time she emerged.

Lee slowed as he saw Faith come out from the women's room. Another false alarm? When she turned away from him and went in the opposite direction, he knew his fears were justified. As he kept his gaze on her, she looked at her watch and picked up her pace. Shit, he knew exactly what she was doing: going for another flight. And from the way she had checked her watch and started walking faster, it must be close to leaving. As he pushed through the crowds, he scanned the aisle ahead. There were ten gates remaining down here. He stopped for a second at the monitors, his gaze flying down the listings, checking the gates off one by one until he stopped at the flashing "boarding" message for a United flight to San Francisco. As his eye drifted farther, he saw

that a flight to Toledo was also boarding. Which one
was it? Well, there was one definite way to find out.

He sprinted ahead, cut through a waiting area and
managed to get past Faith without her seeing him.
He abruptly stopped within sight of the gate for the
San Francisco flight. The men in suits who had
sprinted past him were standing at the departure
door talking to a nervous-looking United employee.
Then the stone-faced men moved off and stood behind a partition, their gaze fixed on the crowd and
departure area. FBI for sure. The San Francisco flight
had to be the one Faith was going for.

But something didn't make sense. If Faith had used
her phony name, how . . . ? Then it hit Lee. She
couldn't use her phony name for both tickets for
flights leaving a few minutes apart. That would have
been a big red flag for the ticket agent. She had used
her real name because she needed ID to get on the
flight. Shit! She was heading right for them. She'd
show her ticket, the agent would signal the FBI and
then it would be over.

Just as he was about to turn, he spotted the two
men in windbreakers and jeans who had rushed past
him earlier. To Lee's experienced eyes, they were
watching the Feds intently, without seeming to do
so. He edged closer, and with the gloomy weather
outside he managed to catch their reflection in the
window. One man held something in his hand. A
chill went down Lee's back as he maneuvered some

more and managed to spot what it was. Or what he thought it was. This case suddenly took on a whole other dimension.

Lee fought his way back down the aisle; seemingly everyone who lived in the Washington metropolitan area had decided to fly today. He saw Faith across the aisle. In another moment she'd be past him. He made a lunge across the wall of people and tripped over a garment bag someone had set down. He fell to the floor hard, his knees taking the brunt of it. When he sprang up, Faith was past him. He had a few seconds, if that.

"Suzanne? Suzanne Blake?" he called out.

At first it didn't register. But then she stopped, looked around. If she saw him, Lee knew she might run. But her stopping had given him the few seconds he needed. He circled and came up behind her.

Faith almost collapsed when he gripped her arm. "Turn around and walk with me," he said.

She pulled at his fingers. "Lee, you don't understand. Please, let me go."

"No, *you* don't understand. The FBI is waiting for you at the San Francisco gate."

The words made her freeze.

"You messed up bad. You made the second reservation in your name. They monitor stuff like that, Faith. They know you're here now."

They headed as quickly as they could back down the aisle to the original departure gate. The plane was boarding. Lee grabbed their bags, but instead of getting on the plane, Lee veered off, pulling Faith along with him. They went back through security and headed toward the elevator.

"Where are we going?" Faith said. "The plane to Norfolk is leaving."

"We're getting the hell out of here before they shut the whole terminal down looking for us."

They took the elevator down to the lower level, went outside and Lee signaled for a taxi. They got in one, Lee gave the man an address in Virginia and the cab pulled off. Only then did Lee look at her.

"We couldn't get on the plane to Norfolk."

"Why not? That ticket was in my other name."

Lee glanced at the driver, an old guy slumped down in his seat listening to country western on the radio.

Satisfied, Lee still spoke in low tones. "Because the first thing they'll do is check at the ticket counter to see who purchased the ticket for Faith Lockhart. Then they'll know Suzanne Blake did. And they'll know Charles Wright is traveling with you. And they'll be given descriptions of us both. And they'll check the reservations for Blake and Wright and the FBI will be waiting for us when we get off the plane in Norfolk."

Faith paled. "They move that fast?"

Lee trembled with rage. "Who the hell do you think you're dealing with here? Larry, Moe and Curly Joe?" He slapped his thigh in sudden anger. "Sonofabitch!"

"What?" Faith said frantically. "What?"

"They have my gun. It's registered in my name. My *real* name. Dammit! Now I've aided and abetted, and the Feds right on our ass." In his despair he rested his head in his hands. "This must be my birthday, things are going so good for me."

Faith started to touch him on the shoulder, but pulled her hand back. She looked out the window instead. "I'm sorry. I'm really, really sorry." She put a hand against the car window, letting the cold from the glass seep into her skin. "Look, just take me to the FBI. I'll tell them the truth."

"That would be great except the FBI's not going to take your word for it. And there's another thing."

"What?" Faith wondered if he was going to tell her about working for Buchanan.

"Not now." Lee was actually thinking of the other men at the gate, what he had seen in the hand of one of the men. "Right now I'd like you to tell me what that was all about back there."

She stared out the window at the choppy gray Potomac. "I'm not sure I can," she said so softly he could barely hear her.

"Well, I'd like you to try," he said very firmly. "I'd like you to try very, very hard."

"I don't think you'd understand."

"I can understand with the best of them."

She finally turned to him, her face flushed, her gaze refusing to catch his. She nervously played with the edge of her jacket. "I just thought it would be better if you weren't with me. You see, I thought you'd be safer that way."

Lee looked away in disgust. "Bullshit!"

"It's true!"

He whirled back around and clutched her shoulder so tightly she winced in pain. "Listen, Faith, they were at my apartment, whoever *they* are. They know I'm involved. Whether I'm with you or not, the danger level really doesn't change for me, it actually gets worse. And you running around trying to ditch me isn't damn well helping."

"But they already knew you were involved. Remember back at your apartment."

Lee shook his head. "Those weren't the Feds."

She looked stunned. "Who, then?"

"I don't know. But the Feds don't show up disguised as UPS men. FBI Rule Number One: Overwhelming force trumps all. They would've come with about a hundred guys and the Hostage Rescue Team and the dogs and body armor and shit like that. And they just come in and take your ass, case closed." Lee's voice grew calmer as he thought things through. "Now, the guys waiting for you at the gate were FBI." He nodded thoughtfully. "They weren't trying to hide who they were." The other two men at the departure gate? All bets were off. But he knew Faith was very lucky to be alive.

"Oh, and by the way, you're welcome for me saving your butt again. Another few seconds and you're back in FBI land with more questions than you have answers for. Maybe I should've just let them take you," he added wearily.

"Why didn't you?" she asked quietly.

Lee almost felt like laughing. The whole experience was like a dream. *But where do I go to wake up?*

"Right now, lunacy seems to be at the top of the list."

Faith attempted a smile. "Thank God for lunatics."

Lee didn't smile back. "From now on, we are Siamese twins. You better get used to seeing a man take a piss because, lady, we are inseparable from here on."

"Lee—"

"I don't want to hear it! Just don't say a damn thing." His voice was trembling. "I'm so close to punching the shit out of you, I swear to God." He made a big show of reaching over and clamping one big hand over her wrist, as though a living handcuff. Then he sat back, staring at nothing.

Faith didn't try to pull her hand away, not that she could have. And she was really terrified he might take a swing at her. This was probably about as angry as Lee Adams had ever gotten in his entire life, she thought. She finally sat back and tried to calm down. Her heart was beating so fast it seemed impossible for her blood vessels to survive the pressure. Maybe she'd save everyone a lot of trouble and just drop from a coronary.

In Washington you could lie about sex, money,

power, loyalties. You could spin falsehoods into truths and simple facts into lies. She had seen it all. It was one of the most frustrating and cruelest places on earth, where one relied on old alliances and quick feet for survival and where every new day, every fresh relationship, could be the one that made you or destroyed you. And Faith had thrived in that world, loved it, in fact. Until now.

Faith could not look at Lee Adams, for fear of what she would see in his eyes. He was all she had. Although she barely knew the man, for some reason she craved his respect, his understanding. She knew she would get neither. She didn't deserve them.

Out of the car window she stared at a plane quickly gaining altitude. In another few seconds it would disappear into the clouds. Soon the passengers would only be able to see that layer of puffy cumulus beneath them, as though the world below had suddenly disappeared. Why couldn't she be on that plane and just keep climbing, to a place where she could start over? Why couldn't a place like that exist? Why?

CHAPTER 23

Brooke Reynolds sat glumly at the small table, chin resting on her palm, and wondered if anything ever was going to go right on this case. They had found Ken Newman's car. It had been professionally cleansed such that her team of "experts" were unable to provide her with any real clues. She had just checked with the lab. They were still messing around with the tape. Worst of all, Faith Lockhart had slipped right through her fingers. At this rate she'd be FBI director in no time. She was certain there would be a stream of messages from the ADIC on down when she returned to her office, and none of them complimentary, she imagined.

Reynolds and Connie were in a private area at Reagan National. They had thoroughly questioned the airline employee who had sold Faith Lockhart her tickets. They had reviewed all the surveillance tapes and the agent had readily picked out Lockhart. Reynolds assumed the woman was Faith Lockhart. The ticket agent had been shown a picture of Lockhart and was reasonably sure she was the same woman.

If it was Lockhart, she had changed her appearance considerably: a haircut and dye job, from what Reynolds had seen on the airport surveillance tape. And now Lockhart had help. For also captured on the video was a tall, well-built man leaving with Lockhart. Reynolds had initiated the obvious inquiries, including checking taxi pickups at the airport during that time. They also had colleagues checking in Norfolk in case the pair had made additional travel arrangements there. So far nothing had turned up. They did, however, have one very promising lead.

Reynolds opened the metal gun case and looked at the SIG-Sauer 9mm while Connie leaned against the wall and scowled at nothing. The gun had already been checked for prints, and they were running the results through the Bureau's databases, but they had something even better: The gun was registered. They had quickly gotten the name and address of the owner from the Virginia State Police.

Reynolds said, "Okay, so the gun's registered to this Lee Adams. We're getting a photo of the guy from DMV. I'm assuming he's the one with Lockhart. What do we know about him so far?"

Connie took a mouthful of Coke from the cup he

was holding and popped two Advil. "PI. Been around awhile. Seems very legit. Some of the guys at the Bureau know him in fact. Say he's a good guy. We'll get his picture to the ticket agent. See if she can positive-ID him. That's all for right now. We'll have more soon." He glanced at the gun. "We found shell casings in the woods behind the cottage. They'd been fired from a pistol. Nine-millimeter. From the number we found, the person emptied half his mag at something."

"Think this is the pistol?"

"We haven't found any slugs to match it to, but ballistics will tell us if the pinprick on the shell casings we found match ones fired from that gun," Connie said, referring to the indentation a gun's firing pin makes on the bottom of the shell casing, a mark about as unique as a fingerprint. "And since we've got his ammo, we can test-fire from the source, which is ideal, you know. And we're running a print check on the casings. That won't definitely confirm if Adams was there, since he could've loaded the pistol earlier and someone else could have fired it at the cottage, but it's still something."

They both knew that shell casings were much better surfaces for getting usable prints than a pistol grip.

"It'd be nice if we could get his prints inside the cottage."

"VCU found nothing. Adams obviously knows how to do this stuff. Had to be wearing gloves."

"If ballistics does match, then Adams looks to be the one who wounded the shooter."

"He didn't fire all those times at Ken, that's for sure, and a SIG is for shit long-distance. If Adams was able to hit Ken with a pistol shot from that distance in the dark, then we've got to get him a job at Quantico on the firing range."

Reynolds looked unconvinced.

Connie went on. "And the lab confirmed that the blood in the woods is definitely human. We also found a slug near the spot where all the pistol shell casings were. Struck a tree and stayed there. We also turned up a number of shell casings near the blood. Rifle ordnance. Full metal jacket, heavy-caliber stuff. And customized, no manufacturer's code or caliber stamp on the casings. But the lab did say the ammo used a Berdan primer instead of an American Boxer."

Reynolds looked at him sharply. "Berdan? So European manufacture?"

"There are so many freaky variations these days, but it looks that way."

Reynolds was very familiar with the Berdan primer. It differed from the American version principally in that it had no integral anvil. The anvil was constructed right into the cartridge case, forming a miniature T-shaped projection in the primer pocket with two flash holes to allow the exploded primer to get to the powder. It was a clever, efficient design, Reynolds thought.

When you pulled the trigger of a weapon, Brooke had learned when she joined the Bureau, the firing pin hit the primer cup, compressing the primer between the cup and anvil and causing the primer to explode. This mini-explosion, in turn, shot through the flash holes and ignited the powder to temperatures in excess of five thousand degrees. A millisecond later the bullet went roaring down the gun barrel, and before you could blink, a human being was probably dead. Guns were by far the weapon of choice for murder in America, and Brooke knew that homicides happened at the rate of fifty-five times a day in the United States. Consequently, Reynolds and her colleagues would never lack for work.

"European-manufactured shells might tie in to the foreign interest angle Lockhart was telling us about," Reynolds said almost to herself. "So Adams and the shooter were going at it and Adams gets the better of it." Reynolds stared thoughtfully at her partner. "Any connection between Adams and Lockhart?"

"None that we can see right now, but we've just started digging."

"Here's another theory, Connie: Adams came out of the woods, killed Ken and then went back through the woods. He could've fallen on something and cut himself. That would account for the blood. I know that doesn't explain the rifle slug, but it's a possibility we can't ignore. For all we know, he was carrying a rifle as well. Or it could have been from a hunter's gun. They hunt in those woods, I bet."

"Come on, Brooke. The guy can't have a gun battle with himself. Remember the two separate piles of different shell casings. And no hunter I know is going to stand there and pump shot after shot at something. They'll kill their buddy or maybe themselves. Most states require plugs in a rifle's magazine to limit shots for that very reason. And those shell casings hadn't been there very long."

"Okay, okay, but I'm just not willing to trust Adams at this point."

"And you think I am? I don't trust my own mother, God rest her soul. But I can't ignore facts either. Lockhart drives away in Ken's car? And Adams just leaves his boots behind before he takes his jaunt through the woods? Come on, you don't believe that."

"Look, Connie, I'm just pointing out the possibilities. I'm not saying I'm sold on any of them. The thing that keeps bugging me is, what spooked Ken? If the shooter's in the woods, it wasn't *him*."

Connie rubbed his jaw. "Now, that's true."

Reynolds suddenly snapped her fingers. "Dammit, the door. How could I have been so blind? When we got to the cottage the screen door was wide open. I remember it clearly. It opens out, so Ken would have seen it when he turned that way. What would he have done? Pull his gun."

"And he might have seen the boots too. It was dark, but the cottage's back porch isn't that big." Connie took another swallow of Coke and rubbed his left temple. "Come on, Advil, do your magic. Well, we'll know for certain if Adams was even there when the lab guys unscramble the video."

"*If* they unscramble it. But why would Adams have been at the cottage in the first place?"

"Maybe someone hired him to shadow Lockhart."

"Buchanan?"

"Probably first on my list."

"But if Buchanan hired the shooter to take out Lockhart, why have Adams there to witness it?"

Connie bunched up his thick shoulders and then let them collapse, like a bear scratching itself against a tree. "That for sure doesn't make a helluva lot of sense."

"Well, let me complicate things further for you. Two tickets were purchased by Lockhart for a trip to Norfolk. But only *one* in her real name for the trip to San Francisco."

"And you got Adams running after our guys on the airport surveillance video."

"Think Lockhart tried to give him the slip?"

"Ticket agent said Adams didn't come up to the counter until after Lockhart had purchased the tickets. And the video shows Adams leading her back from the vicinity of the San Francisco gate."

"So maybe an involuntary partnership of sorts,"

Reynolds said. She had a sudden thought as she looked at Connie. *Like ours, perhaps?* "You know what I'd really like?" Reynolds said. Connie raised his eyebrows. "I'd like to return Mr. Adams's boots. We have his home address?"

"North Arlington. Twenty minutes from here, tops." Reynolds rose. "Let's go."

CHAPTER 24

W HILE CONNIE PARKED THE CAR AT THE CURB, Reynolds stared up at the old brownstone. "Adams must do pretty well. This isn't a cheap area."

Connie looked around and said, "Maybe I should sell my house and buy an apartment around here. Stroll around the street, sit in the park, enjoy life."

"Thoughts of retirement creeping in?"

"Seeing Ken in a body bag isn't making me want to do this forever."

They walked up to the front door. Each of them noted the video camera, and then Connie rang the door buzzer.

"Who is it?" a voice fiercely demanded.

"FBI," Reynolds said. "Agents Reynolds and Constantinople."

The door didn't buzz open as they had expected.

"Show me your badges," the elderly voice proclaimed. "Hold them up to the camera."

The two agents looked at each other.

Reynolds smiled. "Let's play nice and do as we're told, Connie."

The pair held up their credentials, or "creds," to the camera. They both carried them the same way: gold badge pinned to the outside of the ID case, so you got the shield first and the picture ID card last. It was intended to be intimidating. And it was. A minute later they heard a door open from inside the building and a woman's face appeared at the glass of the old-fashioned double doors.

"Let me see them again," she said. "My eyes aren't all that good anymore."

"Ma'am—" Connie began hotly until Reynolds elbowed him. They held up their creds again.

The woman scrutinized them and then opened the door.

"I'm sorry," she said as they came in. "But after all the goings-on this morning, I'm about ready to pack my bags and leave for good. And this has been my home for twenty years."

"What goings-on?" Reynolds asked sharply.

The woman eyed her warily. "Who did you come here to see?"

"Lee Adams," Reynolds said.

"I thought so. Well, he's not here."

"Any idea where he might be, Ms. . . . ?"

"Carter. Angie Carter. And no, I don't have any idea where he's got to. Left this morning and I haven't seen him since."

"So what happened this morning?" Connie said. "It was this morning, right?"

Carter nodded. "Fairly early. Just having my coffee when Lee called down and said he wanted me to watch Max because he was going away." They looked at her curiously. "Max is Lee's German shepherd." Her mouth quivered for a moment. "Poor animal."

Reynolds said, "What happened to the dog?"

"They hit him. He'll be okay, but they hurt him."

Connie edged closer to the old woman. "Who hurt him?"

"Ms. Carter, why don't we go into your apartment and sit down?" Reynolds suggested.

The apartment contained old, comfortable furniture, tiny shelves with odd knickknacks placed just so and the aroma of burnt kale and onions.

After they were seated, Reynolds said, "Maybe it would be better if you just started at the beginning, and we'll ask questions along the way."

Carter told of how she had agreed to keep Lee's dog. "I do it a lot, Lee's gone a lot. He's a private investigator, you know."

"We know. So he didn't say where he was going? Nothing at all?" Connie prompted.

"Never does. *Private* investigator is just what it means, and Lee was a stickler for that."

"Does he have a separate office somewhere?"

"No, he uses his spare bedroom for an office. He also looks after the building. He's the one who put in the camera outside, sturdy locks on the doors, things like that. Never accepted one penny for it either. Anybody has a problem in the building—the tenants are mostly old, like me—they go to Lee, and he takes care of it."

Reynolds smiled warmly. "Sounds like a nice guy. Go on with your story."

"Well, I had just gotten Max settled when the UPS man came. Saw him out the window. And then Lee called me and said to let Max out."

Reynolds interrupted. "Did he call from the building?"

"Don't know. The connection was a little scratchy, like one of those cellular phones, maybe. But the thing is, I didn't see him leave the building. Guess he could have gone out the back and down the fire escape, though."

"How did he sound?"

Mrs. Carter patted her hands together while she thought. "Well, I guess I have to say he was agitated about something. I was surprised he wanted me to let Max back out. I mean, I had just gotten him settled, like I told you. Lee said he needed to give the dog a shot or something. Now that didn't make any sense to me, but I did what Lee told me and then all hell broke loose after that."

"This UPS man, did you see him?"

Mrs. Carter snorted. "He wasn't the UPS man. I mean, he had on the uniform and everything, but he wasn't our regular UPS person."

"Maybe a replacement. A substitute."

"I've never seen a UPS man carrying a gun before, have you?"

"So you saw a gun?"

She nodded. "When he came running back down the steps. He had a gun in one hand, and his other hand was bleeding. But I'm getting ahead of myself. Before that I heard Max barking like I've never heard him bark before. Then there was a scuffle, could hear it clear as day. Feet stomping, a man yelling, Max's claws on the wood floor. Then I heard a thud and then I heard poor old Max howl. Then somebody started beating on Lee's door. The next thing I know, I hear a bunch of feet going up the fire escape. I looked out the window of my kitchen and saw all these men running up the fire escape. It was like I was watching a TV show. I went back to the front door and looked out my peephole. That's when I saw the UPS man go out the front door. Guess he went around back and joined the others. I'm not sure."

Connie leaned forward in his chair. "Did these other men have any type of uniforms on?"

Mrs. Carter looked at him strangely. "Well, you of all people should know."

Reynolds looked at her, confused. "What do you mean?"

But Mrs. Carter hurried on with her story. "When they knocked the back door in, the alarm went off. The police came right off."

"What happened when the police came?"

"The men were still here. At least some of them were."

"Did the police arrest them?"

"Of course not. The police took Max away and let them keep searching the place."

Reynolds exclaimed, "Do you have any idea why the police let them stay?"

"Same reason I let you in the door."

Reynolds looked in shock at Connie and then back at Carter and said, "You mean—"

"I mean," Carter broke in testily, "they were the FBI."

"WHAT EXACTLY ARE WE DOING HERE, LEE?"
Faith asked. They had taken two other cabs after the
one from the airport. The last taxi had dropped them
off in what seemed like the middle of nowhere, and
they had been walking along back streets now for
what seemed like several miles.

Lee glanced at her. "Rule number one when running from the law: Assume they'll find the cabbie or
cabbies who dropped you off. So you never let a cabbie drop you off at your real destination." He pointed
up ahead. "We're almost there." As he walked along,
Lee put his hands up to his eyes and popped out the
contact lenses, returning his eyes to their normal
blue. He put the lenses away in a special case in his
bag. "Those suckers kill my eyes."

Faith stared ahead but saw nothing other than run-down homes, cracked sidewalks and sickly-looking trees and lawns. They were traveling parallel to U.S. Route 1 in Virginia, also known as Jefferson Davis Highway after the president of the Confederacy. It was ironic they were here, Faith thought, since Davis himself knew very well about being chased. In fact he had been chased all over the South after the war until the boys in blue had finally caught up with him and Davis had served a long prison term. Faith knew the history, she just didn't want the same result.

She didn't ordinarily come to this part of northern Virginia. It was heavily industrialized, speckled with on-the-fringe small businesses, truck and boat repair shops, shady-looking car dealerships working out of rusted trailers, and a flea market housed in a decrepit building one failing support beam from condemnation. She was a little surprised when Lee turned and headed for Jeff Davis. She hurried to stay up with him.

"Shouldn't we be getting out of town? I mean, according to you, the FBI can do anything. And then there's the other people you refused to name who are on our track. I'm sure they're incredibly deadly in their own right. And here we are strolling through the suburbs." Lee said nothing and she finally grabbed his arm. "Lee, will you please tell me what's going on?"

He stopped so abruptly she bumped into him. It was like hitting a wall.

Lee glared at her. "Call me stupid, but I just can't shake the feeling that the more information you have, the more likely you'll get another harebrained idea in your head that'll end up getting us both checked into coffins."

"Look, I'm sorry about the airport. You're right, it was stupid. But I had my reasons."

"Your reasons are bullshit. Your whole life is bullshit," he said angrily, and started walking again.

She hurried up next to him, jerked on his arm and they squared off.

"Okay, if you really feel like that, what do you say we just go our separate ways? Here and now. Each take our chances."

He put his hands on his hips. "Because of you I can't go home and I can't use my credit card. I don't have my gun, the Feds are right on my butt and I've got four bucks in my wallet. Let me just jump right on that offer, lady."

"You can have half my cash."

"And where exactly are you going to go?"

"My whole life might be bullshit, and this may shock you, but I *can* take care of myself."

He shook his head. "We stick together. For a lot of reasons. Number one being when and if the Feds pick us up, I want you right there next to me swearing on your mother's grave that yours truly is just an innocent babe stuck in the middle of *your* nightmare."

"Lee!"

"Discussion closed."

He started walking fast and Faith decided against

saying anything else. The truth was she didn't *want* to go it alone. She jogged up to him as they turned onto Route 1. At the light they hurried across the street.

"I want you to wait here," Lee said, putting the bags down. "There's a chance I might get recognized where I'm going, and I don't want you with me."

Faith looked around. Behind her was an eight-foot-high chain-link fence with barbed wire on the top. It housed a boat repair facility. Inside the fence a Doberman patrolled the area. Did boats really require that much security? she wondered. Maybe in this area everything did. The business on the next corner was located inside an ugly cinder-block building with big red banners across the windows proclaiming the best deals in town on new and used motorcycles. The parking lot was filled with the two-wheeled machines.

"Do I *have* to stay here by myself?" she said.

Lee pulled out a baseball cap from his bag and put on his sunglasses. "Yes," he said curtly. "Or was that a ghost back there telling me she can take care of herself?"

With no snappy reply coming to mind, Faith had to content herself with angrily watching as Lee hurried across the street and into the motorcycle shop. As she waited, she suddenly sensed a presence behind her. When she turned, she was staring directly at the large Doberman. It had wandered out of the yard. Apparently the boatyard's tight security didn't include closing the damn gate! When the animal showed its teeth and uttered a low, terrifying growl, Faith slowly reached down and gripped the bags. Holding them in front of her, she backed across the street and into the parking lot of the motorcycle shop. The Dobie lost interest in her and went back inside the boatyard.

Faith breathed a sigh of relief and put down the bags. She noted a couple of fleshy teenagers sporting sparse goatees checking out a used Yamaha at the same time they were ogling her. She pulled her baseball cap down farther, turned away and pretended to examine a shiny red Kawasaki that was, surprise, on sale. Across Jeff Davis was a business that leased heavy construction equipment. She looked at a crane that rose a good thirty feet in the air. Dangling from its cable was a small forklift that had a sign painted across it that read, RENT ME. Everywhere she looked was a world she no longer knew much about. She had traveled a much different circuit: capital cities of the world, high political stakes, demanding clients, enormous amounts of power and money, all perpetually shifting like the continental plates. Things got crushed in between these masses all the time, and no one even knew it. She suddenly realized that the *real* world was a two-ton forklift dangling like a guppy on a string. Rent me. Employ people. Build something.

But Danny had given her a shot at redemption. She was a dime a dozen, yet she had been doing some good in the world. For ten years now she had been helping people who desperately needed it. Perhaps also these ten years she'd been atoning for the vicarious guilt she'd felt growing up, watching her father's shenanigans, however well intentioned, and all the pain they had caused. She had actually been afraid to ever analyze that part of her life too deeply.

Faith heard footsteps behind her and turned around. The man was dressed in jeans, black boots and a sweatshirt with the logo of the motorcycle shop printed across it. He was young, early twenties, big, sleepy eyes, tall, slender and good-looking. And he knew it, she could readily tell, by his cocky manner. His expression clearly evidenced that his interest in Faith was deeper than her choice in two-wheeled transportation.

"Can I help you with anything, ma'am? Anything at all?"

"Just browsing. I'm waiting for my boyfriend."

"Hey, this is a pretty machine over here." He pointed to a BMW cycle that just reeked, even to Faith's untrained eye, of money. Wasted money, in her opinion. But then again, wasn't she the proud owner of a big BMW sedan, which sat in the garage of her very expensive digs in McLean?

He rubbed one hand slowly across the Beemer's gas tank. "Purrs like a kitten. You take care of beautiful things, they take good care of you. Real good." A big smile broke across his features as he said this. He looked her over and winked.

Faith wondered if this was his best pickup line.

"I don't drive them, I just ride on them," she said casually, and then regretted her choice of words.

He smiled broadly. "Well, that's the best news I've heard all day. In fact, you just made my whole year. Just ride 'em, huh?" The young man laughed and clapped his hands together. "Well, how about we go for a spin, sweet thing? You can check out *my* equipment. Just climb on."

Her face flushed. "I don't appreciate your—"

"Now, don't go getting mad. If you need anything, my name's Rick." He held out his card and winked at her again. He added in a low voice, "Home phone's on the back, babe."

She looked at the card in his hand with distaste. "Okay, Rick, but I like full disclosure. Are you man enough to take it?"

Rick didn't look so comfortable now. "I'm man enough for anything, babe."

"Good to hear. My boyfriend is inside. He's about your height, but he's got a real man's body."

The hand holding the card dropped to Rick's side as he scowled at her. Faith easily sensed that his pat lines had been forgotten and his mind was too slow to think of new ones.

Faith eyed him closely. "Yeah, his shoulders are about the size of Nebraska, and did I mention he's an ex-Navy boxing champ?"

"Is that right?" Rick pocketed his card.

"Don't take my word for it; he's right there. Go ahead and ask him." She pointed behind him.

Rick whirled around and watched as Lee came out of the building carrying two helmets and two one-piece riding suits. A map was stuffed into his front jacket pocket. Even under the bulky clothes he was wearing, Lee's impressive build was very apparent. He glared suspiciously at Rick.

"Do I know you?" Lee asked him gruffly.

Rick smiled uneasily and then swallowed with difficulty as he looked Lee over. "N-no, sir," he stammered.

"Then what the hell do you want, kid?"

Faith piped in, "Oh, he was just asking me the sorts of things I liked in my riding equipment, right, Ricky?" She smiled at the young salesman.

"That's right. Yep. Well, see ya." Rick practically ran toward the shop.

"Bye-bye, sweet thing," Faith called after him.

Lee scowled at her. "I told you to wait across the street. Can I not leave you alone for one damn minute?"

"I had an encounter with a Dobie. Retreat seemed the wisest course."

"Right. What, were you negotiating with the guy to jump me so you can get away?"

"Don't get crazy on me, Lee."

"I kind of wished you had. It'd give me an excuse to kick the shit out of somebody. What'd he really want?"

"Junior wanted to sell me something, and it wasn't a motorcycle. What's that?" she asked, pointing at what he was carrying.

"Necessary equipment for motorcycle riders this time of year. At sixty miles an hour, there's a tiny bite in the air."

"We don't have a motorcycle."

"We do now."

She followed him around back to where an enormous Honda Gold Wing SE road bike sat. With its slick chrome and futuristic design, high-tech equipment and full windshield, the motorcycle looked like something Batman might tool around on. It was painted pearl-gray-green with dark gray green trim and had a king and queen seat with a padded backrest. The passenger would fit snugly there, like a ball in a glove. It was so big and elaborately equipped that it looked like an open-air recreational vehicle.

Lee stuck a key in the ignition and started putting on his suit. He handed the other outfit to Faith.

"Just where are we going on this thing?"

Lee zipped up his suit. "*We* are going to your little place in North Carolina."

"All that way on a motorcycle?"

"We can't rent a car without a credit card and ID. Your car and mine are useless. We can't take a train, plane or bus. They'll cover all those places. Unless you can sprout wings, this is it."

"I've never even been on a motorcycle."

He took off his shades. "You don't have to drive it. That's what I'm here for. So what do you say? Want to go for a ride?" He flashed a grin at her.

Faith felt as though a brick had hit her in the head when he said those words. Her skin was afire as she looked at him perched on that machine. And at that exact moment, as though by the will of God, the sun broke through the gloom. A shaft of light came down and ignited those already dazzling blue eyes into flame-filled sapphires. She found she couldn't move. Lord, she could barely breathe; her knees began to quiver.

It was fifth grade, recess. The boy with the man-size eyes the exact color of Lee's had ridden his bike with the banana seat up to where she sat on the swing reading a book.

"Want to go for a ride?" he had asked her. "No," she had said, and then immediately dropped her book and climbed on back. They were an "item" for two months, planning their lives together, vowing their undying love for each other, even though they never exchanged so much as a peck on the lips. Then her mother died, and Faith's father moved them away. She briefly wondered if Lee and he could be one and the same. She had banished the memory so completely from her subconscious that she couldn't even remember the boy's name. It could be Lee, couldn't it? She thought this because the only other time in her entire life when her knees had gone weak was on that playground. The boy had said what Lee had just said, and the sun had hit those eyes just as it had smacked Lee's, and her heart felt as though it would explode if she didn't do exactly as he said. Just how it felt right now.

"Are you okay?" Lee asked.

Faith gripped one of the handlebars to steady herself, and said as calmly as she could, "And they're just going to let you drive off with it?"

"My brother runs the place. It's a demo. We're officially taking it for an extended test drive."

"I can't believe I'm doing this." Just like fifth grade, there was no way she could not get on that bike.

"Consider the alternative, and then the idea of your butt on this Honda starts looking beautiful." He slid his shades on and flipped his helmet's shield down as though putting an exclamation point on this statement.

Faith slipped on the suit, and with Lee's help managed to get the helmet on snugly. He loaded their bags into the Honda's spacious trunk and saddle pouches, and Faith climbed on behind him. He started the engine, gunned it for a moment or so and then hit the gas. When he released the clutch, the power of the Honda threw Faith back against the padded bar and she found herself clamping her arms and legs around Lee and the eight-hundred-pound motorcycle, respectively, as they rocketed onto Jeff Davis heading south.

She almost jumped off the bike when she heard the voice in her ear.

"Okay, calm down, it's a Chatterbox helmet-to-helmet audio link," Lee's voice said. He'd obviously felt her shock. "You ever driven down to your beach house?"

"No, I always flew."

"That's okay. I've got a map. We'll take 95 down and pick up Interstate 64 near Richmond. That'll get us to Norfolk. We'll figure out the best way from there. We'll grab something to eat on the way. We should make it before it gets too dark. Okay?"

She found herself nodding and then remembered to say, "Okay."

"Now, just sit back and relax. You're in good hands."

Instead, she leaned into him, circled her arms around his waist and held tightly. She was suddenly immersed in the recollection of those divine two months in fifth grade. This had to be an omen. Maybe they could drive off and never come back. Start at the Outer Banks, hire a boat and end up on a patch of soil somewhere in the Caribbean no one had ever been before, a place no one would ever see except for them. She could learn to keep a hut, cook with coconut milk or whatever they had there, be a good little homemaker while Lee was off catching fish. They could make love every night under the moonlight. She leaned farther into him. None of that sounded bad. Or too far-fetched, under the circumstances. None of it.

"Oh, and Faith?" Lee said into her ear.

She touched her helmet to his, felt the solid breadth of his torso against her breasts. She was twenty again, the wind was delicious, the warmth of the sun inspiring, her greatest worry a midterm exam. A sudden vision of them lying naked under the sky, skin brown, hair wet, limbs intertwined, made her wish they weren't in body suits with thick zippers, going sixty miles an hour over hard pavement.

"Yes?"

"If you even think about trying to pull another stunt on me like at the airport, I'll use those good hands to wring your neck. Understand?"

She leaned away from him and rested her back against the sissy bar, pushing herself deep into the leather. And away from him. Her shining white knight with the bedeviling blue eyes.

So much for memories. So much for dreams.

CHAPTER 26

DANNY BUCHANAN SURVEYED A FAMILIAR scene. The event was typical of Washington: a political fund-raising dinner at a downtown hotel. The chicken was stringy and cold, the wine cheap, the conversation high-powered, the stakes enormous, the protocol tricky, the egos often impossible. The attendees were either wealthy and/or well connected, or underpaid political staffers who worked long, frantic hours during the day and were rewarded for these prodigious efforts by being compelled to work these sorts of events at night. The Secretary of the Treasury was supposed to have attended, along with some other political heavyweights; ever since he had become engaged to a well-known Hollywood actress with a thing about exhibiting her cleavage at the drop of an intern, the secretary had been more in demand than the keeper of the cash normally was. Then, at the last minute, he had gotten a better offer to speak at another event, which was often the case in the endless game of "where is the political grass greener?" An underling had been sent in his place, a gawky, nervous person no one really knew or cared about.

The event was another opportunity to see and be seen, to check the ever-changing pecking order of a certain subgroup of the political hierarchy. Most never even sat down to eat. They just dropped off their check and then it was off to another fund-raiser. Networking flowed through the room as though from a well-fed spring. Or open wound, depending on how one looked at it.

How many of these events had Buchanan attended over the years? During the frenzy of key fund-raising periods when he used to represent Big Business, Buchanan would attend breakfasts, luncheons, dinners and assorted parties nonstop for weeks. Exhausted, he had sometimes shown up at the wrong event—a reception for the senator from North Dakota instead of a dinner for the South Dakota congressman. After taking over for the world's poor, he had no such problems, for the simple fact that he now had no money to give members. However, Buchanan was well aware that if there was one truism in political fund-raising, it was that there was never enough money. And that meant that there would *always* be the opportunity for influence peddling. Always.

After he got back from Philly, his day had really started, without Faith. He had met with half a dozen different members on the Hill and their staff on a myriad of matters, and set up appointments for future meetings. Staffs were important, particularly committee staff, especially appropriations committee staff. Members came and went. The staff tended to stay forever; they knew the issues and process cold. And Danny knew that you never wanted to surprise a member by trying to dodge the staff. You might be successful once, but you were dead after that, as the angry aides took their revenge by shutting you completely out.

A late luncheon followed, with a paying client whom Faith had typically taken care of. Buchanan had had to make excuses for her absence, and he did so with his usual aplomb and humor. "Sorry, you get the second string today," he told the client. "But I'll try not to mess things up too badly for you."

Though there was no need to bolster Faith's excellent reputation, Buchanan had recounted to this client the story of how Faith had once personally hand-delivered—in a gift box with a big red ribbon, no less—to all five hundred and thirty-five members of Congress detailed polling data that showed the American public was fully in support of funding for global vaccination of all children in the world. She'd included in the gift box accompanying briefing materials and before-and-after photos of vaccinated children from distant lands. Sometimes pictures were the most important weapons Danny and she had. Then she had worked the phone for thirty-six hours straight enlisting support here and overseas and made exhaustive presentations with several of the larger international relief organizations over a two-week period on three continents to show just how such a thing could be accomplished. How important it was. The result: passage of a bill in Congress that supported a study to determine if such an endeavor could work. Now consultants would rack up millions of dollars in fees and kill several forests of trees for the mountains of paper the study would generate (to justify the enormous consulting fees, of course), with no assurances that a single child would receive a single dose of vaccine.

"A small success, to be sure, but a step forward," Buchanan had told the client. "When Faith goes after something, stay out of her way." The client already knew this about Faith, Buchanan was aware. Perhaps he was just saying it to bolster his own spirits. Perhaps he just wanted to talk about Faith. He had been hard on her the last year, very hard. Terrified that she would be drawn into his Thornhillian nightmare, he had outright pushed her away. Well, he had succeeded in driving her right into the arms of the FBI, it seemed. *I'm sorry, Faith.*

After the luncheon it was back to the Hill, where Buchanan waited with a handful of Rolaids on a series of floor votes. He sent in his cards to the floor asking for time from some of the members. He would buttonhole others as they came off the elevator.

"Foreign debt relief is essential, Senator," he individually told more than a dozen members, hustling along beside them and their overly protective entourages. "They're spending more on debt payments than on health and education," Danny would plead. "What good is a strong balance sheet when the population is dying at the rate of ten percent a year? They'll have great credit and not a damn person left to use it. Let's spread the wealth here." There was only one person better at pitching this appeal, but Faith was not here.

"Right, right, Danny, we'll get back to you. Send me some materials." Like the petals of a flower closing up for the night, the entourage would close ranks around the member, and Danny the bee would be off to gather other nectar.

Congress was an ecosystem just as complicated as the one existing in the oceans. As Danny trolled the corridors, he looked at the activity swirling all around. True to their titles, whips were everywhere prodding members to follow the party line. Back in the whip's chambers, Buchanan knew the phones were constantly being worked with the same goal in mind. Gofers scurried down the corridors in search of people more important than themselves. Small groups of people huddled in pockets of the broad hallways, discussing matters of importance with solemn, downcast expressions. Men and women pushed onto crowded elevators with the hope of snaring a few precious seconds with a member whose support they desperately needed. Members talked with each other, laying the groundwork for future deals or reaffirming agreements already struck. It was all chaotic and yet possessed a certain order, as people coupled and uncoupled like robotic arms around hunks of metal on an assembly line. Give a touch here and on to the next one. Danny dared to think that his work might be as exhausting as childbirth; and he would swear it was more exhilarating than skydiving. The man was thoroughly addicted to it. He would miss it.

"Get back to me?" was his typical closing to each member's aide.

"Of course, you can count on it," would be each aide's typical response.

And, of course, he'd never hear back. But they would hear from him. Again and again, until they got it. You just fired your shotgun pellets and hoped one stuck somewhere.

Next, Buchanan had spent a few minutes with one of his "chosen few," going over the language Buchanan wanted to insert in a line amendment in a bill's report. Almost no one ever read the report language, yet it was in the monotonous details that important actions were accomplished. In this case, the language would tell the managers at AID precisely how funding approved by the underlying bill was to be spent.

With the verbiage in good shape, Buchanan mentally checked that off his list and went prowling again for other members. From years of practice, Buchanan navigated with ease the labyrinths of the Senate and House office buildings where even veterans of the Hill sometimes became lost. The only other place where he spent as much time was the Capitol itself. His eyes darted left and right, picking up on everyone he saw, staff members or other lobbyists, swiftly making a calculation as to whether a particular person could help the cause or not. And when you went into chambers with members or caught them in the halls, you had better be ready to roll. They were busy, often harassed, and thinking of five hundred things at once.

Fortunately, Buchanan could summarize the most complex issues in a matter of sentences, a talent for which he was legendary; members, besieged on all sides by special interests of every kind, absolutely demanded this skill. And he could pitch his client's position with passion. All in two minutes while walking down a crowded corridor or while packed inside an elevator or, if he was very lucky, on a long plane flight. Catching the really powerful members was important. If he could get the Speaker of the House to voice support for one of his bills, even informally, Buchanan would use that to leverage other members on the fence. Sometimes that was enough.

"He in, Doris?" Buchanan asked as he popped his head into a member's chambers and eyed the matronly appointments secretary, a veteran of the place.

"He's leaving in five minutes to catch a flight, Danny."

"That's great because I only need two minutes. I can use the other three to catch up with you. I like talking to you better anyway. And God bless Steve, but you're far easier on the eye, my dear."

Doris's heavy face crinkled into a smile. "You smoothie, you."

And he got his two minutes with Congressman Steve.

Buchanan next had stopped at the cloakroom and found out which Senate committees had been assigned to a series of bills he was interested in. There were committees of primary and sequential and, in rare cases, concurrent jurisdiction, depending on what was in a particular bill. Simply determining who had what bill and in what priority of importance was a huge, ever-changing jigsaw puzzle that lobbyists had to constantly figure out. It was often a maddening challenge, and there was no one better at it than Danny Buchanan.

In the course of this day Buchanan had, as always, plied members' offices with his "leave behinds," information and summaries the staffs would need to educate their members on the issues. If they had a question or concern, he would find an answer or an expert, promptly. And Buchanan had concluded every single meeting with the all-important question: "When can I follow up?" Without getting a date certain, he would never hear back from any of them. He would be forgotten, his place taken by a hundred others clamoring just as passionately for their clients.

Then he had spent the late afternoon covering other clients normally handled by Faith. He gave apologies and vague explanations for her absence. What else could he do?

After that he gave remarks at a think-tank-sponsored seminar on world hunger, and then it was back to his office to make phone calls ranging from reminding members' staffs of a variety of issues coming up for vote, to drumming up coalition support from other charitable organizations. A couple of dinners were arranged, future overseas travel booked, along with a visit in January to the White House, where he would personally introduce the president to the new head of an international children's rights organization. It was a real coup that Buchanan and the organizations he supported hoped would generate some good publicity. They were constantly on the lookout for celebrity support. Faith had been particularly good at that. Journalists were rarely interested in the poor from faraway lands, but throw in a Hollywood superstar and the media room would be bursting with scribes. Such was life.

Then Buchanan had spent some time doing his FARA—or Foreign Agent Registration Act—quarterly reports, which were a real pain in the ass, particularly since you had to stamp every page filed with Congress with the ominous label "foreign propaganda," as if you were Tokyo Rose calling for the overthrow of the U.S. government, instead of, in Danny's case, selling his soul to get crop seeds and powdered milk.

After bending a few more ears on the phone, then studying a few hundred pages of briefing materials, he had decided to call it a day. A glamorous day in the life of a typical Washington lobbyist, which usually ended with him collapsing into bed, except that today he did not have that luxury. Instead, he was here in this downtown hotel, attending yet another political fund-raiser, and the reason was standing in the far corner of the room sipping a glass of white wine and looking extremely bored. Buchanan headed over.

"You look like you could use something stronger than white wine," Buchanan said.

Senator Russell Ward turned and a smile broke across his face as he looked at Buchanan. "It's good to see an honest face in this sea of iniquity, Danny."

"How about we trade this place for the Monocle?"

Ward put his glass down on a table. "Best offer I've had all day."

CHAPTER 27

THE MONOCLE WAS A RESTAURANT OF LONG standing on Capitol Hill's Senate side. The restaurant, and the U.S. Capitol Police building, which itself used to be an Immigration and Naturalization building, were the only two structures left in this location that formerly housed a long row of buildings. The Monocle was a favorite place for politicians, lobbyists and VIPs to gather for lunch, dinner and drinks.

The maître d' welcomed Buchanan and Ward by name and ushered the pair to a private corner table. The decor was conservative, the walls adorned with enough photographs of past and present politicians to fill the Washington Monument. The food was good, yet people didn't come for the delights of the menus; they came to be seen, do business and talk shop. Ward and Buchanan were regulars here.

They ordered drinks and perused the menu for a moment.

As Ward studied his menu, Buchanan studied him.

Russell Ward had been called Rusty for as long as Buchanan could remember. And that was a long time, since the two had grown up together. As chairman of the Senate Select Committee on Intelligence, Ward was a powerful influence on the well-being—or not—of all the country's intelligence agencies. He was smart, politically savvy, honest, hard-working, and he came from a very wealthy Northeast family that had lost its fortune when Ward was a young man. He had gone south to Raleigh and methodically built himself a career in public service. He was North Carolina's senior senator and worshiped by the entire state. Under Buchanan's classification system, Rusty Ward would be absolutely labeled a "Believer." He was familiar with every political game ever played. Ward knew all the inside stories on everyone in this town. He knew people's strengths and, more important, their weaknesses. Physically, the man was a wreck, Buchanan knew, with problems ranging from diabetes to the prostate. Yet mentally, Ward was sharp as ever. Those who underestimated the man's massive intellect because of the physical ailments had all lived to regret it.

Ward looked up from his menu. "Anything interesting on your plate these days, Danny?"

Ward's voice was deep and sonorous, and so wonderfully southern, all traces of clipped Yankee long gone. Buchanan could sit and listen to the man for hours. And he had done so on many occasions.

Buchanan replied, "Same old, same old. You?"

"Had an interesting hearing this morning. Senate Intelligence. CIA."

"Is that right?"

"You ever hear of a gentleman by the name of Thornhill? Robert Thornhill?"

Buchanan's features were impassive. "Can't say that I know the man at all. Tell me about him."

"He's one of the old powers there. Associate DDO. Smart, cunning, lies his ass off with the best of them. I don't trust him."

"Doesn't sound like you should."

"I have to give the man his due though. He's done terrific work, outlasted numerous CIA directors. Really served his country extraordinarily well. He's actually a legend over there. They let him do more or less what he wants because of that. Such a policy, however, is dangerous."

"Really? He sounds like a real patriot."

"That's what worries me. People who believe themselves to be true patriots tend to be zealots. Zealots, in my opinion, are one short step from lunatics. History has given us enough examples of that." Ward grinned. "Today he came in to deliver the usual bullshit. He looked so smug I decided I had to tweak him a little."

Buchanan looked very interested. "How'd you do that?"

"I asked him about death squads." Ward paused and looked around for a moment. "We've had problems with the CIA over that in the past. They fund these little insurgency groups, outfit and train 'em, then turn 'em loose, like an old coon dog. Then, unlike a good coon dog, they go and do things they weren't supposed to be doing. At least according to the official agency rules."

"What'd he say to that?"

"Well, it wasn't part of his little script. He looked through his briefing book like he was attempting to shake out a small band of armed men." Ward laughed deeply. "Then he threw me some gobbledygook that really amounted to nothing. Said that the 'new' CIA was merely a collector and analyzer of information. When I asked him if he was conceding that there was something wrong with the 'old' CIA, I thought he might come over the table at me." Ward laughed again. "Same old, same old."

"So what's he up to now that's got you ticked off?"

Ward smiled. "Trying to get me to reveal confidences?"

"Of course."

Ward glanced around again and then leaned forward and spoke quietly. "He was withholding information, what else? You know the spooks, Danny, they want more and more funding but when you start to ask questions about what they're doing with that money, Jesus, it's like you killed their mother. But what else am I going to do when I'm presented with reports from the CIA's inspector general that have so many damn redaction's the paper looks black? So I brought that fact to Mr. Thornhill's attention."

"How did he react to that? Pissed off? Cool and collected?"

"Why are you so curious about him?"

"You started it, Rusty. Don't blame me if I find your work fascinating."

"Well, he said those reports had to be censored to protect the identities of intelligence sources. That it was a very fine line and that the CIA walked it the best it could. I told him that it was kind of like my granddaughter playing hopscotch. She can't hit all the squares just right, so she misses some of them on purpose. I told him it was damn cute. When *little kids* did it.

"Now, I have to give the man his due. He made some sense. He said that it's a delusion that we're going to knock out entrenched dictators with simple satellite photos and high-speed modems. We need old-fashioned assets on the ground. We need people inside their organizations, within their inner circles. That's the only way we win. I understand that well enough. But the arrogance of the man, well, it gets to me. And I'm convinced that even if Robert Thornhill had no reason to lie, the man still wouldn't tell the truth. Hell, he has this little system where he taps his pen against the table and one of his aides pretends to whisper in his ear so he'll have a couple extra breaths to think of some lie. He's been using that same code all these years. I guess he thinks I'm some kind of horse's ass and wouldn't ever catch on."

"I'd like to think this Thornhill fellow knows better than to underestimate you."

"Oh, he's good. I have to admit he got the better of today's jousting. I mean, the man can say absolutely nothing and make it sound as strong and noble as the Ten Commandments. And when he got backed into a corner, he pulled out his national security bullshit counting on the fact that it would scare everybody to death. Bottom line: He promised me all these answers. And I told him I looked forward to working with him." Ward sipped his water. "Yep, he won today. But there's always tomorrow."

The waiter returned with their drinks and they gave their orders. Buchanan worked on a glass of Scotch and water while Ward nuzzled a bourbon, neat.

"So how's your better half? Faith burning the midnight oil for another client looking to ravage us poor, defenseless elected officials?"

"Actually, right now I believe she's out of town. Personal reasons."

"Nothing serious, I hope."

Buchanan shrugged. "Jury's still out on that. I'm

sure she'll pull through." But where was Faith? he wondered once more.

"I guess we're all survivors. I don't know how much longer this tired old carcass of mine will hold out, though."

Buchanan raised his drink. "Outlive us all, word of Danny Buchanan."

"God, I hope not." Ward looked at him keenly. "It's hard to believe that it's been forty years since we left Bryn Mawr. You know, sometimes I envy you having grown up in that apartment over our garage."

Buchanan smiled. "Funny, I was jealous of you for growing up in the mansion with all that money while my family waited on yours. Now which of us sounds drunk?"

"You're the best friend I ever had."

"And you know that sentiment is reciprocated, Senator."

"It's even more remarkable that you've never asked me for a damn thing. You damn well know I sit on a couple committees that could help your causes."

"I like to avoid the appearance of impropriety."

"You must be the only one in this town." Ward chuckled.

"Let's just say our friendship is more important to me than even that."

Ward spoke softly. "I never told you, but what you said at my mother's funeral touched me deeply. I swear, I think you knew the woman better than I did."

"She was a class act. Taught me all I ever needed to know about everything. She deserved a grand send-off. What I said didn't come close by half."

Ward stared into his glass. "If my stepfather could have only lived off my family's inheritance and not tried to play businessman we might have kept the estate, and he wouldn't have taken his head off with a shotgun. But then maybe I wouldn't have gotten to play senator all these years if I'd had a trust fund to blow."

"If more people played the game the way you do, Rusty, the country would be far better off."

"I wasn't fishing for a compliment, but I appreciate you saying it."

Buchanan drummed his fingers against the table. "I drove out to the old place a couple weeks ago."

Ward looked up, surprised. "Why?"

Buchanan shrugged. "Not really sure. I was close by, I had some time. It hasn't changed much. Still beautiful."

"I haven't been there since I left for college. Don't even know who owns it now."

"A young couple. I saw the wife and kids through the gate, playing on the front lawn. Investment banker or Internet mogul, probably. An idea and ten bucks in his pocket yesterday, a red-hot company and a hundred million in stock today."

Ward lifted his glass. "God bless America."

"If I had had the money back then, your mother wouldn't have lost that house."

"I know that, Danny."

"But everything happens for a reason, Rusty. Like you said, you might not have gone into politics. You've had a grand career. You're a Believer."

Ward smiled. "Your little classification system has always intrigued me. You have it all written down somewhere? I'd like to compare it with my own conclusions about my distinguished colleagues."

Buchanan tapped his forehead. "It's all up here."

"All that gold, stored in one man's brain. What a pity."

"You know everything about everybody in this town too." Buchanan paused and then added quietly, "So what do you know about me?"

Ward seemed surprised by the question.

"Don't tell me the world's greatest lobbyist is having self-doubt? I thought the book on Daniel J. Buchanan was unshakable confidence, encyclopedic mind and a keen insight into the psychology of windbag politicians and their innate weaknesses, which could fill the Pacific, by the way."

"Everybody has doubts, Rusty, even people like you and me. That's why we last so long. One inch from the edge. Death at any minute if you let down your guard."

The way he said this made Ward drop his amused look. "You got something you'd like to talk about?"

"Not in a million years," Buchanan said with a sudden smile. "If I start telling the sorry likes of you all my secrets, then I'll have to take my lemonade stand somewhere else and start over. And I'm way too old for that."

Ward leaned back against the soft cushion and looked his friend over. "What makes you do it, Danny? Not money, surely."

Buchanan slowly nodded in agreement. "If I did it solely for the dollars, I would've been gone ten years ago." He swallowed the rest of his drink and looked over at the doorway, where the ambassador from Italy and his substantial entourage stood, along with several senior Hill staffers, a couple of senators and three women in short black dresses who looked like they had been rented for the evening, and very well might have been. The Monocle was filling up with so many VIPs now you could hardly spit without nailing some leader of something. And they all wanted the world. And they all wanted you to get it for them. Eat you up and leave nothing and then call you a friend. Buchanan knew all the lyrics to that song.

He looked up at an old photograph on the wall. A bald-headed man with a beak nose, dour look and ferocious eyes peered down at him. Long dead now, he had once been one of the most powerful men in Washington for decades. And most feared. Power and fear seemed to go hand in hand here. Now Buchanan couldn't even remember the man's name. Didn't that speak volumes.

Ward put down his glass. "I think I know. Your causes have become much more benevolent over the years. You're out to save a world few even care about. You're really the only lobbyist I know who does it."

Buchanan shook his head. "A poor Irish lad who brought himself up by the bootstraps and made a fortune sees the light and then uses his golden years helping the less fortunate? Hell, Rusty, I'm driven more by fear than altruism."

Ward looked at him curiously. "How's that?"

Buchanan sat up very straight, put his palms together and cleared his throat. He had never told anyone this. Not even Faith. Maybe it was time. He would look insane, of course, but at least Rusty would keep it to himself.

"I have this recurring dream, you see. In my dream America keeps getting richer and richer, fatter and fatter. Where an athlete gets a hundred million dollars to bounce a ball, a movie star earns twenty million to act in trash and a model gets ten million to walk around in her underwear. Where a nineteen-year-old can make a billion dollars in stock options by using the Internet to sell us more things we don't need faster than ever." Buchanan stopped and stared off for a moment. "And where a lobbyist can earn enough to buy his own plane." He refocused on Ward. "We keep hoarding the wealth of the world. Anybody gets in the way, we crush them, in a hundred different ways, while selling them the message of America the Beautiful. The world's remaining superpower, right?

"Then, little by little, the rest of the world wakes up and sees us for what we are: a fraud. And they start coming for us. In log boats and propeller planes and God knows how else. First by the thousands, then by the millions and then by the billions. And they wipe us out. Stuff us all down some pipe and flush us for good. You, me, the ballplayers, the movie stars, the supermodels, Wall Street, Hollywood and Washington. The true land of make believe."

Ward stared at him wide eyed. "My God, a dream or a nightmare?"

Buchanan shot him a stern glance. "You tell me."

"Your country, love it or leave it, Danny. There's an element of truth in that slogan. We're not so bad."

"We also suck up a disproportionate share of the wealth and energy in the world. We pollute more than any other country. We trash foreign economies and never look back. But still, for a lot of big and small reasons that I really can't explain, I do love my country. That's why this nightmare disturbs me so much. *I don't want it to happen.* But it's getting harder and harder to feel any hope."

"If that's the case, why *do* you do it?"

Buchanan stared at the old photograph again and said, "Do you want something pithy or philosophical?"

"How about the truth?"

Buchanan looked at his old friend. "I deeply regret never having children," he began slowly, then paused. "A good friend of mine has a dozen grandchildren. He was telling me about a PTA meeting he had attended at his granddaughter's elementary school. I asked him why he was bothering with doing that. Wasn't that the parents' job? I said. You know what he told me? He said that with the way the world is now, we all have to think about things beyond our lifetime. Beyond our children's lifetime, in fact. It's our right. It's our duty, my good friend told me."

Buchanan smoothed out his napkin. "So maybe I do what I do because the sum of the world's tragedies outweighs its happiness. And that's just not right." He paused again, moistness creeping into his eyes.

"Other than that, I haven't the faintest idea."

CHAPTER 28

Brooke Reynolds was just finished saying grace, and they all started on their meals. She had burst through the door ten minutes earlier, determined to eat dinner with her family. Her regular hours at the Bureau were eight-fifteen A.M. to five P.M. That was the funniest joke at the Bureau: regular hours. She had changed into jeans and a sweatshirt and exchanged her suede flats for Reeboks. Reynolds took much pleasure in scooping out spoonfuls of peas and mashed potatoes for all their plates. Rosemary poured out milk for the kids while her teenage daughter Theresa helped three-year-old David cut up his meat. It was a nice, quiet family gathering, which Reynolds had come to cherish and which she did everything possible to make each evening, even if it meant going back to work later.

Reynolds rose from the table and poured herself a glass of white wine. While half her brain focused on finding Faith Lockhart and her new confederate, Lee Adams, the other part was looking ahead with much anticipation to Halloween, less than a week away. Sydney, her six-year-old daughter, was dead set on being Eyore, for the second year in a row. David would be the bouncy Tigger, a character that fit the perpetual-motion child perfectly. After that, Thanksgiving, perhaps a trip to her parents' in Florida, if she could find the time. Then Christmas. This year Reynolds was taking the kids to see Santa Claus. She had missed last year because of—what else?—Bureau business. This year she would pull her 9mm on anyone who tried to stop her appointment with Kris Kringle. All in all, a good plan, if she could just make it work. Conception was easy; execution was the key that so often fell out of the lock.

As she put the cork back in the bottle, she looked sadly around a home that would not be hers much longer. Her son and daughter sensed that the change was coming. David hadn't slept through the night in over a week. Reynolds, home after working fifteen-hour days, would hold the quivering, wailing little boy, trying to calm him, rock him back to sleep. She tried to tell him that things would be just fine, when she was as uncertain as anyone whether they would be. It was sometimes terrifying being a parent, particularly in the midst of a divorce and all the pain it caused, which you saw every day etched into the faces of your children. More than once Reynolds had thought about calling off the divorce for that reason alone. But hanging on for the sake of the children wasn't the answer, she felt. At least not for her. They would have a better life without the man than they'd had with him. And her ex, she thought, might be a better father after the divorce than he had been before. Well, at least she could hope. Reynolds simply did not want to let her children down.

When Reynolds caught her daughter Sydney looking apprehensively at her, she smiled as naturally as she could. Sydney was six going on sixteen, so mature beyond her years that it scared Reynolds to death. She picked up on everything, missed nothing of significance. Reynolds had never in her career interrogated a suspect as thoroughly as Sydney did her mother nearly every day. The child dug deep, trying to understand what was going on, what their future would hold, and Reynolds had no ready answers for any of it.

More than once, she had found Sydney holding her crying brother in his bed late at night, attempting to soothe him, relieve his fears. Reynolds had recently told her daughter that she didn't need to assume that responsibility too, that her mother would always be there. Her statement had a hollow ring, and Sydney's face plainly showed a lack of belief. The fact that her daughter had not accepted this statement as dead, solid truth had aged Reynolds several years in several seconds. The memory of the palm reader and her predictions of premature death had come back to roost.

"Rosemary's chicken is awesome, isn't it, honey?" Reynolds said to Sydney.

The little girl nodded.

"Thank you, ma'am," Rosemary said, pleased.

"Are you okay, Mom?" Sydney asked. At the same time, she moved her little brother's milk away from the edge of the table. David had a propensity for spilling any liquid within his reach.

That subtle act of motherhood and her daughter's earnest question moved Reynolds almost to tears. She had been on such an emotional roller coaster of late that it didn't take much to set her off. She took a sip of wine, hoping it would prevent her from actually collapsing into a crying fit. It was like being pregnant again. The littlest thing affected her as if it were life or death. But then her common sense kicked in. She was a mom, things would work out. She had the luxury of a devoted live-in nanny. Sitting around whining, feeling sorry for yourself, wasn't the answer. So their life wasn't perfect. Whose was? She thought of what Anne Newman was going through right now. Suddenly Reynolds's problems didn't seem so bad.

"Everything's really good, Syd. Really good. Congratulations on your spelling test. Ms. Betack said you were the star of the day."

"I like school a lot."

"And it shows, young lady."

Reynolds was about to sit back down when the phone rang. She had caller ID and checked the read-out screen. The ID screen came up blank. The caller must have ID block or his number was unlisted. She debated whether to answer it or not. The problem was that every FBI agent she knew had an unlisted number. Ordinarily, though, anyone from the Bureau would call her on her pager or cell phone, both of which numbers she closely guarded; and calls to those two she would always answer. It was probably a random computer dialer and she would be told to wait until a real person came on and tried to sell her a time-share in Disney World. Still, something made her reach out and pick up the phone.

"Hello?"

"Brooke?"

Anne Newman sounded distressed. And as she listened to the woman, Reynolds sensed that there was something in addition to her husband's violent death—poor Anne, what worse could there be?

"I'll be there in thirty minutes," Reynolds said.

She grabbed her coat and car keys, took a bite out of a slice of the bread on her plate and kissed her children.

"Will you be back in time to read us a story, Mom?" Sydney asked.

"Three bears, three pigs, three goats." David promptly recited his favorite nighttime storytelling ritual to Brooke, his favorite story reader. His sister Sydney favored reading the stories herself, every night, sounding out each word along the way. Little David now took a big gulp of milk, loudly burped and then excused himself in a fit of laughter.

Reynolds smiled. Sometimes when she was tired she would tell the stories so fast they almost blurred together. The pigs built their houses, the bears went for their walk while Goldilocks burglarized the joint and the three billy goats gruff trounced the evil troll and lived happily ever after in their new pasture of grass. Sounded nice. Where could she buy some? And then, undressing for bed, Reynolds would endure spasms of crushing guilt. The reality was that her kids would be grown and gone before she blinked her eyes twice, and she routinely shortchanged them on three short fairy tales because she wanted to do something so unimportant as sleep. Sometimes it was better not to think too much. Reynolds was a classic over-achiever and a perfectionist, to boot, while a "perfect parent" was the world's greatest oxymoron.

"I'll try my best. I promise."

The disappointed look on her daughter's face made Reynolds turn and flee the room. She stopped at the small room on the first floor that served as her study. From the top of a cabinet she removed a squat, heavy metal box, which she unlocked. Removing her SIG 9mm, she loaded in a fresh mag, pulled the slide back to chamber a round, clicked the safety on, slid the

weapon in her clip holster and was out the door before she could think any more about another interrupted meal in a long string of disappointments for
her children. Superwoman: career, kids, she had it all.
Now, if she could only clone herself. Twice.

CHAPTER 29

LEE AND FAITH HAD MADE TWO STOPS ON THE way to North Carolina, once for a late lunch at a Cracker Barrel and another at a large strip mall in southern Virginia. Lee had seen a billboard off the highway advertising a week-long gun show. The parking lot was packed with pickup trucks, RVs and cars with fat tires and engines erupting through their hoods. Some of the men were dressed in Polo and Chaps, and others in Grateful Dead T-shirts and ragged jeans. Americans of all backgrounds apparently loved their guns.

"Why here?" Faith asked as Lee got off the bike.

"Virginia law requires that licensed gun dealers conduct on-the-spot background checks on people trying to buy weapons," he explained. "You have to fill out a form, have your gun permit and two forms of identification. But the law doesn't apply to gun shows. All they want is your money. Which, by the way, I need."

"Do you *really* have to have a gun?"

He stared at her as though she had just hatched from an egg. "Everybody coming after *us* has them."

Unable to dispute this devastating logic, she said nothing more, gave him the cash and huddled on the bike as he went inside. Leave it to the man to say something that would paralyze her very soul.

Inside, Lee purchased a Smith & Wesson double-action autopistol with a fifteen-round mag, chambering 9mm Parabellums. The autopistol tag was misleading. You had to pull the trigger each time to fire. The "auto" term referred to the fact that the pistol automatically loaded a new round with each pull of the trigger. He also bought a box of ammo and a cleaning kit and then returned to the parking lot.

Faith watched closely as he packed the gun and ammo away in the motorcycle's storage compartment.

"Feel safer now?" she asked dryly.

"Right now I wouldn't feel safe sitting in the Hoover Building with a hundred FBI agents staring at me. Gee, I wonder why."

They made Duck, North Carolina, by nightfall, and Faith gave Lee directions to the house in the Pine Island community.

When they pulled up in front, Lee stared at the immense structure, tugged off his helmet and turned to her. "I thought you said it was small."

"Actually, I think you referred to it as small. I said it was comfortable."

She climbed off the Honda and stretched out her body. Every bit of her, especially her butt, was one solid knot.

"It must be at least six thousand square feet." Lee continued to stare at the three-story, wooden-shingle-siding house that had dual stone chimneys and a cedar shake roof. Two broad veranda-style porches ran across the second and third floors, which gave it a plantation feel. There were gabled turrets and walls of lattice and glass; and immense displays of fountain grass erupted from the ground. Lee watched as the automatic sprinklers came on, along with the exterior landscape lighting. Behind the house he could hear the pounding surf. The house was situated at the end of a quiet cul-de-sac, although there were similar monster homes painted yellow, blue, green and gray lined up on the beach side in both directions as far as the eye could see. Although the air was warm and slightly humid, they were approaching November, and virtually all the other homes were dark.

Faith said, "I've never really bothered to add up the square footage. I rent it out April through September. It covers the mortgage and nets me about thirty thousand a year—just in case you're interested." Taking off her helmet and running her hands through her sweaty hair, she said, "I need a shower and some food. The kitchen should be stocked. You can put the bike in the carport."

Faith unlocked the front door and went inside while Lee parked the Honda in one of two bays of the carport and then carried in the bags. The inside of the house was even more beautiful than the outside. Lee was also grateful to see that the place had a security system. As he looked around, he took in the soaring ceilings, pickled wood beams and paneling, an enormous kitchen, Italian tile floors in some places, high-dollar Berber carpeting elsewhere. He counted six bedrooms, seven bathrooms and discovered an outdoor Jacuzzi on the back porch big enough for at least six drunken adults to flop around in. There were also three fireplaces, including a gas one in the master suite. The furniture was overstuffed rattan and wicker, all seemingly designed to beckon one to catnap.

Lee opened a set of French doors off the kitchen, stepped onto the deck and looked down into the enclosed courtyard. A kidney-shaped pool was situated down there. The chlorinated water sparkled under the glow of the pool lights. A Creepy Crawly made its way through the water, sucking up bugs and debris.

Faith joined him on the deck. "I had the people come out this morning and get everything going. They maintain the pool all year 'round anyway. I've skinny-dipped down here in December. It's gloriously peaceful."

"There doesn't seem to be anybody else in the other houses."

"Certain parts of the Outer Banks are pretty full about nine or even ten months out of the year now, what with the nice weather. But you always have the chance of hurricanes this time of year, and this area is pretty expensive. The houses rent out for a small fortune, even in the off season. Unless you can get a big group together to rent them, your average family isn't going to be staying here. Mostly, you see the owners come down this time of year. But with kids in school, it's tough to do that during the week. So empty we have."

"Empty I like."

"The pool's heated, if you want to take a dip."

"I didn't bring my trunks."

"Not into skinny-dipping, huh?" She smiled and was very relieved that it was too dark for her to really see his eyes. If his baby blues had hit her just right, she might have pushed him in the pool, dived after him and everything else be damned.

"There are plenty of places in town to get some swimming stuff. I keep clothes down here, so I'm okay. We'll buy you some things tomorrow."

"I think I'm fine with what I brought."

"You don't want to stick out here, do you?"

"I'm not sure we'll be here long enough for that."

Faith looked out toward the wooden walkways leading past the sand dunes to where the Atlantic

Ocean pitched and bellowed. "You never know. I don't think there's a better place to sleep than at the beach. There's nothing like the sound of waves crashing in your ears to drive you into unconsciousness. Back in D.C. I never sleep well. Too many things to worry about."

"Funny, I sleep just fine there."

She glared at him. "To each his own."

"What's for dinner?"

"First, a shower. You can have the master suite."

"It's your place. I'm fine on a couch."

"With six bedrooms, I don't think that would make much sense. Take the one at the end of the hall upstairs. It opens out onto the back porch. The Jacuzzi's out there. Feel free. Even without trunks. Don't worry, I won't peek."

They went inside. Lee grabbed his bag and followed her upstairs. He showered and put on a clean pair of khakis, a sweatshirt and sneakers without socks, since he had forgotten to bring the latter. He didn't bother to dry his new buzz cut. He caught himself looking in the mirror. The haircut didn't look so bad on him. In fact, it had taken a few years off. He slapped his hard gut, even did an exaggerated flex in the mirror.

"Yeah, right," he said to his reflection. "Even if she were your type, which she sure as hell ain't." He left his room and was about to head downstairs when he stopped in the hallway.

Faith's bedroom was at the other end of the corridor. He could still hear her shower running. She was probably taking her time under the hot water after the long ride. She had held up well, he had to admit, hadn't complained too much. He was edging down the hallway the whole time he was thinking this, because it had just occurred to him that Faith might at this very minute be escaping out the back door while using the running shower as a ruse. For all he knew, she had arranged for a rental car that was parked down the street, and she was about to drive off, leaving him with not much of a life. Was she just like her old man? Running away into the night when things got tough?

He knocked on her door. "Faith?" There was no answer, so he knocked louder. "Faith? Faith!" The water was still running. "Faith!" he yelled. He tried the door. It was locked. He pounded on the door again and yelled her name.

Lee was about to hustle down the stairs when he heard footsteps and the door was flung open. Faith stood there, her hair soaked and hanging in her face, water dripping down her legs, a towel covering, barely, the front of her.

"What?" she demanded. "What's wrong?"

Lee found himself staring at the elegant bone development of her shoulders, the now fully revealed Audrey Hepburn neck, the tightness of her arms. Then his gaze slid down to her upper thighs and he quickly concluded that her arms had nothing on her legs.

"What the hell is it, Lee?" she said loudly.

He snapped back. "Oh. I was just wondering, um, how about I make dinner?" He smiled weakly.

She stared incredulously at him as a puddle of water collected on the carpet at her feet. As she wrapped the mostly wet towel around her, Faith's small, firm breasts were now fully outlined against the thin wet fabric. That's when Lee began thinking seriously about taking another shower, only this time with water cold enough to turn certain parts of his anatomy the same color as his eyes.

"Fine." She slammed the door in his face.

"Very fine," Lee said quietly to the door.

He went downstairs and examined the contents of the refrigerator. He decided on a menu and started pulling food and pans. He had been living alone for so long that he had finally decided, after years of Golden Arches food, that he had better learn how to cook properly. He actually found it therapeutic, and he fully expected to live an extra twenty years now that he had cleaned his arteries of all the grease. At least until he met Faith Lockhart. Now all bets on a long life were off.

Lee laid out talapia on a baking sheet, brushed the fish with butter he had melted in a pan and let it soak in. Then he added garlic, lemon juice and some other secret spices handed down to him through generations of Adamses and put the fish in the wall oven to broil. He sliced up tomatoes and a slab of mozzarella, arranged them nicely on a serving plate and doused them with olive oil and seasoning. Next he prepared a salad and then slit a length of French bread, buttered it, added garlic and placed it in the lower oven. He got out two plates, silverware and cloth napkins he found in a drawer and set the table. There were candles on the table, but lighting them seemed like a cheesy idea. This wasn't a honeymoon, and they still had that nationwide manhunt thing to consider.

He opened a small, built-in wine cooler next to the fridge and selected a chilled bottle of white. As he was pouring out two glasses of wine, Faith came down the stairs. She wore an unbuttoned blue denim shirt with a white T-shirt underneath, a pair of loose-fitting white slacks and red sandals. He noted she still wore no makeup, at least that he could detect. A silver bangle bracelet dangled at her wrist. She also wore turquoise earrings done in a loopy southwestern design.

She looked surprised at the kitchen activity. "A man who can shoot a gun, lose the Feds and cook too. You just never cease to amaze me."

He handed her a wine glass. "A good meal, a quiet evening and then we get down to serious business."

She glanced coolly at him as he clinked his glass against hers. "You clean up well," she said.

"Another one of my talents." He went to check the

fish while Faith went over to the wall of windows and stared out.

They ate quietly, both of them apparently feeling a little awkward now that they had arrived at their destination. Getting here, ironically enough, seemed to be the easy part.

Faith insisted on cleaning up the kitchen while Lee turned on the TV.

"Did we make the news?" Faith asked.

"Not that I can see. But there must have been reports of the FBI agent being found. A murdered Fed is still pretty damn rare even in this day and age, thank God. I'll get a newspaper tomorrow."

Faith finished cleaning up, poured herself another glass of wine and joined him.

"Okay, our bellies are full, the booze has us about as mellow as we're going to get, so now's the time to talk," Lee said. "I need to hear the whole story, Faith. As sweet and simple as that."

"So you feed a girl a nice meal, fill her with wine and you think she's yours for the asking?" She smiled coyly.

He frowned. "I'm serious, Faith."

Her smile disappeared, along with her coyness. "Let's go for a walk on the beach."

Lee started to protest but then stopped. "Okay. It's your turf, home rules apply." He headed up the stairs.

"Where are you going?"

"Be right back."

When Lee came back down, he had on a wind-
breaker.

"You didn't need a jacket, it's still pretty warm."

He spread open the front of the jacket, revealing
the clip holster and the Smith & Wesson in it. "Didn't
want to spook any sand crabs we come across."

"Guns frighten me to death."

"Guns also prevent death, when *properly* used. Usually sudden, violent death."

"No one could have followed us. No one knows
we're here."

His reply chilled her to the bone.

"I hope to God you're right."

CHAPTER 30

REYNOLDS DIDN'T USE HER BUBBLE LIGHT BUT would have if a patrol car had tried to pull her over, as she was exceeding the speed limit by more than twenty miles per hour on the few open stretches of the Beltway before having to slow down in a sea of red brake lights. She checked her watch: seven-thirty. When wasn't there a rush hour in this damn area? People got up earlier and earlier to go to work, or stayed later and later before going home to avoid the traffic. Pretty soon the two groups would smack right into each other and the twenty-four-hour-a-day highway parking lot would officially begin. Luckily Anne Newman's house was only a few exits down from hers.

As she drove, Reynolds thought about her visit to Adams's apartment building. Reynolds had thought she had seen and heard everything by now, but Angie Carter's statement about the FBI had stunned her, and the shock of it had moved her and Connie into hyperspeed. They'd notified their superiors at the Bureau and quickly determined that no FBI operation had been conducted at Adams's address. Then the shit had really hit the fan. The impersonation of FBI agents got the attention of the director himself, and he had personally issued orders on the case. Even though the back door to Adams's apartment had been knocked off its hinges and they could have walked right in, a search warrant was fast-tracked and executed, again with the director's personal blessing. Reynolds was actually relieved about that because she didn't want to have any slip-ups on this one. Any mistakes would come home to roost right on her head.

The apartment was thoroughly searched by one of the Bureau's crack forensics teams, pulled off another high-profile case. In the end they didn't find much. There was no tape in the answering machine. That had really ticked Reynolds off. If the phony FBI people had taken the tape, there must have been something important on it. Her search team had continued to strike out. There were no travel documents, maps consulted, nothing that would hint as to where Adams and Lockhart were going. They had found fingerprints matching Faith Lockhart's, so that was something. They were checking into Adams's background. He had family in the area; maybe they knew something.

They had discovered the roof hatch in the empty apartment next door to Adams's. Clever. Reynolds had also noted the extra locks, video surveillance, steel door and frame and the copper shield over the alarm panel. Lee Adams knew what he was doing.

They had retrieved the bag of hair and hair coloring from one of the trash cans behind the apartment. That, together with the snips they had seen of the airport surveillance tapes, showed that Adams was now a blond, Lockhart a brunette. Not that this helped much. They were checking into whether either of them had other residences listed in their names elsewhere in the country. That was a needle in a haystack, she knew, even if they had used their real names. She doubted they would be that stupid. And even if they had used their aliases, the names Suzanne Blake and Charles Wright were too common to aid Reynolds very much.

The police officers who responded to the call at Adams's apartment were pulled in and questioned. The men posing as FBI agents had fed them a story that Lee Adams was wanted in connection with a kidnapping ring across state lines. The FBI posers' credentials looked real, both police officers were quick to point out. And they carried the firepower and the professional swagger one normally associated with federal law enforcement. They were searching the place expertly and had made no move to run when the cruiser had shown up. The imposters talked the talk and walked the walk in all respects, said the two police officers, who were both veterans on the street. They had been given the name of the supposed special agent in charge. It was run through the FBI personnel database and came up negative. No surprise there. The police officers had given descriptions of the men they had seen, and a Bureau technician was creating computer images of them. Still, all in all, it was a dead end, with frightening implications. Implications that struck very close to home for Reynolds.

She had received another visit from Paul Fisher. He came with orders right from Massey, as he was quick to point out. Reynolds was to proceed with all due speed, but with the utmost caution, to find Faith Lockhart, and she could be assured of all the support she needed.

"Just don't make any more mistakes," he had said.

"I wasn't aware I had made any mistakes, Paul."

"An agent killed. Faith Lockhart falls into your lap and you let her get away. What would you call those?"

"Leaked information caused Ken to die," she had fired back. "I fail to see how that was my fault."

"Brooke," Fisher had said, "if you really believe that, then you might want to request reassignment right now. The buck stops with you. As far as the Bureau is concerned, if there is a leak, every member of your squad, including you, is at the top of the list. And that's how the Bureau's following that up."

As soon as he left her office, Reynolds had thrown her shoe against the closed door. Then she had thrown the other one, just to be sure he was aware of her extreme displeasure. Paul Fisher was officially off her sexual fantasy list.

Reynolds raced down the exit ramp, hung a left on Braddock Road and fought through some late traffic backup until she turned off and entered the quiet residential neighborhood of the slain FBI agent. She slowed when she reached the Newmans' street. The house was dark, a single car in the driveway. Reynolds parked her government-issue sedan at the curb, got out and hustled up to the door.

Anne Newman must have been watching for her, because the door opened before Reynolds could ring the bell.

Anne Newman didn't attempt to make small talk or ask Reynolds if she wanted anything to drink. She led the FBI agent directly to a small back room that had been set up as an office with a desk, metal file cabinet, computer and fax machine. On the wall were framed baseball cards and other sports memorabilia. On the desk were stacks of silver dollars encased in hard plastic and neatly labeled.

"I was looking through Ken's office. I don't know why. It just seemed . . . ."

"You don't have to explain, Anne. There are no set rules for what you're going through."

Anne Newman wiped away a tear as Reynolds studied her. Clearly the woman was near the breaking point, on all fronts. She was dressed in an old robe, her hair unwashed, eyes red and puffy. Yesterday afternoon, the most pressing decision she probably had to make was what to have for dinner, Reynolds assumed. God, it could all turn on a dime. Ken Newman wasn't the only one being buried. Anne was right there beside him. The only catch was she still had to go on living.

"I found these photo albums. I didn't even know they were back here. They were in a box with some other things. I know this might look bad, but . . . but if it helps in finding out what happened to Ken . . ." She faded out for a moment as more tears plunked down onto the photo album she was holding with its tattered, seventies-style psychedelic cover.

"Calling you was the right thing to do," Anne finally said with a bluntness that was both painful and gratifying for Reynolds to hear.

"I know this is terribly difficult for you." Reynolds eyed the album, not wanting to prolong this any more than absolutely necessary. "Can I see what you found?"

Anne Newman sat down on a small sofa and opened the album and pulled up the clear plastic sheet that kept the photos securely inside. On the page she had opened to was an eight-by-ten photo of a group of men in hunting garb holding rifles. Ken Newman was one of the men. She pulled out the photo, revealing a piece of paper and a small key pressed into the album page. She handed Reynolds both and watched her closely as the FBI agent examined them.

The piece of paper was an account statement for a safe-deposit box at a local bank. The key, presumably, fit that box.

Reynolds looked at her. "You didn't know about this?"

Anne Newman shook her head. "We have a safe-deposit box. But not at that bank. And of course that's not all."

Reynolds looked back at the bank statement and she jerked involuntarily. The name of the boxholder was not Ken Newman. Nor was the billing address for the house she was in. "Who's Frank Andrews?"

Anne Newman looked like she would burst into tears again. "God, I have no idea."

"Did Ken ever mention that name to you?" Anne shook her head.

Reynolds took a deep breath. If Newman had a safe-deposit box under a false name, he would have needed one thing to set up the account.

She sat on the sofa next to Anne and took her hand. "Have you found any identification around here that might match the name Frank Andrews?"

The tears welled in the stricken woman's eyes and Reynolds truly felt for her.

"You mean with Ken's picture on it? Showing that he was this Frank Andrews person?"

"Yes, that's what I mean," Reynolds said softly.

Anne Newman put her hand in her robe and pulled out a Virginia driver's license. The name on it was Frank Andrews. The license number, which in Virginia was the person's Social Security number, was on there. And in the small accompanying photo Ken Newman was staring back at her.

"I thought about going to open the safe-deposit box myself, but then I realized they wouldn't let me. I'm not on the account. And I wouldn't be able to explain that it was my husband, but just under a fake name."

"I know, Anne. I know. You were right to bring me in. Now, where exactly did you find the fake ID?"

"In another one of the photo albums. They weren't family albums, of course. I keep those, been through them a zillion times. These albums were pictures of Ken and his hunting and fishing buddies. They took trips every year. Ken was good about taking pictures. I never knew he kept them in albums. I wasn't all that interested in looking at those pictures, you see." She stared wistfully at the far wall. "Sometimes it seemed Ken was happier with his buddies shooting at ducks or at his coin and card shows than he was at home." She caught a quick breath, put a hand over her mouth and looked down.

Reynolds could sense Anne had never meant to share that personal bit of information with her, a semi-stranger. She said nothing. Experience told her to allow Anne Newman to work her way through this. A minute later the woman started speaking again.

"I never would have found it, I suppose, unless . . . what happened to Ken . . . you know. I guess life is funny sometimes."

Or terribly cruel. "Anne, I need to check this out. I'm going to take these items, and I don't want you to mention it to anyone. Not friends, family . . ." She paused, choosing her words as carefully as she could. "Or anyone else at the Bureau. Not until I dig a little bit."

Anne Newman looked up at her with frightened eyes. "What do you think Ken was involved in, Brooke?"

"I don't know yet. Let's not jump to conclusions on this. The safe-deposit box might be empty. Ken might have leased it a long time ago and then forgotten about it."

"And the fake ID?"

Reynolds licked her dry lips. "Ken worked some undercover over the years. This might be a souvenir of those days." Reynolds knew this was a lie, and Anne Newman probably did too, she thought. The license had a recent issue date on it. And those working undercover in the FBI didn't usually take home the props with their secret identities on them once their tasks were completed. The fake license, she was fairly certain, was unrelated to his FBI duties. It was her job to discover what it *was* connected to.

"Anne, not a word to anyone. It's for your own safety as much as anything."

Anne Newman clutched her arm as Reynolds stood. "Brooke, I've got three kids. If Ken was mixed up in something . . ."

"I'll put the house under twenty-four-hour surveillance. Anything remotely suspicious catches your eye, you call me." She handed her a card with her direct-dial numbers on it. "Day or night."

"I didn't know where else to turn. Ken thought a lot of you, he really did."

"He was a damn good agent and he had a terrific career." If she discovered that Ken Newman had been a sell-out, however, the Bureau would crush his memory, his reputation, everything about his professional life. That would, of course, destroy his private side as well, including the woman Reynolds was looking at, and her children. But that was life. Reynolds didn't make the rules, didn't always agree with the rules, but she lived by them. However, she would check out the safe-deposit box by herself. If there was nothing suspicious in there, she would tell no one. She would continue to investigate why Newman was using an alias, but that would be done on her own time. She wasn't going to destroy his memory without a very compelling reason. She owed the man that.

She left Anne Newman sitting on the sofa, the photo album open in her lap. The ironic thing was, if Newman was the leak on the Lockhart case, he had probably helped himself to an early death. Now that Reynolds thought about it, whoever might have hired him had probably hoped to eliminate the mole and the main target in one efficient thrust. Only a slug deflecting off a pistol barrel had saved Faith Lockhart from joining Ken Newman on a slab. And perhaps the assistance of Lee Adams as well?

Whoever had orchestrated it clearly knew what he was doing. Which was bad for Reynolds. Contrary to popular fiction and film, most criminals weren't that accomplished and couldn't so easily outmaneuver the police at every turn. The majority of murderers, rapists, burglars, robbers, drug dealers and other felons were usually uneducated or scared; or drugged-out punks or drunks terrified of their own shadows when off the needle or bottle, yet demons when high. They left many clues behind and were usually caught, or turned themselves in, or were ratted on by their "friends." They were prosecuted and did jail time or, in rare cases, were executed. They were in no sense of the word professionals.

Reynolds knew that this was not the case here. Amateurs didn't find ways to pay off veteran FBI agents. They didn't hire hit men who lurked in the woods waiting for their prey. They didn't impersonate FBI agents with credentials so authentic they had scared off the cops. Sinister theories of conspiracy swirled in her head, sending a shiver of fear down her back. No matter how long you did this, the fear was always there. To be alive was to be afraid. To not be afraid was to be dead.

As she walked out, Reynolds passed under a blinking fire detector that was in the hallway. There were three other such devices in the house, including one in Ken Newman's office. While they were plugged into the home's electrical wiring and did function as designed, they all also housed sophisticated surveillance cameras with pinhole lenses. Two of the wall outlets on each level were similarly "modified." The modifications had taken place two weeks ago when the Newmans had taken a rare three-day vacation. This type of surveillance mode was based upon PLCs, power line carrier technology favored by the FBI. And the Central Intelligence Agency.

Robert Thornhill was on the prowl. And his attention would now turn to Brooke Reynolds.

As she climbed in her car, Reynolds understood very clearly that she was perhaps at the crossroads of her career. She would probably need every bit of ingenuity and inner strength she could muster to survive this. And yet the only thing she really wanted to do right now was drive home and tell her two beautiful children the story of the three pigs, just as slowly, accurately and colorfully as she possibly could.

THE WIND, IT TURNED OUT, WAS BLOWING hard along the beach, and the temperature had dropped drastically. Faith buttoned her overshirt; then, despite the cold, she took off her sandals and held them in one hand.

"I like to feel the sand," she explained to Lee. The tide was low, so they had a broad beach on which to meander. The sky held scattered clouds, the moon almost full, the stars winks of light staring down upon them. Far out on the water they saw the blink of what was probably a ship's light or stationary buoy. Except for the wind, it was completely quiet. No cars, no blaring TVs, no planes, no other people.

"It's really nice out here," Lee finally said as he watched a sand crab do its funny sideways scuttle into its tiny home. Stuck in the sand was a piece of

PVC pipe. Lee knew that fishermen would stick their poles in the hollow tube when they were fishing from the beach.

"I've thought of moving here permanently," said Faith. She broke ranks with him and ventured into the water up to her ankles. Lee slipped off his shoes, rolled up his pants legs and joined her.

"Colder than I thought it would be," he said. "No swimming out here."

"You wouldn't believe how invigorating a swim in cold water can be."

"You're right, I wouldn't."

"I'm sure you've been asked this a million times, but how did you become a private investigator?"

He shrugged and looked out toward the ocean. "Sort of fell into it. My dad was an engineer and I was a gadget guy, like him. But I never had the book smarts he did. I was sort of a rebel too, like you. But I didn't go to college. I joined the Navy."

"Please tell me you were a Navy SEAL. I'd sleep better."

Lee smiled. "I can barely shoot straight. I can't build a nuclear device out of toothpicks and gum wrappers, and the last time I checked, I couldn't disable a man simply by pressing my thumb against his forehead."

"I guess I'll keep you anyway. Sorry to interrupt."

"Not much more to it. I studied telephony, communications, that sort of thing in the Navy. Got married, had a kid. I left the service and worked at the phone company as a repairman. Then I lost my daughter in a messy divorce. I quit my job, answered an ad at a private security firm for someone experienced in electronic surveillance. I figured with my technical background I could learn what I needed to know. The job really got into my blood. I started my own private investigation firm, got some decent clients, made mistakes along the way but then got a firm footing. Now you see me today as the head of a mighty empire."

"How long have you been divorced?"

"A long time." He looked at her. "Why?"

"Just curious. Ever gotten close to the altar since then?"

"No. I guess I'm terrified of making the same mistakes." He stuffed his hands into his pockets. "Quite honestly, the problems came from both ends. I'm not easy to live with." He smiled. "I think God makes two kinds of people: those who should marry and procreate and those who should remain alone and have sex only for fun. I think I'm in the latter group. Not that I've been having much 'fun' lately."

Faith looked down. "Save some room for me."

"Not to worry. There's plenty of space left."

He touched her elbow. "Let's talk. We're running out of time."

Faith led him back up onto the beach and plopped

down cross-legged on a patch of dry sand. He sat next to her.

"Where would you like to begin?" she asked.

"How about the beginning?"

"No, I meant do you want me to tell you all first, or do you want to spill *your* secrets first?"

He looked startled. "*My* secrets? Sorry, I'm fresh out."

She picked up a stick, drew the letters *d* and *b* in the sand and then glanced at him. "Danny Buchanan. What do you really know about him?"

"Just what I told you. He's your partner."

"He's also the man who hired you."

Lee couldn't find his voice for a few seconds. "I told you I didn't know who had hired me."

"That's right. That's what you *told* me."

"How do you know he hired me?"

"While I was in your office, I listened to a message from Danny, and he sounded quite anxious to know where I was and what you had found out. He left his phone number for you to call him back. He was more distressed than I've ever heard him. I guess I would be too if someone I had arranged to have killed was still alive and kicking."

"You're sure it was him on the phone?"

"After fifteen years of working with him I think I know his voice. So you didn't know?"

"No, I didn't."

"You know that's really hard to believe."

"I guess it is," he agreed. "But it happens to be the truth." He scooped up some sand and let it run through his fingers. "So I take it that phone call is why you tried to give me the slip at the airport? You don't trust me."

She licked her dry lips and glanced at the holstered gun, which was visible as the wind whipped Lee's jacket around. "I *do* trust you, Lee. Otherwise I wouldn't be sitting on a lonely beach in the dark with an armed man who's still pretty much a stranger to me."

Lee let his shoulders slump. "I was hired to follow you, Faith. That's all."

"Don't you first find out if the client or his intentions are legitimate?"

Lee started to say something and then stopped. That was a reasonable question. The fact was business had been slow recently and the assignment and cash had been timely. And the file he had been given had a photo of Faith. And then he had seen her in person. Well, what the hell could he say? Most of his targets weren't as attractive as Faith Lockhart. In the photo her face had suggested vulnerability. After meeting her, he knew that impression wasn't necessarily true. But it was a very potent combination for him, beauty and vulnerability. For any man.

"Normally, I like to meet with a client, get to

know him and his agenda before I agree to accept a job."

"But not here?"

"It was a little difficult, since I didn't know who had hired me."

"So instead of returning the cash, you accepted the offer and started following me—blindly, as it were."

"I didn't see any harm in just following you."

"But they could have been using you to get to me."

"It's not exactly like you were in hiding. Like I said, I thought you might be having some sort of affair. When I went inside the cottage, I knew that wasn't the case. The rest of the night's events damn sure reinforced that conclusion. That's all I really know."

Faith stared out toward the ocean, to the horizon, where water met sky. It was a visual collision of sorts that happened every day and was comforting for some reason. It gave her hope when she probably had no other reason to feel it. Other than the man sitting beside her, perhaps.

"Let's go back to the house," she said.

CHAPTER 32

THEY SAT IN THE SPACIOUS FAMILY ROOM. FAITH picked up a remote control, hit a button and the flames in the gas fireplace crept to life. She poured another glass of wine, offered one to Lee, but he declined. They sat on the overstuffed couch.

Faith took a sip of wine and stared out the window, her eyes focusing on nothing. "Washington represents the richest, most enormous pie in the history of mankind. And everyone in the whole world wants a slice of it. There are certain people who hold the knife that portions out that pie. If you want a slice, you have to go through them."

"That's where you and Buchanan come in?"

"I lived, breathed and ate my career. Sometimes I worked more than twenty-four hours in a day because I'd cross the International Date Line. I can't tell you the hundreds of details, nuances, mind-reading, gut checks and sheer nerve and perseverance that lobbying on the scale we did requires." She put down her wine glass and focused on him. "I had a great teacher in Danny Buchanan. He almost never lost. That's remarkable, don't you think?"

"I guess never losing at anything is pretty remarkable. We can't all be Michael Jordan."

"In your line of work can you guarantee to your client that a certain result will occur?"

Lee smiled. "If I could foresee the future, I'd start playing the lottery."

"Danny Buchanan could guarantee the future."

Lee stopped smiling. "How?"

"He who controls the gatekeepers controls the future."

Lee slowly nodded in understanding. "So he was paying off people in government?"

"On a more sophisticated scale than anyone's done before."

"Congressmen on the payroll? That sort of thing?"

"Actually, they did it for free."

"What—"

"Until they left office. Then Danny had a whole world of goodies lined up for them. Lucrative do-nothing jobs in companies he had set up. Income from private portfolios of stocks and bonds, and cash funneled through legitimate businesses under the cover of services rendered. They could play golf all day, make a couple of sham phone calls to the Hill, take a few meetings and live like kings. Hey, it's like a super 401(k). You know how Americans are so into their stocks. Danny worked them hard while they were on the Hill, but he would give them the best golden years money could buy."

"How many of them have 'retired'?"

"None, as yet. But everything is set up for when they do. Danny's been doing this only about ten years."

"He's been in D.C. a lot longer than ten years."

"I mean he's been bribing people for only ten years. Before then, he was a much more successful lobbyist. The last ten years, he's made a lot less money."

"I thought guaranteeing results would bring him a lot *more* money."

"The last ten years have been pretty much a charitable decade for him."

"The man must have deep pockets."

"Danny has pretty much gone through his money. We started representing paying clients again so we could continue what we were doing. And the longer his people do what they are told, the more they will receive later. And by waiting until they're out of office to be paid, the chances any of them will be caught go down considerably."

"They must really trust Buchanan's word."

"I'm sure he's had to show them proof of what's waiting for them. But he's also an honorable man."

"All crooks are, aren't they? Who are some of the people on his retirement plan?"

She looked at him suspiciously. "Why?"

"Just humor me."

Faith named two of the men.

"Correct me if I'm mistaken, but aren't they the current vice president of the United States and the Speaker of the House?"

"Danny doesn't work with middle management. He actually started working with the vice president before he rose to that office, back when he was a House whip. But when Danny needs the man to pick up the phone and put the screws to someone, the man does."

"Holy shit, Faith. What the hell did you need that kind of firepower for? Are we talking military secrets?"

"Actually, something much more valuable." She picked up her wine glass. "We represent the poorest of the world's poor. African nations, in issues of humanitarian aid, food, medicine, clothing, farm equipment, crop seed, desalinization systems. In Latin America, money for vaccines and other medical supplies. The export of legal birth control devices, sterile needles and health information in the poorest countries."

Lee looked skeptical. "You're saying you were bribing government officials to help third world countries?"

She set down her wine glass and looked directly at him. "Actually, the official lexicon has changed. The rich nations have developed very politically correct terminology for their destitute neighbors. The CIA publishes a manual on them, in fact. So instead of 'third world,' you have new categories: LDCs are 'less-developed countries,' meaning they're in the bottom group in the hierarchy of developed countries. There are officially one hundred and seventy-two LDCs, or the vast majority of countries in the world. Then there are the LLDCs. They're the 'least developed countries.' They're the bottom of the barrel, dead in the water. There are *only* forty-two of them. This may surprise you, but about half of the people on this planet live in abject poverty."

"And that makes it right?" Lee said. "That makes bribery and cheating right?"

"I'm not asking you to condone any of it. I don't really care if you agree with it or not. You wanted the facts, I'm giving them to you."

"America gives lots of foreign aid. And we don't *have* to give a dime."

She gave him a fierce look, one he had never seen from her before. "If you talk facts with me, you lose," she said sharply.

"Come again?"

"I've been researching this—living this—for more than ten years! We pay farmers in this country more *not* to grow crops than we do on humanitarian relief overseas. Of the total federal budget, foreign aid represents about one percent, with the vast majority of that going to two countries, Egypt and Israel. Americans spend a hundred times as much money on makeup or fast food or video rentals in a year's time than we do on feeding starving children in third world countries in a decade. We could wipe out a dozen serious childhood diseases in undeveloped countries around the world with less money than we spend on Beanie Babies."

"You're naïve, Faith. You and Buchanan are probably just filling the lining of some dictator's pockets."

"No! That's an easy excuse, and one that I'm so sick of. The money we do manage to get goes directly to legitimate humanitarian relief organizations, and never to the government directly. I've personally seen enough health ministers in African countries wearing Armani and driving a Mercedes while babies starve at their feet."

"And there aren't starving children in this country?"

"They get a lot of aid, and rightfully so. All I'm saying is that Danny and I had our agenda, and ours involved the *foreign* poor. Human beings are dying, Lee, by the millions. Children all over the world are perishing for no reason other than neglect. Every day, every hour, every minute."

"And do you really expect me to believe you two did this out of the goodness of your hearts?" He looked around the house. "This isn't exactly a soup kitchen, Faith."

"The first five years I worked with Danny I did my

job, represented the big clients and I made a lot of money. A *lot* of money. I'll be the first to admit I'm one materialistic hardass. I like the money, and I loved what the money could buy."

"And then what happened? You found God?"

"No, he found me." Lee looked bewildered, and Faith quickly continued. "Danny had begun lobbying on behalf of the foreign poor. He was getting nowhere. No one cared, he kept telling me. The other partners at our firm were getting tired of Danny's charitable endeavors. They wanted to represent IBM and Philip Morris, not Sudan's starving masses. Danny came to my office one day, said he was forming his own firm and wanted me to go with him. We weren't taking any clients, but Danny told me not to worry, that he'd take care of me."

Lee appeared mollified. "That much I can believe: You didn't know he was bribing people, or at least planning to."

"Of course I knew about it! He told me everything. He wanted me to go into this with eyes wide open. That's how he is. He's not some crook."

"Faith, do you know what you're saying? You *went along*, even though you knew you'd be breaking the law?"

She fixed a cold gaze upon him. "If I could fix it so that cigarette companies could keep selling cancer on a stick to anybody with a fresh set of lungs and gun manufacturers could roll out machine guns to anyone with a heartbeat, I guess I felt nothing was beneath me. And the goal here was something I could actually be proud of."

"Materialistic hardass goes soft?" Lee said with contempt.

"It's been known to happen," she shot back.

"How did you two work it?" Lee said in a baiting tone.

"I was Mister Outside, working all the people we didn't have in our back pocket. I was also good at getting celebrities to appear at some events, even travel to some of the countries. Photo ops, meet-and-greets with members." She sipped her wine. "Danny was Mister Inside. He worked all the people on the take while I pushed from the outside."

"And you kept this up for ten years?"

Faith nodded. "About a year ago Danny started running out of money. A lot of our lobbying expenses he paid out of his own pocket. It wasn't like our clients could afford to pay us anything. And he had to invest a lot of his own money into these 'trust' funds, as he called them, for the members we were bribing. Danny took that part very seriously. He was their trustee. Every cent he promised would be there."

"Honor among thieves."

Faith ignored the barb. "That's when he told me to concentrate on paying clients while he carried the torch on the other matters. I offered to sell my house, and this house, to help raise money. He refused. He said I'd done enough." She shook her head. "Maybe I should still sell it—believe me, no one could ever do enough."

She fell silent for a bit and Lee chose not to break it. She stared across at him. "We really were accomplishing a lot of good."

"What do you want, Faith? You want me to break out in applause?"

Her eyes flashed at him. "Why don't you get on that stupid motorcycle and get the hell out of my life?"

"All right," Lee said calmly, "if you thought so highly of what you were doing, how did you turn out to be a witness for the FBI?"

Faith covered her face with her hands, as though she were about to start bawling. When Faith finally looked at him she seemed so distressed, Lee felt his anger slip away.

"For some time Danny had been acting strangely. I suspected that maybe someone was on to him. That scared the hell out of me. I didn't want to go to prison. I kept asking him what was wrong, but he wouldn't talk to me about it. He kept withdrawing, became more and more paranoid, finally even asking me to leave the firm. I felt so alone, for the first time in a long time. It was like I had lost my father again."

"So you went to the FBI, tried to cut a deal. You for Buchanan."

"No!" she exclaimed. "Never!"

"What, then?"

"About six months ago there was a lot of news coverage about the FBI breaking a major public corruption case, involving a defense contractor bribing several congressmen to help it win a large federal contract. A couple of employees at the defense contractor contacted the FBI and revealed what was going on. They were actually part of the conspiracy early on, but were granted immunity in exchange for their testimony and assistance. That sounded like a good deal to me. Maybe I could get a deal too. Since Danny wouldn't confide in me, I decided to go for it. The lead agent was named in the article: Brooke Reynolds. I called her.

"I didn't know what to expect from the FBI, but I knew one thing: I wouldn't tell them much right away, no names or anything, not until I saw what the lay of the land was. And I had leverage. They needed a live witness with a head full of dates, times, names, meetings, records of votes and agendas to make this work."

"And Buchanan was ignorant of all this?"

"I guess not, considering he hired someone to kill me."

"We don't know that he did."

"Oh, come on, Lee, who else could it be?"

Lee thought back to the other men he had seen at the airport. The device in the man's hand was a high-tech blowgun of sorts. Lee had seen a demonstration of one at a seminar on counterterrorism. The gun and ammo were constructed solely from plastic to allow passage through metal detectors. You hit the palm trigger and the air compression fired a tiny needle either tipped or filled with a deadly toxin, like thallium or ricin, or the all-time favorite of assassins, curare, because it reacted so damn fast in the body that there was no known antidote. In a crowd, the act could be carried out and the assassin gone before the victim fell dead.

"Go on," he said.

"I offered to bring Danny into the fold."

"And how did they react to that?"

"They made it very clear that Danny was going down."

"I'm not following your logic. If you *and* Buchanan were going to turn witness, who were the Feds going to prosecute: the foreign countries?"

"No. Their representatives didn't know what we were doing. As I said, the money didn't go directly to the governments. And it's not like CARE or the Catholic Relief Services or UNICEF would ever condone bribery. Danny was their unofficial and unpaid lobbyist-in-residence, but they had no idea what he was doing. He represented about fifteen such organizations. It was tough going. They all had their agendas, took a scattergun approach. They typically proposed hundreds of single-issue bills, instead of a few comprehensive ones. Danny got them organized, working together, sponsoring a small number of bills containing more comprehensive legislation. He taught them what they had to do to be more effective."

"So tell me exactly who were you going to testify against, then?"

"The politicians we paid off," she said simply. "They did it just for the money. It's not like they gave a damn about children with dead eyes living in Hepatitis Heaven. I saw it every day in their greedy faces. They just expected a rich reward—thought it was their due."

"Don't you think you're coming down a little heavy on these guys?"

"Why don't *you* stop being so naïve? How do you think people get elected in this country? They get elected by the groups who *organize* the voters, who shape citizens' decisions on who and what to vote for. And do you know who those groups are? They're big business and special interests, and the wealthy who fill the coffers of political candidates every year. Do you really think ordinary people attend five-thousand-dollar-a-plate dinners? And then do you really think these groups give all that money out of the goodness of *their* collective hearts? When the politicians get into office, you better believe they're expected to deliver."

"So you're saying all politicians in this country are corrupt. That still doesn't make what you did right."

"No? What congressman from the state of Michigan would vote to do anything to seriously hurt the automobile industry? How long do you think she'd be in office? Or high-tech in California? Or farmers in the Midwest? Or tobacco in the South? It's like a self-fulfilling prophecy in a way. Business and labor and other special interests have a lot at stake. They're focused, they have big dollars, they have PACs and lobbyists blasting their messages to Washington nonstop. Big and small business employ just about everybody. Those same people vote in elections. They vote their pocketbooks. Voilà, there's your big, dark conspiracy of American politics. I see Danny as the first visionary ever to outsmart greed and selfishness."

"But what about the foreign aid? If this story came out, wouldn't that kill the pipeline?"

"That's the thing! Can you imagine all the positive attention it would get? The poorest countries on earth forced to bribe greedy American politicians to get the help they so desperately needed because it was unavailable any other way. You get stories like that in the media, then maybe some real, substantive changes would be made."

"That all sounds pretty far-fetched. I mean, come on."

"Maybe so, but my options weren't exactly flowing over. It's real damn easy to second-guess, Lee."

Lee sat back as he mulled this over. "Okay, okay. Do you *really* think Buchanan would try to kill you?"

"We were partners, friends. Actually, more than that. In many ways he was like a father to me. I . . .

I just don't know. Maybe he found out I went to the FBI. He would think I betrayed him. That could have driven him over the edge."

"There's a major problem with the theory that Buchanan is behind all this."

She looked over at him curiously.

"I *hadn't reported back* to Buchanan, remember? So unless he has someone else working for him, he doesn't know you're dealing with the FBI. And it takes time to set up a professional-caliber hit. You can't just call your local shooter and ask him to pop somebody for you and charge it to your Visa."

"But he might have known a hired killer already, and then he planned to somehow set you up for the murder."

Lee was shaking his head before she finished. "He would have had no idea I would be there that night. And if you had been killed, he'd have the problem of me finding out about it and maybe going to the police with the result that everything gets traced back to him. Why bring all that misery on himself? Think about it, Faith, if Buchanan was planning to kill you, he would not have hired me."

She slumped in a chair. "My God, what you're saying makes perfect sense." Terror seeped into Faith's eyes as she thought about what all this meant. "Then you're saying . . . ?"

"I'm saying that somebody else wants you dead."

"Who? Who?" She almost shouted this at him.

"I don't know," he said.

Faith abruptly stood and stared into the fire. The shadows of the flames lapped against her face. When she spoke her voice was calm, almost resigned. "Do you see your daughter much?"

"Not much. Why?"

"I thought marriage and kids could wait. And then months turned to years and years to decades. And now this."

"You're not in your golden years yet."

She looked at him. "Can you tell me I'll be alive tomorrow, a week from tomorrow?"

"Nobody has that guarantee. We can always go to the FBI, and now maybe we should."

"I can't do that. Not after what you've just told me."

He stood and gripped her shoulder. "What are you talking about?"

She moved away from him. "The FBI won't let me bring Danny in. Either he goes to jail or I do. When I thought he was behind trying to have me killed, I probably would have gone back and testified. But I can't do that now. I can't be part of him going to prison."

"If there hadn't been an attempt on your life, what were you going to do?"

"I was going to give them an ultimatum. If they wanted my cooperation, then Danny would have to be given immunity."

"And if they turned you down, like they did?"

"Then Danny and I would have been long gone. Somehow." She stared directly at him. "I'm not going back. For a lot of reasons. Not wanting to die being right at the top."

"And exactly where the hell does that leave me?"

"This isn't such a bad place, is it?" Faith said weakly.

"Are you crazy? We can't stay here forever."

"Then we better think of another place to run to."

"And what about my home? My life? I *do* have a family. Do you expect me to just kiss it all good-bye?"

"Whoever wants me dead will assume you know everything I do. You won't be safe."

"That's *my* decision, not yours."

"I'm sorry, Lee. I never thought anyone else would be dragged into this. Especially not someone like you."

"There has to be another way."

She headed for the stairs. "I'm very, very tired. And what else is there to talk about?"

"Dammit, I can't just walk away and start over."

Faith was halfway up the stairs. She stopped, turned and looked down at him.

"Do you think things will look better in the morning?" she asked.

"No," said Lee frankly.

"Which is why there's nothing left for us to talk about. Good night."

"Why do I think you made your decision not to go back a long time ago? Like the minute you met me."

"Lee—"

"You sucker me into going with you, pull that stupid stunt at the airport and now I'm trapped too. Thanks a helluva lot, lady."

"I didn't plan it like this! You're wrong."

"And you really expect me to believe you?"

"What do you want me to say?"

Lee stared up at her. "Granted it's not much, but I like my life, Faith."

"I'm sorry." She fled upstairs.

CHAPTER 33

L<small>EE</small> GRABBED A SIX-PACK OF R<small>ED</small> D<small>OG</small> FROM THE refrigerator and slammed the side door on his way out. He stopped at the Honda, wondering whether he should just climb on the big machine and run until his gas, money or sanity were gone. Then another possibility occurred to him. He could go to the Feds alone. Turn Faith in and claim ignorance about all of this. And he *was* ignorant. He hadn't done anything wrong. And he owed the woman nothing. In fact, she had been a source of misery, terror and near-death experiences. Turning her in should be an easy decision. So why the hell wasn't it?

He went out the rear gate and onto the walkway leading past the dunes. Lee intended to go down to the sand, watch the ocean and drink beer until either his mind ceased to function or he came up with a

brilliant plan that would save them both. Or at least
him. For some reason, he turned to look back at the
house for a moment. The light was on in Faith's bedroom. The mini-blinds were down but not closed.

As Faith came into view, Lee stiffened. She didn't
close the blinds. She moved through the room, disappeared into the bathroom for a minute and then
reappeared. As she started to undress, Lee looked
around to see if anyone was watching him watching
her. The police responding to a Peeping Tom call
would put the finishing touches on a spectacular day
in the charmed life of Lee Adams. The other homes
were dark, however; he could safely continue his
voyeurism. Her shirt came off first, then her pants.
She kept shedding clothes until all the window was
filled with skin. And she didn't slip into any pajamas
or even a T-shirt. Apparently this highly paid lobby-
ist-turned-Joan-of-Arc slept in the raw. Lee had a
fairly clear view of things the towel had only hinted
at. Maybe she knew he was out here and was putting
on a peep show for him. What, as compensation for
destroying his life? The bedroom light went out and
Lee popped a beer, turned and headed for the beach.
The show was over.

He had finished the first beer by the time he hit the
sand. The tide was starting to roll in, and he didn't
have to venture far to be in water past his ankles. He
cracked another beer and went in farther, up to his
knees. The water was freezing, but he went in farther

still, almost to his crotch, and then stopped, for a practical reason: A wet pistol wasn't particularly useful.

He sloughed back to the sand, dropped the beer, slipped off his waterlogged sneakers and started to run. He was tired, but his legs moved seemingly of their own accord, his limbs scissoring, his breath coming in great chunks of foggy air. He did a quick mile, one of his fastest ever, it seemed to him. Then he dropped to the sand, sucking oxygen from the damp air. He felt hot and then chilled. He thought about his mother and father, his siblings. He envisioned his daughter Renee when she was young, falling off her great horse and calling for Daddy, her cries finally dying away to nothing when he did not come. It was as though his flow of blood had been reversed; it was all backing up, not knowing where to go. He felt the walls of his body giving way, unable to hold everything inside.

He stood on shaky legs, jogged unsteadily back to the beer and his shoes. He sat on the sand for a while, listened to the ocean scream at him and downed another two cans of Red Dog. He squinted into the darkness. It was funny. A few beers and he could see clearly the end of his life at the edge of the horizon. Always wondered when it was going to happen. Now he knew. Forty-one years, three months and fourteen days and the Man upstairs had pulled his ticket. He looked to the sky, waved. *Thanks a lot, God.*

He rose and moved on to the house but didn't go inside. Instead he went to the enclosed courtyard, put his pistol on the table, stripped off all his clothes and dived into the pool. The water temperature, he figured, hovered around eighty-five degrees. His chills quickly disappeared and he went under, touched bottom, did an awkward handstand, blowing freshly chlorinated water out his nostrils, and then floated on the surface, staring at a sky smeared with clouds. He swam some more, practiced his crawl and breast strokes and then drifted over to the side and downed another beer.

He crawled up on the pool deck and thought of his ruined life and of the woman who had done it to him. He dived back in, did another few laps and then climbed out of the pool for good. He looked down, surprised. That was a real kicker. He looked up at the dark window. Was she asleep? How could she be? How in the hell could she be, after all this?

Lee decided he would find out for certain. No one could screw up his life and then fall into peaceful sleep. He looked down at himself again. Shit! He glanced at his soggy, sandy clothes and then up at the window. He finished another can of beer in quick gulps, his pulse seemingly spiking with each swallow. He wouldn't need the threads. He'd leave his pistol down here too. If things got out of hand, he didn't want lead to start flying. He pitched the last can of Red Dog over the fence, unopened. Let the birds pry it open and get a buzz. Why should he have all the fun?

He opened the side door quietly and took the stairs two at a time. He thought about kicking her bedroom door in but found it unlocked. He pushed the door open, peered in, letting his eyes adjust to the darkness here. He could make her out on the bed, one long hump. *One long hump.* To his alcohol-saturated mind, that phrase was immensely funny. He took three quick strides and was next to the bed.

Faith stared up at him. "Lee." It wasn't a question, how she said it. It was a simple statement that he didn't know the meaning of.

He knew she could see he was naked. Even in the darkness he trusted she could see he was fully aroused. With a sudden thrust of his arm he stripped the cover off her.

"Lee?" she said again, this time a question.

He looked down at the fine curves and softness of her naked body. His pulse rose, the blood rocketed through his veins, delivering devilish potency to a man severely wronged. He roughly bulled between her legs, flopped down chest-to-chest. She made no move to resist, her body limp. He started to kiss her on the neck and then stopped. It was not that sort of thing. No tenderness. He clenched her wrists hard.

She just lay there, saying nothing, not telling him to stop. This angered him. He breathed heavily in her face. He wanted her to know it was the beer, not her.

He wanted her to feel, to know this was not about her or how she looked or how he felt about her or anything else. He was a red-eyed drunken sonofabitch and she was easy meat. That was all. He loosened his grip. He wanted her to scream, to slug him as hard as she could. Then he would stop. But not before.

Her voice broke through the sounds of what he was doing. "I'd appreciate if you'd get your elbows off my chest."

He wouldn't stop, however, kept going. Hard elbow against soft tissue. The king and the peasant. *Give it to me, Faith. Clean my clock.*

"You don't have to do it like this."

"Whad'cha have in mind?" he slurred back. Navy shore leave in New York City was the last time he had even come close to being this drunk. Intense pain clacked against his temples. Five beers and a few glasses of wine and he was pretty damn well blitzed. God, he was getting old.

"Me on top. You're obviously too intoxicated to know what you're even doing." Her tone was blunt, reproachful.

"On top? Always the boss, even between the sheets? The hell with you." He squeezed her wrists so tightly his thumbs and index fingers touched together. To her credit she didn't even make a whimper, though he could sense the pain coursing through her in how her body tensed under him. He pawed her breasts and buttocks, roughly pummeled her legs and torso. He

made no move, though, to enter her. And it wasn't because he was too drunk to accomplish the mechanics;
it was because not even alcohol could make him do
that to a woman. He kept his eyes closed, didn't want
to look at her. But he dipped his face to hers. Lee
wanted Faith to smell the stink of his sweat, to soak
in the barley and hops base of his lust.

"I just thought you might enjoy it more, that's all,"
she said.

"Dammit!" he roared. "Are you just gonna let me
do this?"

"Would you have me call the police?"

Her voice was like a twirling drill bit against his
already throbbing skull. He hovered over her, arms
locked, the cords of his triceps bulging.

He felt a tear escape his eye, touch his cheek, like
a single wandering snowflake—homeless, just like
him. "Why aren't you kicking the shit out of me,
Faith?"

"Because it's not your fault."

Lee started to feel sick to his stomach, his arms
weakening. She moved her arm, and he let it go, releasing her without Faith having to say a word. She
touched his face, very gently, like a feather dropped
from the sky. With a simple motion she rubbed the
single tear away. When she spoke, her voice was
hoarse. "Because I took your life."

He nodded in understanding. "So if I run with you,
do I get this every night? My little dog biscuit?"

"If that's what you want." She suddenly took her hand away, let it drop to the bedding.

He made no move to take it again.

He finally opened his eyes and stared down at the numbing sadness in her gaze, the lingering pain in the tightness of her neck and face; pain he had inflicted and she had taken, silently; the outline of her own hopeless tears against pale cheeks. They all were like searing heat that somehow flashed right past his skin, collided with his heart, vaporizing it.

He pulled himself off her, staggered into the bathroom. He barely made it to the toilet, where the beer and dinner came out much faster than it had gone in. Then Lee passed out on the very expensive Italian tile floor.

The tingle of the cold washcloth against his forehead brought him around. Faith was behind him, cradling him. She seemed to be wearing some kind of long-sleeved T-shirt. He could make out her long, muscular calves and her skinny, curved toes. Lee felt a thick towel across his middle. He was still nauseous, and cold, his teeth chattering. She helped him sit up and then stand, her arm around his waist. He was wearing a pair of Jockeys. She must have done it; he wouldn't have been capable. As it was, he felt like he'd been hog-tied to a whirlybird for about two days. Together they made it back to the bed and she helped him in, covering him with the sheet and comforter.

"I'll sleep in another room," she said softly.

He said nothing, refusing to open his eyes once more.

He could hear her move to the door. Right before she left, he said, "I'm sorry, Faith." He swallowed; his tongue felt big as a damn pineapple.

Before she closed the door, he heard her say so very quietly, "You won't believe this, Lee, but I'm more sorry than you."

BROOKE REYNOLDS LOOKED CALMLY AROUND
the interior of the bank. It had just opened and there
were no other customers in the branch. In another
life she might have been casing the place for future
robbery. The thought actually brought a rare smile
to her face. She had several scenarios she could
have played out, but the very young man sitting behind the desk, with the title of assistant branch manager on a name plate in front of him, had decided the
matter.

He looked up as she approached. "Can I help you?"

His eyes grew appreciably larger when the FBI creds
came out, and he sat up much straighter, as though attempting to show her that he indeed had a backbone
beneath the boyish facade. "Is there a problem?"

"I need your assistance, Mr. Sobel," Reynolds said,

eyeing the name on the brass plate. "It has to do with an ongoing Bureau investigation."

"Of course, certainly, whatever I can do," he said.

Reynolds sat down across from him and spoke in a quiet, direct manner. "I have a key here that fits a safe-deposit box at this branch. It was obtained during the investigation. We think whatever's in the box might lead to serious consequences. I need to get inside that box."

"I see. Well, um—"

"I have the account statement with me, if that'll help."

Bankers loved paper, she knew; and the more numbers and statistics, the better. She handed it across to him.

He looked down at the statement.

"Do you recognize the name Frank Andrews?" she asked.

"No," he said. "But I've only been at this branch for a week. Bank consolidation, it never ends."

"I'm sure; even the government is cutting way back."

"I hope not with you people. Lot of crime out there."

"I guess, being in bank management, you see a lot."

The young man looked smug and sipped his coffee. "Oh, the stories I could tell you."

"I bet. Is there any way to tell how often Mr. Andrews visited the box?"

"Absolutely. We transfer those logs to the computer now." He punched in the account number on his computer and waited while it crunched the data. "Would you like some coffee, Agent Reynolds?"

"Thanks, no. How large a box is it?"

He glanced at the statement. "From the monthly fee, it's our deluxe, double width."

"I guess it can hold a lot."

"They're very roomy." He leaned forward and spoke in a low voice. "I bet this has to do with drugs, doesn't it? Laundering, that sort of thing? I've taken a class on the subject."

"I'm sorry, Mr. Sobel, it's an ongoing investigation, and I really can't comment. You understand."

He quickly leaned back. "Absolutely. Sure. We all have rules—you wouldn't believe what we have to deal with at this place."

"I'm sure. Anything come up on the computer?"

"Oh, right." Sobel looked at the screen. "He's actually been in here quite a bit. I can print the log out for you, if you'd like."

"That would be a big help."

As they walked toward the vault a minute later, Sobel started looking nervous. "I'm just wondering if I should check upstairs first. I mean, I'm sure they'd have no problem and all, but still, they're incredibly strict with safe-deposit box access."

"I understand, but I thought the assistant branch manager would have the authority. I won't be taking anything out, just reviewing the contents. And depending on what I find, the box may have to be impounded. It's not the first time the Bureau's had to do this. I'll take full responsibility. Don't worry."

That seemed to relieve the young man and they proceeded into the vault. He took Reynolds's key and his own master and pulled out the large box.

"We have a private room where you can look at it."

He showed her into the small room and Reynolds closed the door. She took a deep breath and noticed that her palms were sweaty. In this box might be something that could shatter any number of lives and perhaps careers. She slowly raised the lid. What she saw made her swear under her breath.

The cash was neatly bundled with thick rubber bands, old, not new bills. She did a quick count. Tens of thousands. She put the lid back down.

Sobel was standing outside the booth when she opened the door. He returned the box to the vault.

"Can I see the sign-in register for this box?"

He showed her the signature log. It was Ken Newman's handwriting; she knew it well. A murdered FBI agent and a box full of cash under an alias. God help them.

"Did you find anything helpful?" Sobel asked.

"I need this box impounded. Anyone shows up wanting to get inside, you're to call me immediately at these numbers." She handed him her card.

"This is serious, isn't it?" Sobel suddenly looked

very unhappy that he had been assigned to this branch.

"I appreciate your help, Mr. Sobel. I'll be in touch."

Reynolds returned to her car and drove as quickly as possible toward Anne Newman's house. She called from her car and confirmed the woman would be home. The funeral was scheduled to take place in three days. It would be a big affair, with top officials from the Bureau as well as law enforcement agencies from across the country attending. The funeral motorcade would be especially long and would pass between columns of somber, respectful federal agents and men and women in blue. The FBI buried its agents who died in the line of duty with the great honor and dignity they deserved.

"What did you find out, Brooke?" Anne Newman wore a black dress, her hair was nicely styled, and there was a touch of makeup on her face. Reynolds could hear talk coming from the kitchen. There were two cars parked out front when she had arrived. Probably family or friends offering condolences. She also noted platters of food on the dining room table. Cooking and condolences seemed, ironically, to go hand in hand; grief was better digested on a full stomach, apparently.

"I need to see records of your and Ken's bank accounts. Do you know where they are?"

"Well, Ken always handled the finances, but I'm sure they're in his office." She led Reynolds down the hallway and they went into Ken Newman's home office.

"Do you have more than one bank you deal with?"

"No. That much I do know. I always get the mail. It's just the one bank. And we only have a checking account, no savings. Ken said the interest they paid was a joke. He was really good about money. We own some good stocks, and the kids have their college accounts."

While Anne looked for the records, Reynolds idly glanced around the room. Stacked on one bookshelf were numerous hard plastic containers in various colors. While she had noted the coins encased in clear plastic on her previous visit, she hadn't really focused on these.

"What's in those containers?"

Anne looked at where she was pointing. "Oh, those are Ken's sports cards. Coins too. He was really good at it. He even took a course and became certified to grade both cards and coins. Just about every weekend he was at some show or another." She pointed up to the ceiling. "That's why there's a fire detector in here. Ken was really afraid of fire, in this room especially. All that paper and plastic. It could go up in a minute."

"I'm surprised he found the time for collecting."

"Well, he made the time. He really loved it."

"Did you or the kids ever go with him?"

"No. He never asked us to."

Her tone made Reynolds drop that line of inquiry. "I hate to ask this, but did Ken have life insurance?"

"Yes. A lot."

"At least you won't have to worry about that. I know it's little enough consolation, but so many people never think about those things. Ken obviously wanted you all to be taken care of if anything happened to him. Acts of love often speak louder than words." Reynolds was sincere, yet that last statement had sounded so incredibly lame that she decided to shut her mouth on the subject.

Anne pulled out a three-inch red notebook and handed it to Reynolds.

"I think this is what you're looking for. There are more in the drawer. This is the most current one."

Reynolds looked down at the binder. There was a laminated label affixed to the front flap of the notebook indicating that it contained checking account statements for the current year. She flipped it open. The statements were neatly labeled and organized chronologically by month, the most recent month on top.

"The canceled checks are in the other drawer. Ken kept them divided by year."

Damn! Reynolds kept her financial records stuffed in an assortment of drawers in her bedroom and even in the garage. Tax time at the Reynolds household was an accountant's worst nightmare.

"Anne, I know you have company. I can look through these by myself."

"You can take them with you if you want."

"If you don't mind, I'll look at them here."

"Okay. Would you like something to drink or eat? Lord knows we've got plenty of food. And I just put on a fresh pot of coffee."

"Actually, coffee would be great, thanks. Just a little cream and sugar."

Anne suddenly looked nervous. "You still haven't told me if you found out anything."

"I want to make absolutely sure before I say anything. I don't want to be wrong." As Reynolds looked into the poor woman's face, she felt tremendous guilt. Here she was letting the man's wife unknowingly assist her in possibly tarnishing her husband's memory.

"How are the kids holding up?" Reynolds asked, doing her best to shake this traitorous feeling.

"How any children would be, I suppose. They're sixteen and seventeen, so they understand things better than a five-year-old would. But it's still hard. For all of us. Only reason I'm not still bawling is that I ran out of tears this morning. I sent them to school. I decided it couldn't be any worse than sitting around here while a parade of people came through talking about their dad."

"You're probably right."

"You can only do the best you can. I knew there was always the possibility. God, Ken was an agent for twenty-four years. The only time he ever got hurt on duty was when his car got a flat and he wrenched his back changing the tire." Anne smiled briefly at this memory. "He was even talking about retirement. Maybe moving away when the kids were both in college. His mother lives in South Carolina. She's getting to the age where she needs some family close by."

Anne looked like she might start crying again. If she did, Reynolds wasn't sure she wouldn't join her, given her own mental state right now.

"You have children?"

"Boy and girl. Three and six."

Anne smiled. "Oh, still babies."

"I understand it gets tougher as they get older."

"Well, let's put it this way, it gets more complex. You go from spitting, biting, potty-training, to battles over clothes, boys, money. About age thirteen they suddenly can't stand being around Mom and Dad. That one was tough, but they finally came back. Then you worry yourself sick over alcohol and cars and sex and drugs."

Reynolds managed a weak smile. "Gee, I can't wait."

"How long have you been with the Bureau?"

"Thirteen years. Joined after one incredibly boring year as a corporate lawyer."

"It's a dangerous business."

Reynolds stared at her. "It certainly can be."

"You're married?"

"Technically, yes, but in a couple of months, no."

"Sorry to hear that."

"Believe me, it's best all around."

"You're keeping the children?"

"Absolutely."

"That's good. Children belong with their mothers, I don't care what the politically correct folk say."

"In my case, I wonder—I work long, unpredictable hours. All I know is that my children belong with me."

"You say you have a law degree?"

"From Georgetown."

"Lawyers make good money. And it's not nearly as dangerous as being an FBI agent."

"I suppose not." Reynolds finally realized where this was going.

"You might want to think about a career change. Too many nuts out there now. And too many guns. When Ken started at the Bureau, there weren't kids just out of diapers running around with machine guns shooting people down like they were in some damn cartoon."

Reynolds had no answer for that. She just stood there hugging the notebook to her chest, thinking of her kids.

"I'll bring your coffee."

Anne closed the door behind her and Reynolds sank into the nearest chair. She was having a sudden vision of her body being put inside a black pouch while the palm reader delivered the bad news to her bereaved children. *I told your mother so.* Shit! She shook off these thoughts and opened the notebook. Anne returned with her coffee, and then, left to herself, Reynolds made considerable progress. What she found out was very disturbing.

For at least the last three years, Ken Newman had made deposits, all in cash, to his checking account. The amounts were small—a hundred dollars here, fifty there—and they were made at random times. She pulled out the log Sobel had given her and ran her eye down the dates Newman had visited the safe-deposit box. Most of them corresponded with the dates he had also deposited cash into his checking account. Visit the box, put fresh cash in, take some old cash out and deposit it in the family bank account, she surmised. She also figured he would have gone to another bank branch to deposit the money. He couldn't very well take cash out of his box as Frank Andrews and deposit it as Ken Newman, all at the same branch.

It all added up to a significant amount of money, yet not a vast fortune. The thing was, the total balance of the checking account was never very large because there were always checks written on the account that depleted this balance. Newman's FBI payroll checks were on direct deposit, she noted. And there were numerous checks written to a stock brokerage firm. Reynolds found those records in another file drawer and quickly determined that while Newman was far from wealthy, he'd had a nice stock portfolio going, and the records showed he religiously added to it. With the long bull market still steaming along, his investments had grown considerably.

Except for the cash deposits, what she was looking at wasn't really that unusual. He had saved money and invested it well. He wasn't wealthy, but he was comfortable. Dividends from the investment account were also deposited to the Newmans' checking account, further muddling the income picture. Simply put, it would be difficult to conclude that there was anything suspicious about the agent's finances unless one really took a very close look. And unless one knew about the safe-deposit box cash, the amount of money seemingly at issue just didn't warrant that level of scrutiny.

The confusing thing was the amount of cash she had seen in the safe-deposit box. Why keep that much in the box where it was earning no interest? What puzzled her almost as much as the cash was what she *wasn't* finding. When Anne came to check on her, she decided to ask her directly.

"I'm not finding any mortgage or credit card payments recorded here."

"We don't have a mortgage. That is, we did, a thirty-year one, but Ken made extra payments and finally paid it off early."

"Good for him. When was that?"

"About three or four years ago, I think."

"What about credit cards?"

"Ken didn't believe in them. What we bought, we

bought with cash. Appliances, clothes, even cars. We never bought new, only used."

"Well, that's smart. Saves a ton in finance charges."

"Like I said, Ken was really good with the money."

"If I'd known how good, I would've had him help me."

"Do you need to look at anything else?"

"One more thing, I'm afraid. Your tax returns for the last couple of years, if you have them."

The large amount of cash in the box made sense now to Reynolds. If Newman paid cash for everything, then he would have no need to deposit it in his checking account. Of course, for things like the mortgage, the utilities and the phone bill, he needed to write a check, so he would have to deposit cash to cover those checks. And this also meant that for the money he didn't deposit into his checking account there was no record that he ever had the money in the box at all. Cash was cash, after all. And that meant that the IRS would have no way of knowing Newman ever had it either.

He wisely hadn't changed his lifestyle. Same house, no fancy cars, and he hadn't gone on the insane shopping binges that had toppled so many thieves. And with no mortgage or credit card payments, he had a lot of free cash flow; on a cursory examination, this would seem to explain the ability to make the regular stock investments. Someone would have to really dig as Reynolds had to uncover the truth.

Anne found tax returns for the last six years in the

metal filing cabinet standing against one wall. These were as well organized as the rest of the man's financial records. A quick look at the returns for the last three years confirmed Reynolds's suspicions. The only income listed was Newman's FBI salary and some miscellaneous investment interest and dividends and bank interest.

Reynolds put the files back and slipped on her coat. "Anne, I'm so sorry I had to come and do all this in the middle of everything you're having to deal with."

"I asked *you* for help, Brooke."

Reynolds felt another stab of guilt. "Well, I don't know how much help I've been."

Anne gripped her arm. "Now can you tell me what's going on? Has Ken done anything wrong?"

"All I can tell you right now is that I found some things I can't explain. I won't lie to you, they are very troubling."

Anne slowly took her hand away. "I guess you'll have to report what you've found."

Reynolds stared at the woman. Technically what she should do was go directly to OPR and tell them everything. The Office of Professional Responsibility was officially under the umbrella of the Bureau but was actually run by the Department of Justice. OPR investigated allegations of misconduct by Bureau personnel. They had a reputation for being very thorough. An OPR investigation could put a scare into even the toughest FBI agent.

Yes, from a simple technical point of view, it was a no-brainer. If life could only be so simple. The devastated woman standing before Reynolds made her decision much less simple. In the end she went with her human side and put aside the Bureau manual for now. Ken Newman would be buried a hero. The man had been an agent for over two decades; he at least deserved that.

"At some point, yes, I'll have to report my findings. But not right now." She paused and gripped the woman's hand. "I know when the funeral is. I'll be there with everyone else, paying our respects to Ken."

Reynolds gave Anne a reassuring hug and then walked out, her mind whirling so fast she felt a little dizzy.

If Ken Newman was on the take, he had been doing it for a while. Was he the leak on Reynolds's investigation? Had he sold out other investigations as well? Was he just a freelancing mole selling to the highest bidder? Or was he a regular snitch working for the same party? If so, why was such a party interested in Faith Lockhart? There were foreign interests involved. Lockhart had told them that much. Was that the key? Was Newman working for a foreign government all this time, a foreign government that was also coincidentally caught up in Buchanan's scheme?

She sighed. The whole thing was snowballing into something so big, she halfway felt like running home and pulling the covers over her head. Instead she would get in her car, drive to the office and continue chipping away at this case, as she had hundreds of others over the years. She had won more than she had lost. And that was the best anyone in her line of work could ever hope for.

CHAPTER 35

LEE HAD AWOKEN VERY LATE WITH THE MOTHER of all hangovers and decided to run it off. At first, each of his strides on the sand sent lethal darts through his brain. Then, as he loosened up, breathed the chilly air, felt the salty wind on his face, at about the one-mile point in his run, the effects of his crushed grape and Red Dog shooters disappeared. When he got back to the beach house, he went around to the pool and retrieved his clothes and his gun. He sat in a sling chair for a while, letting the sun warm him. When he went back inside, he smelled coffee and eggs.

Faith was in the kitchen, pouring a cup of coffee. She had on jeans and a short-sleeved shirt and was barefoot. When she saw him come in, she pulled out another mug and filled it. For a moment, this simple act of companionship pleased him. And then his actions of the night before washed that feeling away, like ocean waves brutally wiping out sand castles.

"I figured you'd sleep all day," she said. Her tone was excessively casual, he thought, and she didn't look at him when she spoke.

This qualified for the most awkward moment in Lee's entire life. What was he supposed to say? *Hey, sorry about that little sexual assault thing last night.*

He came into the kitchen area, fingered the mug, half hoping the large lump in his throat would end up strangling him to death. "Sometimes the best remedy for doing something incredibly stupid and inexcusable is to run until you drop." He glanced at the eggs. "Smells good."

"Doesn't compare to the meal you made last night. But then again, I'm no whiz in the kitchen. I guess I'm a room-service kind of girl. But I'm sure you already figured that out." As she moved over to the stove, he noted she walked with a slight limp. He also couldn't fail to notice the bruises on her uncovered wrists. He laid the pistol down on the counter before he could impulsively use it to blow his brains out.

"Faith?"

She didn't turn around, just kept scrambling the eggs around in the pan.

"If you want me to leave, I'll leave," said Lee.

While she seemed to consider this, he decided to say what he had been thinking during his run.

"What happened last night, what I *did* to you last night, there's no excuse for. I've never, ever done anything like that in my life. That's not who I am. I can't blame you if you don't believe that. But it's the truth."

She suddenly turned to him, her eyes glistening. "Well, I can't say I hadn't imagined something happening between us, even in the nightmare we're in. I just didn't think it would be like that. . . ." Her voice broke off and she just as quickly turned away from him.

He looked down and nodded slightly, her words doubly devastating to him. "You see, I'm in a bit of a dilemma here. My gut and my conscience tell me to get out of your life so you won't have to be reminded of what happened last night every time you see me. But I don't want to leave you alone with all this. Not when someone's out to kill you."

She turned the burner off and set out two plates, shoveled the eggs on them, buttered two pieces of toast and put everything on the table. Lee didn't move. He just watched her, moving slowly, her cheeks wet from her tears. The bruises on her wrists were like permanent shackles around his soul.

He sat down across from her and picked at his eggs.

"I could have stopped you last night," she said bluntly. The tears slid down her cheeks and she made no attempt to wipe them away.

Lee felt his own eyes begin to burn with the beginnings of tears. "I wish to God you had."

"You were drunk. I'm not saying that's an excuse for what you did, but I also know you wouldn't have done it if you had been sober. And you also didn't go all the way. I choose to believe you would never sink so low as that. In fact, if I weren't absolutely sure of that, I would've shot you with your gun when you passed out." She paused, seemed to be searching for the right combination of words. "But maybe what I've done to you is much more awful than what you could have done to me last night." She pushed her plate away and looked out the window at what was shaping up to be a beautiful day.

When she next spoke, it was in a wistful, faraway tone that was curiously both hopeful and tragic. "When I was a little girl, I had my whole life planned out. I was going to be a nurse. And then a doctor. And I was going to get married and have ten kids. Dr. Faith Lockhart was going to save lives during the day and then come home to a wonderful man who loved her and be the perfect mother to her perfect children. After moving around all those years with my father, I just wanted *one* home. I'd live there the rest of my life. My children would always, always know where to find me. It seemed so simple, so . . . achievable, when I was only eight years old." She finally used her paper napkin to dab at her eyes, seeming only then to feel the wetness on her face.

She looked back at Lee. "But I have this life instead." Her gaze roamed the lovely room. "I actually had a pretty good run. Made a lot of money. What do I have to complain about? That's the American Dream, isn't it? Money? Power? Owning beautiful things? I even ended up doing a little good, even if I did it illegally. But then I went and ruined everything. The best of intentions, but I struck out in the end. Just like my father. You're right, the nut didn't fall far from the tree." She paused again, played with her silverware, precisely placing the fork and butter knife perpendicular to one another.

"I don't want you to leave." On this she rose, quickly crossed the room and then raced up the stairs.

Lee heard her bedroom door slam shut.

Lee took a deep breath, stood and was surprised to find his legs so rubbery. It wasn't from the run, he knew. He showered, changed and came back downstairs. Faith's door was still closed and he had no intention of interrupting whatever she was doing in there. With his nerves unraveling, he decided to spend an hour with the mundane task of thoroughly cleaning his gun. The downside to salt and water was that they were tough on weapons, and automatic pistols were notoriously finicky anyway. If the ammo wasn't of a very high quality, you could count on the thing misfiring and then jamming—or a little sand and grit could cause the same malfunction. And you couldn't clear an autopistol by simply pulling the trigger and bringing up a clean cylinder, as you would a revolver. By the time you got your gun all straightened out, you'd be dead. And with Lee's luck to date, it would happen right when he absolutely needed the thing to fire true and straight. However, on the plus side, the 9mm Parabellums fired by the compact Smith & Wesson had excellent stopping power. Whatever they hit would drop. He prayed he wouldn't have to use the gun, however. Because that would probably mean someone was shooting at him.

He reloaded the fifteen-shot magazine, inserted it in the grip and chambered a round. He clicked on the safety and holstered the gun. He thought about taking the Honda down to the store for a newspaper but decided he didn't quite have the energy or desire to undertake even such a simple task. He also didn't want to leave Faith alone. When she came downstairs, he wanted to be here.

When Lee went to get a drink of water at the kitchen sink, he glanced out the window and almost had a heart attack. Across the roadway, above a wall of tall, thick brush that ran about as far as the eye could see, suddenly exploding into his line of vision was a small plane! That's when Lee remembered the runway Faith had told him about. It was across from the house and shielded by the brush.

Lee hurried to the front door to watch the landing. By the time he got outside, the plane had already disappeared. Then whizzing above the top of the brush was the tail of the plane. It flashed in front of him and then continued past at a fast clip.

He went up on the second-story front porch and watched as the plane taxied to a stop and the passengers deplaned. A car was waiting to pick them up. Bags were off-loaded and stored in the car, which left with the passengers through a small paved opening in the brush not far from Faith's house. The pilot got out of the twin-prop plane, checked a few things and then climbed back in. A few minutes later the plane taxied to the other end of the runway and turned around. The pilot opened the throttle and came roaring down the runway in the same direction he had landed, and then lifted gracefully into the air. The plane headed out toward the water, made a turn and quickly disappeared into the horizon.

Lee went back inside and tried to watch some TV, while at the same time listening for Faith. After roaming through about a thousand channels, he concluded there was absolutely nothing worth watching, and he played a game of solitaire. He enjoyed losing so much, he played another dozen games, with the same result. He wandered downstairs and shot some pool in the game room. When lunchtime came around, he fixed a tuna sandwich and some beef barley soup and ate out on the deck overlooking the pool. He watched the same plane land once more around one o'clock. It shed its passengers and soared once more. He thought about knocking on Faith's door to see if she was hungry and then decided against it. He went for a swim in the pool and then lay on the cool concrete and caught some rays from the intense sun. He felt guilty every minute for enjoying it.

The hours passed, and when it started to grow dark, he began contemplating cooking dinner. He would go and get Faith this time, and make her eat. He was just about to head up the stairs when her door opened and she came out.

The first thing that caught his eye was what she was wearing: a white cotton dress, knee-length and clingy, paired with a light blue cotton sweater. Her legs were bare, and she wore simple sandals that managed to look very classy. Her hair was nicely styled; a touch of makeup highlighted her features and pale red lipstick completed the look. She held a small clutch purse. The sweater covered the bruises on her wrists. Probably why she had picked it, he thought. He was thankful that her limp seemed to be gone.

"Going out?" Lee asked.

"Dinner. I'm starving."

"I was going to make something."

"I'd rather eat out. I'm getting cabin fever."

"So where are you going?"

"Well, actually I thought *we* might go."

Lee looked down at his faded khakis, deck shoes and short-sleeved Polo shirt. "I look sort of ragged next to you."

"You look fine." She glanced at the holstered gun. "I'd leave the six-shooter behind, though."

He looked at her dress. "Faith, I'm not sure how comfortable you'll be on the Honda in that."

"The country club's only a half mile up the road. It has a public restaurant. I thought we could walk. Looks to be a beautiful evening."

Lee finally nodded, understanding that getting out made perfect sense, for a lot of reasons. "Sounds good. Give me a sec." He ran upstairs, slipped off his gun and put it in a drawer in his room. He splashed water on his face, wet down his hair a little, grabbed his jacket and joined Faith at the front door, where she was activating the alarm. They left the house and crossed the service road. Reaching the sidewalk, which ran parallel to the main road, they strolled along under a sky that had changed from blue to pink as the sun sank. Landscape lighting had come on in the common areas and so had the underground sprinklers. The sound of the pressurized water was soothing to Lee. The lighting lent a nice mood to the walk, he thought. The whole place seemed to possess almost an ethereal glow, as though they were in a perfectly lit scene from a movie.

Lee looked up in time to see a twin-prop airplane coming in for a landing. He shook his head.

"Scared the hell out of me the first time I saw that thing this morning."

"It would have scared me too, except the first time I came here I was flying on it. That's the last flight for the evening. It's getting too dark now."

They reached the restaurant, which was decorated with a distinctly nautical theme: a big ship's wheel at the front entrance, diving helmets hung on the wall, fish netting suspended from the ceiling, knotty pine walls, rope banisters and hand rails and an enormous aquarium filled with castles, plant life and an odd assortment of fish peeking out here and there. The servers were young, energetic and attired in cruise line uniforms. The one attending Faith and Lee's table was particularly bubbly. She took their drink orders. Lee opted for iced tea. Faith ordered a wine spritzer. That done, the waitress proceeded to sing the specials for the day in a pleasant if wavering alto. After she left, Faith and Lee looked at each other and had to laugh.

While they waited for their drinks, Faith looked around the room.

Lee shot her a glance. "See anybody you recognize?"

"No. I never really went out when I came down here. I was afraid I'd run into someone I knew."

"Stay cool. You look very different from Faith Lockhart." He looked her over. "And I should have said this before, but you look really . . . well, you really look pretty tonight. I mean really fine." He suddenly looked embarrassed. "Not that you don't look good all the time. I meant . . ." Thoroughly tongue-tied, Lee lapsed into silence, sat back and perused his menu.

Faith looked over at him, feeling just as awkward

as he did, she was sure, but a smile still eased across her lips. "Thank you."

They were there for two pleasant stolen hours, discussing innocuous subjects, telling stories of times past and learning more about each other. Since it was the off-season and a weekday, there were few other patrons. They finished their meal, then had coffee and shared a thick slice of coconut cream pie. They paid in cash and left a very generous tip, which would probably make their waitress sing all the way home.

Faith and Lee walked slowly back, enjoying the crisp night air and digesting their meals. Instead of going to the house, though, Faith led Lee down to the beach after dropping her purse off by the back door of the beach house. She slipped off her sandals and they continued their stroll on the sand. It was completely dark now, the wind light and refreshing, and they had the beach entirely to themselves.

Lee looked over at her. "Going out was a good idea. I really enjoyed myself."

"You can be very charming when you want to be."

He looked annoyed for a moment until he realized she was kidding him. "I guess going out together made for a fresh start of sorts too."

"That did cross my mind." She stopped and sat down on the beach, sinking her feet into the sand. Lee remained standing, looking out to the ocean.

"So what do we do now, Lee?"

He sat next to her, slipped off his shoes and curled his toes under the sand. "It would be great if we could stay here, but I don't think we can."

"Then where? I'm fresh out of houses."

"I've been thinking about that. I've got some good buddies in San Diego. Private investigators like me. They know everybody. If I ask, I'm sure they'll help us slip across the border into Mexico."

Faith didn't look very enthusiastic about that idea. "Mexico? And from there?"

Lee shrugged. "I don't know. We can maybe get some fake documents and use them to get to South America."

"South America? And you work the cocaine fields while I labor in a brothel?"

"Look, I've been there. It's not just drugs and prostitutes. We'll have lots of options."

"Two fugitives from justice with God knows who else after them?" Faith looked down at the sand and shook her head doubtfully.

"If you have a better idea, I'm listening," said Lee.

"I've got money. A lot of it in a numbered account in Switzerland."

He looked skeptical. "They really have those things?"

"Oh, yes. And all those global conspiracies you've probably heard about? Secret organizations ruling the planet? Well, they're all true." She smiled and tossed sand on him.

"Well, if the Feds search your home or office, will

they find records for it? If they know the account numbers, they can put a tag on it. Trace the money."

"The whole purpose of a Swiss numbered account is to ensure absolute confidentiality. If Swiss bankers ran around giving out that information to anyone who asked for it, their whole system sort of topples."

"The FBI isn't just anyone."

"Not to worry, I didn't keep any records. I have the access information with me."

Lee looked unconvinced. "So do you have to go to Switzerland to get the money? Because that would be, you know, sort of impossible."

"I went there to open the account. The bank appointed a fiduciary, a bank employee, with a power of attorney to handle the transaction in person. It's pretty elaborate. You have to show your access numbers, give positive ID, then provide your signature, which they compare with the one they have on file."

"So from then on you call the fiduciary and he does all that for you?"

"Right. I've done small transactions in the past, just to make sure it works. It's the same guy. He knows me and my voice. I give him the numbers and where I want the money to go. And it happens."

"You know you can't deposit it in Faith Lockhart's checking account."

"No, but I have a bank account down here under the name of SLC Corporation."

"And you're a signatory as an officer?"

"Yes, as Suzanne Blake."

"The problem is, the Feds know that name. Remember, from the airport."

"Do you know how many Suzanne Blakes there are in this country?"

Lee shrugged. "That's true."

"So at least we'll have money to live off. It won't last us forever, but it's something."

"Something is good."

They fell silent for a bit. Faith alternated between nervously looking at him and then out toward the ocean.

He glanced at her, having noticed her scrutiny. "What is it? Do I have coconut pie on my chin?"

"Lee, when the money comes, you can take half and leave. You don't have to come with me."

"Faith, we've already been through this."

"No, we haven't. I practically ordered you to come with me. I know it would be difficult to go back without me, but at least you'll have the money to go somewhere. Look, I can even call the FBI. I'll tell them you had no involvement. You were just blindly helping me. And that I gave you the slip. Then you can go back home."

"Thanks, Faith, but let's take it one step at a time. And I can't leave until I know you're safe."

"Are you sure?"

"Yes, I'm really sure. I won't go unless you tell me to. And then even if you do, I'll still stalk you, to make sure you're okay."

She reached out and took his arm. "Lee, I can never thank you enough for all you've done for me."

"Just consider me the big brother you never had."

The look they shared, though, held more than sibling affection. He looked down at the sand, trying to get his head straight. Faith looked back out at the water. When Lee looked over at her a minute later, Faith was moving her head from side to side and smiling.

"What are you thinking?" he asked.

She stood and looked down at him. "I'm thinking that I'd like to dance."

He stared up at her in amazement. "Dancing? How much *did* you have to drink?"

"How many nights do we have left here? Two? Three? Then it's off to play fugitive for the rest of our lives? Come on, Lee, last chance to party." She slipped off her sweater and let it fall to the sand. The white dress had spaghetti straps. She slipped them off her shoulders, gave him a heart-stopping wink and held out her hands for Lee to take. "Let's go, big boy."

"You're crazy, you truly are." However, Lee gripped her hands and stood. "Fair warning, I haven't danced in a long time."

"You're a boxer, right? Your footwork is probably better than mine. I'll lead first, and then you take over."

Lee took a few halting steps and dropped his hands. "This is silly, Faith. What if somebody's watching? They'll think we're nuts."

She looked at him stubbornly. "I've spent the last fifteen years of my life worrying about what everybody thought about everything. So right now, I don't give a damn about what anybody thinks about anything."

"But we don't even have any music."

"Hum a tune. Listen to the wind, it'll come."

And surprisingly it did. They started slowly at first, Lee feeling clumsy and Faith unused to leading. Then, as they started to get more familiar with each other's movements, they began making wider circles in the sand. After about ten minutes, Lee's right hand was perched comfortably on Faith's hip, hers was around his waist, and their other pair of hands were interlocked and held chest high.

Then they grew noticeably braver and started doing some spins and twirls and other moves reminiscent of Big Band swing and Lindy hop. It was difficult, even in the hard-packed sand, but they gave it an inspired effort. Anyone watching would have thought them either intoxicated or reliving their youth and having the time of their lives. And, in a way, both observations would have been true.

"I haven't done this since high school," Lee said, smiling. "Although Three Dog Night was the big thing back then, not Benny Goodman."

Faith said nothing as she twirled and dipped around him, her moves growing more and more daring, more and more seductive; a flamenco dancer in white flaming heat.

She hiked her skirt up to give herself more freedom of movement, and Lee felt his heart race at the sight of her pale thighs.

They even ventured out into the water, splashing mightily as they went about their increasingly intricate dance steps. They had some tumbles into the sand and even into the salty, chilly water, but they got back up and kept going. Occasionally a truly spectacular combination, perfectly executed, left them both breathless and grinning like schoolkids at a prom.

They finally reached the point where they both grew silent, their smiles faded and they drew closer to each other. The spins and twirls stopped, their heavy breaths eased and they found their bodies touching as their dance circles grew smaller. Finally they stopped altogether and simply stood there rocking slightly side to side, the last dance of the evening, arms around each other, faces close, eyes directly on one another as the wind whistled around them, the waves pitched and crashed hard, the stars and the moon watched from above.

Faith finally stepped away from him, her eyelids heavy, her limbs starting to once again erotically move to a silent tune.

Lee reached out to take her back. "I don't feel like dancing anymore, Faith." His meaning was crystal clear.

She reached out to him too, and then, quick as the snap of a whip, she shoved him hard in the chest and he flopped backward into the sand. She turned and ran, her peals of laughter descending over him as he looked after her, stunned. He grinned, jumped up and raced after her, catching her at the stairs going up to the beach house. He slung her over his shoulder and carried her the rest of the way, her legs and arms flailing in mock protest. They had forgotten the house alarm was set and went in the back door. Faith had to race like mad to the front door to disarm it in time.

"God, that was close. Like we really want the police coming by," she said.

"I don't want anybody coming by."

Gripping his hand tightly, Faith led Lee up to her bedroom. They sat on the bed in the darkness for a few minutes holding one another, gently rocking back and forth as though extending their movements on the beach to this more intimate place.

Finally she eased back from him, cupped his chin with her hand. "It's been a while, Lee. It's been a long time, in fact." Her tone was almost one of embarrassment, and Faith did feel embarrassed at this admission. She didn't want to disappoint him.

He stroked her fingers gently, held her gaze with his as the sounds of the waves reached them through the open window. It was comforting, she thought, the water, the wind, the touches of skin; a moment she may not experience again for a very long time, if ever.

"It'll never be easier for you, Faith."

This surprised her. "Why do you say that?"

Even in the darkness the glow of his eyes surrounded her, held her—protectively, she felt. The fifth-grade romance finally consummated? And yet she was with a man, not a boy. A unique man, in his own right. She looked him over. No, definitely not a boy.

"Because I can't believe you've ever been with a man who feels the way I do about you."

"Easy to say," she murmured, though in fact his words had touched her deeply.

"Not for me," Lee said.

These few words were spoken with such depth of sincerity, with not a trace of the glibness, the self-servedness of the world she had thrived in for the last fifteen years, that Faith honestly didn't know how to react. But the time for talk had passed. She found herself sliding Lee's clothes off, and then he disrobed her. He massaged her shoulders and neck as he did so. Lee's big fingers were surprisingly gentle. She would've expected them to be rough.

All of their movements were unhurried, natural, as though they had done this thousands of times over the course of a long, happy marriage, seeking just the right spots to work, to please the other.

They slid under the covers. Ten minutes later Lee slumped down, breathing heavy. Faith was under him, gasping for air as well. She kissed his face, his chest, his arms. Their sweat mingled, their limbs intertwined, they lay there talking and slowly kissing for another two hours, falling in and out of sleep as they did so. About three in the morning they made love again. And then both collapsed into deep, exhausted sleep.

CHAPTER 36

Reynolds was sitting at her desk when the phone call came. It was Joyce Bennett, the lawyer representing Reynolds in her divorce.

"We have a problem, Brooke. Your husband's attorney just called, ranting and raving about you hiding assets."

Brooke's face collapsed in disbelief. "Are you serious? Well, tell him to let me in on it. I could use the extra money."

"This isn't a joke. He faxed me some account statements he says he just discovered. Under the children's names."

"For God's sake, Joyce, those are the kids' college accounts. Steve knew about those. That's why I didn't list them with my assets. Besides, they only have a few hundred dollars in them."

"Actually, the statements I'm looking at show a balance of fifty thousand dollars in each."

Reynolds's mouth went dry. "That's not possible. There must be some mistake."

"The other troubling thing is that the accounts are set up as Uniform Transfer to Minor's Act accounts. That means they're revocable at the discretion of the donor and trustee. You're the listed trustee, and I'm assuming you would be the donor of the funds as well. In essence, it's your money. You should have told me about these, Brooke."

"Joyce, there was nothing to tell. I have no idea where that money came from. What do the statements show as the origin of funds?"

"Several wire transfers of roughly equal amounts. It doesn't show where they came from. Steve's attorney is threatening to go to court and claim fraud. Brooke, he also says he's called the Bureau."

Reynolds squeezed the phone and sat rigidly. "The Bureau?"

"You're sure you don't know where the money came from? How about your parents?"

"They don't have that kind of money. Can we trace the funds?"

"It's *your* account. I think you better do something. Keep me posted."

Reynolds hung up the phone and stared blankly at the papers on her desk, her mind reeling from this latest development. When the phone rang again a few minutes later, she almost didn't answer it. She knew who it was.

Paul Fisher spoke more coldly than ever to her. She was to come to the Hoover Building immediately. That was all he would tell her. As she walked down the stairs to the parking garage, her legs threatened to collapse under her several times. Every instinct she had told her she had just been summoned to her own professional execution.

The conference room at the Hoover Building was small and windowless. Paul Fisher was there, along with the ADIC, Fred Massey. Massey sat at the head of the table, twirling a pen between his fingers, his gaze locked on her. She recognized the two other people in the room: a Bureau lawyer and a senior investigator from OPR.

"Sit down, Agent Reynolds," Massey said firmly.

Reynolds sat. She wasn't guilty of anything, so why did she feel like Charlie Manson with a bloody knife in his sock?

"We have some things to discuss with you." He glanced at the Bureau lawyer. "I have to advise you, however, that you have the right to have counsel present, if you so wish."

She tried to act surprised, but couldn't really, not after the phone call from Joyce Bennett. Her forced reaction certainly increased her guilt in their eyes, she felt sure. She wondered about the timing of that phone call from Bennett. Not a big believer in conspiracies, Reynolds suddenly began to reconsider that stance.

"And why would I need counsel?"

Massey eyed Fisher, who turned to Reynolds. "We received a phone call from the attorney representing your husband in the divorce."

"I see. Well, I just received a call from my attorney, and I can assure you I'm as much in the dark as anyone else about how that money got into those accounts."

"Really?" Massey looked at her skeptically. "So you're saying it's a mistake that someone very recently dumped a hundred thousand dollars into accounts under your children's names, monies which are solely controlled by you?"

"I'm saying I don't know what to think. But I will find out, I can assure you."

"The timing, as you can understand, has us deeply troubled," Massey said.

"Not as troubled as me. It's my reputation at stake."

"Actually, it's the reputation of the Bureau we're concerned about," Fisher bluntly pointed out.

Reynolds gave him a cold stare and then looked back at Massey. "I don't know what's going on. Feel free to investigate; I've got nothing to hide."

Massey glanced down at a file in front of him. "Are you quite certain of that?"

Reynolds looked at the file. This was a classic interrogation technique. She had used it herself. Bluff the subject by suggesting you had incriminating evidence that would catch him in a lie and hope he'd cave. The only thing was, she didn't know if Massey was really bluffing or not. She suddenly knew what it was like to be on the other side of the interrogation. It wasn't fun.

"Am I quite certain of what?" she said, buying time.

"That you have nothing to hide?"

"I really resent that question, sir."

He tapped the file with his index finger. "You know what has deeply distressed me about Ken Newman's death? The fact that on the night he was murdered, he had taken your place. At your instruction. But for that order, he would be alive today. Would you?"

Reynolds's face turned red and she stood, towering over Massey. "Are you accusing me of being involved in Ken's murder?"

"Please sit down, Agent Reynolds."

"Are you?"

"I'm saying the coincidence, if it is one, has me concerned."

"It *was* a coincidence, since I didn't happen to know there was someone waiting there to kill him. If you recall, I showed up almost in time to stop it."

"Almost in time. That was convenient. Almost like a built-in alibi. A coincidence, or perfect timing? Perhaps too perfect timing?" Massey's gaze burned into her.

"I was working another case and finished sooner than I thought I would. Howard Constantinople can corroborate that."

"Oh, we plan to talk to Connie. You and he are friends, aren't you?"

"We're professional colleagues."

"I'm sure he wouldn't want to say anything that would implicate you in any way."

"I'm *sure* he'll tell you the truth if you just ask him."

"So you're saying there is no connection between Ken Newman's murder and the money showing up in your account?"

"Let me put it a little more strongly than that. I'm saying it's all bullshit! If I were guilty, why would I have anyone put a hundred grand into one of my accounts so close to the time Ken was killed? Don't you think that's a little obvious?"

"But it wasn't really your account, was it? It was in your children's names. And according to your personnel records, you're not due for a Bureau five-year check for another two years. I rather doubt the money would be in the account at that time, and by then I'm sure you'd have a good answer in case anyone did discover that money had once been there. The point is, if your husband's attorney hadn't dug it up, no one would know. That hardly qualifies as obvious."

"Okay, if it's not a mistake, then someone is setting me up."

"And who exactly would be doing that?"

"The person who killed Ken, and who tried to kill Faith Lockhart. Maybe he's afraid I'm getting too close."

"So Danny Buchanan is trying to set you up, is that what you're saying?"

Reynolds glanced at the Bureau lawyer and the representative from OPR. "Do they have clearance to hear this?"

"Your investigation has taken a backseat to these more recent charges," Fisher said.

Reynolds glared at him with rising anger. "Charges! They're unsubstantiated garbage."

Massey opened the file. "So are you saying that your *private* investigation into Ken Newman's finances is garbage?"

On this Reynolds froze and then abruptly sat down. She pressed sweaty palms against the table and tried to get her emotions under control. Her temper was not doing her any good. She was playing right into their hands. Indeed, Fisher and Massey exchanged what she saw as pleased glances at her obvious distress.

"We talked to Anne Newman. She told us everything you've done," Fisher said. "I can't even begin to tell you how many Bureau rules you've broken."

"I was trying to protect Ken and his family."

"Oh, please!" Fisher exclaimed.

"It's true! I was going to go to OPR, but not until after the funeral."

"That was so very considerate of you," Fisher said sarcastically.

"Why don't you go to hell, Paul."

"Agent Reynolds, keep a civil tongue in your head," Massey commanded.

Reynolds sat back and rubbed her forehead. "May I ask how you found out about what I was doing? Did Anne Newman come to you?"

"If you don't mind, we'll ask the questions." Massey leaned forward and made a pyramid with his fingers. "What exactly did you find in the safe-deposit box?"

"Cash. A lot. Thousands."

"And Newman's financial records?"

"A lot of unexplained income."

"We've also talked to the bank branch you visited. You told them not to allow access to the box to anyone except yourself. And you told Anne Newman not to tell anyone about it, not even anyone at the Bureau."

"I didn't want anybody getting to that money. It was material evidence. And I told Anne to keep quiet until I had a chance to dig further. It was for her own protection, until I found out who was behind it."

"Or did you want the time to get the money for yourself? With Ken dead and Anne Newman apparently not even aware her husband had the safe-deposit box, you would be the only one who knew the money was there." Massey stared directly at her; his tiny eyes resembled twin bullets coming for her.

Fisher piped in: "It's curious that when Newman dies you access a box with thousands of dollars in it that he had under a fake name, and about the same time, accounts controlled by you fill up with a hundred thousand dollars."

"If you're somehow trying to say I had Ken killed because of the money in the box, you're way off base. Anne called and asked for my help. I never knew Ken had a safe-deposit box until she told me about it. I had no idea what was in the box until after Ken was already dead."

"So you say," Fisher said.

"So I know," Reynolds replied hotly. She looked at Massey. "Am I being formally charged with anything?"

Massey sat back and put his hands behind his head. "You must realize how very, very bad this all looks. If you were sitting in my chair, what would your conclusions be?"

"I can see how you might have your suspicions. But if you just give me the chance—"

Massey closed his file and stood. "You're suspended, Agent Reynolds, effective immediately."

Reynolds was stunned. "Suspended? I haven't even been formally charged. You don't even have any specific evidence that I've done anything wrong. And you're suspending me?"

"You should be grateful it's not worse," Fisher said.

"Fred," Reynolds said, half rising from her chair, "I can understand your taking me off this assignment. You can transfer me somewhere else while you investigate, but don't suspend me. Everybody in the Bureau will assume I'm guilty. It's not right."

Massey's face did not soften at all. "Please turn in your credentials and sidearm to Agent Fisher. You are not to return to your office. And you are not to leave the area for any reason."

The blood drained from Reynolds's face and she fell back into her chair.

Massey went to the door. "Your highly suspicious actions, coupled with the murder of an agent and reports of unknown people impersonating FBI agents, do not allow me the option of merely reassigning you, Reynolds. If you're innocent as you claim, then you'll be reinstated with no loss in pay, seniority or responsibility. And I'll make absolutely certain there's no permanent damage to your reputation. If you're guilty, well, you know better than most what awaits you." Massey closed the door behind him.

Reynolds stood to leave, but Fisher blocked her way. "Creds and gun. Now."

Reynolds slipped them out and handed them over. It was as though she were giving up one of her children. She looked at Fisher's triumphant features. "Gee, Paul, try not to enjoy it so much. You'll look like less of a fool when I'm exonerated."

"Exonerated? You'll be lucky if you're not under arrest by day's end. But we want this case to be air-tight. And if you're thinking of running, we'll be watching. So don't even try."

"I wouldn't dream of it. I want to be here to see your face when I come and get my gun and badge back. Don't worry, I won't ask you to kiss my ass."

Reynolds walked down the hallway and out of the building, feeling as though every pair of eyes in the entire Bureau were fully upon her.

CHAPTER 37

LEE GOT UP BEFORE FAITH, SHOWERED, CHANGED his clothes and then stood next to the bed, watching her as she slept. For a few seconds he allowed himself to forget about everything except the wonderful night the two had spent together. He knew it had changed his life forever, and that thought scared him to death.

He went downstairs, moving a little slowly. Parts of him were aching that hadn't in a long time. And it wasn't just from the dancing. He went into the kitchen and made coffee. While it was brewing, he thought about last night. In his mind, Lee had made a very strong commitment to Faith Lockhart. Perhaps an old-fashioned sentiment to some, but sleeping with a woman meant you had deep feelings for her, at least as far as Lee was concerned.

He poured a cup of coffee and went out to sit on the deck off the kitchen. It was already late morning and a warm sunny day, but off in the distance, Lee could see darkening clouds approaching. Ahead of the storm was the twin-prop plane as it floated in for a landing with another load of passengers. Faith had told him that during the summer months, the planes might make ten or so trips a day. Now it was down to three: morning, noon and early evening. And so far none of the plane passengers had remained on this street. They had driven off to other places, which suited Lee just fine.

As he sipped his coffee, Lee concluded that he did have such feelings for Faith, even though he had only known her a few days. Stranger things had happened, he guessed. And their relationship had certainly begun on the shakiest of grounds. After all she had put him through, Lee knew he would be justified in hating the woman. And after what he had done to her that night, drunk or not, she would be right to loathe him. Did he love Faith Lockhart? He knew that right now he didn't want to be away from her. He wanted to protect her from harm. He wanted to hold her, spend every minute with her and, yes, have incredibly energetic sex with her as often as his body could manage. Did that constitute love?

On the other hand, she had participated in a bribery scheme involving government officials and was wanted by the FBI, among others. Yes, he

thought with a sigh, things had gotten very complicated indeed. Right before they were taking off to
God knew where. It wasn't like they could go to a
church or even a justice of the peace and get married.
*That's right, Father, we're the fugitive couple. Could you
please hurry it up?*

Lee rolled his eyes and slapped his forehead. Marriage! Good God, was he nuts? Maybe that was how
he felt, but what about Faith? Maybe she was into
one-night stands, although everything he had observed about the woman argued against such a conclusion. Did she love him? Maybe she was infatuated,
caught up in his role as her protector. Last night
could be explained away by alcohol, the intoxication
of the danger swirling around them or perhaps just
simple lust. And he wasn't going to ask her how she
felt. She had enough going on.

He focused on the immediate future. Was traveling cross-country on the Honda to San Diego the
best plan? Mexico and then South America? He felt
a pang of guilt when he thought of the family he
would be leaving behind. Then he thought about
something else: his reputation, what his family
would think. If he ran, he would be admitting guilt
of sorts. And if they did get caught while running,
who would believe them?

He slumped back in his chair and suddenly pondered a very different strategy. A few minutes before,
flight seemed the wisest choice. Faith, understand-

ably, didn't want to go back and help send Buchanan to prison. Lee really didn't have much interest in doing that either, not after hearing why the man had been bribing the politicians. In truth, Danny Buchanan probably should be sainted instead. That's when an idea started to form in his head.

Lee went back inside and picked up his cell phone from the coffee table. He had one of those mega-minute deals with no long distance or roaming charges, so that he rarely even used his hard-line phone anymore. It had voice mail, text mail, caller ID. It even had a news banner where you could check out late-breaking stories, or how your stocks were doing, not that he had any.

When he had first started out as a private investigator, Lee had used an IBM typewriter; Touch-Tone phones were cutting edge; and fax machines spit out curly thermal paper and were the domain of only the largest companies. That was less than fifteen years ago. Now he was holding a global communications command center in the palm of his hand. Change that fast just couldn't be healthy. But still, who could live without these damn things now?

He plopped down on the couch and stared at the slowly revolving ceiling fan's rattan blades, contemplating the pros and cons of what he was thinking about doing. Then he made up his mind, and slipped his wallet out of his back pocket. The piece of paper was in there with the number his client, who he knew now was Danny Buchanan, had originally given him. The one he had been unable to trace. Then doubt seized him. What if he was wrong about Buchanan's not being involved in the attempt on Faith's life? He stood and paced. When he looked out the window at the blue sky, he saw only possible disaster looming in the approaching storm clouds. Still, Buchanan had hired him. He was technically working for the man. Maybe it was time to report in. He said a silent prayer, picked up his cell phone and punched in the numbers from the piece of paper.

CHAPTER 38

Connie did not look happy as Paul Fisher leaned foward and addressed him in a conspiratorial tone.

"We have every reason to believe that she's in on it, Connie. Despite what you've told us."

Connie glared at the man. He hated everything about Fisher, from his perfect hair and rocky-ledge chin down to his ramrod-straight posture and wrinkle-free shirts. He had been sitting in here for half an hour. He had told Fisher and Massey his side of the story, and they had told him theirs. They were not going to find any middle ground.

"That's bullshit with a capital *B*, Paul."

Fisher sat back and looked at Massey. "You heard the facts. How can you sit there and defend her?"

"Because I know she's innocent, how about that?"

"Do you have any facts to back that up, Connie?" Massey wanted to know.

"I've been sitting here telling you the facts, Fred. We had a hot lead at Agriculture on another case. Brooke didn't even want Ken to go with Lockhart that night. She wanted to go."

"Or so she told you," Massey replied.

"Look, I've got twenty-five years' worth of experience that says Brooke Reynolds is as clean as they come."

"She investigated Ken Newman's finances without telling anyone."

"Come on, it's not the first time an agent's gone off the manual. She gets a hot one and wants to follow it up. But she doesn't want to bury Ken's reputation along with the body. Not until she's sure."

"And the hundred thousand dollars in her kids' accounts?"

"Planted."

"By whom?"

"That's what we have to figure out."

Fisher shook his head in frustration. "We're going to have her followed. Every minute until we break this."

Connie leaned forward and did his best to keep his big hands from flying to Fisher's neck. "What you should be doing, Paul, is following up the leads from Ken's murder. And trying to track down Faith Lockhart."

"If you don't mind, Connie, we'll run the investigation."

Connie looked over at Fred Massey. "You want a tail on Reynolds, I'm your guy."

"You! No way!" Fisher protested.

"Hear me out, Fred," Connie said, his gaze locked on Massey. "I admit, things look bad for Brooke. But I also know there's not a finer agent in the Bureau. And I don't want to see a good agent's career go down the toilet because somebody made the wrong call. I've been down that road myself. Right, Fred?"

Massey looked intensely troubled at this last statement. He seemed to shrink in his chair under Connie's withering gaze.

"Fred," Fisher said, "we need an independent source—"

Connie interrupted, "*I* can be independent. If I'm wrong, then Brooke goes down, and I'll be the first one to break the news to her. But I'm betting she's going to come back and pick up her badge and gun. In fact, in ten years I see her running this whole damn place."

"I don't know, Connie," Massey began.

"I think *somebody* owes me that opportunity, Fred," Connie said very quietly. "What do you think?"

There was a long moment of silence while Fisher looked back and forth between the two men.

"All right, Connie, you follow her," Massey said.

"And you report back to me at regular intervals. Exactly what you see. No more. No less. I'm counting on you. For old times' sake."

Connie rose from the table and flicked a victorious glance at Fisher. "Thanks for the vote of confidence, gentlemen. I won't disappoint."

Fisher followed Connie out into the hallway.

"I don't know what you just pulled in there, but remember this: Your career already has one black mark against it, Connie. It can't afford another. And anything you report to Massey, I want to know about."

Connie crowded the much taller Fisher back against the wall.

"Listen up, Paul." He paused, ostensibly to pick a piece of lint off Fisher's shirt. "I understand that, technically, you're my superior here. Don't confuse that, though, with reality."

"You're treading a dangerous line, Connie."

"I like danger, Paul, that's why I joined the Bureau. That's why I carry a gun. I've killed somebody with mine. How about you?"

"You're not making sense. You're throwing your career away." Fisher felt the wall behind him; his face was growing red as Connie continued to lean into him like a listing oak against a picket fence.

"Is that right? Well, let me make some sense of this for you. Somebody is setting Brooke up. Now, who could that be? It's got to be the leak here at the Bureau. Somebody wants to discredit her, bring her down. And if you ask me, Paul, you're trying awfully hard to do just that."

"Me? You're accusing me of being the leak?"

"I'm not accusing anybody of anything. I'm just reminding you that until we do find that leak, nobody, and I mean nobody, from the director down to the guys who clean the johns here, is above suspicion in my book."

Connie moved away from Fisher. "Have a nice day, Paul. I'm off to catch some bad guys."

Fisher stared after him, slowly shaking his head, something close to fear in his eyes.

CHAPTER 39

THE PHONE NUMBER LEE CALLED WAS LINKED TO a pager, so that Buchanan would know the instant the number was called. When the pager went off, Buchanan was at home packing his briefcase for a meeting at a downtown law firm that was doing pro bono work for one of Buchanan's clients. He had given up hope of the damn beeper ever sounding. When it did, he thought he would suffer a stroke.

Now Buchanan's dilemma was apparent. How to check the message and call back without Thornhill knowing about it. Then he thought of a plan. He called his driver. It was Thornhill's man, of course. It always was. They drove downtown to the law firm.

"I'll be a couple of hours. I'll phone when I'm done," he told the driver.

Buchanan went into the building. He had been

here before, knew the layout well. He didn't go to the elevator bank, but instead went through the main lobby and passed through a door in the back that also served as a rear entrance to the parking garage. He took the elevator down two levels and stepped off. He went through the underground lobby area and out into the parking level. Right next to the door leading out from the lobby was a pay phone. He put in his coins and dialed the number that would allow him to check the message. His reasoning was clear: If Thornhill could intercept a random hard-line call under a thousand tons of concrete, he was the devil himself and Buchanan had no chance of beating him anyway.

On the message Lee's voice was tight, his words few. And the impact on Buchanan was enormous. He had left a number. Buchanan dialed it. A man answered the phone immediately.

"Mr. Buchanan?" Lee asked.

"Is Faith all right?"

Lee gave a sigh of relief. He was hoping that would be the man's first question. That told him a lot. But still, he had to be cautious. "Just to verify it's really you: You sent me a package of information. How did you send it, and what was in it? And let me have the answers fast."

"Personal courier. I use Dash Services. The packet had a photo of Faith, five pages of background information on her and my firm, the contact phone num-

ber, a summary of my concerns and what I wanted
you to do. It also had five thousand dollars in cash in
denominations of fifties and twenties. I also called
you three days ago at your office and left a message
on your machine. Now please tell me that Faith is all
right."

"She's fine, for now. But we have some problems."

"Yes, we do. For starters, how do I know you're
Adams?"

Lee thought quickly. "I have a great Yellow Pages
ad with a corny magnifying glass and everything. I
have three brothers. The youngest works at a motorcycle shop in south Alexandria. He goes by Scotty,
but his nickname in college was Scooter because he
played football and could run so damn fast. If you
want you can call him, check it out and call me
back."

"Not necessary. I'm convinced. What happened?
Why did you run?"

"Well, you would have too if someone tried to kill
you."

"Tell me everything, Mr. Adams. Leave nothing
out."

"Well, I know *who* you are, but I'm not sure I trust
you. What can you do about that?"

"You tell me *why* Faith went to the FBI. That
much I do know. And then I'll tell you who you're
really up against. And it's not me. When I tell you
who it is, you'll wish it were me."

Lee debated this for a moment. He could hear Faith getting up and heading probably to the shower. *Well, here goes.* "She was scared. She said you had been acting strangely, jumpy for a while. She had tried to talk to you about it, but you blew her off, even asked her to leave the firm. That made her even more fearful. She was afraid the authorities were on to you. She went to the FBI with the idea of bringing you in to testify too. Against the people you were bribing. You both cut a deal and walk."

"That would never have worked."

"Well, as she's fond of telling me, it's easy to second-guess."

"So she's told you everything?"

"Pretty much. She thought maybe you were the one who tried to kill her. But I put that notion to rest." *I hope I was right.*

"I had no idea Faith had even gone to the FBI until after she disappeared."

"It's not just the FBI after her. There are some other people too. They were at the airport. And they were carrying something I've only seen at a seminar on counterterrorism."

"Who sponsored the seminar?"

This question puzzled Lee. "The counterterrorism stuff was put on by the official spooks. You know, I guess the guys at CIA."

Buchanan said, "Well, at least you have encountered the enemy and you're still alive. That's good."

"What are you talking . . ." The blood suddenly seemed to pool over Lee's temples. "Are you saying what I think you're saying?"

"Let's just put it this way, Mr. Adams: Faith is not the only one working for a prominent federal agency. At least her involvement was voluntarily. Mine wasn't."

"Oh, shit."

"To put it mildly, yes. Where are you?"

"Why?"

"Because I need to get to you."

"And how can you do that without bringing the ACME assassin squad down on us? I assume you're under surveillance."

"Unbelievably, astonishingly tight surveillance."

"Okay, so you're not coming anywhere near us."

"Mr. Adams, the only chance we have is to work together. That can't be done from a distance. I have to come to you, because I don't think it wise for you to come here."

"You're not convincing me."

"I won't come if I can't lose them."

"Lose them? Look, who do you think you are, Houdini reincarnated? Well, let me tell you, not even Houdini could lose *both* the FBI *and* the CIA."

"I'm neither a spy nor a magician. I'm a humble lobbyist, but I have one advantage: I know this city better than anyone alive. And I have friends in both high and low places. And right now, they are equally valuable to me. Rest assured, I will get to you alone. And then we might be able to survive this. Now I want to speak to Faith."

"I'm not sure that's a good idea, Mr. Buchanan."

"Yes, it is."

Lee whirled around and saw Faith standing on the stairs in a T-shirt. "It's time, Lee. In fact, it's way past time."

He took a deep breath and held out the phone.

"Hello, Danny," she said into the phone.

"God, Faith, I'm sorry. For all of this." Buchanan's voice cracked in midsentence.

"I should be apologizing. I started this whole nightmare by going to the FBI."

"Well, we have to finish it. We may as well do it together. How is Adams? Is he capable? We're going to need some support."

Faith glanced over at Lee, who was anxiously watching her. "In my informed opinion, we have no problems there. In fact, that's probably our one ace in the hole."

"Tell me where you are, and I'll be down as quickly as possible."

She did. She also told Buchanan everything she and Lee knew. When she hung up, she looked over at Lee.

He shrugged. "I figured it was our only shot. Either that or we spend the rest of our lives running."

She sat on his lap, curled her legs up and laid her

head against his chest. "You did the right thing. Whoever's involved in this, they'll find a tough opponent in Danny."

Lee's hopes, however, had plummeted. The CIA. Hired assassins, legions of people expert in all sorts of nasty things: computers, satellites, covert operations, air guns with poisoned bullets, all coming for them. If he was smart, he'd throw Faith on the Honda and run like hell.

"I'm going to grab a shower," Faith said. "Danny said he'd be down as soon as he could."

"Right," Lee said, a faraway look in his eyes.

As Faith headed up the stairs, Lee picked up his phone, glanced at it and froze. Lee Adams had never been more stunned in his life. And with the events of the last few days, the bar on what surprised him had risen to about the level of the sun. The text message on the cell phone's screen was concise. And it came close to stopping even Lee's very strong heart.

Faith Lockhart for Renee Adams, it said. There was a phone number to call. They wanted Faith in exchange for his daughter.

CHAPTER 40

REYNOLDS SAT IN HER LIVING ROOM CRADLING A CUP of tea and staring into a fire that was slowly dying. The last time she could remember being home at this time of the day was when she had been on maternity leave with David. Her son had been as surprised to see her come through the door as Rosemary. David was now napping, and Rosemary was busy doing laundry. Just another normal day for them. Reynolds simply stared into the embers of the fire, wishing that something, anything about her life could be normal.

It had started to rain hard, which fit in perfectly with her deep depression. Suspended. She felt naked without her gun and credentials. All those years at the Bureau, never a blemish, and now she was a step away from a ruined career. Then what would she do? Where could she go? Without her job, would her husband try to take the kids? Could she stop him if he did?

She put her cup down, kicked off her shoes and sank back on the couch. The tears started to come fast and heavy, and she put an arm across her face both to soak them up and muffle her sobs. The ringing doorbell made her sit up, wipe at her face and head to the door. She looked through the peephole and found herself staring at Howard Constantinople.

Connie stood in front of the fire he had just stoked, warming his hands. An embarrassed Reynolds quickly dabbed at her eyes with a tissue. He could not have missed her red eyes and splotchy cheeks, she knew, but he had tactfully said nothing.

"Did they talk to you?" she asked.

Connie turned and dropped into a chair, nodding as he did so. "And I came damn close to being suspended myself. I was about two seconds from punching out Fisher, that shit-faced excuse for an agent."

"Don't go and crater your career for me, Connie."

"If I had slugged the guy, believe me, it would've been for me, not you." He popped a big knuckle, as though emphasizing the point, and then looked across at her. "The thing that kills me is, they actually believe you're somehow involved in this. I told them the truth. Something came up, we were working another case. You wanted to go with Lockhart because you had the relationship with her, but we had this potential whistleblower over at Agriculture we were committed to. I told them you were fretting like all get-out because you didn't know if Ken going with Lockhart out there was the right thing to do."

"And?"

"And they weren't listening. They've already made up their minds."

"Because of the money? Did they tell you about that?"

Connie nodded slowly and suddenly hunched forward. For a big man his movements could be quick, agile. "I don't like kicking you while you're down, but why in the hell did you go sniffing around Newman's accounts without telling somebody? Like me, for instance? You know detectives go in pairs for lots of reasons, not the least of which is to cover the other's ass. Now you've got nobody to corroborate shit for you, except Anne Newman. And as far as they're concerned, she doesn't count."

Reynolds threw up her hands. "I never in a million years thought this would happen. I was trying to do right by Ken and his family."

"Well, if he was being paid off, maybe Ken doesn't deserve that sort of consideration. And that's coming from a good friend of his."

"We don't know that he was bad yet."

"Cash in a safe-deposit box under a fake name? Yeah, I guess everybody does that, don't they?"

"Connie, how did they know I was investigating

Ken's finances? I can't believe Anne would have called the Bureau. She asked me for help."

"I asked Massey, but he's a clam. Figures I'm the enemy too. I nosed around a bit, though, and I think they got a phone tip. Anonymous, of course. Massey told me you were screaming frame-up. And you know what, I think you're right, even if they don't."

The sight of Connie at the door had been welcome. The fact that he was still loyal meant a lot to her. And she wanted to do right by him too. Especially him. "Look, this isn't going to help your career, being seen with me, Connie. I'm sure Fisher has a tail on me."

"Actually, I'm your tail."

"You're kidding."

"No, the hell I am not. I talked the ADIC into it. Called in a few markers. For old times' sake, Massey said. In case you didn't know, Fred Massey was the guy who asked me to take the dive on the Brownsville case all those years ago. If he thinks this evens us up, he's brain-dead. But don't get all excited. They know I have every incentive to cover *my* ass on this. And that means if you fall, they don't have to go putting blame anywhere else. Including on yours truly." Connie paused and made a mock show of surprise. "ADIC? Come to think of it, that acronym really fits. Massey's a little shit too."

"You don't have much respect for your chain of

command." Reynolds smiled. "What do you think of me, Agent Constantinople?"

"I think you screwed up big-time, and you just gave the Bureau a face-saving scapegoat," he said bluntly.

Reynolds's face grew serious. "You don't sugar-coat."

"Do you want me to waste time doing that?" Connie stood. "Or do you want to clear your name?"

"I *have* to clear my name. If I don't, I could lose it all, Connie. My kids, my career. All of it." Reynolds could feel herself trembling again and she took several deep breaths to counteract the panic she was feeling. She felt like a high schooler who had just learned she was pregnant. "But I'm suspended. No creds, no gun. No authority."

In answer Connie pulled on his overcoat. "Well, you've got me. I've got creds, a gun and, while I'm only a humble field agent after two and a half decades of doing this crap, I can do authority with the best of them. So get your coat and let's try to track down Lockhart."

"Lockhart?"

"I figure we deliver her, the pieces start to fall into place. The more they do, the more the blame gets shifted off you. I've talked to the VCU boys. They're spinning their wheels waiting on lab results and crap like that. And now Massey has them going hot and heavy on your angle and to hell with Lockhart for now. You know nobody's even gone to her house looking for clues?"

Reynolds looked miserable. "We were so reactive on the whole thing. Ken killed. Lockhart gone. The fiasco at the airport. Then people calling themselves the FBI at Adams's apartment. We never really had a chance to take the proper investigative steps."

"So I figure we follow up some leads while they're still hot. Like checking out Adams's family in the area. I've got the list of names and addresses. If he went on the run, he might have gotten one of them to help."

"You could get into deep trouble for this, Connie."

He shrugged. "Not the first time. Besides, we don't have a squad supervisor anymore. I don't know if you heard, but she was suspended for being stupid."

They exchanged smiles.

Connie continued. "So, as second-in-command, I'm entitled to investigate an active case I happened to be assigned to. My instructions are to find Faith Lockhart, so that's what I'm going to do. They just don't know I'm doing it with you. And I talked to the VCU guys. They know what I'm up to, so we won't run into another team going through Adams's relatives."

"I need to tell Rosemary I might be gone overnight."

"Then go." He looked at his watch. "I guess Sydney's still in school. Where's your boy?"

"Sleeping."

"Whisper in his ear that Mommy's gonna kick some butt."

When Reynolds returned, she went straight to the closet and got her coat. She hustled toward her study and then stopped.

"What's wrong?" Connie asked.

She looked at him, slightly embarrassed. "I was going to get my gun. Old habits die hard."

"Not to worry. You'll get yours back soon enough. But you have to make me a promise. When you go to get your gun and creds, take me with you. I want to see their faces."

She opened the door for him. "Deal."

Buchanan MADE A NUMBER OF OTHER PHONE
calls from the parking garage as he worked out his
arrangements. He then went up to the law firm and
spent time on an important matter he suddenly cared
nothing about. He was driven home, his mind working the whole time as he devised his plan against
Robert Thornhill. That was one area of his being that
the CIA man could never penetrate or control:
Buchanan's mind. That fact was enormously comforting. Buchanan was slowly regaining his confidence. Maybe he could give the man a run for his
money.

Buchanan unlocked the front door to his home and
went inside. He lay his briefcase down on a chair and
passed the darkened library. He turned on the light
to gaze at his beloved painting, to give him strength

for what lay ahead. As the light came on, Buchanan stared in disbelief at the empty frame. He staggered over to it, put his hands through the frame and touched the wall. He had been robbed. Yet he had a very good security system, and it had not been tripped.

He raced across to the phone to call the police. As his hand touched the receiver, it rang. He picked it up.

"Your car will be around in a couple of minutes, sir. Going to the office?"

At first Buchanan's mind didn't register.

"To the office, sir?"

"Yes," Buchanan was finally able to say.

He put the phone down and stared over at where his painting had hung. First Faith, and now his painting. All Thornhill's doing. *All right, Bob, first point to you. Now it's my turn.*

He went upstairs, washed his face and changed his clothes, carefully selecting what he needed to wear. He had a custom-built entertainment system in his bedroom housing a TV, stereo, VCR and DVD player. It was relatively safe from burglars since one couldn't take the components out without unscrewing numerous wooden pieces, a very time-consuming process. Buchanan did not watch TV or movies. And when he wanted music, he put a 33 platter on his old phonograph.

Sticking his hand in the slot of the VCR, Buchanan pulled out his passport, credit card and ID, all under an alias, and a slim bundle of hundred-dollar bills and put it all in a zippered inner pocket of his coat. Coming back downstairs, he looked outside and saw his car waiting. He would let him wait a few more minutes, just for the hell of it.

When that time had passed, Buchanan picked up his briefcase and walked out to the car. He climbed in and the car drove off.

"Hello, Bob," Buchanan said as calmly as he could.

Thornhill glanced down at the briefcase.

Buchanan nodded his head toward the tinted window.

"I'm going to the office. The FBI will expect me to take my briefcase. Unless you assume they haven't tapped my phone line by now."

Thornhill nodded. "You have the makings of a good field operative in you, Danny."

"Where is the painting?"

"In a very safe place, which is far more than you deserve under the circumstances."

"What exactly does that mean?"

"That exactly means Lee Adams, private investigator. Hired by you to follow Faith Lockhart."

Buchanan feigned being taken aback for a minute. As a young man he'd had notions of being an actor. Not in the movies, but on the stage. For him, lobbying was the next best thing. "I didn't know she had gone to the FBI when I did that. I was only concerned for her safety."

"And why was that?"

"I think you know the answer."

Thornhill looked offended. "Why in the world would I want to harm Faith Lockhart? I don't even know the woman."

"Do you have to know someone before you destroy her?"

Thornhill's tone was mocking. "You were wrong to have done it, Danny. The painting will probably be returned to you. But for now, learn to live without it."

"How did you get into my house, Thornhill? I have a security system."

Thornhill looked as though he might burst out laughing. "A *home* security system? Oh, dear."

It was all Buchanan could do not to fling himself on the man.

"You amuse me, Danny, you really do. Running around trying to save the have-nots. Don't you understand? That's what makes the world go 'round. The rich and the poor. The powerful and the powerless. We'll always have them, until the world ends. And nothing you do will change that. Just as people will always hate each other, will betray each other. If it weren't for the evil qualities in humanity, I wouldn't have a job."

"I was just thinking that you missed your calling as a psychiatrist," said Buchanan. "For the criminally insane. You'd have so much in common with your patients."

Thornhill smiled. "That's how I got on to you, you know. Someone you tried to help ended up betraying you. Jealous of your success, your wanting to do good, I suppose. He didn't know about your little scheme, but he aroused my curiosity. And when I focus on someone's life, well, kept secrets are not an option. I tapped your home, your office, even your clothing, and found myself a treasure trove. We so enjoyed listening to you."

"Fascinating. Now tell me where Faith is."

"I was hoping you could tell me that."

"What do you want with her?"

"I want her to come and work for me. There is a friendly competition between the two agencies, but between the FBI and my agency, I would have to say that we play much fairer with our people. I've been working on this project longer than the Bureau. I don't want all my efforts to be in vain."

Buchanan chose his words carefully. He knew he was in great personal danger here. "What can Faith possibly give you that I already haven't?"

"In my line of work, two is always better than one."

"Would your math include the FBI agent you had killed, Bob?"

Thornhill took out his pipe and fiddled with it.

"You know, Danny, you would be well advised to keep yourself focused on your part of this puzzle only."

"I consider *every* part my part. I read the newspapers. You told me Faith had gone to the FBI. An FBI agent is killed working on an undisclosed case. Faith disappears at the same time. You're right, I hired Lee Adams to find out what was going on. I haven't heard from him. Did you have him killed too?"

"I'm a public servant. I don't have people killed."

"The FBI got on to Faith somehow, and you couldn't allow that, because your whole plan goes down the tubes if they find out the truth. And did you really think I believed you'd let me walk away with a slap on the back for a job well done? I didn't survive this long in the business by being a damned idiot."

Thornhill put his pipe away. "Survival, interesting concept. You consider yourself a survivor, and yet you come to me and make all these sorts of unfounded accusations—"

Buchanan leaned forward and placed his face right next to Thornhill's. "I've forgotten more about the subject of survival than you ever knew. I don't have armies of people with guns running around doing my bidding while I sit safely behind the walls of Langley analyzing the field of battle like it was a chess game. The minute you came into my life, I made contingency plans that will absolutely *destroy* you if anything happens to me. Didn't you ever consider the possibility that someone might be half as agile as yourself? Or have all your successes really gone to your head?"

Thornhill simply stared at him, so Buchanan kept going. "Now, I consider myself a partner of sorts with you, no matter how loathsome that thought is. And I want to know if you killed the FBI agent, because I want to know exactly what I have to do to get out of this nightmare. And I want to know if you killed Faith and Adams as well. And if you don't tell me, the minute I leave this car, my next stop will be the FBI. And if you think yourself so invincible as to try and kill me while the Feds are back there, then go ahead. However, if I die, you go down too."

Buchanan leaned back and allowed himself a smile. "You know the old story of the frog and the scorpion, don't you? The scorpion needs a ride across the water and tells the frog he won't sting it if the frog will provide that ride. And the frog knows that if the scorpion does sting it, that the scorpion will drown, so he gives it the ride. Halfway across the water, the scorpion, against all reason, does sting the frog. As it's dying, the frog cries out, 'Why did you do it? Now you'll die too.' And the scorpion simply tells him, 'It's my nature.'" Buchanan made a mock show of waving. "Hello, Mr. Frog."

The two men sat staring at each other for the next mile, until Thornhill broke the silence.

"Lockhart needed to be eliminated. The FBI agent was with her. So he had to die too."

"But you missed Faith?"

"With your private investigator's help. But for your

blunder, this crisis would never have happened."

"It never *occurred* to me that you would be planning to kill anyone. So you have no idea where she is?"

"It's only a matter of time. I have a number of irons in the fire. And where there's bait, there's always hope."

"Meaning what?"

"Meaning I'm done talking with you."

The next fifteen minutes passed in complete silence. The car drove into the underground parking garage of Buchanan's building. A gray sedan waited on the lower level, its engine running. Before Thornhill got out, he gripped Buchanan's arm.

"You claim to have the ability to destroy me if anything happens to you. Well, here's my side. If your colleague and her new 'friend' bring all that I've worked for crashing down, you will all be eliminated. Immediately." He removed his hand. "Just so we understand one another. Mr. Scorpion," Thornhill added scornfully.

A minute later, the gray sedan pulled out of the parking garage. Thornhill was already on the phone.

"Buchanan is not to be out of sight for even one second." He clicked off and began to think of how to attack this new development.

THIS IS THE LAST PLACE," CONNIE SAID AS THEY pulled up to the motorcycle shop in his sedan.

They got out and Reynolds looked around. "His younger brother?"

Connie nodded as he checked his list. "Scott Adams. Manages the place."

"Well, let's hope he's a little more helpful than the others."

They had covered all of Lee's relatives in the area. None had seen or heard from him in the last week. Or at least that's what they said. Scott Adams might be their last chance. However, when they got inside they were told he was out of town for a friend's wedding and wouldn't be back for a couple of days.

Connie handed the young man behind the counter his card. "Tell him to call me when he gets in."

Rick, the salesman who had obnoxiously flirted with Faith, looked down at the card. "Does this have to do with his brother?"

Connie and Reynolds eyed him. "Do you know Lee Adams?" Reynolds asked.

"Can't say I know him. He don't know my name or nothing. But he's come by a few times. Just a couple days ago, in fact."

The two agents looked Rick up and down, gauging his credibility.

"Was he alone?" Reynolds asked.

"No. He had some chick with him."

Reynolds took out a photo of Lockhart and handed it over to him. "Think short hair, not long, black, not auburn."

Rick nodded as he stared at the photograph. "Yep, that's her. And Lee's hair was different too. Short and blond. And he had a beard and mustache too. I'm real good at noticing things."

Reynolds and Connie looked at each other, trying hard to hide their excitement.

"Any idea where they might have gone?" Connie asked.

"Maybe. But I sure know why they came here."

"Really? Why's that?"

"They needed wheels. Took a bike. One of the big Gold Wings."

"Gold Wing?" Reynolds repeated.

"Yeah." Rick rifled through a stack of color

brochures on the counter and flipped one around so Reynolds could see. "This one here. The Honda Gold Wing SE. If you're going long distance, nothing beats this baby. Trust me."

"And you say Adams took one. Got a color, license plate number?"

"I can look the plate up. The color's the same as on the brochure. That was a demo. Scotty let him take it."

"You said you might have an idea where they went," Reynolds prompted.

"What do you want with Lee?"

"We want to talk with him. And the lady he's with," she said amiably.

"They do something wrong?"

"Won't know until we talk to them," Connie replied. He stepped forward a little. "It's an ongoing FBI investigation. You a friend of theirs or something?"

Rick paled at the suggestion. "Hell, no, that chick is bad news. A real attitude. While Lee was inside, I went out to the sales lot and tried to help her. Real professional-like, and she jumped all over me. And Lee's no better. When he came out, he gave me some lip. I came close to kicking his ass, in fact."

As Connie looked at the beanpole Rick, he recalled the surveillance tape of the physically imposing Lee Adams. "Kick his ass? Is that right?"

Rick looked defensive. "He's got some weight on me, but he's an old guy. And I'm into tae kwon do."

Reynolds studied Rick closely. "So you're saying that Lee Adams was inside for a while, and the woman was out in the lot by herself?"

"That's right."

Reynolds and Connie traded a quick glance. "If you have information as to where they went, the Bureau would greatly appreciate it," Reynolds said, growing impatient. "That and the plate number on the bike. Like right now, if you don't mind. We're sort of in a hurry."

"Sure. Lee also got a map for North Carolina. We sell 'em here, but Scotty just gave it to him. That's what Shirley, the girl who usually works the desk, said."

"Is she in today?"

"Nope. Sick. I'm it."

"Can I get one of those Carolina maps?" Reynolds asked. Rick pulled one out and handed it to her. "How much?"

He smiled. "Hey, it's on the house. Just being a good citizen. You know, I'm thinking about joining the FBI."

"Well, we could always use a good man," Connie said with a blank expression, his gaze averted.

Rick looked up the plate number on the demo and gave it to Connie. "You guys let me know what happens," Rick said as they started to leave.

"You'll be the first," Connie called back over his shoulder.

The two agents settled back in the car.

Reynolds looked at her partner. "Well, Lockhart isn't being held by Adams against her will. He left her outside by herself. She could've taken off."

"They sure look to be a team of sorts. At least right now."

"North Carolina," Reynolds said almost to herself.

"Big state," Connie said back.

Reynolds looked at him with a wry expression. "Well, let's see if we can cut it down some. At the airport, Lockhart bought two tickets for a flight to Norfolk International."

"So why the map for North Carolina?"

"They couldn't take the plane. We'd have been waiting for them in Norfolk. At least Adams seemed to know that. He was probably aware we have an arrangement with the airlines, and that's how we scored Lockhart at the airport."

"Lockhart screwed up by using her real name for the second ticket. But that was probably all she could do, unless she had a third fake ID," Connie added.

"So no plane. Can't use a credit card, so no rental car. Adams figures we have the bus and railroad terminals covered. So they get the Honda from his brother and a map for their true destination: North Carolina."

"Meaning that when they got to Norfolk by plane they were either going to drive or hop another plane to someplace in Carolina."

Reynolds shook her head. "But that doesn't make

sense. If they were going to North Carolina, why not just take a plane directly there? There are tons of flights to Raleigh and Charlotte out of National. Why go through Norfolk?"

"Well, maybe you'd go through Norfolk if you weren't going to Charlotte or Raleigh or anyplace near them," Connie ventured, "but still wanted to go to someplace in North Carolina."

"But why not still go through one of those two major airports?"

"Well, what if Norfolk is a lot closer to where they wanted to go than Charlotte or Raleigh are?"

Reynolds thought a moment. "Raleigh's roughly in the middle of the state. Charlotte is west."

Connie snapped his fingers. "East! The coast. The Outer Banks?"

Reynolds found herself nodding in agreement. "Maybe. The Outer Banks has thousands of beach houses where one could hide."

Connie suddenly looked less hopeful. "Thousands of beach houses," he muttered.

"Well, the first thing you can do is call the Bureau's airline liaison and find out what flights run out of Norfolk for the Outer Banks. And we have some times to work with. Their flight was scheduled to get into Norfolk at noon. I don't see them cooling their heels any longer than necessary at a public place, so the flight out had to be relatively close to noon or so. Maybe one of the commuters has regular service. We already checked with the major airlines. They didn't reserve with any of them out of Norfolk."

Connie picked up the car phone and placed the call. It didn't take long before they got an answer.

Connie's features looked hopeful again. "You're not going to believe this, but there's only one commuter service to the Outer Banks from Norfolk International."

Reynolds smiled broadly and shook her head. "Finally, some luck in this damn case. Talk to me."

"Tarheel Airways. They fly out of Norfolk to five places in Carolina: Kill Devil Hills, Manteo, Ocracoke, Hatteras and a place called Pine Island, near Duck. There're no regular departures. You call ahead and the plane is waiting for you."

Reynolds spread open the map and scanned it. "Okay, there are Hatteras and Ocracoke. They're the farthest south." She put a finger on the map. "Kill Devil Hills is here. Manteo south of that. And Duck is here, to the north."

Connie looked at where she was pointing. "I've been down there on vacation. You cross the bridge over the sound and head north for Duck. South for Kill Devil. They're fairly equidistant from each other at that point."

"So what do you think? North or south?"

"Well, if they were going to North Carolina, it was probably at Lockhart's prompting." Reynolds looked at him curiously. "Because Adams took the map,"

Connie explained. "If he knew the area, he wouldn't have done that."

"Nice, Sherlock, what else?"

"Well, Lockhart has some serious money. One look at her house in McLean will tell you that. If I were her, I'd have a safe house under my phony name in case the roof caved in."

"But we're still at square one: north or south?"

They sat there stewing over this until Reynolds suddenly slapped her forehead. "God, how stupid. Connie, if you have to call Tarheel to arrange for a flight, our answer's right there."

Connie's eyes grew wide. "Damn, talk about blind." He picked up the phone, got the number for Tarheel and placed the call, relaying the date and approximate time and the name Suzanne Blake.

He hung up and looked at her. "A reservation for two people with Tarheel was made by our Ms. Blake two days ago to fly out of Norfolk around two P.M. They were pissed because she never showed. They normally take a credit card, but she'd flown with them before, and so they just took her on her word."

"And their destination?"

"Pine Island."

Reynolds couldn't help but smile. "God, Connie, we might actually pull this off."

Connie put the car in gear. "Only bad thing is, I don't rate one of the Bureau's planes. We're stuck with the old Crown Vic here. I figure six hours or so, not counting stops." He checked his watch. "With stops, that'll put us there about one in the morning."

"I'm not supposed to leave the area."

"Bureau Rule Number One: You can go anywhere so long as you have your guardian angel along."

Reynolds looked troubled. "What do you think about calling in reinforcements?"

He eyed her quizzically. "Well, I guess we could call Massey and Fisher and let them take all the credit."

Reynolds suddenly smiled. "Give me a minute to call home and then let's roll."

IT HAD TAKEN LEE MANY AGONIZING HOURS, BUT he had finally tracked down Renee. Her mother had flatly refused to give him her phone number at college, but in a series of calls to the admissions office, among others, Lee had lied, begged and threatened until the number had been given up. It figured. He hadn't called his daughter for a long time, and when he did, it had to be for something like this. Boy, she was really going to cherish her old man now.

Renee's roommate at UVA swore on her grave that Renee had left for class accompanied by two members of the football team, one of whom she was dating. After telling the young woman who he was and leaving a number for Renee to call, Lee had hung up the phone and then gotten the telephone number for the Albermarle County Sheriff's office. He talked his way to a deputy sheriff and told the woman that someone had made threats against Renee Adams, a student at UVA. Would they please send someone to check on her? The woman asked questions that Lee could not answer, including wanting to know who the hell he was. *Just check the latest most-wanted list,* he wanted to tell her. Sick with worry, he tried his best to impress upon her the sincerity of what he was saying. Then he hung up and stared down at the digital missive once more: "Renee for Faith," he slowly said to himself.

"What?"

He jerked around and stared at Faith, there on the stairs, her eyes wide, her mouth open.

"Lee, what is it?"

Lee was out of ideas at the moment. He simply held up the phone for Faith, his face an anguished mess.

She looked at the message and then stared at him. "We have to call the police."

"She's okay, I just talked to her roommate. And I called the police. Somebody's blowing smoke at us. Trying to spook us."

"You don't know that."

"You're right, I don't," he said miserably.

"Are you going to call the number back?"

"That's probably what they want me to do."

"You mean so they can trace the call? Can you trace a cellular call?"

"It's possible, if you have the right equipment. Phone carriers have to be able to trace a cell call to determine the location of a 911 caller. It uses a time difference of arrival method by measuring signal distances between cell towers and kicks out a string of possible locations. . . . Shit, my daughter's head might be in the guillotine and I sound like a damn walking science magazine."

"But not an exact location."

"No, at least I don't think so. It's not as precise as satellite positioning, that's for certain. But who the hell really knows? Some geeky asshole invents some new piece of shit every second that rips away a little bit more of your privacy. I know, my ex-wife married one."

"You should call, Lee."

"And what the hell am I supposed to say? They want to trade you for her."

She put one hand on his shoulder, rubbed his neck and then leaned against him. "Call them. And then we'll see what we can do. Nothing is going to happen to your daughter."

He looked at her. "You can't guarantee that."

"I *can* guarantee that I will do everything I can to make sure she's not harmed."

"Including walking into their hands?"

"If it comes to that, yes. I'm not going to let an innocent person get hurt because of me."

Lee slumped back against the couch. "I'm supposed to be so good under pressure too and I can't even think straight."

"Call them," Faith said very firmly.

Lee took a long breath and punched in the numbers. With Faith sitting beside him and listening in, they waited as the phone rang once and then was answered.

"Mr. Adams?" Lee didn't recognize the voice. It had a mechanical quality to it, making him think it was being altered somehow. It sounded inhuman enough to make his skin tingle with absolute dread.

"This is Lee Adams."

"Nice of you to leave your cell phone number at your apartment. It made contacting you much more convenient."

"I just checked on my daughter. She's fine. And the cops are on the scene. So your little kidnapping plan—"

"I have no need to kidnap your daughter, Mr. Adams."

"Then I'm not sure why I'm talking to you."

"You needn't abduct someone to kill her. Your daughter can be eliminated today, tomorrow, next month, next year. While going to class, lacrosse practice, driving on holiday, even while she's sleeping. Her bed is right next to a window, first floor. She often stays late at the library. It couldn't be easier, really."

"You sick bastard! You sonofabitch!" Lee looked like he wanted to break the phone in two.

Faith gripped his shoulders, trying to calm him down.

The voice continued with irritating calm. "Histrionics won't help your daughter. Where is Faith Lockhart, Mr. Adams? That's all we want. Give her up and all your problems go away."

"And I'm supposed to just accept that as gospel?"

"You really don't have a choice."

"How do you know I've even got the woman?"

"Do you want your daughter to die?"

"But Lockhart got away."

"Fine, next week you can bury Renee."

Faith jerked at Lee's arm and pointed at the phone.

"Wait, wait!" Lee said. "Okay, okay, if I have Faith, what do you propose?"

"A meeting."

"She's not going to come voluntarily."

"I don't really care how you get her there. That's your responsibility. We'll be waiting."

"And you'll just let me walk away?"

"Drop her off and drive away. We'll take care of the rest. You don't interest us."

"Where?"

Lee was given an address outside of Washington, D.C., on the Maryland side. He knew it well: very isolated.

"I have to drive it. And the cops are everywhere. I need a few days."

"Tomorrow night. Twelve sharp."

"Dammit, that's not a lot of time."

"Then I suggest you start right now."

"Listen, if you lay a hand on my daughter, I'll find you, somehow I will. I swear it. First I'll break every bone in your body, and then I'll really hurt you."

"Mr. Adams, consider yourself the luckiest human being on the face of the earth that we don't see you as a threat. And do yourself a favor: When you walk away don't ever, ever look back. You won't turn to salt, but it still won't be pretty." The line went dead.

Lee put the phone down. For a few minutes he and Faith just sat there without speaking. "Now what do we do?" Lee finally managed to say.

"Danny said he'd be here as soon as he could."

"Great. I've got a deadline: tomorrow, midnight."

"If Danny's not here in time we'll drive to the place they gave you. But first we'll call in some reinforcements."

"Like who, the FBI?" Faith nodded. "Faith, I'm not sure we could explain all this to the Feds in one year, much less one day."

"It's all we have, Lee. If Danny gets here in time and has a better plan, so be it. Otherwise I'll call Agent Reynolds. She'll help us. I'll make it work."

She squeezed his arm. "Nothing is going to happen to your daughter. I promise."

Lee gripped her hand, hoping with all his heart that the woman was right.

CHAPTER 44

Buchanan had a number of meetings on Capitol Hill scheduled for the early evening, pitching to an audience that didn't want to receive his message. It was like throwing a ball at a wave. It would either be kicked back in your face or lost at sea. Well, today was the end. No more.

His car dropped him off near the Capitol. He went up the front steps and over to the Senate side of the building, where he climbed the broad staircase to the second floor, which was mostly restricted space, and continued to the third floor, where people could freely wander.

Buchanan knew he was being followed by more people now. While there were lots of dark suits around, he had trekked these halls long enough to sense who should be here as opposed to those who looked out of place. He assumed they were the FBI and Thornhill's men. After the encounter in the car, the Frog would have deployed more resources. Good. Buchanan smiled. He would, from now on, refer to the CIA man as the Frog. Spies liked code names. And he couldn't think of a more appropriate one for Thornhill. Buchanan just hoped that his stinger was potent enough, and that the Frog's shiny, inviting back wouldn't prove too slippery.

The door was the first one a person would come to upon reaching the third floor and turning left. A middle-aged man in a suit stood next to it. There was no brass plate to identify whose office this was. Right next door was the office of Franklin Graham, the Senate sergeant-at-arms. The sergeant-at-arms was the Senate's principal law enforcement, administrative support and protocol officer. Graham was a good friend of Buchanan's.

"Good to see you, Danny," the man in the suit said.

"Hello, Phil, how's that back of yours?"

"Doc says I should have the surgery."

"Listen to me, don't let them cut you. When you're feeling the pain, have a nice, pleasing shot of Scotch, sing a song at the top of your lungs and then make love to your wife."

"Drinking, dancing and loving—sounds like good advice to me," Phil said.

"What'd you expect from an Irishman?"

Phil laughed. "You're a good man, Danny Buchanan."

"You know why I'm here?"

Phil nodded. "Mr. Graham told me. You can go right in."

He unlocked the door and Buchanan passed through, and then Phil closed the door and stood guard. He didn't notice the two pairs of people who had idly watched this exchange.

The agents reasonably figured they could wait for Buchanan to come out and then take up their surveillance once more. They were on the third floor, after all. It wasn't like the man could fly away.

Inside the room, Buchanan grabbed a raincoat off the hook on the wall. Lucky for him it was drizzly outside. There was also a yellow hard hat on another wall hook. He slipped this on as well. Then he pulled Coke-bottle glasses and work gloves from his briefcase. At least from a distance, with his briefcase under the raincoat, he would change from lobbyist to laborer.

Going to another door at the end of the room, Buchanan removed the chain locking this door and opened it. He went up the stairs and then opened a hatchlike door, which revealed a ladder leading up.

Buchanan put his feet on the rungs and started climbing. At the top, he popped another hatch and found himself on the roof of the Capitol.

The attic room was how the pages accessed the roof to change the flags that flew over the Capitol. The inside joke was that the flags were constantly changed, some flying only for seconds, so that members could send generous constituents back home a continuous supply of Stars and Stripes that had "flown" over the Capitol. Buchanan rubbed his brow. God, what a town.

Buchanan looked down at the front grounds of the Capitol. People were scurrying here and there, running for meetings with people they desperately needed help from. And with all the egos, factions, agendas, crisis upon crisis and stakes greater than anything that had come before in the world's history, everything somehow seemed to work out. A large anthill came to mind as Buchanan looked down upon the scene. This well-oiled machine of democracy. At least the ants did it for survival. *But maybe in a way, we do too,* he thought.

He looked up at Lady Liberty on her century-and-a-half perch atop the Capitol's dome. She had recently been removed via helicopter and stout cable, and the grime of a hundred fifty years had been thoroughly cleaned away. Too bad the sins of people weren't as easy to scrape off.

For one insane moment, Buchanan contemplated jumping. He might have too, except the desire to beat Thornhill was simply too strong. And that would be the coward's way out anyway. Buchanan was many things, but a coward was not one of them.

There was a catwalk that ran across the roof of the Capitol, and it would take Buchanan to the second part of his journey. Or, more accurately, his escape. The House wing of the Capitol building had a similar attic room, which its pages used to raise and lower its flags. Buchanan quickly went across the catwalk and through the hatch on the House side. He climbed down the ladder and into the attic room, where he removed the hard hat and gloves, but kept on the glasses. He pulled a snap-brim hat from his briefcase and put it on. Pulling up the collar on the raincoat, he took a deep breath, opened the door to the attic room and passed through. People milled here and there, but no one really gave him a second glance.

In another minute he had left the Capitol through a rear doorway known only to a few veterans of the place. A car was waiting for him there. A half hour later he was at National Airport, where a private plane, its twin engines revving, awaited its sole passenger. Here was where the friend in *high* places earned his money. The plane received clearance for takeoff a few minutes later. Soon thereafter Buchanan looked out the window of the plane as the capital city slowly disappeared from view. How many times had he seen that sight from the air?

"Good riddance," he said under his breath.

CHAPTER 45

THORNHILL WAS HEADING HOME AFTER A VERY productive day. With Adams now in the fold, they would soon have Faith Lockhart. The man might try to dupe them, but Thornhill didn't think so. He had heard the very real fear in Adams's voice. Thank God for families. Yes, all in all, a productive day. The ringing phone would soon change all that.

"Yes?" Thornhill's confident look vanished as the man reported to him that somehow, some way, Danny Buchanan had utterly vanished, from the very top floor of the Capitol, no less.

"Find him!" Thornhill roared into the phone before slamming it down. What could the man's game be? Had he decided to begin his escape a little early? Or was it for another reason? Had he contacted Lockhart somehow? That was intensely troubling. Shared information between the two was not good for Thornhill. He thought back to their meeting in the car. Buchanan had displayed his usual temper, his little word games—mere bluster, really—but had otherwise been fairly subdued. What could have precipitated this latest development?

In his agitation, Thornhill drummed his fingers on the briefcase he had in his lap. As he looked down at the hard leather, his mouth dropped open. The briefcase! The damn briefcase! He had provided one for Buchanan. It had a backup recorder in it. The conversation in the car. Thornhill admitting he had had the FBI agent killed. Buchanan had tricked him into betraying himself and then taped him. Taped him with CIA-issued equipment. That two-faced sonofabitch!

Thornhill grabbed the phone; his fingers were shaking so badly he misdialed twice. "His briefcase, the tape in it. Find it. And him. You must get it. You *have* to get it."

He dropped the phone and slumped back in the seat. The master strategist of over a thousand clandestine operations was absolutely stunned by this development. Buchanan could take him down with this. He was running loose with the evidence to crush him. But Buchanan would go down too, had to, there was no way around it.

Wait. The scorpion! The frog! Now it all made

sense. Buchanan was going to go down and take Thornhill with him. The CIA man loosened his tie, wedged himself into the seat and fought the panic he felt flooding his body.

This is not how it will end, Robert, he told himself. *After thirty-five years this is not damn well how it's going to end. Calm down. Now is when you need to think. Now is where you earn your place in history. This man will not beat you.* Slowly, steadily, Thornhill's breathing returned to normal.

It could be that Buchanan would simply use the tape as insurance. Why spend the rest of his life in prison when he could quietly disappear? No, it made no sense that he would take the tape to the authorities. He had as much to lose as Thornhill, and he couldn't possibly be that vindictive. Thornhill had a sudden thought: Perhaps it was the painting, the idiotic painting. Maybe that was what had started this whole thing. Thornhill should never have taken the damned thing. He would leave a message on Buchanan's machine at once, telling him his precious object had been returned. Thornhill left the message and arranged for the painting to be brought back to Buchanan's home.

As Thornhill sat back and looked out the window, his confidence was restored. He had one ace in the hole. A good commander always held something in reserve. Thornhill made another phone call and received some positive news, a piece of intelligence that had just come in. His face brightened, the visions of doom receding. It would be all right after all. His mouth eased into a smile. The snatch of victory from the jaws of defeat; it could either age a man several decades overnight or give him bronze balls. Or sometimes both.

In another few minutes Thornhill was getting out of his car and going up the sidewalk to his lovely house. His impeccably dressed wife met him at the door and gave him a perfunctory peck on the cheek. She had just come back from a country club function. In fact, she was always coming back from a country club function, he thought, muttering to himself. While he agonized over terrorists sneaking into the country with nuclear-bomb-making materials, she lounged at fashion shows where young, vacuous women with legs stretching to their inflated bosoms pranced about in outfits that didn't even bother to cover their derrieres. He was out every day saving the world, and his spouse ate finger sandwiches and drank champagne in the afternoon with other ladies of considerable means. The idle rich were as stupid as the uneducated poor—more brainless than cows, in fact, was Thornhill's opinion. At least cows had a reasonable understanding that they were the slaves. *I'm an underpaid civil servant,* Thornhill mused, *and if I ever let my defenses down, the only thing left of the wealthy and powerful in this country would be the echoes of their screams.* It was a mesmerizing thought.

He barely heard his wife's inconsequential ramblings on "her day" as he put down his briefcase, mixed a drink and escaped to his study and closed the door. He never told the woman about *his* day. She'd chat about it to her one-name, oh-so-chic glorified barber, who would tell another client, who would let it slip to someone else and the world would stop tomorrow. No, he never talked shop with the wife. But he did indulge her in just about everything else. But finger sandwiches indeed!

Ironically, Thornhill's home office was much like Buchanan's. There were no plaques, testimonials or souvenirs of his long career on display. He was a spy, after all. Was he supposed to act like the idiotic FBI and wear T-shirts and hats emblazoned with CIA? He almost choked on his whiskey at the thought. No, his career had been invisible to the public, but highly visible to those who mattered. The country was far better off because of him, though the ordinary folk would never know it. That was all right. To seek accolades from the great and ignorant public was the vice of a fool. He did what he did because of pride. Pride in himself, in his devotion to his country.

Thornhill thought back to his beloved father, a patriot who carried his secrets, his distinguished triumphs to the grave. Service and honor. That was what it was all about.

Soon, with a little luck, the son would notch another triumph in his own career. When Faith showed up, she would be dead within an hour. And Adams? Well, he would have to die too. Certainly Thornhill had lied to the man on the phone. Thornhill understood quite clearly that deceit was nothing more nor less than a highly effective tool of the trade. One just had to make sure that lies at work didn't interfere with one's personal life. But Thornhill had always been good with compartmentalization. Just ask his country club wife. He could initiate a covert action in Central America in the morning and play, and win, at bridge at the Congressional Country Club in the evening. Now, dammit, *that* was compartmentalization!

And whatever anyone said about him within the confines of the Agency, he had always been good with his people. He pulled them out of situations when they needed to be pulled. He had never left an agent or case officer spinning in the wind, helpless. But he also kept them in the field when he knew they could carry it home. He had developed an instinct for such things, and it had hardly ever proved wrong. He also didn't play political games with intelligence collection. He had never told the politicians simply what they wanted to hear, as others at the Agency had— sometimes with disastrous consequences. Well, he could only do what he could. In two years it would be someone else's problem. He would leave the organization in as strong a state as he could. His parting gift. There was no need to thank him. Service and honor. He lifted his drink in memory of his late father.

CHAPTER 46

Stay low, Faith," Lee said as he edged close to a window overlooking the street. He had his gun out and was watching a car drop a man off out front. "Is that Buchanan?" he asked.

Faith anxiously peered over the windowsill and then immediately relaxed.

"Yes."

"Okay, answer the front door. I'll cover you."

"I told you it was Danny."

"Great, then go let *Danny* in. I'm not taking any unnecessary chances."

Frowning at this remark, Faith went to the front door and opened it. Buchanan slipped through and she closed and locked the door behind him. They exchanged a prolonged hug as Lee watched from the stairs, his gun in plain sight in his belt clip. Their bodies shook together, and tears streamed down their faces. He felt a pang of jealousy at this embrace. It quickly passed, though, as he sensed the exchange of affection was clearly that of a father and his daughter; a reunion of souls separated by life's circumstances.

"You must be Lee Adams," Buchanan said, extending his hand. "I'm sure you regret the day you ever took on this assignment."

Lee came down and shook his hand. "Nah. This one's been a piece of cake. I'm actually thinking about specializing in this area, especially considering no one else would be stupid enough to do it."

"I thank God you were there to protect Faith."

"Actually, I've gotten pretty good at saving Faith." Lee and Faith exchanged smiles, then Lee looked back at Buchanan. "But the fact is we have one additional complication. A very important one," Lee added. "Let's go to the kitchen. You might want to hear it over a drink."

As they sat at the kitchen table, Lee filled Buchanan in on the situation with his daughter.

Buchanan looked furious. "That bastard."

Lee eyed him keenly. "This bastard have a name? I'd love to know it, for future reference."

Buchanan shook his head. "Trust me, you don't want to go down that route."

"Who is behind all this, Danny?" Faith touched his arm. "I think I have a right to know."

Buchanan looked at Lee.

"Sorry," Lee said, putting up his hands, "that's your call."

Buchanan gripped Faith's arm. "They're very powerful people and they happen to work for this country. That's all I can really say without endangering you even more."

Faith sat back astonished. "*Our* own government is trying to kill us?"

"The gentleman I've been dealing with tends to go his own way. But he does have resources, lots of them."

"So Lee's daughter is in real danger?"

"Yes. This man will usually say rather less than what he actually intends."

"Why'd you come here, Buchanan?" Lee wanted to know. "You got away from the guy. At least for our sakes I hope you did. You could've lost yourself in a million different places. Why come here?"

"I got you both into this. I intend to get you out."

"Well, whatever plan you have better include saving my daughter or else you can count me out. I'll park myself inside her skin for the next twenty years if I have to."

Faith said, "I thought I could call the FBI agent I was working with, Brooke Reynolds. We can tell her what's going on. She could place Lee's daughter in protective custody."

"For the rest of her life?" Buchanan shook his

head. "No, that won't work. We have to cut the hydra's heads off and then burn the stubs. Otherwise we're just wasting time."

"And exactly how do we do that?" Lee asked.

Buchanan opened his briefcase and pulled out the tiny cassette tape from a hidden crevice. "With this. I was able to record the gentleman I've been talking about. On this tape he admits that he had the FBI agent killed, among other incriminating things."

For the first time Lee looked hopeful. "Are you serious?"

"Trust me, I would never joke about this man."

"So we use this tape to keep the hound at bay. He hurts us, we destroy him? He knows that. Then we've pulled his fangs."

Buchanan slowly nodded. "Exactly."

"And you know how to contact him?" asked Lee.

Buchanan nodded. "I'm sure that he's figured out what I did and is right now trying to deduce what my intention is."

"Well, *my* intention is that you call up this asshole right this second and tell him to stay the hell away from my daughter. I want it in blood. And I don't trust the sonofabitch, so I still want something like a company of SEALs outside her dorm room for good measure. And I still plan on heading up there myself. Just in case. They want Renee? They go through me."

"I'm not sure that's a good idea," Buchanan said.

"I don't remember asking for your permission," Lee fired back.

"Lee, please," Faith said. "Danny's just trying to help."

"I wouldn't be in this nightmare if this guy had been straight with me up front. So excuse the hell out of me if I don't treat him like he's my best buddy."

"I don't blame you for feeling that way," Buchanan said. "But you called me for help, and I'll do whatever I can to help you. And your daughter. That I swear."

Lee's guarded manner relaxed somewhat in the face of this seemingly frank declaration.

"Okay," he said grudgingly. "I admit you get points for coming here. You'll get more points when you call off the assassins. And then after that we should get the hell out of here. I've already called this psycho once on my cell phone. I'm assuming that at some point he'll be able to narrow our location down from that. When you call him, it'll give them even more info to work with."

"Understood. I have a plane at my disposal at a private airstrip not too far from here."

"Your friends in high places?"

"*Friend.* Senior senator from this state, Russell Ward."

"Good old Rusty," Faith said, smiling.

"You're sure you weren't followed?" Lee glanced at the front door.

"No one could have followed me. I'm not sure of much anymore, but I am certain of that."

"If this guy is as good as you seem to think he is, I wouldn't feel too certain of anything." Lee held out his cell phone. "Now please make the call."

CHAPTER 47

THORNHILL WAS IN HIS STUDY AT HOME WHEN Buchanan's phone call came in. His communication link was such that the call was not traceable to Thornhill, if Buchanan was perhaps sitting at FBI headquarters. And Thornhill's phone also had a voice scrambler that would make voice ID impossible. On the other hand, Thornhill's people were working on tracing Buchanan's location, but as yet they hadn't been successful. Even the CIA had its limits, what with the explosion in the field of communications technology. There were so many electronic signals flying through the air, it made it damn near impossible to trace a wireless call to a precise location.

The National Security Agency would be able to trace the call with its stadium-size circular antennae.

The super-secret NSA possessed technological might that made anything the CIA had pale by comparison, Thornhill well knew. It was said that the intelligence the NSA perpetually swept out of the air could fill the Library of Congress every *three* hours, gobbling up avalanches of information-bytes. Thornhill had availed himself of the NSA's services before. However, the NSA (the inside joke was that the acronym stood for "no such agency") was often difficult for anyone to control. Thus Thornhill didn't want to involve them in this highly sensitive matter. He would handle it himself.

"You know why I'm calling?" Buchanan said.

"A tape. A highly personal one."

"It's good doing business with someone who considers himself omniscient."

"I would appreciate some small bit of evidence, if it's not too much trouble," Thornhill said placidly.

Buchanan played a snatch of the earlier conversation between the two men.

"Thank you, Danny. Now, your terms?"

"Point one, you don't go near Lee Adams's daughter. That is called off. Now and forever."

"Do you happen to be with Mr. Adams and Ms. Lockhart right now?"

"Second, all three of us are off limits as well. If anything remotely suspicious happens, then the tape goes directly to the FBI."

"During our last conversation you said you already had the means to destroy me."

"I lied."

"Do Adams and Lockhart know of my involvement?"

"No."

"How can I trust you?"

"It would only have put them in more danger to tell them. All they want to do is survive. It seems a common enough goal these days. And I'm afraid you'll just have to take my word for it."

"Even though you just admitted lying to me?"

"Exactly. Tell me, how does it feel?"

"And my long-term plan?"

"I really don't give a damn at this point."

"Why did you run?"

"Put yourself in my place; what would you have done?"

"I would never have allowed myself to be put in your place," said Thornhill.

"Thank God we can't all be like you. Do we have an agreement?"

"I don't have much choice, do I?"

"Join the club," said Buchanan. "However, you can be absolutely certain that if anything happens to any of us, it's over for you. But if you play fair, you accomplish your goal. Everyone lives to celebrate."

"Good doing business with you too, Danny."

Thornhill clicked off and sat there seething for a few moments. Then he made another call but came away disappointed. The trace had not been made. Well, that was all right. He hardly expected it to be so easy. He still had his ace in the hole. He made one more phone call and this time the information brought a broad smile to his lips. As Danny had said, Thornhill did know all there was to know, and he thanked God for his omniscience. When you planned for every possible contingency you were difficult to beat.

Buchanan was with Lockhart, of that he was almost certain. His two golden birds were occupying the same nest. That made his task infinitely simpler. Buchanan had outsmarted himself.

He was just about to refill his scotch when his wife popped her head in. Would he like to go to the club with her? There was a bridge tournament going on. She had just gotten a call. A couple had canceled and wanted to know if the Thornhills could take their place.

"Actually," he said, "I'm very much engaged in a game of chess." His wife looked around the empty room. "Oh, it's long-distance, dear," Thornhill explained, nodding at his desktop computer. "You know the things one can do with technology these days. You can do battle and never even see your opponent."

"Well, don't stay up too late," she said. "You've been working very hard and you're not a young man anymore."

"I see light at the end of the tunnel," Thornhill replied. And this time he was telling the absolute truth.

CHAPTER 48

Reynolds and Connie reached Duck, North Carolina, around one in the morning after only a single stop for fuel and food and reached Pine Island a short while later. The streets were dark, the businesses closed. They were fortunate in finding an all-night gas station, however. While Reynolds got two coffees and some pastries, Connie found out from the clerk on duty where the airplane runway was located. They sat in the gas station lot, ate, and mulled things over.

"I checked in at WFO," Connie told Reynolds as he stirred sugar into his coffee. "Interesting twist. Buchanan's disappeared."

She swallowed a bite of her pastry and stared at him. "How the hell did that happen?"

"Nobody knows. That's why so many people are catching grief over it."

"Well, at least they can't blame that one on us."

"Don't be too sure of that. Laying blame is a fine art in D.C., and the Bureau ain't no exception."

Reynolds had a sudden thought. "Connie, do you think Buchanan could be trying to rendezvous with Lockhart? That may be why he disappeared."

"If we could nail them both at the same time, you might get appointed director."

Reynolds smiled. "I'll settle for having my suspension lifted. But Buchanan might be on his way here. What time did they say they lost the tail?"

"Early evening."

"Then he could already be here; hours ago if he took a plane."

Connie sipped his coffee, while he thought this over. "Why would Buchanan and Lockhart be doing anything together?" he asked slowly.

"Don't forget, if we're right about Buchanan hiring Adams, then maybe Adams called Buchanan and they hooked up that way."

"*If* Adams is innocent in all this. But he sure as hell wouldn't call Buchanan if he thought the guy had anything to do with trying to knock off Lockhart. After all we've found out, I'm gauging the guy as her protector, of sorts."

"I think you're right about that. But maybe Adams found out something that made him believe Buchanan didn't order the hit. If that was the case, he might try to team with Buchanan to figure out together what the hell was going on and who else was out there trying to kill Lockhart."

"Somebody else behind this? One of the foreign governments Buchanan was working with, maybe? If the truth came out, they'd be sitting out there with world-class egg on their face. That's plenty of incentive to kill somebody," Connie said.

"I wonder," Reynolds began, as Connie watched her closely. "There's just been something about this case that's never added up," she said. "We've got somebody impersonating FBI agents. Somebody who seems to know our every move."

"Ken Newman?"

"Maybe. But that doesn't seem to make sense either. Ken's had cash coming in for a long time. Has he been somebody's mole for that long a period of time? Or is it somebody else?"

"And don't forget about whoever's trying to frame you. Moving money around accounts like that takes some expertise."

"Exactly. But I just don't see operatives of a foreign government being able to do all that, and no one the wiser."

"Brooke, countries conduct industrial espionage against us every day. Shit, our staunchest allies even do it, ripping off our technology because they're not smart enough to do it on their own. And our borders are so open it doesn't take much to get in. You know that."

Reynolds let out a deep sigh as she stared into the darkness lying right outside the gas station's harsh ring of lights. "I suppose you're right. I guess instead of trying to figure out who's behind this, we should try to find Lockhart and company and just ask them."

"Now, that's a plan I can relate to." Connie put the car in gear and they sped off into the darkness.

After locating the runway, Reynolds and Connie cruised the dark streets looking for the Honda Gold Wing. Virtually all of the beach houses appeared vacant now, which made their search both easier and more difficult. It cut down the number of places they had to focus on, but it also made the agents stand out more.

Connie finally spotted the Honda in the carport of one of the beach houses. Reynolds eased out of the car and got a close enough look to confirm that the license tag matched the bike Lee Adams had borrowed from his brother's shop. Then they drove to the other end of the street, hit the lights and talked it over.

"Maybe it's as simple as me going in the front and you going in the back," Reynolds said as she studied the dark house. Her skin was tingling with the thought that a bare fifty feet away were two or possibly the three key people in this whole investigation.

Connie shook his head. "I don't like that. The Honda being there means Adams is in there too."

"We've got his gun."

"A guy like that, first thing he would've done is get another one. And we go in, even if we surprise him, he knows the lay of the land better than we do. He might get one of us." He added, "And you don't even have a gun, so we're not splitting up."

"You're the one who said you thought Adams wasn't a bad guy."

"Thinking something and being absolutely certain of it are two different things. And that difference is not something I'm willing to risk anybody's life over. And rushing in on anybody, good or bad, in the middle of the night, mistakes can happen. I intend on getting you back to your kids in one piece. And I wouldn't mind doing the same."

"So how do we play it? Wait for daylight and call in reinforcements?"

"Calling in the locals will probably mean every TV station down here will be on the block an hour after we do. That won't earn us many points at HQ."

"Well, I guess we can wait for them to ride off on the Honda and then pull them."

"Other things being equal, I'm inclined to watch the place and see what happens. If they come out, we move in. If we get real lucky, Lockhart will surface without Adams and we can take her. After that, I'm figuring we can bait Adams out pretty easy."

"And if they don't come out, together or singly?"

"Then we'll cross that bridge when we come to it."

"I don't want to lose them again, Connie."

"It's not like they can just take off down the beach or swim to England. Adams went to a lot of trouble to get those wheels. He's not going to abandon the bike because he doesn't have another way to replace it. Where he goes, that Honda goes. And that Honda ain't going anywhere without us seeing it."

They settled down and waited.

CHAPTER 49

His pistol resting on his belly, Lee had spent a few fitful hours on the couch downstairs. Every few minutes he thought he heard someone breaking in, and each time it proved to be nothing more than his very tired imagination doing its best to drive him crazy. Since he couldn't sleep, he had finally decided to get ready to leave for Charlottesville. He grabbed a quick shower and changed his clothes. He was packing his bag when a soft knock came on his door.

Faith was dressed in a long white robe; her puffy cheeks and tired-looking eyes were stark testaments to her inability to sleep.

"Where's Buchanan?" he asked.

"Actually dozing, I think. I never came close."

"Tell me about it." He finished packing and closed his bag.

"Are you sure you don't want me to come with you?" she asked.

He shook his head. "I don't want you anywhere near this guy and his goons if they show up. I got through to Renee last night. First time I've talked to her in I don't know how long and I have to tell her she might be the target of some psycho because of something her stupid dad did."

"How did she take it?"

On this Lee brightened. "Actually, she seemed happy to hear from me. I didn't tell her everything that was going on. I didn't want to panic her too much, but I think she's looking forward to seeing me."

"I'm glad to hear that. I'm really happy for you, Lee."

"The cops at least took my call seriously. Renee said a patrolman came by and a marked car's been cruising the area."

He put his bag down, took her hand. "I don't feel good about leaving you."

"It's your daughter. We'll be fine. You heard Danny. He's got this person over a barrel."

Lee looked unconvinced. "The last thing you should do right now is let down your guard. The car will be here at eight to take you and Buchanan to the plane. You head back to D.C."

"And then what?"

"Go to a motel in the suburbs. Register under a false name and then call me on my cell phone. As soon as things are okay with Renee I'll head back. I already talked it over with Buchanan. He's in agreement."

"And then?" Faith persisted.

"Let's just take it a step at a time. I told you there are no guarantees in this."

"I was actually talking about *us.*"

Lee played with the strap on his bag. "Oh," was all that came out, and it sounded idiotic.

"I see."

"You see what?" Lee demanded.

"Wham, bam, thank you, ma'am."

"Where do you get off thinking like that? Don't you know what kind of a man I am by now?"

"Actually, I thought I did. But I guess I forgot. You're in the loner group: sex only for fun. Right?"

"Why are we doing this? Like we don't have enough going on. We can talk about it later. It's not like I'm not coming back."

Lee didn't mean to put her off, but—hell, why couldn't she see there was no time for this right now?

Faith sat down on the bed.

"Like you said, no guarantees," she said.

He put a hand on her shoulder. "I am coming back, Faith. I didn't come this far to desert you now."

"Okay," was all she said. She stood and gave him a quick hug. "Please, please, be careful."

Faith let him out the rear door. As she turned to go back in, Lee's gaze was riveted on her. He took in everything, from the bare feet to the short dark hair and all points in between. For one troubling moment, he wondered if this was the last time he would ever see her.

Lee climbed on the Honda and quickly started up the bike.

As Lee roared out of the driveway and hit the street, Brooke Reynolds raced back to the Crown Vic and threw open the door. Breathless, she looked inside.

"Shit, I knew the minute I left the car to get a closer look at the house this would happen. He must have come out a rear door. He didn't even turn on the carport light. I never saw him until the bike cranked up. So what do we do? House or the bike?"

Connie looked down the road. "Adams is already out of sight. And that bike is a lot more agile than this tank."

"I guess that leaves the house and Lockhart."

Connie suddenly looked worried. "We're presuming she's still inside. In fact, we don't even know if she was ever inside."

"Shit, I knew you were going to say that. She damn well better be. If we just let Adams go and Lockhart isn't in that house, *I* will swim to England. And you're going to have to be right beside me. Come on, Connie, we have to go in the house."

Connie climbed out of the car, pulled his gun and looked around nervously. "Shit, I don't like this. It could be a setup. We could be walking right into an ambush. And we've got no backup."

"We don't have much choice, do we?"

"All right, but dammit, stay behind me."

They headed for the house.

CHAPTER 50

Dressed in black sweats and tennis shoes, the three men raced along the beach, keeping low to the sand. Although the dawn was fast approaching, they were virtually invisible in their dark clothing against the backdrop of the ocean, and the pounding surf covered all sounds of their movements.

They had arrived in the area barely an hour ago and had just received some very disturbing news. Lee Adams had left the house. Lockhart wasn't with him. She must still be in the house. Or at least they hoped she was. Buchanan, they had been told, might be there as well. They would take those two over Adams. He could wait. They would eventually get him. In fact, they would not stop until they got him.

Each team member was equipped with an automatic pistol and a knife specially designed to take out the carotid in one efficient stroke. Each man was well skilled in exactly how to execute just such a lethal blow. Their orders were clear. Everyone in the house had to die. Perfectly executed, it could be a clean operation. They could be back in Washington by late morning.

They were proud men, professionals in their own right and long in the service of Robert Thornhill. As a team they had survived some dangerous times in the last twenty years with their wit, skill, physical strength and stamina. They had saved lives, made certain parts of the world safer, helped to ensure that the United States would become the world's sole remaining superpower. This would mean a fairer, more just world for many. Like Robert Thornhill, they had joined the Agency to perform a service, to engage in a public trust. To them, there was no higher calling.

All three men were also part of the group Lee and Faith had eluded at Adams's apartment. The episode had embarrassed them, tarnishing their reputation for near perfection. They had been hoping for a shot at redemption, and now they did not intend to waste it.

One man stayed near the top of the stairs to keep watch, while the other two hurried down the boardwalk to the rear of the house. The plan was simple, direct, unencumbered by layers of detail. They would hit the house hard and fast, starting on the ground floor and moving up. When they ran into anyone, they wouldn't ask questions or seek identification.

Their suppressor-equipped pistols would fire one time for each victim, and then they would move on until every living thing in the house no longer was. Yes, it was definitely conceivable they could be back in Washington before lunch.

LEE SLOWED DOWN THE HONDA AND THEN stopped in the middle of the road, his feet coming down lightly on the asphalt. He looked back over his shoulder. The street was long, black and empty. Daylight would be coming soon, though. He could see it in the softening edges of the sky, like the streaked edges of a Polaroid slowly lapping to vibrancy.

So why couldn't he have waited? He could have stayed until the car came to take Faith and Buchanan to the airstrip. It would only delay his trip to Charlottesville by a couple of hours at most. And it would certainly increase his peace of mind. Why the hell was he running away so fast? Renee was protected. What about Faith?

His gloved hand tapped against the Honda's throttle. It would also give him a chance to talk to the woman, to let Faith know that he cared very much for her.

He turned the Honda around and headed back. When he reached the street, he slowed the bike. The car was parked at the far end of the street. It was a big sedan that just screamed federal government. True, it was at the opposite end of the street and he wouldn't have passed it heading to the main road, but how the hell had his "expert" eyes missed that? God, was he really getting that old?

He drove directly at the car, figuring that if it was the Feds, he could cut off easily enough and lose them. As he drew closer, however, it was clear the car was empty. Starting to panic, he swung the Honda around, rode up into the driveway of the beach house two lots down from Faith's and jumped off. Throwing down his helmet and pulling his pistol, Lee raced around to the rear courtyard of the house and then on to the boardwalk that crisscrossed the rear common areas connecting all the houses to the main steps going to the beach, like human veins leading to the heart's arteries. His own heart was pumping at a feverishly high pace.

He jumped off the boardwalk, squatted low behind some sawgrass and peered at the back of Faith's beach house. What he saw chilled him to the bone. The two men were dressed all in black and were sliding over the rear wall of Faith's courtyard. Were they the Feds? Or were they the men who had been prepared to assassinate Faith at the airport? *Please, God, don't let it be them.* The two men had already disappeared over the wall. In seconds they would be in the house. Had Faith reset the alarm system after she let him out? No, he thought, she probably hadn't.

Lee jumped up and dashed toward the house. As he crossed the boardwalk, he sensed something coming at him from the left as the darkness began to lift even more. That sensation was probably the only thing that saved his life.

The knife plunged into his arm instead of his neck as he ducked and rolled. He came up bleeding, but the rigid material of the bike suit had absorbed a good deal of the blow. His attacker didn't hesitate but leaped straight at him.

However, Lee timed it just right, managed to raise his good arm, pushed hard, levered the man over him, throwing him into the sawgrass, which was about as unpleasant as having a sharp knife driven into your flesh. Lee lunged for his gun, which he had lost when the guy had slammed into him. Lee had no qualms about shooting the guy down and raising a ruckus. Right now he would welcome any assistance the local police cared to provide.

His opponent made a stunning recovery, however, bursting out of the sawgrass with startling velocity and colliding with Lee before he could retrieve his pistol. The two men landed at the edge of the steps. Lee saw the knife thrust coming again but was able to grip the man's wrist before the blade hit him. The guy was strong; Lee could feel the steely tendons in the man's forearm and in the rocklike triceps as he grabbed the man's upper arm in an attempt to force the knife out of his hand. But Lee wasn't exactly a weakling either. He hadn't shoved tons of barbells around for years for nothing.

The guy he was battling was an experienced fighter as well because he managed to get in two or three efficient gut punches with his free hand. After the first one, though, Lee tightened his abdominals and obliques and felt little pain from the other jabs. He had spent over two decades doing stomach crunches and having medicine balls slammed into his belly. After that punishment, the human fist offered very little difficulty for him, no matter how hard it was thrown.

Thinking that two could play at that game, Lee let go of the man's upper arm and landed a body uppercut to the diaphragm. He felt the wind go out of the guy, but the grip on the knife remained unbroken. Then Lee landed three successful kidney punches, about the most painful ones you could throw and still leave your opponent conscious. The knife fell from the man's hand, clattering down the steps.

Then both men rose to their feet, breathing hard, still clinging to each other. Like a burst of wind, the man executed a nifty loopkick that knocked Lee's legs out from under him. He went down with a grunt but popped right back up when he saw the guy go for his pistol. Being seconds from death gave Lee's body resiliency he could never summon in less dangerous times. He hit the guy low and hard, linebacker to running back in a textbook impact, and they both went over the edge of the steps, bouncing painfully down each pressure-treated plank and landing in a pile of twisted arms, legs and torsos in the sand and then eating mouthfuls of salty water as they rolled into the water, the rising tide being almost up to the steps.

Lee had seen the pistol tumble away during the fall, so he kicked himself free and stood in ankle-deep water. The guy rose too, but not as swiftly. Lee, however, was tightly on guard. The guy knew karate; Lee had felt it in the kick at the top of the stairs; he was seeing it in the defensive posture the man now assumed, making himself into a little ball, leaving no angles, nothing of much width to hit. His brain working faster than conscious thought, Lee figured he had about four inches and fifty pounds on the guy, but if the man nailed him with a lethal foot to the head, Lee would go down. And then he and Faith and Buchanan were all dead. But if he didn't finish the guy within the next minute, Faith and Buchanan would be dead anyway.

The man aimed a crushing side kick to Lee's torso; however, his having to slosh through water to deliver the kick gave Lee the little extra time he needed. Lee had to get in close, grab what he could and not give Chuck Norris Jr. enough space to do his martial arts magic. Lee was a boxer; in-close fighting, where whipping legs couldn't do much damage, was where he could be absolutely devastating. Lee braced himself and absorbed the rib-rattling leg shot to the body but then held on to the limb with his bloodied arm, clinching it to his side in a viselike grip. With his free hand, he landed a cartilage-shattering blow to the guy's knee, driving it backward to a degree knees were not designed to go. The man screamed. Then Lee delivered a crunching straight jab to the guy's face, feeling the nose flatten under the impact. Finally, in a flash of almost choreographed movement, Lee dropped the leg, curled low and then erupted out of that position with a cannonball left hook that carried all two hundred and twenty pounds of his bulk plus whatever multiplying factor pure fury brought to the battle. When his fist hit facial bone, which promptly yielded under the terrible impact, Lee knew he had won. Nobody short of a professional heavyweight had a jaw that hard.

The man went down as though shot through the head. Lee instantly flipped him on his stomach and pushed his head under the water. He didn't have time to actually drown the guy, so he brought his elbow down with all his might dead center on the back of the man's neck. The resulting sound was unmistakable, even with the water lapping all over them, as though God wanted Lee to damn well know what he'd done, and didn't want him to ever forget it.

The body went limp and Lee rose over the dead man. Lee had been in more than his share of fights both in and out of the boxing ring, but he had never killed anyone before. As he looked down at the body, he knew it was nothing to be proud of. Lee was just grateful it wasn't him lying dead.

Sick to his stomach and suddenly feeling the full force of the pain in his wounded arm, Lee looked up the steps leading to the beach houses. He had only two other beasts to conquer and then he could call it a day. And it was clear they weren't the Feds. FBI agents didn't run around trying to kill people with fancy knives and karate kicks; they pulled their shields and guns and told you to stop right in your tracks. And if you were smart, you did.

No, they were the other guys. The CIA robokillers. He raced up the steps, found his pistol and hustled as fast as he could to the beach house, hoping with every labored breath that he was not too late.

CHAPTER 52

FAITH HAD CHANGED INTO JEANS AND A SWEAT-shirt and now sat on her bed staring at her bare feet. The sounds of the motorcycle had disappeared as though into an enormous vacuum. As she looked around the room, it was as though Lee Adams had never even been here, had never been real. She had spent so much time and energy trying to lose the man, and now that he was gone, all of her spirit seemed to have been swept into the void Lee had left behind.

At first she thought the sound she heard in the stillness of the house was Buchanan stirring. Then she thought it might actually be Lee returning. It had sounded like the back door. As she rose from the bed, it suddenly occurred to her that it couldn't be Lee because she hadn't heard the motorcycle pull into the carport; as this thought hit, her heart started thudding uncontrollably.

Had she locked the door? She couldn't remember. She knew she hadn't set the alarm. Could it be just Danny stumbling around? For some reason Faith knew it wasn't.

She eased over to the doorway and peered out, her ears straining to hear any sound. She knew she hadn't imagined the noise. Someone had come in the house, she was sure of it. Someone was in the house right now. She looked down the hallway. There was another alarm control panel in the bedroom Lee had used. Could she reach it, activate the system, the motion detector? She dropped to her knees and crawled out into the hallway.

Connie and Reynolds had gone in the side door and made their way down the lower-floor hallway. Connie had his gun pointed ahead. Reynolds was behind him, feeling naked and useless without her own pistol. They eased open each door on the lower level and found each room empty.

"They must be upstairs," Reynolds whispered into Connie's ear.

"I hope there's somebody here," he whispered back, his voice carrying an ominous tone.

They both froze when a sound came from somewhere within the house. Connie motioned upstairs with his finger and Reynolds nodded in agreement. They approached the stairs and headed up. Fortunately, the stairs were carpeted and absorbed the sounds of their footsteps. They reached the first landing and paused, listening intently. Silence. They moved forward again.

The family area was empty, as far as they could see. They moved along one wall, their heads swiveling in near-synchronized motion.

Right above them, in the upstairs hallway, Faith was flat on her stomach on the floor. She peered over the edge and relaxed slightly as she saw that it was Agent Reynolds. When she saw the two other men moving up the stairs from the lower level, her fear instantly returned.

"Look out," Faith yelled.

Connie and Reynolds turned back to look at her and saw where she was pointing. Connie swung his gun in the direction of the two men, who also had their guns out, pointed directly at the two agents.

"FBI," Reynolds barked out to the men in black. "Drop your weapons." Usually when she said that, she felt fairly confident of the response. Now, with two guns against one, she was not nearly as confident.

The two men didn't drop their weapons. They moved forward as Connie swung his gun back and forth between the two.

One of the men looked up at Faith. "Come down here, Ms. Lockhart."

"Stay up there, Faith," Reynolds called out, her

gaze finding Faith's and holding on it. "Go to your room and lock the door."

"Faith?" Buchanan appeared in the hallway, his white hair disheveled, his eyes blinking.

"You too, Buchanan. Now," the same man commanded. "Down here."

"No!" Reynolds said, moving forward. "Listen up, an HRT unit is on its way here right now. We're looking at an ETA of about two minutes. If you won't put your weapons down, then I suggest you run like hell unless you want to go up against those guys."

The man looked at her and smiled. "There's no HRT unit coming, Agent Reynolds."

Reynolds could not hide her astonishment. That astonishment immeasurably increased with the man's next words.

"Agent Constantinople," the man said, looking over at Connie, "you can leave now. We have it under control, but we appreciate your assistance."

Slowly, Reynolds turned and looked at her partner, her mouth open in absolute shock.

Connie stared back at her, a distinct look of resignation on his features.

"Connie?" Reynolds took a quick breath. "It can't be, Connie. Please tell me it's not."

Connie fingered his pistol and he shrugged. Gradually his taut posture relaxed. "My plan was to get you out of this alive *and* get your suspension lifted."

He looked over at the two men. One of them shook his head decisively.

"You're the leak?" Reynolds said. "Not Ken?"

"Ken was no leak," Connie said.

"But the money in the safe-deposit box?"

"That came from his card and coin trading. He operated all in cash. I actually did some shows with him. I knew. He was cheating the tax guys. So who the hell cared? More power to him. Most of it was going to college funds for his kids anyway."

"You let me think he was the leak."

"Well, I didn't want you to think it was me. Obviously, that would not have been good."

One of the men ran upstairs and disappeared into one of the bedrooms. A minute later he emerged carrying Buchanan's briefcase. He escorted Faith and Buchanan down the stairs. The man popped open the briefcase and took out the cassette. He played a little of the tape to confirm what was on it. Then he cracked open the cassette, pulled out the tape and threw the long strands into the gas fireplace and hit the remote switch. They all watched in silence as the tape was quickly reduced to a gooey mess.

As Reynolds watched the tape disappear, she couldn't help but think she was being shown the next few minutes of her life. The *last* few minutes of her life.

Reynolds looked at the two men and then at Connie. "So they just tailed us all the way down? I didn't see anybody," she said bitterly.

Connie shook his head. "There was a transmitter in my car. They've been listening in. They let us find the right house and then followed."

"Why, Connie? Why turn traitor?"

Connie's tone was reflective. "I put in twenty-five years at the Bureau. Twenty-five damn good years, and I'm still at square one, still a grunt in the field. I got a dozen years on you and you're my boss. Because I wouldn't play the political game south of the border. Because I wouldn't lie and just go along, they tanked my career." He shook his head and looked down. When he stared back up at her, he looked apologetic. "Understand, I got nothing against you, Brooke. Nothing. You're a damn fine agent. I didn't want it to end like this. The plan was for us to stay outside and let these guys do their thing. When I got the all-clear, we'd go in and find the bodies. Your name would be cleared, everything would work out fine. Adams taking off like that blew our plan apart." Connie stared with unfriendly eyes at the man in black who had identified him by name. "But if this guy hadn't said anything, maybe I still could have figured out a way for you to walk away with me."

The man shrugged. "Sorry, I didn't know that was important to you. But you'd better get going. It's getting light outside. Give us half an hour. Then you can call the cops. Make up any cover story you want."

Reynolds never took her eyes off Connie. "Let me make up a cover story for you, Connie. It goes like this: We found the house. I go in the front while you cover the rear. I don't come out. You hear shots, you go in. Find us all dead." Reynolds's voice broke as she thought of her children, of never seeing them again. "You see someone leaving, empty your pistol at him. But you miss, give chase, are almost killed, but luckily barely survive. You call the cops. They get here. You call HQ, fill them in. They send people down. You get bitched at a little for coming down here with me, but you were just standing by your boss. Loyalty. Who could really blame you? They investigate and never reach a satisfactory answer. Probably think I'm the leak for sure, came down for a payoff. You can tell them it was my idea to come here, that I knew exactly where to go. I go in the house, get popped. And you, a poor innocent dupe, almost lose your life too. Case closed. How's that sound, Agent Constantinople?" She almost spat this last part out.

One of Thornhill's men looked over at Connie and smiled. "Sounds good to me."

Connie never took his eyes off Reynolds. "I'm sorry, Brooke, I really am."

Reynolds's eyes filled with tears and her voice cracked again when she spoke. "Tell Anne Newman that. Tell *my* kids that, you bastard!"

His eyes downcast, Connie moved past them and started to head down the stairs.

"We'll do them here, one by one," the first man said.

He looked at Buchanan. "You first."

"I take it that was a special request from your boss," Buchanan said.

"Who? I want a name," Reynolds demanded.

"What does it matter?" the second man said. "It's not like you're going to be around to testify—"

The instant he said this, the bullet hit him in the back of the head.

The other man whirled, trying to aim his gun, but was too late and took a blast right in the face. He dropped, dead, next to his partner.

Connie came back up the stairs, a wisp of smoke still trailing from his pistol's muzzle. He looked down at the two dead men. "That was for Ken Newman, you assholes." He looked up at Reynolds. "I didn't know they were going to kill Ken, Brooke. I swear that on a stack of Bibles. But after it happened, there was nothing I could do but bide my time and see what happened."

"And let me chase a wild goose? Watch me get suspended. My career ruined."

"There wasn't much I could do about that. Like I said, my intent was to get you out of this, get you reinstated. Let you be the hero. Let Ken take the charge as snitch. He was dead, what did it matter?"

"It would matter to his family, Connie."

Connie's features turned angry. "Look, I don't have to stand here and explain shit to you or anybody else. I'm not proud of what I did, but I had my reasons.

You don't have to agree with them, and I'm not asking you to, but don't stand there and lecture me about something you know nothing about, lady. You want'a talk pain and bitterness? I got about fifteen years of it on you."

Reynolds blinked and stepped back, eyeing the pistol.

"Okay, Connie, you just saved our lives. That'll count for a lot."

"You think so, do you?"

She pulled out her cell phone. "I'm going to call Massey and get a team down here."

"Put the phone away, Brooke."

"Connie—"

"Put the damn phone down. Now!"

Reynolds let the phone drop to the floor. "Connie, it's over."

"It's never over, Brooke, you know that. Stuff that happened years ago will always come back to bite you in the ass. People find out stuff and look you up and suddenly your life is over."

"Is that why you're involved in this? Somebody was blackmailing you?"

He slowly gazed about. "What the hell does it matter?"

"It matters to me!" said Reynolds.

Connie let out a deep sigh. "When my wife got cancer, our insurance wouldn't cover all the specialized treatments. The doctors thought the treatments might give her a chance, a few more months. I mortgaged the house to the hilt. I cleaned out our bank accounts. It still wasn't enough. What was I supposed to do? Just let her die?" Connie angrily shook his head. "So some coke and other stuff turned up missing from the Bureau evidence room. Some people found out about it later. And suddenly I had a new employer." He paused and looked down for a moment. "And the most damnable thing is June died anyway."

"I can help you, Connie. You can end this right now."

Connie smiled grimly. "Nobody can help me, Brooke. I made my deal with the devil."

"Connie, let them go. It's over."

He shook his head. "I came here to do a job. And you know me well enough to know that I always finish what I start."

"Then what? How will you talk yourself out of these?" She looked at the two dead men. "And now you're going to kill three *more* people? That's crazy. Please."

"Not as crazy as giving up and spending the rest of my life in prison. Or maybe getting the chair." He shrugged his big shoulders. "I'll think of something."

"Please, Connie. Don't do this. You can't do this. I know you. You can't."

Connie looked at his pistol and then knelt down

and picked up one of the dead men's guns that had a suppressor attached. "I've got to. And I am sorry, Brooke."

They all heard the click. Connie and Reynolds instantly recognized it as the cock of a semi-automatic pistol.

Lee barked, "Drop the pistol. Now! Or I put a tunnel in your head."

Connie froze and let the gun fall to the floor.

Lee came up the stairs and put the muzzle of his pistol against the agent's head. "I'm real tempted to shoot you anyway, but you did save me the trouble of tangling with two more gorillas." Lee looked at Reynolds. "Agent Reynolds, I'd appreciate if you'd pick up the pistol and keep it trained on your boy here."

Reynolds did so, her eyes burning into her partner's. "Sit down, Connie. Now!" she ordered.

Lee went over and put his arms around Faith.

"Lee," was all she said, leaning into him.

"Thank God I decided to come back."

"Can someone tell me what the hell this is all about?" Reynolds said.

Buchanan stepped forward. "I can, but it may not do any good. The proof I had was on that tape. I was planning on making copies, but I didn't have the chance to before I left Washington."

Reynolds looked down at Connie. "You obviously know what's going on. If you cooperate, it'll help your sentencing."

"I might as well strap myself in the chair," Connie said.

"Who? Dammit, who is behind this that everybody's so scared to death of?"

"Agent Reynolds," Buchanan said, "I'm sure that particular gentleman is waiting to hear the outcome of all this. If he doesn't get it soon, he'll send out more men. I suggest we stop that from happening."

Reynolds looked at him. "Why should I trust you? What I should do is call the cops."

Faith said, "The night Agent Newman was killed, I told him I wanted Danny to come in and testify with me. Newman told me that would never happen."

"Well, he told you right."

"But I think if you know all the facts, you won't think that way. What we did was wrong, but there was *no other way.* . . ."

"Well, that makes it all perfectly clear," Reynolds replied.

"That can wait," Buchanan said with urgency. "Right now we have to take care of the man behind these people." He looked down at the dead men.

"You can add one more to that count," Lee said. "He's outside taking a dip in the ocean."

Reynolds looked exasperated. "Everybody except for me seems to know everything." She turned to Buchanan with a scowl. "Okay, I'm listening. What's your suggestion?"

Buchanan started to answer when they all heard the

sound of a plane coming in. Their eyes went to the window, where the dawn had broken.

"It's just the commuter service. It's daylight. First flight in. The runway's across the street," Faith explained.

"That I *do* know," Reynolds said.

"I suggest we use your friend there," Buchanan said, nodding at Connie, "to communicate with this person."

"And tell him what?"

"That his operation was a total success, except that his men were killed in the ensuing battle. He'll understand that, of course. Losses happen. But that Faith and I were killed and the tape was destroyed. That way he'll feel safe."

"And me?" Lee said.

Buchanan glanced at him. "We'll let you be our wild card."

"And why exactly should I do that?" Reynolds wanted to know. "When I could take you and Faith, and him"—she flicked her pistol at Connie—"to the WFO, get my job back and walk away a hero?"

"Because if you do that, the man who has caused all of this will go free. Free to do something like this again."

Reynolds looked confused and troubled.

Buchanan watched her closely. "It's up to you."

Reynolds looked at each of them and then her gaze

came to rest on Lee. She noted the blood on his sleeve, the cuts and bruises on his face.

"You saved all of our lives. You're probably the most innocent person in this room. What do you think?"

Lee looked at Faith and then at Buchanan before coming back to Reynolds. "I don't think I can give you a great reason to do it, but if you want my gut, I'd say to go along with them."

Reynolds sighed and looked over at Connie. "You have a way of contacting this monster?" Connie said nothing. "Connie, you work with us on this, it'll help you. I know you were just prepared to kill all of us, and I shouldn't give a damn about what happens to you." She paused and looked down for a moment. "But I do. Last chance, Connie, what do you say?"

Connie's big hands clenched and unclenched nervously. He looked at Buchanan. "What exactly do you want me to say?"

Buchanan told him precisely, and Connie sat down on the couch, picked up the phone and dialed. When the line was answered, he said, "This is . . . "—Connie looked embarrassed for a moment—"this is Ace-in-the-Hole." A few minutes later Connie put down the phone and looked at each of them. "Okay, it's done."

"Did he seem to buy it?" Lee asked.

"Yes, but you can never be sure with these guys."

"Good enough; that gives us some time," Buchanan said.

"Well, right now we have some things to tend to," Reynolds said. "Like a number of dead bodies. And I've got to report in. And get you"—she looked at Connie—"into a cell."

Connie glared at her. "So much for loyalty," he said.

She glared back. "You made your choices. What you did for us *will* help you. But you're going to be in prison a long time, Connie. At least you get to live. That's more of a choice than Ken had."

She looked at Buchanan. "Now what?"

"I suggest we leave here immediately. Once we're out of the area, you can call the police. When we get back to Washington, Faith and I will meet with the FBI, tell them what we know. We must keep everything completely secret. If he knows we're working with the FBI, we'll never get the proof we need."

"This guy had Ken killed?"

"Yes."

"Is he with a foreign interest?"

"Actually, you both have the same employer."

Reynolds looked at him, stunned. "Uncle Sam?" she said slowly.

Buchanan nodded. "If you trust me, I will do my best to bring him to you. I have my own personal score to settle with him."

"And what exactly do you expect in return?"

"For me? Nothing. If I go to prison, I go to prison.

But Faith goes free. Unless you can guarantee me that, you can just call the police right now."

Faith grabbed his arm. "Danny, you're not taking the fall for this."

"Why not? It was my doing."

"But your reasons—"

"Reasons are no defense. I knew I was taking a chance when I broke the law."

"Well, so did I, dammit!"

Buchanan turned back to Reynolds. "Do we have a deal? Faith does not go to prison."

"I'm really not in a position to offer you anything." She pondered the issue for a moment. "But I can promise you this: If you are shooting straight with me, I'll do everything in my power to see that Faith goes free."

Connie stood up, suddenly looking pale. "Brooke, I need to hit the john, like quick." He was wobbly on his feet; one hand slid to his chest.

She glanced at him suspiciously. "What's the matter?" She scrutinized his pallid features. "Are you all right?"

"To tell you the truth, I've been better," he mumbled, his head rolling to one side, his left side drooping.

"I'll go with him," Lee said.

As the pair started to the stairs, Connie seemed to lose his balance and he pressed his hand hard against the center of his chest, his face contorted in pain.

"Shit. Oh, God!" He dropped to one knee, moaning, saliva dripping out of his mouth; he started gurgling.

"Connie!" Reynolds started toward him.

"He's having a heart attack," Faith cried out.

"Connie!" Reynolds said again as she stared at her stricken partner, who was fast sinking to the floor, his body twitching uncontrollably.

The movement was fast. It seemed too fast for a man in his fifties, but then again, desperation could mix with adrenaline in a flash.

Connie's hand dipped to his ankle. A compact pistol was in a holster there. The gun was out and aimed before anyone could react. Connie had multiple targets, but he chose Danny Buchanan and fired.

The only one who reacted as fast as Connie did was Faith Lockhart.

From where she was standing next to Buchanan, she saw the pistol come out before anyone else. She saw the barrel pointed at her friend. In her mind she could hear the explosion that would launch the bullet that would kill Buchanan. How she moved that fast was inexplicable.

The bullet hit Faith in the chest; she gasped once and then dropped at Buchanan's feet.

"Faith!" Lee screamed. Instead of tackling Connie, he lunged for her.

Reynolds's gun was trained on Connie. As he swung the pistol around in her direction, the image of the palm reader flashed through her mind. That all-too-short life line. MOTHER OF TWO, FEDERAL AGENT DEAD. She saw the headline fully and boldly in her mind. The whole thing was almost paralyzing. Almost.

She and Connie locked gazes. He was bringing up his pistol, lining it up with her. He would pull the trigger, she had no doubt. He clearly had the nerve, the balls to kill. Did she? Her finger tightened on her own trigger as the entire world seemed to slow to the pace of an underwater world, where gravity was either suspended or magnified. Her partner. An FBI agent. A traitor. Her children. Her own life. Now or never.

Reynolds pulled the trigger once and then a second time. The recoil was short, her aim perfect. As the bullets entered Connie's body, his bulk quivered, his mind perhaps still sending messages, not yet realizing that it was dead.

Reynolds thought she saw Connie stare searchingly at her as he started to go down, the gun falling from his hand. That image would haunt her forever. Only when Agent Howard Constantinople hit the floor and didn't move again did Brooke Reynolds take a breath.

"Faith, Faith!" Lee was tearing at her shirt, exposing the horribly bloody wound in her chest. "Oh my God. Faith." She was unconscious, her breathing barely detectable.

Buchanan stared down in blank horror.

Reynolds knelt beside Lee. "How bad?"

Lee looked up in anguish. He couldn't speak.

Reynolds assessed the wound. "Bad," she said. "Slug's still in her. The hole's right near her heart."

Lee looked at Faith. Her skin was already beginning to pale. He could fee the warmth of life spilling out from her with each shallow breath she took. "Oh, God. No. Please!" he cried out.

"We've got to get her to a hospital. Fast," Reynolds said. She had no idea where the closest hospital was, let alone a trauma center, which was what Faith really needed. And searching the local area by car would be akin to signing the woman's death warrant. She could call the paramedics, but who knew how long it would take for them to get here? The roar of the plane engine outside made Reynolds glance at the window. The plan formed in her head within seconds. She raced back to Connie and lifted his FBI credentials from his body. For one brief moment she gazed at her former colleague. She shouldn't feel bad for what she had done. He had been well prepared to kill her. So why did she feel crushed by remorse? But Connie was dead. Faith Lockhart wasn't. At least not yet. Reynolds hustled back over to where Faith lay. "Lee, we're taking the plane. Hurry!"

The group raced outside, Reynolds in the lead. They could hear the plane's engines revving up as it prepared to take off. Reynolds sprinted ahead. She headed for the wall of brush until Lee screamed at her and pointed toward the access road. She raced in that

direction and a minute later found herself on the runway. She looked down at the opposite end. The plane
was turning, getting ready to roar down the tarmac,
lift into the air; their only hope would be gone in seconds. She ran down the asphalt, directly at the aircraft, waving the pistol, the badge, screaming,
"FBI!" at the top of her lungs. The plane came racing at her, as Buchanan and Lee, carrying Faith, burst
onto the runway.

The pilot finally focused on the woman waving a
pistol and coming at him. He pulled back on the
throttle and the aircraft stopped its roll; the engines
whined down.

Reynolds reached the plane, held up the badge and
the pilot slid open his window.

"FBI," she said hoarsely. "I have a badly wounded
person. I need your aircraft. You're going to fly us to
the nearest hospital. Now."

The pilot looked at the badge, the gun and nodded
dumbly. "Okay."

They all climbed on the plane, Lee cradling Faith
against his chest. The pilot turned the aircraft around
again, went back to the end of the runway and started
his takeoff roll once more. A minute later the plane
lifted into the air and rushed toward the embrace of
the quickly lightening sky.

CHAPTER 53

The PILOT RADIOED AHEAD AND A LIFE-SUPPORT ambulance unit was waiting on the tarmac at the airstrip in Manteo, which was thankfully only a few minutes of flight time away. Reynolds and Lee had used some bandages from the first-aid kit on the plane to try to stop the bleeding, and Lee had given Faith oxygen from the small canister on board, but none of it seemed to have any effect. She had not yet regained consciousness; they could barely get a pulse now. Her limbs were beginning to grow cold, even as Lee clung to her, tried to give her heat from his own body, as though that would do any good.

Lee rode in the ambulance with Faith over to Beach Medical Center, which had an emergency and trauma center. Reynolds and Buchanan were driven there in a car. On the way to the hospital, Reynolds called Fred

Massey in Washington. She told him just enough that he was already running to catch a Bureau plane. Just him, Reynolds had insisted; no one else could come. Massey had accepted this condition without comment. Perhaps it had been the tone of her voice, or simply the stunning content of her very few words.

Faith was immediately taken to the emergency room, where doctors labored over her for almost two hours, trying to get her vitals up, her heart regulated, the internal bleeding stopped. None of it looked good. Once, the crash cart even had to be called.

Through the doors Lee watched in the numbest horror as Faith repeatedly jerked under the impact of the electrical current surging through the paddles. Only when he saw the heart monitor go from flat line to its regular peaks and valleys did he find he could even move.

Barely two hours later they had to cut her chest open, spread her ribs wide and massage her heart to get it going. Every hour seemed to bring a new crisis as she barely clung to life.

Lee paced the floor incessantly, hands shoved in his pockets, head down, talking to no one. He had said every prayer he could remember. He had made up some new ones. He was helpless to do anything for the woman, and that's what tore at him. How could he have let this happen? How could Constantinople, that old, bulky sonofabitch, have gotten that shot off? And him right beside the guy? And Faith, why had she taken the round? Why? Buchanan should be the guy lying on that gurney with people swarming over him, trying desperately to push life back into his wrecked body.

Lee slumped against the wall and slid down to the floor, covering his face with both hands as his big body shook.

In a private room, Reynolds waited with Buchanan, who had barely spoken a word since Faith had been shot. He just sat there and stared at the wall. To look at Buchanan, no one would have guessed that anger was building in him: the absolute hatred he was holding for Robert Thornhill, a man who had destroyed everything he cared about.

About the time Fred Massey arrived, Faith was taken to the ICU. She was stabilized for the time being, the doctor told them. The bullet was one of those vicious dum-dums, he said. It had tumbled through her body like a runaway bowling ball, doing considerable damage to organs, and the internal hemorrhaging had been severe. She was strong and for now she was alive. She had a chance, that was all, he cautioned. They would know more soon.

As the doctor walked away, Reynolds put a hand on Lee's shoulder and handed him a fresh cup of coffee.

"Lee, if she survived until now, I have to believe she's going to make it."

"No guarantees," he mumbled to himself, unable to look at the woman.

They went to the private room, where Reynolds introduced Buchanan and Lee to Fred Massey.

"I think Mr. Buchanan should start telling you his story," Reynolds said to Massey.

"And he's willing to do that?" Massey asked skeptically.

At this Buchanan perked up. "Something more than willing. But before I do, tell me one thing. What's more important to you? What I did, or arresting the person who killed your agent?"

Massey leaned forward. "I'm not sure I'm prepared to discuss any sort of deal with you."

Buchanan put his elbows on the table. "When I tell you my story, you will be. But I'll do so on only one condition. You let me deal with this man. In my own way."

"Agent Reynolds informed me this person works for the federal government."

"That's right."

"Well, that's pretty damn unbelievable. Do you have proof?"

"You let me do this my way, and you'll have your proof."

Massey looked over at Reynolds. "The bodies at the house. Do we know who they are yet?"

She shook her head. "I just checked in. The police and agents from D.C., Raleigh and Norfolk are on the scene. But it's too early yet to have that info. But everything's on the QT. The locals have been told nothing. We're controlling all flows of information. You won't see anything on the news about the bodies or about Faith being alive and in this hospital."

Massey nodded. "Good work." As though suddenly remembering something, he opened his briefcase, pulled out two objects and handed them to her.

Reynolds looked down at her pistol and creds.

"I'm sorry any of this happened, Brooke," Massey said. "I should have trusted you and I didn't. Maybe I've been out of the field too damn long. Pushing too many papers and not listening to my instincts anymore."

Reynolds holstered her gun and put the creds in her purse. She once more felt complete. "Maybe I wouldn't have either, in your position. But it's in the past, Fred, let's move on. We don't have much time."

"Rest assured, Mr. Massey," Buchanan said, "you'll never identify those men. Or if you do, they'll have no ties to the person I'm talking about."

"How can you be so sure of that?" Massey demanded.

"Trust me, I know how this man operates."

"Look, why don't you just tell me who it is and I'll handle it from there?"

"No," Buchanan said firmly.

"What do you mean no? We're the FBI, mister, we do this for a living. If you want any sort of deal—"

"You will listen to me." Buchanan hardly raised his voice, but his eyes bored into Massey with such overwhelming force that the ADIC lost his train of thought and fell silent. "We have one chance to bring him in. One! He's already infiltrated the FBI. Constantinople may not be the only mole. There may be others."

"I highly doubt that—" Massey began.

Now Buchanan raised his voice. "Can you guarantee me that there aren't? Can you?"

Massey sat back, looking uncomfortable. He glanced at Reynolds, who shrugged.

"If they could turn Connie, they could turn anybody," she said.

Massey looked miserable, shaking his head slowly. "Connie . . . I still can't believe it."

Buchanan tapped the tabletop. "And if there is another spy in your ranks and you try to trap this man on your own, you will absolutely fail. And your chance will be gone. Forever. Do you really want to risk that?"

Massey rubbed his smooth chin, thinking it over. When he looked up at Buchanan, his expression was wary but interested.

"Do you really think you can nail this guy?"

"I'm prepared to die trying. And I need to work the phones. Call in some very special help." Buchanan smiled to himself. A lobbyist to the very end. He turned to Lee. "And I need your help, Lee. If you're willing."

Lee looked surprised. "Me? What can I do to help anybody?"

"I spoke with Faith about you last night. She told me about your 'special' abilities. She said you were a good man to have in a bad situation."

"I guess she was wrong about that. Otherwise she wouldn't be lying up there with a hole in her chest."

Buchanan put a hand on Lee's arm. "I can barely function with the guilt I have, for her having stepped in front of that bullet. But I can't change that now. What I can do is try to make sure she didn't risk her life for nothing. There's great danger for you. Even if we get this man, he has many at his back. There'll always be some out there."

Buchanan settled back in his chair and watched Lee closely. Massey and Reynolds stared at the PI too. Lee's muscular arms and broad shoulders were in stark contrast to the fragility of the look deep within his eyes.

Lee Adams took a deep breath. What he really wanted to do was stand next to Faith's bed and never leave until she woke up, saw him, smiled, said she'd be okay. And then, so would he. But, Lee knew, one rarely got what one wished for in this life. So instead, he looked at Buchanan and said, "I guess I'm your man."

CHAPTER 54

THE BLACK SEDAN PULLED UP TO THE FRONT OF the house. Robert Thornhill and his wife, dressed in formal evening clothes, came out the front door. Thornhill locked the house, then the two got in the car and were driven away. The Thornhills were attending an official dinner at the White House.

The sedan passed the phone-line control pedestal belonging to the community where the Thornhills lived. The metal box was large, bulky and painted light green. It had been placed there about two years ago when the phone company had upgraded the communications lines for this old neighborhood. The metal box had been a sudden eyesore in an area that prided itself on splendid homes and high-dollar landscaping. Thus, the residents had paid for a number of large bushes to be planted around the aboveground pedestal. These bushes now hid the box completely from the road, which meant that the telephone servicemen had to approach it from the rear side, which faced the woods. Aesthetically pleasing, the bushes were also very welcome to the man who had watched the sedan pass by and then had opened the box and begun delicately picking his way through its electronic guts.

Lee Adams identified the line going to the Thornhills' residence with a special piece of his own customized equipment. His background in communications hardware was serving him well. The Thornhills' home had a good security system. However, every security system had an Achilles' heel: the phone line. Always the phone line. Thank you, Ma Bell.

Lee went through the steps in his head. When an intruder broke into someone's home, the alarm went off and the computer dialed the central monitoring station to inform him of the break-in. Then the security person at the monitoring station called the home to see if everything was okay. If the owner answered, he had to give his special code or else the police would be sent. If no one answered the phone, the police would be sent automatically.

Simply put, Lee was making sure that in this home security system the computer's phone call would never reach the monitoring station, yet the computer would think that it had. He was accomplishing this by building an in-line component or phone simulator. He had dropped the Thornhill home from the landline feed, effectively severing outside phone communication. Now he had to trick the alarm computer into thinking it had phone service. To do this, he installed the in-line component and threw the switch, effectively giving the Thornhills' home a dial tone and phone line that went absolutely nowhere.

He had also found out that the Thornhills' alarm system had no cellular backup, just the regular landline. That was a big hole. A cellular backup was incapable of being fooled, since it was a wireless system with no way for Lee to access its feed line. Virtually all alarm systems in the country had the very same backbone land- and data-lines. And, thus, they all had back doors in. Lee had just completed his.

He packed up his tools and made his way through the woods to the rear of the Thornhills' home. He located a window that was not visible from the street. He had a copy of the Thornhills' floor plan and alarm layout. It had been provided to him by Fred Massey. By accessing this window, he could reach the upstairs alarm panel without passing any motion detector points.

He pulled a stun gun from his backpack and held it flush against the window. The windows were all wired, even the second-floor ones, he knew. And both top and bottom window components had contacts. Most homes only had contacts at the bottom window casement; if that had been the case here, Lee would have simply picked the window lock and slid down the top window, without breaking any contacts.

He pulled the trigger on the stun gun and then moved it to another position on the window where he thought the contact elements were probably located. In all, he fired eight shots into the window frame from the stun gun. The electrical charge from the gun would melt the contacts, fusing them together and rendering them inoperable.

He picked the sash lock, held his breath and slid the window up. No alarm sounded. He quickly climbed through the window and closed it. Pulling a small flashlight from his pocket, he found the stairs and headed up. The Thornhills, he quickly observed, lived in extremely comfortable luxury. The furnishings were mostly antique; real oil paintings hung on the walls; and his feet melted into the thick and, he assumed, expensive carpet.

The alarm panel was where all such alarm panels were located: on the upper floor in the master bedroom. He unscrewed the plate and found the wire for the sound cannon. Two snips and the alarm system had suddenly developed laryngitis. Now he was free to roam. He went downstairs and passed in front of the motion detector, waving his arms in defiance, even giving it the finger, pretending it was Thornhill there scowling at him, helpless to do anything about the intrusion. The red light came on and the alarm system was activated, although the system no longer could scream its warning. The computer would soon be dialing the central station, only its call would never get there. It would dial the number eight times, get no answer and then it would stop trying and go back to sleep. At the central station, everything would seem perfectly normal: a burglar's dream.

Lee watched as the red light on the motion detector disappeared. Each time he passed in front of it, though, it would go through the same routine, with the same result. Call eight times and then stop. Lee smiled. So far, so good. Before the Thornhills came home he would reattach the wires for the sound cannons: Thornhill would be suspicious if the normal beeping sound didn't occur when he opened the door. But for now, Lee had work to do.

CHAPTER 55

THE WHITE HOUSE DINNER WAS VERY MEMO-
rable for Mrs. Thornhill. Her husband, on the other
hand, was working. He sat at the long table and
made inconsequential conversation when called
upon, but spent most of his time listening intently
to the guests. There were a number of foreign visitors tonight, and Thornhill knew that good intelligence might come from unusual sources, even a
White House dinner. Whether the foreign guests
knew he was with the CIA, he wasn't sure. That was
certainly not public knowledge. The guest list that
would be printed in the *Washington Post* the next
morning would identify them only as Mr. and Mrs.
Robert Thornhill.

Ironically, the invitation to the dinner had not
come because of Thornhill's position at the Agency.

Who was invited to White House functions such as this, and why, were the greatest of mysteries in the capital city. However, the Thornhills' invitation had been extended because of his wife's well-known philanthropic work for the District of Columbia poor— a charitable endeavor in which the first lady herself was much involved as well. And Thornhill had to admit, his wife was dedicated to this cause. When she wasn't at the country club, of course.

The ride home was uneventful; the couple talked of mundane things while most of Thornhill's mind was focused on the phone call from Howard Constantinople. Losing his men had been a blow to Thornhill, both personally and professionally. He had worked with them for years. How all three had been killed was beyond his comprehension. He had people down in North Carolina right now finding out as much as possible.

He had not heard anything further from Constantinople. Whether the man had run was unknown. But Faith and Buchanan were dead. And so was the other FBI agent, Reynolds. At least he was almost certain they were dead. The fact that no newspaper reports had come out regarding at least six dead bodies at a beach house in an affluent area in the Outer Banks was particularly troubling. It had been over a week, and nothing. It might be the Bureau's doing, covering up what was quickly building to a PR nightmare for them. Yes, he could see them doing that. Unfortunately, without Constantinople he had lost his eyes and ears at the Bureau. He would have to do something about that soon. It would take time to cultivate a new mole, yet nothing was impossible.

Well, the trail could never lead back to him. His three operatives had cover buried so deeply that the authorities would be incredibly fortunate if they managed to dig through even the surface layer. They would find nothing after that. Well, the three had died heroes. He and his colleagues had toasted their memory in the underground chamber upon learning of their deaths.

There was one more troubling loose end: Lee Adams. He had gone off on his motorcycle, presumably to Charlottesville to make sure his daughter was safe. He had never arrived in Charlottesville, that Thornhill knew for a fact. So where was he? Had he come back and managed to kill Thornhill's men? And yet one man taking out all three of them was incomprehensible. But Constantinople had not mentioned Adams in the call.

As the car drove along, Thornhill felt much less confident than he had at the beginning of the evening. He would have to watch the situation very carefully. Perhaps there would be some message waiting for him at home.

As the car pulled into their driveway, Thornhill glanced at his watch. It was late, and he had an early morning. He had to testify tomorrow before Rusty

Ward's committee. He had finally tracked down the answers the senator wanted, meaning he was prepared to throw out so much bullshit that the room would have to be fumigated after he had finished.

Thornhill disarmed the security system, kissed his wife good night and watched as she went up the stairs to her bedroom. She was still a very attractive woman, slender, fine-boned. Retirement would be coming soon. Perhaps it wouldn't be so bad. He'd had nightmares about it; his sitting in agony at interminable bridge games, country club dinners, fund-raisers; or hacking his way through infinite rounds of golf, his insufferably perky wife at his side for all of it.

However, as he watched the woman's nicely shaped backside gliding up the stairs, Thornhill suddenly saw more enticing possibilities for his golden years. They were relatively young, wealthy; they could travel the world. He even thought he might turn in early tonight, and take advantage of the physical urges he was suddenly feeling as he watched Mrs. Thornhill gracefully ascend the stairs to their bedroom. He liked the way she slid her high heels off, exposing black-hosed feet; moved a hand along her curvy hip; let her hair down in back, her shoulder muscles tensing with each movement. Those hours at the country club certainly hadn't all been wasted. He would just pop in his study to check his messages and then head upstairs.

He clicked on the light in his study and went over to his desk. He was about to check for any messages on his secure phone when he heard a noise. He turned to the French doors that opened out onto the garden. The doors were opening and a man was stepping through.

Lee put a finger to his lips and smiled, his gun pointed directly at Thornhill. The CIA man stiffened, his eyes darting left and right, looking for escape, but there was none to be had. If he ran or screamed, he would be dead; he could see that in the man's eyes. Lee crossed the room and closed, then locked the door to the study. Thornhill watched him silently.

Thornhill received a second shock when another man stepped through the French doors, closing and locking them too.

Danny Buchanan looked so calm as to be almost asleep, yet a high level of energy danced behind his eyes.

"Who are you? What are you doing in my house?" Thornhill demanded.

"I expected something a little more original, Bob," said Buchanan. "How often is it that you see a ghost from the very recent past?"

"Sit," Lee ordered Thornhill.

Thornhill eyed the gun one more time, then went over and sat on the leather couch facing the two men. He undid his bow tie and dropped it on the couch, trying, with some difficulty, to assess the situation and decide on a course of action.

"I thought we had a deal, Bob," Buchanan said. "Why did you send your team of killers down? A lot of people lost their lives unnecessarily. Why?"

Thornhill looked at him suspiciously and then at Lee.

"I don't know what you're talking about. I don't even know who the hell you are."

It was clear what Thornhill was thinking: Lee and Buchanan were wired. Perhaps they were working with the FBI. And they were in his house. His wife was upstairs undressing, and these two men were in his house asking him these sorts of questions. Well, they would get nothing for their troubles.

"I"—Buchanan stopped and glanced at Lee—"we came here, as the sole survivors, to see what sort of arrangement we can work out. I don't want to keep looking over my shoulder for the rest of my life."

"Arrangement? How about I yell up to my wife to call the police? You like that arrangement?" Thornhill eyed Buchanan closely and then pretended recognition. "I know I've seen you somewhere before. In the newspapers?"

Buchanan smiled. "That certain tape Agent Constantinople told you was destroyed?" He slid his hand in his coat pocket and pulled out a cassette. "Well, he didn't get it exactly right."

Thornhill stared at the cassette as if it were plutonium about to be shoved down his throat. He reached into his own jacket.

Lee raised the pistol.

Thornhill gave him a disappointed look and slowly edged out his pipe and lighter, taking a moment to light up. Several soothing puffs later, he eyed Buchanan.

"Since I don't even know what you're talking about, why don't you play the tape? I'd be interested to know what's on it. It might explain why two complete strangers have broken into my house." *And if that tape had me talking about killing an FBI agent, neither of you would be here, and I'd already be under arrest. Bluff, bluff, bluff, Danny.*

Buchanan slowly tapped the cassette against his palm, while Lee looked nervous.

"Come now, don't tease me with something and then pull it away," said Thornhill.

Buchanan dropped the cassette on the desk. "Maybe later. Right now I want to know what you're going to do for us. Something that will make us not go to the FBI and tell them what we know."

"And what might that be? You talked about people getting killed. Are you insinuating that I might have killed somebody? I'm assuming that you know I'm employed by the CIA. Are you foreign agents attempting some sort of bizarre blackmail scheme? The problem with that is, you need to have something to blackmail me with."

Lee said, "We know enough to bury you."

"Well, then I suggest you go get your shovel and start digging, Mr. . . . ?"

"Adams, Lee Adams," Lee said with a fierce scowl.

"Faith is dead, you know, Bob," Buchanan said. As he said this, Lee looked down. "She almost made it. Constantinopole killed her. He also killed two of your men. Payback for your killing the FBI agent."

Thornhill looked suitably bewildered. "Faith? Constantinople? What the hell are you talking about?"

Lee came and stood directly in front of Thornhill. "You bastard! You kill people like stepping on ants. A game. That's all it is to you."

"Please put the gun away and leave my house. Now!"

"Damn you!" Lee aimed his pistol directly at Thornhill's head.

Buchanan was next to him in an instant. "Lee, please don't. That won't do any good."

"I would listen to your friend if I were you," Thornhill said as calmly as he could. He had had a gun pulled on him once before, when his cover had been blown in Istanbul many years ago. He had been lucky to get out alive. He wondered if his luck would hold tonight.

"Why should I listen to anybody?" Lee growled.

"Lee, please," Buchanan said.

Lee's finger hovered on the trigger for an instant,

his gaze locked with Thornhill's. Finally, he lowered the gun, slowly.

"Well, I guess we'll have to go to the Feds with what we have," Lee said.

"I just want you out of my house."

"And all I want," Buchanan said, "is your personal assurances that no one else will be killed. You've got what you want. You don't have to harm anyone else."

"Right. Right, whatever you say. I won't kill anybody else," Thornhill said sarcastically. "Now if you'll please leave my house. I don't want to upset my wife. She has no idea she's married to a mass murderer."

"This is no joke," Buchanan said angrily.

"No, it really isn't, and I hope you get the help you so obviously need," said Thornhill. "And please take care that your gun-toting friend doesn't hurt anyone." *That should sound very nice on the tape. I am actually caring about others.*

Buchanan picked up the cassette.

"Not leaving the evidence of my crimes?"

Buchanan swiveled around and eyed him severely. "Under the circumstances, I don't think it will be necessary."

He looks like he wants to kill me, Thornhill thought. *Good, very good.*

Thornhill watched as the two men hurried down his driveway and disappeared onto the darkened street. A minute later he heard a car start up. He raced toward the phone on his desk and then stopped. Was it tapped? Was this whole thing a charade to trick him into a mistake? He stared at the window. Yes, they could be out there right now. He hit a button under his desk. All the drapes in the room descended and then a small whooshing sound commenced at each of the windows: white noise. He slid open his drawer and pulled out his secure phone. It had so many security and scrambling features that not even the NSA jocks could lift a conversation on it from the air. Similar to the technology used on military aircraft, the phone threw out electronic chaff that jammed attempts to intercept its signal. *So much for electronic eavesdropping, you amateurs.*

"Buchanan and Lee Adams were in my study," he said into the phone. "Yes. In my home, dammit! They just left. I want all the men we can spare. We're only minutes from Langley. You should be able to find them." He paused to relight his pipe. "They sang some bullshit song about the cassette tape where I admitted to having the FBI agent killed. But Buchanan was just bluffing. The tape is gone. I figured they were wired, and I played dumb with everything. It almost cost me my life. That idiot Adams was two seconds away from blowing my head off. Buchanan said Lockhart was dead, which is good for us, if it's true. But I don't know if they're somehow working with the FBI. But without that tape they've got no evidence of what we've done. What? No, Buchanan was begging for us to leave him alone. We could go ahead with the blackmail plan, just let him live. It was pitiful, actually. When I first saw them, I thought they had come to kill me. That Adams is dangerous. And they told me Constantinople killed two of our men. Constantinople must be dead, so we need to get another spy at the FBI. But whatever you do, you find them. And this time no mistakes. They are dead. And after that, it's time to execute the plan. I can't wait to see those pitiful faces on Capitol Hill when I hit them with this."

Thornhill clicked off and sat at his desk. It was funny, their coming here that way. A desperate act. From desperate men. Did they really think they could bluff a man such as himself? It was rather insulting. But he had won in the end. The reality was that tomorrow or soon thereafter they would be dead and he wouldn't be.

He rose from behind the desk. He had been brave, cool under pressure. *Survival is always intoxicating*, Thornhill thought as he turned out the light.

CHAPTER 56

THE DIRKSEN SENATE OFFICE BUILDING WAS bustling as usual on this crisp morning. Robert Thornhill walked with special purpose down the long hallway, swinging his briefcase cavalierly at his side. Last night had been quite something, a success in many ways. The only downside was that they had failed to find Buchanan and Adams.

The rest of the night had been simply marvelous. Mrs. Thornhill had been impressed with his animalistic zeal. The woman had even gotten up early and made him breakfast, dressed in a sheer, clingy black outfit. That hadn't happened in years—making his breakfast or the clingy number.

The hearing room was at the far end of the hallway. Rusty Ward's little fiefdom, Thornhill thought derisively. He ruled with a Southern fist, meaning velvet-gloved, yet with granite knuckles underneath. Ward would lull you to sleep with his ridiculously syrupy drawl and when you least expected it, he would pounce and shred you. His intense gaze and oh-so-precise words could melt the unsuspecting foe right in his uncomfortable, government-issue hot seat.

Everything about Rusty Ward painfully assaulted Thornhill's old-school, Ivy-League sensibilities. But this morning he was ready. He would talk death squads and redactions until the cows came home, to borrow one of Ward's favorite lines; and the senator would be left with no more information at the end of the day than when he had started.

Before entering the hearing room, Thornhill took one energizing deep breath. He envisioned the setting that he was about to confront: Ward and company behind their little bench, the chairman pulling at his suspenders, his fat face looking here and there as he rustled through his briefing papers, missing nothing in the confines of his pathetic kingdom. When Thornhill entered, Ward would look at him, smile, nod, give him some little innocent greeting intended to disarm Thornhill's defenses, as if that were even a possibility. *But I guess he has to go through the motions. Teaching an old dog new tricks indeed.* That was another of Ward's stupid little sayings. How dreary.

Thornhill pulled open the door and strode confidently down the aisle of the hearing room. About halfway down, he realized that the room held many more people than usual. The small space was literally bursting with bodies. And as he looked around, he noted numerous faces he did not recognize. As he approached the witness table, he received another shock. There were already people sitting there, their backs to him.

He looked up at the committee. Ward stared back at him. There was no smile, no inane greeting from the portly chairman.

"Mr. Thornhill, take a seat in the front row, will you? We have one person testifying before you."

Thornhill looked dazed. "Excuse me?"

"Just sit down, Mr. Thornhill," Ward said again.

Thornhill looked at his watch. "I'm afraid I have limited time today, Mr. Chairman. And I wasn't told about anyone else testifying." Thornhill glanced at the witness table. He didn't recognize the men sitting there. "Perhaps we should just reschedule."

Ward looked past Thornhill. The latter turned and followed his gaze. The uniformed Capitol Hill police officer ceremoniously closed the door to the hearing room and then stood with his broad back against it, as though daring anyone to try to get past him.

Thornhill looked back around at Ward. "Am I missing something here?"

"If you are, it will be made crystal clear in a minute," Ward replied ominously. Then he looked over at one of his aides and nodded.

The aide disappeared through a small doorway behind the committee. He was back in a few seconds. And then Thornhill received what amounted to the greatest shock of his life, as Danny Buchanan walked through the doorway and made his way to the witness table. He never even looked at Thornhill, who just stood there in the middle of the aisle, his briefcase now resting motionless against his leg. The men rose from the witness table and took seats in the audience.

Buchanan stood in front of the witness table, raised his right hand, was sworn in and then sat down.

Ward glanced over at Thornhill, who still hadn't moved.

"Mr. Thornhill, will you please sit down so we can get started here?"

Thornhill couldn't take his eyes off Buchanan. He shuffled sideways toward the one remaining empty seat in the front row. The large man sitting at the end of the row moved aside so Thornhill could pass by. As Thornhill sat, he glanced over at the man and found himself staring at Lee Adams.

"Good to see you again," Lee said in an undertone before settling back in his chair and turning his attention toward the front of the room.

"Mr. Buchanan," Ward began. "Can you tell us why you're here today, sir?"

"To provide testimony regarding a shocking conspiracy at the Central Intelligence Agency," Buchanan replied in a calm, assured tone. Over the years he had

testified before more committees than all the Watergate folk combined. He was on familiar ground, his
best friend in the world doing the questioning. This
was his time. Finally.

"Then I guess you should start at the beginning, sir."

Buchanan placed his hands neatly in front of him,
leaned forward and spoke into the microphone.

"Approximately fifteen months ago I was approached by a high-level official at the CIA. The gentleman was quite familiar with my lobbying
practice. He was aware that I knew many of the
members on the Hill intimately. He wanted me to
help him with a very special project."

"What sort of project?" Ward prompted.

"He wanted me to help him gather evidence
against congressmen that could be used to blackmail
them."

"Blackmail? How?"

"He knew of my efforts to lobby on behalf of impoverished countries and world humanitarian organizations."

"We all are aware of your efforts in that regard,"
Ward said magnanimously.

"As you can imagine, it's a tough sell up here. I've
used most of my own money in that crusade. The
man knew that too. He felt I was desperate. An easy
mark, I believe is what he said."

"Precisely how would this blackmail scheme work?"

"I would approach certain congressmen and bureaucrats who could help influence foreign-aid dollars and other overseas relief. I would only approach those who needed money. I would tell them that in return for their help, they would be compensated after they left office. They didn't know it, of course, but the CIA would finance these 'retirement' packages. If they agreed to help, then I would wear a wire provided by the CIA and record incriminating conversations with these men and women. They would also be placed under surveillance by the CIA. All this 'illegal' activity would be captured and subsequently used against them by the man at the CIA."

"How so?"

"Many of the people I was supposed to bribe for foreign aid also serve on committees overseeing the CIA. For example, two of the members of this very committee, Senators Johnson and McNamara, also sit on the appropriations committee for foreign operations. The gentleman from the CIA gave me a list of names of all the people he wanted to target. Senators Johnson and McNamara were on that list. The plan was to blackmail them and others into using their committee positions to help the CIA. Increased budgets for the CIA, greater responsibilities, less congressional oversight. That sort of thing. In return, I would be paid a large sum of money."

Buchanan looked at Johnson and McNamara, men he had recruited so easily ten years ago. They stared back at him with exactly the proper look of shock and anger. Over the last week Buchanan had met with every single one of his bribees and had explained what was happening. If they wanted to survive, they would back up every word of the lie he was now telling. What choice did they have? They would also continue to support Buchanan's causes, and they wouldn't be getting a dime from him for doing so. Their efforts would really turn out to be "charitable." There was a God.

And he had confided in Ward as well. His friend had taken it better than Buchanan had thought possible. He had not condoned Buchanan's actions, yet he had decided to stand by his old friend. There were greater crimes to punish.

"This is all the truth, Mr. Buchanan?"

"Yes sir," Buchanan said, with the look of a saint.

Thornhill sat impassively in his seat. The man's expression was akin to the condemned walking alone to the gas chamber—a mixture of bitterness, terror and disbelief. Buchanan had obviously cut a deal. The politicians were backing his story. He could see it in Johnson's and McNamara's faces. How could Thornhill attack their claims without revealing his own participation? He could hardly jump up and say, "That's not how it happened. Buchanan was already bribing them, I just caught him and used him for my own blackmail purposes." His Achilles' heel. It had never occurred to him. The frog and the scorpion, only the scorpion was going to survive.

"What did you do?" Ward asked Buchanan.

"I immediately went to the people on the list and told them what had happened, including Senators Johnson and McNamara. I'm sorry we were unable to bring you into the loop at the time, Mr. Chairman, but absolute confidentiality was the key. We collectively decided to set up a sting of sorts. I would pretend to go along with the CIA's plan, and the targets would pretend to be part of the plan. Then, while the CIA was gathering its blackmail material, I would secretly gather evidence against the CIA. When we felt the case was strong enough, we planned to go to the FBI with what we had."

Ward took off his glasses and dangled them in front of his face. "Damn risky business, Mr. Buchanan. Was this blackmail operation officially sanctioned by the CIA, do you know?"

Buchanan shook his head. "It was clearly the work of one official there."

"What happened then?"

"I gathered my evidence, but then my associate, Faith Lockhart, who was unaware of any of this, became suspicious of me. She thought, I suppose, that I was actually involved in a blackmail scheme. I, of course, couldn't confide in her. She went to the FBI with her story. They commenced an investigation. The man from the CIA found out about this development and arranged to have Ms. Lockhart killed. Thankfully, she escaped, but an FBI agent was killed."

The entire room began buzzing at this.

Ward looked pointedly at Buchanan. "Are you telling me that an official from the CIA was responsible for the murder of an FBI agent?"

Buchanan nodded. "Yes. Several other deaths have also occurred, including"—Buchanan looked down for a moment, his lips trembling—"Faith Lockhart. That is what has prompted my appearance here today. To stop the killing."

"Who is this man, Mr. Buchanan?" Ward said with as much indignity and curiosity as he could feign.

Buchanan turned and pointed directly at Robert Thornhill.

"Associate Deputy Director of Operations Robert Thornhill."

Thornhill erupted from his chair, waving an angry fist in the air, and roared, "That is a damnable lie. This entire event is a circus, an abomination the likes of which I have never witnessed in all my years in government. You bring me here under false pretenses and then subject me to the preposterous, outrageous accusations of this person. They—they were in my home last night. This Buchanan person, and this man!" Thornhill pointed a finger angrily at Lee. "This man held a gun to my head. They threatened me with this same insane story. They claimed to have evidence of this nonsense, but when I called their bluff, they ran off. I demand that you place them under immediate arrest. I intend to press full charges. And now, if you'll excuse me, I have legitimate business elsewhere."

Thornhill tried to get past Lee, but the PI stood up and blocked his way.

Thornhill looked at Ward. "Unless you do something right this instant, Mr. Chairman, I will be forced to call the police on my portable phone. I doubt if it would look very good on the evening news."

"I have proof of all that I've said," Buchanan said.

"What," Thornhill cried out, "the silly tape you threatened me with last night? If you have it, produce it. But whatever's on it is obviously forged."

Buchanan opened a briefcase, which rested on the table in front of him. Instead of an audiocassette, he took out a videocassette and handed it to an aide of Ward's.

Everyone in the room watched as another aide wheeled a television, with a VCR attached, out into a corner of the room where everyone could see the screen. The aide took the tape and inserted it in the VCR, hit the remote, and stepped back. Everyone in the room watched breathlessly as the screen came to life.

On the TV Lee and Buchanan were just leaving Thornhill's study. Then Thornhill was at his desk, reaching for his phone, hesitating, then after a moment extracting from a desk drawer a different phone. He spoke into it anxiously. His conversation of the night before was played out before the entire room. His blackmail scheme, the killing of the FBI agent, his ordering the murders of Buchanan and Lee Adams. The look of triumph on his face as he put down the phone was in monumental contrast to the look the man wore now.

As the screen went to black, Thornhill continued to stare at the TV, his mouth slightly open, his lips moving but no words coming out. His briefcase, with all its important papers, fell to the floor, forgotten.

Ward tapped his pen against the microphone, his eyes squarely on Thornhill. There was some satisfaction in the senator's features, but it could not overcome the horror there as well. Ward appeared sickened by what he had just watched.

"I suppose that since you've admitted that these men were in your home last night, then you won't claim this piece of evidence is a forgery, Mr. Thornhill?" Ward said.

Danny Buchanan sat quietly at the table, his eyes downcast. His face showed relief, tinged with sadness; and there was about his bearing a weariness. He too had clearly had enough.

Lee watched Thornhill intently. The other task he had performed at the Thornhill residence last night had been a relatively simple one. The underlying technology was PLC, the same as that used by Thornhill to bug Ken Newman's home. It was a wireless system with a 2.4-gigahertz transmitter, covert camera and antenna installed in a device that looked just like the smoke alarm in Thornhill's study and actually performed the functions of a smoke detector while it simultaneously conducted surveillance. It was powered by the home's regular electrical current and produced clear, crisp video and audio of everything in its range. Thornhill had stopped his incriminating conversation from leaving his house, but it had never occurred to him that there was a miniature Trojan horse of sorts *inside* his house.

"I will be available to testify at the trial," said Danny Buchanan. He rose, turned and started to walk up the aisle.

Lee put a hand on Thornhill's shoulder. "Excuse me," he said politely. Thornhill gripped Lee's arm.

"How did you do it?" Thornhill said.

Lee slowly pulled away from his grip and joined Buchanan. The two men quietly walked out together.

CHAPTER 57

ONE MONTH TO THE DAY AFTER BUCHANAN'S testimony to Ward's committee, Robert Thornhill bounded down the steps of the federal courthouse in Washington, leaving his lawyers in his liberated, if anxious, wake. The car was waiting for him. He slid inside. He had been granted bail, after four weeks of sitting behind bars. Now it was time to get to work. Now it was damn well time for revenge.

"Have they all been contacted?" Thornhill asked the driver.

The man nodded. "They're already there. Waiting for you."

"Buchanan and Adams? Status?"

"Buchanan is in Witness Protection, but we have some leads. Adams is right out in the open. Available anytime to take out."

"Lockhart?"

"Dead."

"You're certain?"

"We haven't actually dug up her body, but every-thing else points to her having died from her wounds at the hospital in North Carolina."

Thornhill leaned back against his seat with a sigh. "Lucky her."

The car entered a public garage, where Thornhill left the vehicle. He stepped directly into a van wait-ing there for him, which then pulled out from the garage and headed in the opposite direction. So much for any tail the FBI had.

Within forty-five minutes he was at the small abandoned strip mall. He stepped into the elevator and was zipping several hundred feet down into the earth. The lower he was carried, the better Thornhill felt. This thought deeply amused him.

The doors parted and he literally burst out of the confines of the elevator. The men, his colleagues, were all there. His chair at the head of the table was empty. His trusty comrade Phil Winslow was in the seat to the immediate right. Thornhill allowed him-self a grateful smile. Back in business, ready to go.

He sat down, looked around.

"Congratulations on getting bail, Bob," Winslow said.

"Four weeks later," Thornhill said bitterly. "I think the Agency needs to upgrade its legal counsel."

"Well, that video was very damaging," said Aaron Royce, the younger man who had butted heads with Thornhill at the previous meeting here. "I'm actually surprised you were able to get bail at all. And, quite frankly, I'm a little stunned that the Agency even saw fit to provide counsel."

"Of course it was damaging," Thornhill said scornfully. "And the Agency provided counsel because of loyalty. It doesn't forget its people. Unfortunately, however, it means I have to disappear. The lawyers think we have a shot at suppressing the video, but I think all would agree that, despite having technical legal deficiencies, the subject matter of the tape was a little too detailed to allow me to continue in my present capacity." Thornhill looked saddened for a moment. His career over, and not in the way he had planned. But then his features reassumed their usual steeliness; his resolve flooded back into him like an oil gusher. He looked around the room in triumph. "But I will lead the battle from a distance. And we will win the war. Now, I understand Buchanan went underground. But Adams didn't. We'll go the path of least resistance. Adams first. Then Buchanan. I want someone at the U.S. marshal's service. We have people there. We locate good old Danny and make his life disappear. Next, I want to make damn *sure* Faith Lockhart is no more." He looked at Winslow. "Are my travel documents ready, Phil?"

"Actually, no, Bob," Winslow said slowly.

Royce stared at Thornhill. "This operation has cost us too much," he said. "Three operatives dead. You indicted. The Agency's turned upside down. The FBI is all over us. It's a total and complete disaster. This makes Aldrich Ames seem like a bounced check."

Thornhill noticed that every man in the room, Winslow included, was looking at him with a very unfriendly face. "We will survive this, make no mistake about that," Thornhill said in an encouraging tone.

"I'm quite sure *we* will survive it," Royce said forcefully.

Royce was definitely beginning to bother Thornhill. He was showing backbone in a way that had to be quickly quashed. But for now Thornhill decided to ignore him. "The damn FBI," complained Thornhill. "Bugging my house. Is the Constitution not applicable to them?"

"Thank God you didn't mention my name during the phone call that night," Winslow said.

Thornhill looked at him again, struck by the curious tone in his friend's voice. "About my documents . . . I should prepare to leave the country as soon as possible."

"That won't be necessary, Bob," Royce said. "And frankly, despite your constant outbursts to the contrary, until you screwed everything up, we had quite a good working relationship with the FBI. Cooperation is the key these days. Turf battles make losers of everyone. You made us into dinosaurs and you're dragging us down into the mud with you."

Thornhill gave him an exasperated look and then glanced at Winslow. "Phil, I don't have time for this. You deal with him."

Winslow coughed nervously. "I'm afraid he's right, Bob."

Thornhill froze for a moment and then looked around the table before settling back on Winslow. "Phil, I want my documents and my cover, and I want them right now."

Winslow looked at Royce and gave a slight nod of the head.

Aaron Royce rose from his chair. He didn't smile; he showed no signs of triumph. Just as he had been trained.

"Bob," he said, "there's been a change in plan. We won't be needing your assistance in this matter any further."

Thornhill's face flushed with anger. "What the hell are you talking about? I'm running this operation. And I want Buchanan and Adams dead. Now!"

"There will be no more killing," Winslow said fiercely. "No more killing of innocent people," he added quietly.

He stood. "I'm sorry, Bob. I truly am."

Thornhill stared at him, the first tremors of the truth hitting him. Phil Winslow had been his class-mate at Yale, his fraternity brother. The two men were members of Skull & Bones. Winslow had been his best man. They'd been lifelong friends. Lifelong.

"Phil?" Thornhill said cautiously.

Winslow motioned to the other men, who rose too. They all headed for the elevator.

"Phil?" Thornhill said again, his mouth going dry.

When the group reached the elevator, Winslow looked back. "We can't let this matter go any further. We can't let it go to trial. And we can't let you steal away. They'll never stop looking for you. We need closure, Bob."

Thornhill half rose from his chair. "Then we can fake my death. My suicide."

"I'm sorry, Bob. We need complete and *honest* closure."

"Phil!" Thornhill screamed out. "Please!"

When all the men were inside the elevator, Winslow looked at his friend one last time. "Sacrifices are sometimes necessary, Bob. You know that better than anyone. For the good of the country."

The elevator doors closed.

CHAPTER 58

LEE CAREFULLY HELD THE BASKET OF FLOWERS in both hands as he walked down the hospital corridor. Once she'd regained enough strength, Faith had been transferred to a hospital outside of Richmond, Virginia. There she was listed under an alias, though, and an armed guard was stationed outside her room at all times. The hospital was considered far enough away from Washington to maintain absolute secrecy on her whereabouts, yet near enough for Brooke Reynolds to keep a close watch on her.

This was the first time Lee had been allowed in to see her, despite his frantic pleas to Reynolds. At least she was alive. And getting better every day, he had been told.

Thus he was very surprised when he approached her room and there was no guard outside. He knocked on the door, waited, then pushed it open. The room was empty, the bed stripped. He walked around the room in a daze for a few seconds and then ran back out into the hallway where he nearly collided with a nurse. He grabbed the woman's arm.

"The patient in 212? Where is she?" he asked.

The nurse glanced at the empty room and then back at him, her expression a sad one. "Are you family?"

"Yes," he lied.

She looked at the flowers and her expression grew even more distressed. "Didn't anyone call you?"

"Call me? About what?"

"She passed away last night."

Lee's face paled. "Passed away," he said numbly. "But she was out of danger. She was going to make it. What the hell are you talking about—passing away?"

"Please, sir, there are other patients here." She took his arm and steered him away from the room. "I don't know the exact details. I wasn't on duty. I can refer you to someone here who can answer your questions."

Lee pulled his arm free. "Look, she can't be dead, okay? That was just a story. To keep her safe."

"What?" The woman looked puzzled.

"I'll take it from here," a voice said.

They both turned and looked at Brooke Reynolds standing there. She held out her badge for the nurse to see. "I'll take it from here," she said again. The nurse nodded and walked quickly away.

"What the hell is going on?" Lee demanded.

"Let's go to a quiet place and talk this over."

"Where is Faith?"

"Lee, not here! Dammit, do you want to ruin everything?" She pulled on his arm, but he wasn't budging, and she knew she couldn't physically make him.

"Why should I go with you?"

"Because I'm going to tell you the truth."

They got in Reynolds's car and she pulled out of the parking lot.

"I knew you were coming today, and I was planning on being at the hospital ahead of you, waiting. I didn't quite make it. I'm sorry you had to hear about it from a nurse; that's not what I intended." Reynolds looked down at the flowers he still held tightly, and her heart went out to him. She wasn't an FBI agent for this moment—she was simply a fellow human being sitting next to someone whose heart, she knew, was being torn apart. And what she had to tell him would only make it worse.

"Faith has been placed in Witness Protection. Buchanan too."

"*What?* Buchanan I can understand! But Faith isn't a witness to anything!" Lee's relief was matched only by his outrage. This was all wrong.

"But she is in need of protection. If certain people knew she was still alive—well, you know what could happen."

"When's the damn trial?"

"Actually, there isn't going to be a trial."

He stared over at her. "Don't tell me that sonofa-bitch Thornhill copped some sort of sweetheart deal. Don't tell me that."

"He didn't."

"So why no trial?"

"A trial needs a defendant." Reynolds tapped her fingers against the steering wheel and then slid on a pair of sunglasses. She proceeded to fiddle with the heating control.

"I'm waiting," Lee said. "Or don't I qualify for an explanation?"

Reynolds sighed and straightened up. "Thornhill is dead. He was found in his car on a back-country road with a single gunshot wound to the head. Suicide."

Lee was stunned into silence. After a minute he was able to mutter, "The coward's way out."

"I think everyone's relieved, actually. I know the people at CIA are. To say this whole thing rocked them to their super-secretive bones is an understate-ment. I guess for the good of the country, it's better to be spared a lengthy, embarrassing trial."

"Right, dirty laundry and all," Lee said acidly. "Hooray for the country." Lee gave a mock salute to a flag flying in front of a post office they passed. "So if Thornhill's out of the way, why does Faith need Witness Protection?"

"You know the answer to that. When Thornhill

died, he took the identity of everyone else involved in this with him to the grave. But they're out there, we know they are. Remember the videotape you orchestrated? Thornhill was talking to somebody on that phone, and that somebody is still out there. The CIA is doing an internal investigation to try to ferret them out, but I'm not holding my breath. And you know these people will do their best to get to Faith and Buchanan. For pure revenge, if nothing else." She touched his arm. "And you too, Lee."

He glanced over at her, read her mind. "No. There is no way I'm going into Witness Protection. I can't deal with a new name. I have a hard enough time remembering my real one. Might as well wait for Thornhill's sidekicks. Least I'll have some fun before I die."

"Lee, this is no joke. If you don't go underground, you'll be in great danger. And we can't follow you around twenty-four hours a day."

"No? After all I did for the Bureau? Does this also mean I don't get the FBI decoder ring and free T-shirt?"

"Why are you being such a smartass about this?"

"Maybe I don't give a shit anymore, Brooke. You're a smart lady, didn't that one ever occur to you?"

Neither said a word for the next couple of miles.

"If it were up to me, you'd get anything you wanted, including your own island somewhere with servants, but it's not up to me," Reynolds finally said.

He shrugged. "I'll take my chances. If they want to come after me, so be it. They'll find me a little tougher bite than they think."

"Isn't there anything I can say to change your mind?"

He held up the flowers. "You can tell me where Faith is."

"I can't do that. You know I can't do that."

"Oh, come on, sure you can. You just have to *say* it."

"Lee, please—"

He smashed his big fist against the dashboard, cracking it. "Dammit, Brooke, you don't understand. I have to see Faith. I have to!"

"You're wrong, Lee, I do understand. And that's why this is so hard for me. But if I tell you and you go to her, that puts her in danger. And you too. You know that. That breaks all the rules. And I'm not going to do that. I'm sorry. You don't know how terrible I feel about all this."

Lee laid his head against the back of the seat and the two remained silent for another several minutes as Reynolds drove aimlessly.

"How is she?" he finally asked quietly.

"I won't lie to you. That bullet did a lot of damage. She's recovering, but slowly. They almost lost her a couple more times along the way."

Lee put his hand over his face, slowly shook his head.

"If it's any consolation, she was as upset as you are about this arrangement."

"Boy," Lee said, "that just makes everything wonderful. I'm the friggin' king of the world."

"That's not how I meant it."

"You're really not going to let me see her, are you?"

"No, I'm really not."

"Then you can drop me at the corner."

"But your car's back at the hospital."

He opened the car door before she came to a stop. "I'll walk."

"It's miles," Reynolds said, her voice strained. "And it's freezing outside. Lee, let me drive you. Let's go get some coffee. Talk about this some more."

"I need the fresh air. And what's there to talk about? I'm all talked out. I may never talk again." He climbed out and then leaned back in. "You *can* do something for me."

"Just name it."

He handed her the flowers. "Could you see that Faith gets these? I'd appreciate it." Lee shut the door and walked off.

Reynolds gripped the flowers and looked at Lee as he trudged away, head down, hands stuffed in his pockets. She saw his shoulders quiver. And then Brooke Reynolds lay back against the seat as the tears trickled down her face.

CHAPTER 59

Nine months later Lee was staking out the hideaway townhouse of a man soon to be involved in an acrimonious divorce proceeding with his many-times-cheated-on wife. Lee had been hired by the very suspicious spouse to collect dirt on her hubby, and it hadn't taken him long to fill up bag after bag, as Lee watched a parade of pretty young things flounce through the premises. The wife wanted a nice-size financial settlement from the guy, who had about five hundred million bucks' worth of stock options at some high-tech Internet outfit he had co-founded. And Lee was very happy to help her get it. The adulterous husband reminded him of Eddie Stipowicz, his ex-wife's billion-dollar man. Collecting evidence on this guy was a little bit like hurling rocks at little Eddie's bloated head.

Lee took out his camera and shot some pictures of a tall, blond, miniskirted number sauntering up to the townhouse. The photo of the bare-chested guy standing at the door awaiting her, beer can in hand, a goofy, lascivious smile on his fat face, would be exhibit numero uno for the wife's lawyers. No-fault divorce laws had seriously depressed the business of PIs running around digging up dirt, but when it came time to split the marriage loot, the slimy ooze still carried weight. Nobody liked being embarrassed with that stuff. Especially when there were kids involved, as there were here.

The long-legged blonde couldn't have been more than twenty, about his daughter Renee's age, while the hubby was pushing fifty. God, those stock options. Must be nice. Or maybe it was the man's bald head, diminutive stature and soft pooch. You couldn't figure some women. *Nah, must be the dough,* Lee told himself. He put the camera away.

It was August in Washington, which meant just about everybody, other than cheating husbands and their bimbos, and PIs who spied on them, was out of town. It was hot, muggy, miserable. Lee had his window rolled down, praying for even the slightest movement of air, as he munched on trail mix and bottled water. The hardest thing with this type of surveillance was the lack of pee-pee breaks. That's why he preferred bottled water. The empty plastic containers had come in handy more than once for him.

He checked his watch; it was close on midnight. Most lights in the apartments and townhouses in the area had long since gone out. He was thinking about heading on, himself. He had gotten enough stuff in the last few days, including some embarrassing shots of a late-night romp in the townhouse's outdoor hot tub, to make the guy easily fork up three quarters of his net worth. Two naked girls who looked young enough to be thinking about the senior prom, frolicking in the bubbly water with a guy old enough to know better—this probably wouldn't sit too well with the upstanding stockholders of the husband's nice little high-tech concern, Lee imagined.

His own life had taken on a routine bordering on obsessive monotony, or so he had dubbed it. He got up early, worked out hard, pounding the bag, crunching the stomach and hoisting the weights until he thought his body would raise the white flag and then present him with an aneurysm. Then he went to work and kept at it nonstop until he barely made it to dinner at the McDonald's late-night drive-through near his apartment. Then he went home, alone, and tried to sleep, but found that he was never able to actually accomplish total unconsciousness. So he would prowl the apartment, look out the window, wonder about a whole bunch of things he couldn't do a damn thing about. His life's "what if" book was filled up. He'd have to go buy another one.

There had been some positives. Brooke Reynolds had made it her mission to send as much business his way as possible, and it had been quality, good-paying stuff. She also had had a number of ex-FBI agent buddies now in corporate security offer him full-time employment with, of course, stock options. He had turned them all down. The gesture was appreciated, he had told Reynolds, but he worked alone. He was not a suit type. He didn't like eating the kinds of lunches that required silverware. Traditional elements of success would undoubtedly be hazardous to his health.

He had seen Renee a great deal, and each time, things had gotten better between them. For about a month after everything had shaken out, he had barely left her side, making sure that nothing would happen to her because of Robert Thornhill and company. After Thornhill had killed himself his concerns had faded, although he was always on her to stay alert. She was going to come and visit him before school started up again. Maybe he'd drop Trish and Eddie a postcard, telling them what a fabulous job they'd done raising her. Or maybe he wouldn't.

Life was good, he kept telling himself. Business was good, he was in good health, his daughter was back in his life. He wasn't six feet under helping to fertilize grass. And he had served his country. All good shit. Which made him wonder why he was so unhappy, so out-and-out miserable. Actually, he knew, but there was absolutely nothing he could do about it. Wasn't that a kicker? Story of his life. Know the blues, but just can't change them.

A car's headlights flicked across his side mirror. His gaze immediately went to the car that had just pulled up behind him. It wasn't a cop wondering why he had been parked here for several hours. He frowned and looked over at the townhouse. He wondered if his naughty tech mogul had noticed him and called in some reinforcements to help teach the curious PI a little lesson. Lee hoped that was the case. He had his crowbar in the seat next to him. This might actually be fun. Kicking the crap out of somebody might be the depression antidote he needed; get those endorphins going. At least it might get him through the night.

He was surprised when only one person emerged from the passenger side and headed his way. The person was small, slender, hidden inside an ankle-length coat with a hood, not exactly your recommended attire for a ninety-degree thermometer and one hundred percent humidity. His hand tightened on the crowbar. As the figure came up to his passenger door, he hit the door lock. The next moment, his lungs had locked up and he was gasping for air.

The face looking in at him was very pale and very thin. And very Faith Lockhart. He unlocked the door and she slid in.

He looked at her, finally found his voice down near his knees. "God, is it really you?"

She smiled, and suddenly she didn't seem so pale, so drawn, so frail. She slid off her long, hooded coat. Underneath she had on a short-sleeved shirt and khaki shorts. Her feet were in sandals. Her legs were very pale and thinner than he remembered; all of her was. Months in a hospital had decimated her, he realized. Her hair had grown out and was longer, though far from its original length. She looked better with her real hair color, he thought. Actually, he would have taken the woman bald.

"It's me," she said quietly. "At least, what's left."

"Is that Reynolds back there?"

"Nervous and upset that I talked her into it."

"You look beautiful, Faith."

She smiled in a resigned fashion. "Liar. I look like hell. I can't even bear to look at my chest. God!" She said the words in a joking manner, but Lee could sense the anguish behind the light tone.

He very gently touched her face with his hand. "I'm not lying, and you know it."

She put her hand around his and gripped it with amazing strength. "Thank you."

"'How are you really doing? I want facts, nothing but."

She stretched her arm slowly, the pain in her face so evident from such a simple movement. "I'm officially retired from the aerobics circuit, but I'm hanging in there. Actually, each day it gets better. The doctors expect a full recovery. Well, in the ninety percentile anyway."

"I never thought I'd see you again."

"I couldn't let that happen."

He slid over to her, put his arm around her. She winced a little as he did this, and he quickly backed off.

"I'm sorry, Faith, I'm sorry."

She smiled and put his arm back around her, patting his hand as she did so. "I'm not that fragile. And the day you can't put your arm around me is the day I call it a life."

"I'd ask you where you're living, but I don't want to do anything that could put you in danger."

"Helluva way to have to live, don't you think?" Faith asked.

"Yes."

She leaned against him, resting her head against his chest. "I saw Danny right after I got out of the hospital. When they told us Thornhill had killed himself, I didn't think he was ever going to stop smiling."

"Can't say I felt any different."

She looked at him. "How are *you*, Lee?"

"Me! Nothing happened to me. Nobody shot me. Nobody tells me where I have to live. I'm doing fine. I got the best deal of all."

"Lie or the truth?"

"Lie," he said softly.

They exchanged a quick kiss and then a longer one. The movements were so easy, Lee thought, their heads turning at just the right angle, their arms going around each other with no wasted motion, like pieces in a puzzle someone was sliding together. They could be waking up at the beach house, the morning after. The nightmare never having occurred. How was it possible that one could know another person for such a short period of time and have it feel like several lifetimes? God would only let that happen once, if ever. And in Lee's case, God had taken it away. It wasn't fair, it wasn't right. He pressed his face into her hair, soaking up every particle of her scent.

"How long are you here?" he asked.

"What did you have in mind?"

"Nothing fancy. Dinner at my place, a quiet talk. Letting me hold you all night."

"As wonderful as that sounds, I'm not sure I'm up to that last part just yet."

He looked at her. "I'm being literal, Faith. I just want to hold you. That's all. That's all I've been thinking about all these months. Just holding you."

Faith looked as though she might start crying. Instead she brushed away the lone tear that had tumbled down Lee's face.

Lee glanced in the rearview mirror. "But I guess that's not in Reynolds's agenda, is it?"

"I doubt it."

He looked back at her. "Faith," he said softly, "why did you step in front of that bullet? I know you care for Buchanan and all, but why?"

She took a shallow breath. "Like I said, he's unique, I'm ordinary. I couldn't let him die."

"I wouldn't have done it."

"Would you have done it for me?" she asked.

"Yes."

"You sacrifice for people you care about. And I care a great deal about Danny."

"I guess the fact that you had all the means to disappear—fake ID, Swiss bank account, safe house—and instead went to the FBI to try and save Buchanan should have clued me in on that."

She clutched his arm. "But I survived. I made it. Maybe that makes me just a little extraordinary, in a way?"

He cupped her face with his hand. "Now that you're here, I really don't want you to go, Faith. Like I would give everything I have, do anything I can, if you wouldn't leave me."

She traced his mouth with her fingers, kissed his lips, stared at his eyes, which even in the darkness seemed to have the blinding heat of the sun behind them. She never thought she would ever see those eyes again; maybe the fact that she might, if she were to survive, had been the only thing that had saved her, had not let her die. Right now she wasn't sure what else she had to live for. Other than the apparently depthless love of this man. And right now it meant everything to her.

"Start the car," she said.

Puzzled, he looked at her but said nothing. He turned the key in the ignition, put the car in gear.

"Go ahead," Faith said.

He pulled the car away from the curb and the vehicle behind them immediately did the same.

They drove along, the car following them.

"Reynolds must be pulling her hair out," Lee said.

"She'll get over it."

"Where to?" he said.

"How much gas do you have in the car?" Faith asked.

He looked surprised. "I was on a stakeout. Full tank."

She was settled against him, her arm curling around his middle, her hair tickling his nose; she smelled so wonderful he felt dizzy.

"We can drive to the lookout spot off the GW Parkway." She looked at the star-filled sky. "I can show you the constellations."

He looked at her. "Been chasing stars lately?"

She smiled at him. "Always."

"And after that?"

"They can't keep me in Witness Protection against my will, can they?"

"No. But you'd be in danger."

"How about *we'd* be in danger?"

"In a second, Faith. In a second. But what happens when we run out of gas?"

"For now, just drive."

And that's exactly what he did.